Between Rock and a Hard Place

M. J. Schiller

Please Note

This is a work of fiction. Names, characters, places, and incidents either are the product of the author's imagination or are used fictitiously, and any resemblance to actual persons, living or dead, business establishments, events or locales is entirely coincidental.

The reverse engineering, uploading, and/or distributing of this book via the internet or via any other means without the permission of the copyright owner is illegal and punishable by law. Please purchase only authorized electronic editions, and do not participate in or encourage electronic piracy of copyrighted materials. Your support of the author's rights is appreciated.

No part of this book may be reproduced or transmitted in any form or by any electronic or mechanical means, including photocopying, recording or by any information storage and retrieval system, without the written permission of the publisher, except where permitted.

DEDICATION

For all those who serve in the law enforcement field, with respect and gratitude for all you do.

But especially for my stepbrother, Senior Corporal Mike Irwin, of the Dallas Police Department, who made sure I was using real cop talk, not TV cop talk, much to my disappointment. (It sounded much cooler before.)

And for Sergeant Jeff Klepec, of the Bloomington (Illinois) Police Department, who also fields questions for me about police procedure, with utmost patience.

CHAPTER ONE

The brass called Lieutenant Heath McGowan in on the case because it was a splashy, high-profile murder. He knew how to handle VIPs with diplomacy, and still not let them walk all over him. A rare talent he'd heard, especially when it was found in one so young. It was a skill he often was called upon to put into use, as in cases like this one, in which a woman was murdered in the condominium of the famous rock star, Jasmine Barrett.

The detective flashed his badge at the door of the condo as he crossed the threshold. His partner, rookie detective Adam Cozwell, followed on his heels. Heath was sporting a grey blazer, stretched to the maximum as it spanned his upper body, and matching grey pants. Underneath he wore a bright blue shirt with a wide collar that lent his slate gray eyes a bluish tint, something his brother had teased him about earlier in the evening.

The suit screamed cop so loudly, showing his shield at the door was superfluous, especially since he was acquainted with the uniform posted there. But, regs were regs, and he was setting an example for Adam.

The opulent condominium was humming with police life, as he knew it would be. His pulse beat a little faster with the excitement of a new case. Crime scene technicians were busy doing what they could to record the scene, but were told to leave things as they were until he arrived. He said a quiet hello to those he knew by name as he passed them and nodded to those he recognized from other crime scenes. The whole time his gaze was taking in details and recording them, an attribute that earned him the nickname "Hawk" or "Hawkeye." Some guys on the squad would probably be hard-pressed to come up with his given name, but "The Hawk" was known in circles wide and small.

His keen vision took mental note of the plush white carpeting that still had vacuum trails visible in it despite the large amount of traffic that had been in and out. He surveyed and logged in his mind a list of the expensive-looking furniture in neutral colors, as well as pricey glass and wrought iron tables. Very few personal items graced the walls and tabletops, though he saw a large black and white print, perhaps an Ansel Adams, hanging on the central wall. It was an interesting shot of bare trees along a sidewalk lined with empty park benches.

On the large beige couch he spotted her, Jasmine Barrett, or "Jazz," as her fans called her. She didn't appear to be at all like her press photos or videos, where she was usually clad in scanty clothing, with wildly flowing hair, and her legendary pouting mouth parted suggestively. Instead, she wore one of those big, fluffy white robes often found in luxury hotels, provided one had the means to stay there. Her hair was not even shoulder length, he was surprised to find. After thinking it through, it made sense she might wear wigs as part of her "image." The color was not a flamboyant blond or red, as he'd seen in the past, but instead it was a rather staid brown color, although it was wet, which probably muted the hue some. In the call she placed to the precinct, Jasmine Barrett stated she was in the shower prior to discovering the body. Some junior officers chuckled and wolf-whistled at that, which compelled him to give them a tongue-lashing, despite the fact he had some rather steamy fantasies of his own on the way to the scene, centered on that famously fabulous body.

As he watched her, he noticed the slight tremble in her hands as she clutched a white coffee cup and then attempted to bring it to her lips. No doubt someone slipped something in there to calm her, but her eyes still shone with terror. She alternately looked at all the people surrounding her, and then stared at the empty table in front of her. Her damp hair was wavy and slicked back from her pale face, offsetting her large eyes and wide, red lips. She lifted those eyes and caught his for a second. Hers were an arresting shade of green. And, indeed, it was as if his heart was cuffed and read its rights as he peered into them, but then her gaze darted elsewhere. He saw anguish and horror and disbelief in her features, something that never failed to strike him to the core when he met a victim.

"Hawk."

He turned at the sound of the familiar voice.

"Man, am I glad you're here." The speaker slapped Heath on the shoulder, giving Adam a slight nod. Chief of Police Gary Larson was a balding, but physically fit, sixty-three-year-old who never quit his habitual gum chewing, despite having stopped smoking some years ago. "I'd have dealt with this myself if it weren't for IAB breathing down my neck on the whole Menendez thing."

Menendez was a fellow policeman who responded to an incoming call, and found his own fiancé being sexually assaulted. He shot and killed the suspect. Heath and Adam were the first arrivals on the scene after shots were fired, and it wasn't a pretty one. The girl was found tied to the couples' own bed, badly beaten, her blood splattered everywhere. She physically recovered from the attack, but now, the pair had decided to put their wedding on hold until the investigation into Menendez's actions played out. Yeah, the chief definitely had a lot on his plate with that one.

"Glad to be able to help, Chief."

"Okay, let me get you up to speed here, Hawk," he said in a rush, obviously wanting to rid himself of the sticky case as soon as possible. "Jasmine Barrett, as you can see." He motioned to the couch, pausing to consider, with poorly-hidden desire, the young singer in the robe across the room. Adam caught Heath's eye, raising a brow. The chief was not subtle. "She found the vic, a..." he flipped open a worn notebook, "...Patricia Norman, in the rear bedroom, Ms. Barrett's bedroom." He gestured vaguely in the direction of a hall. "Scene's a real mess." He sighed, glancing at the star again. "Poor thing has only said a few words." He shook his head. "'Course with her jackass of an uncle—name's Brody Barrett, by the way—blabbering on and on..."

Heath took in the tall figure to the girl's left, one arm stretched protectively behind her. Or, after watching a few minutes, a more accurate assessment might be that it was stretched possessively around her since he made no move to comfort her in any fashion. He had a long face with strong lines, dark-grey eyes, and a cleft in his chin. He wore a tasteful burgundy shirt and black, pleated pants, but Heath couldn't help thinking he would be more at home at a horse track. The feeling was so strong he began to wonder if he'd seen the guy at one at some point.

"This dude's such a good mouthpiece," the chief was saying, "he oughta go to law school."

Heath snorted, giving Brody one last, withering look as he sat blathering to some uniform opposite him. The officer was seated in a large, cream-colored chair taking note of Brody's every word as if auditioning for a position in the stenographers' pool.

Police Chief Larson led them into a hall. "Right this way."

Heath and Adam followed the chief's lengthy strides to the murder scene. The door opened on a wide room that smelled of new paint and blood. A huge circular bed was the focal point, with a short, pewter, vine-covered, curved footboard, and a much taller headboard made of the same material. In the middle of the bed, the victim's nude body was posed like some twisted mannequin. The killer put her in a seated position, back resting against the headboard, her arms and legs splayed crudely to the sides. Her head was cocked at an angle, held in place by a bright pink, silk scarf tied about her neck to one of the rails behind her. Fire engine red lipstick was roughly smeared around her mouth, and her eyes bulged out of what once must have been a pretty face, but now was a bizarre effigy of sorts. Oddly, her curly blond hair was immaculate. A white rose, dipped in the blood and dripped over the bedspread, lay at an angle across the bed.

Heath was almost startled when the chief began talking again. "The victim was twenty-six years old. Lived here, in the building. She was a photographer and personal friend of Ms. Barrett's." Adam made entries in a small notebook he'd removed from his pocket. "Ms. Barrett was in the shower. She claims she heard nothing, as does her dipshit of an uncle. There was no sign of forced entry."

The chief broke off as Heath approached the bed, crouching to get a better view of the girl's features. He glanced up and noticed the coroner, a tall, thin Black woman, standing close by, jotting her own notes. "Cause of death?" he asked.

"Strangulation." She pointed with her pencil to the victim's chest. "The knife wound happened shortly after death. The blade entered here and then was thrusted vertically, as if to be certain it hit the heart. But the heart had stopped pumping or the blood splatter would have gone considerably farther. As it is, the blood is focused in one large pool on the mattress. The knife was left on the bed."

Heath spotted an area where blood dripped from the victim onto the lavender comforter in a line, traveling to what appeared to be the location of the discarded knife. It apparently was already bagged.

"The knife was clean." The coroner paused and bit the tip of her pencil eraser, eyeing Adam to make sure he was getting everything. "This was personal. The knife was pushed in so hard the hilt left an impression on her skin."

She waved her pencil in a circle near the edges of the wound where Heath distinguished the marks left by the crosspiece of the blade. He stood to inspect the wall adjacent to the bed, where a set of filmy curtains was draped. The killer wrote in blood with large letters at a slant, "JAZZ." The crimson liquid dripped sickeningly down the wall from the letters.

"After you've gotten everything you need here, pictures, and evidence..." Heath instructed, not looking away from the gruesome scrawling, "...let's make sure we try to clean this."

"Yes, sir."

Heath and Adam followed the chief back out to the living room, Adam still scratching furiously in his notebook. This was the upside of having a rookie with him. He could think without having to be concerned about recording everything. He noted the location of the shower as they passed. As he walked toward Jasmine Barrett, he noticed her position hadn't changed. She still sat with her legs curled to one side, holding onto her cup like a lifeline. For some reason, his attention was drawn to her feet. They were pretty, slender and well-groomed. Again he was surprised to find no flash of color on her nails, as he might have expected a rock star to have. Instead, he saw a rich woman's pampered feet; no hangnails there, no jagged edges, simply clean and classy. His focus drifted to the soft curves of her calves and continued to roll upward until his view ended at the fluffy, white fabric of her robe. Her gaze flitted to them as they approached.

Heath reminded himself to be patient with her. If there was one thing he hated, it was spoiled brat, prima donnas. But, spoiled or not, this one had just been through hell, and he could spare her some compassion, although he may have to work on it a little.

"Ms. Barrett...I'd like to introduce you to Detectives Heath McGowan and Adam Cozwell. Detective McGowan is the man I told you of who will be in charge of the investigation. He's the best," the chief added plainly.

The girl swung her feet in front of her to shake his hand and hastily set her cup on an end table, spilling it.

"Dammit, Jasmine!" her uncle barked.

She tried to staunch the flow of liquid onto the carpeting with her hands.

"Here, I'll get it," he snapped, brusquely hopping from the couch and moving in the direction of the kitchen. Heath pulled a handkerchief from his pocket, quickly passing it to her to mop up the spill.

"Oh. Thank you." Her hands shook more violently as she struggled with the gush of what he now recognized as hot chocolate, and, almost without volition, he covered them with his larger ones. Jasmine Barrett lifted her head and he could see the tears in that sea-green of her eyes that she was struggling to hold in. Her skin was so soft. It was like cupping a dove.

"Let me help you." He crouched by the table next to her.

Brody Barrett reentered the room. "Oh, detective. Let me get you a towel. Jasmine," he snarled. "You're in the way!" He climbed past her with a stack of towels, and she backed off. Seeing the soaked hankie she held, he snatched it with a huff, giving her a towel. "Let me get you a new handkerchief, detective."

"No. That's not necessary. Really." Heath straightened, but then shifted to sit on the corner of the coffee table in front of the couch. He sat in an open, relaxed stance, one knee pointed at Jasmine, one slung carelessly over the other side of the table, facing a chair. He glanced at Adam who stood posed with pen and notebook. "Ms. Barrett, I'd like to ask you a few questions if you feel like you're able to—"

"My niece has experienced a horrible ordeal," Brody Barrett cut in, sounding like a sound bite for the eleven o'clock news. "Besides, she has already answered all of this officer's questions."

"Actually," Heath responded, injecting a hint of coolness, "it seemed as if *you* were providing many of the answers. I assure you, I will be reading Officer Davis' report, but I have a few questions of my own."

"Uncle Brody," the singer inserted, startling them both. "If I can help them catch whoever did this to Trish..."

"As you wish." He arched his brows, staring at her icily before returning to his seat next to her. Jasmine dropped her gaze, looking at her hands as they fidgeted with the ends of her belt. Then she seemed to purposefully still them before folding them carefully on top of each other.

"Could you tell me what happened?" Anticipating Brody's interruption, Heath stopped him with a glare and added, "In your own words?"

She smoothed invisible wrinkles in her robe for several seconds prior to speaking. "I was taking a shower—I had just finished exercising—Tr-Trish and I were planning to watch a movie—" Her voice caught and her fists clenched in her lap. "I went to my room...t-to change. I had taken an extra-long shower. I had a sore neck from a show...oh, my God." She lifted her face and he could see her come to some sort of epiphany. "If I had left the bathroom earlier, maybe I could have prevented him from killing her. Maybe I could have fought him off...or called the police or something." She became nearly hysterical.

"Detective..." Brody placed his arm around his niece, gripping her shoulder. Again Heath saw it more as a restraint than a comfort. "My niece needs to get some sleep."

"Sleep?" she said weakly. "I c-can't sleep. How could I sleep?" She sounded confused.

"We'll get you something to sleep, Jazz."

"I don't want to sleep."

"Detective, as you can see, she really is no help to you in her condition."

"All right," he admitted. "The questions can wait until the morning. I'll read Officer Davis' report in the meantime." He squeezed Jasmine's forearm. "I am sorry for your loss, ma'am."

She nodded, seeming unable to trust her voice, as he rose to leave. Brody stood, shaking hands with the chief.

"The crime scene investigators will probably be here for another couple of hours. I'm sorry for the inconvenience, but some of the evidence taking is very time sensitive—"

Heath tuned the conversation out while sneaking another peek at the girl. She sat as if in a daze, oblivious to all the activity surrounding her, wearing that broken expression many victims displayed, like all the neurons in her brain were pinging about, unable to connect and make sense of anything. He was sorry for her. *Hell, her world is usually filled with manicurist appointments and Caramel Latte Frappuccino's, or whatever—not friends murdered in your own bed.* He half wished she would glance up again and catch his eye so he could give her a reassuring smile, but she didn't. She looked small and lost, set adrift on the ocean of the couch.

"—but if you can't reach Lieutenant McGowan or Cozwell for some reason, feel free to call me. We will keep a uniformed policeman posted until such time as Lieutenant McGowan tells you otherwise."

All of the men shook hands. He wondered if he should say anything else to Jasmine Barrett, but decided that in her state, she probably wouldn't hear him anyway. The Chief wanted to give the crime scene people some final instructions, so Heath and Adam left on their own. They were halfway down the hall when he heard the door open behind him and the sound of someone running in his direction. He turned to see Jasmine Barrett rushing towards him. She touched him lightly.

"You'll find him, won't you?" she asked frantically, grasping at the top of her robe to hold it together. "You'll find whoever did this to Tricia?" She gazed at him with such stark desperation in her eyes he was speechless for a second.

Her uncle rushed through the door after her. "Jasmine!"

As Heath peered at her wordlessly, he felt an unfamiliar tug on his heart.

"Jasmine. I'm sorry, detective." Brody grabbed her roughly by the shoulders. "You need to leave the man alone," he said sharply, but then, seeming to notice the frown of disapproval, bordering on anger, on Heath's face, he changed his tone. "Come on, darling, now. Let's go back inside." He shuffled her toward the door. At the threshold she peeked at Heath one more time before disappearing into her condo.

CHAPTER TWO

Heath and Adam continued to amble down the hall to the elevator. He rewound the evening and played it back: the girl, the uncle, the victim. Then as the elevator doors closed to take them to the ground floor, and Adam pored over his notes, he erased it all and started thinking of home and his six-year-old son, Jack.

Ever since his young wife Juliette had left them when Jack was only six weeks old, he had been trying to fill the role of both mother and father, and sometimes he felt as though he failed miserably at both. At least he had his brothers, Luke and older brother Kole, architect/playboy, to lean on when it seemed to him everything he was doing was all wrong. They would assure him that everything he was doing *was* all wrong, but Jack would turn out okay in spite of it. Apparently they believed such lopsided encouragement was part of their brotherly duty.

As they exited the elevator, Adam asked, as if reading his thoughts, "Luke with Jack?"

"Yeah." He shrugged. "Fortunately, they called after I had the chance to tuck him in." Adam understood what it was like to try to balance the life of a cop with home life. He had a pregnant wife and his own toddler running around.

"It's a good thing you have him there to watch Jack."

Luke was living with him. A jazz pianist and composer, he could spend the entire time Jack was at school, and Heath was at work, playing away on the grand piano that had been placed in the front room when he moved in. Heath nodded.

"You're right. It works well for all of us. But I couldn't do this job at all without him."

In the evenings, Luke would take a break and help his culinary-challenged brother to fix supper for the three of them, and even, sometimes, join in on the routine of bath time, story-time, and bedtime. It gave Heath a much-needed break, and Jack a second caring adult in his life. And Lord knows he needed that.

"And he's not just a baby sitter. He's really there for Jack."

"That's nice, man. I wish I had a Luke," he muttered.

They left the building and decided to walk the three short blocks to the precinct house.

"I'm sure Davis will have the report entered, a fresh pot of coffee brewing, and the boss's shoes shined."

Adam laughed. "That guy is such an overachiever."

As they crossed the street Heath peeked at his phone. "Eleven-thirty. With any luck, we'll pull into bed at, maybe...one-thirty or two. At least it's Friday night. Jack will get a box of sugared cereal in the morning and sit and watch cartoons until I show my face at ten or so. We'll have a couple of hours together before I return to do some follow up on this case."

"Henry doesn't know how to work the television yet. He'll be awake at the crack of dawn."

Heath chuckled. "I remember those days."

As he walked, he shrugged into his jacket a little more as the wind blowing off the St. Louis waterfront was chillier than he had anticipated. September in St. Louis was a crap shoot. It could be eighty degrees; it could be forty.

"Yeah." Adam smiled. It was clear he didn't mind much. "Sam—" he referred to his wife, Samantha "—will keep him quiet though."

Heath swiveled to look up at Jasmine Barrett's loft. Lights were still ablaze. Perhaps he'd stop in on the way to his car and check on her. He liked going back to a scene after it had been cleared so that he could walk himself through the crime in the quiet, without any distractions.

"So, who would have wanted to kill Tricia Norman, and then leave her like that—on display—for Jasmine to find?"

"A crazed fan?"

"Writing Jazz on the wall as they had seen it in lights at a concert?" Heath finished for him. "Murdering an innocent woman to get their idol's attention?" They waited at a corner for the light to become green as a car turned in front of them.

"Maybe." Adam commented. "Whoever it was, it would appear Tricia Norman knew them, let them in."

"Unless it was someone who worked at the hotel who had a key." He shrugged. "No use speculating until we read some of the report." The light changed and they entered the crosswalk. His thoughts wandered to the rock star.

"What do you think of Jasmine Barrett?"

Adam whistled. "As hot in person as on stage. Maybe more so." A car honked at them, the driver gesturing, even though Heath and Adam had the light. They both stared at the driver.

Heath contemplated informing the nimrod that they were cops, but decided it wasn't worth the hassle. They continued on. "She was not what I expected. No entourage—" he had anticipated that being a tremendous headache for them. "—just her uncle, Jasmine, and Tricia Norman. No bodyguard. Hmm. We'll have to review the report on that."

Adam nodded. They were silent for a few seconds. "That uncle's a prick."

Heath grunted his agreement, but found his thoughts absorbed by Jasmine. Her onstage persona, tough, sexy, edgy, bold, he'd seen little of that. Except maybe the sexy. She'd appeared quiet, innocent, controlled, even, by her uncle.

"Yeah. What about that uncle? He claimed to be on the phone. That will be easy enough to verify. We can pull the phone records in the morning. But what motive would Brody Barrett have? Another method to intimidate his niece, to control her?"

Adam glanced at him. "She's twenty-four years old, maybe she was having ideas of cutting him loose and managing the business herself."

"I doubt it. Not the girl I saw tonight. She cowered to her uncle." They paused again at a light. "But still, I don't like Brody Barrett." And his instincts were rarely wrong.

They reached the steps of the precinct house, clamoring up them. Heath enjoyed the sound their shoes made as they echoed off the surrounding buildings.

"Quiet tonight," he remarked.

"No Cards' game."

"True. Nothing to draw people downtown. But still and all, quiet for a Friday night."

"True."

A half-hour later they sat with cups of bad coffee from a vending machine, and the Barrett report. Heath skimmed it over, searching for any new information.

Adam leaned forward, reading from the report. "Bodyguard had gone home for the evening. Ms. Barrett and Ms. Norman were planning on spending the evening in and thus did not require his services.'"

Heath set the paperwork on his desk. "Further evidence Tricia Norman knew who was at the door. She felt safe enough to open it, despite the fact that no bodyguard was around. Or...what about the bodyguard? Could he have a grudge against Ms. Barrett and returned to the condominium intending to do her harm?"

"Then why not simply kill her?"

He rose and plucked his suit coat off the back of his chair. "Too many questions at this point. We'll start narrowing the possibilities tomorrow. I'm going home to bed."

Adam smiled broadly. "I thought you'd never say that."

They covered the three blocks to the condo more quickly this time, thoughts of a warm, comfy bed and a morning with his son spurring Heath on. Still, as he rounded the corner and caught sight of her building, his gaze couldn't help but to be drawn skyward. Fewer lights were on now. They were finishing things. Unable to resist, he turned to his partner. "I'm going up for a few minutes. You go on home."

"You sure? I can come with you?"

"Nah. Go on home and I'll call you tomorrow."

"Okay, Hawk." He ambled toward his car. "Tomorrow."

"See ya." Heath hopped the steps to the front door and took the elevator. Nodding at the uniform posted outside this time, he quietly opened the door just as a crime scene investigator, with black-coffee-colored skin and dreadlocks, was about to walk through with his kit.

"How's it goin', Darrius?"

"Hey, Hawk," the young man whispered with a friendly bob of his head as he passed, used to seeing him at the tail end of a crime scene cleanup.

Heath searched for the reason for the hushed tone. The room was dark, except for one lamp left on by the couch, illuminating the sleeping figure of Jasmine Barrett, still clad in her robe. He slid in and closed the door behind him with a soft click. He stood frozen for several seconds, then, slowly moved toward her. When he was within a couple feet of her, he stopped, hands jammed in his pockets, staring. She was curled on her side, with no blanket, one palm underneath her cheek, the other resting below it on her arm.

Even when you sleep you're in the spotlight, he thought with a degree of pity. She seemed more peaceful than a woman who had seen her best friend's strangled body should.

He glanced at the coffee table and examined a bottle of pills left there. Valium. He replaced the pill bottle and took the empty coffee cup near it, sniffing. Yeah, she had some brandy, all right. He peered at her again and had a moment of panic, wondering if she might have purposefully over-medicated herself in despair. He crouched to listen for breathing then laid two fingers on her wrist to feel for a pulse. Slow but steady. He remained crouched next to the sofa, drinking in her face.

God, was she beautiful. Those perfectly arched eyebrows and high cheekbones, and lush, full lips...

But, he told himself, trying to deny the attraction for a woman who was so clearly not his type, *any woman with enough money could buy that for herself. The right cosmetics...surgeons...* A small section of her hair had fallen forward and he caught himself as he was about to push it back. He stood abruptly. What the hell was he thinking? He had no business touching this woman. As if he were fleeing from the scene of a crime, instead of hastening toward one, he turned away from her and headed down the hall.

As in the living room, one light had been left on in the bedroom. The mattress had been removed and a valiant attempt had been made to expunge the name from the wall, but a lighter patch of paint still remained as a telltale sign. Heath began to go through the crime in his mind, asking, and then answering his own questions.

How had the killer gotten Tricia Norman into the bedroom? There were no signs of a struggle or drag marks in the carpeting in the hall, so he assumed she was lured into the bedroom somehow. He read in Officer Davis' report that the scarf wrapped around her neck belonged to Ms. Barrett, and had been draped over the knob of the footboard. A weapon of opportunity, then. The killer strangles her from behind. Maybe she fell on the bed. Then he undresses her, poses the body, and stabs it with a knife he had in his possession. He then dips his finger in the victim's blood and writes on the wall, all while Jasmine Barrett is in the shower. Pretty bold. Two people in the home, but the killer comes and goes without notice.

Heath climbed on the bed and calculated the height of the perpetrator by reaching to the bleached spot on the wall and tracing her name. Adjusting for the missing mattress, he judged the killer had to be at least six-foot. Swiveling to scrutinize the room again, his sharp gaze registered something. Stretching, he inspected the base of the pewter and bleached wood ceiling fan. No light fixture was attached to it, as the room relied on two tall pewter lamps on either side of the bed for its light, and yet a small glass opening was in the center. Some kind of sensor, maybe? Curious, he twisted the base to unscrew it.

It came loose and he found a mechanism inside it, attached to the base. After examining the box, he determined it was a mini-camera. It was a live feed, so there would be no tape or film to view on this end. A red light was on. He guessed it was operated by remote control, which would have to be used within a short range. Did Jasmine Barrett like to record her sexual exploits? The thought had him hurriedly screwing it back in again. Something he would definitely have to ask Ms. Barrett about, he thought uncomfortably.

The detective surveyed the bedroom one last time. He noted a vase of cream-colored roses on the dresser, counting eleven. So the killer probably took one from the vase to dip in the blood, again taking advantage of what was available to him.

Heath left the bedroom and entered the adjacent bathroom. It was a large room with a spa tub and a marble, stand-alone shower. He ran his hand along the marble double-sink vanity picking up a fancy bottle of perfume with a bulb mister and smelling it. He found himself closing his eyes and imagining her face again...those gorgeous, but haunted eyes that had seemed to peer into his depths, begging him to help her somehow. The scent was all her, sexy yet light and innocent at the same time. He cleared his throat and hastily set the mister down. He was letting his hormones get the best of him. He was a professional and he needed to act like one. Briskly, he crossed to the shower.

The bath mat was still wet from when she had stepped on it, which he wasn't allowing himself to think of even for one second. He turned the water on. Between the thundering of the shower head and the insulation of the marble, he doubted Jasmine Barrett could have heard much outside of the room. He left the water running and went into the bedroom. Yes, the killer would have been able to hear the water through the pipes. He would know when Jasmine was finished with her shower and would have time to escape while she toweled off, an image he also had to force from his mind. He returned to the bathroom to stop the flow of the water. Satisfied, he extinguished the light and shut the door behind him.

As he twisted, Heath saw the couch at the end of the hall, centered in the frame of the walls and ceiling, soft light spilling on it from the left. She still lounged, like some goddess caught napping. He strode forward. He couldn't quite figure out what he found so fascinating about Jasmine Barrett sleeping there, why he was pulled again to sit on the coffee table by her and follow the rhythmic rise and fall of her shoulders and chest. The motion was slight, but it reassured him enough he wasn't compelled again to take her pulse.

"She's beautiful, isn't she?"

He jumped. He'd been so mesmerized by the figure on the couch he hadn't heard Brody Barrett approach from beyond it. Brody bent over her and brushed his hand along her face and then ran it down the length of her body in a manner that made Heath's skin crawl. The asshole hadn't even bothered to keep his voice low. Jasmine murmured something and rolled onto her back. Her robe fell open a little with the movement and Heath stood, feeling suddenly like a voyeur. The uncle looked at him with a leering quality, making him strangely uncomfortable with leaving them alone.

"The guard will be right outside the door," he stated, though it was unnecessary, and then added, rather pointedly, "And I'll come again tomorrow."

"We'll see you then." The style in which Brody referred to the two of them, almost like they were a couple, gave him the creeps. Maybe he was letting his imagination, combined with his libido, run away with him. He left without saying anything further, glancing at her again as the door closed. He saw Brody standing with arms crossed in front of Jasmine, watching him.

CHAPTER THREE

It had all been so easy.

The girl, Jasmine's photographer-slash-friend, had answered the door and luckily recognized him, although they'd only met briefly that morning when Brody introduced him as a family friend. She let him into the condo with a smile, telling him, when he asked for Jasmine, that she was in the shower, and it would probably be awhile, as Jazz always took long showers.

He knew then he would kill her. He hadn't intended to do it that night, but the opportunity presented itself so he'd thought, why not?

"Is Brody home?" he asked casually.

"Yeah. Do you want me to get him?" She started toward the area he knew Brody's room was in.

"No, no. That won't be necessary. I don't want to disturb him." What he actually meant was he didn't want Brody to be disturbed by the sounds of her murder, but he couldn't quite tell her that, could he?

He knew he needed to get her at a distance from that end of the condo, and it came to him like a flash of lightening. Brilliant. He told her—Tricia, he'd thought Jasmine called her—he came to see Jasmine's new bedroom set. As he'd hoped, she had offered to show it to him. As she sauntered along the hall in front of him, babbling on and on about Jasmine's choice in paint and how much she'd liked the bedspread and blah, blah, blah, he'd slipped his driving gloves from his coat pocket and put them on his hands.

He immediately saw the scarf on the end of the bed. When she wasn't paying attention, he stole it, smelling the silk. *Ahhh. My sweet Jasmine.* He had anticipated using the knife, but it seemed far more appropriate to kill her with a piece of Jasmine's own clothing.

"That's a lovely design on the headboard. It's hearts, isn't it?" There were no hearts, of course, but he needed her to look in that direction. The scarf slid without difficulty around the slim column of her neck and he brought his knee up violently into her back to brace himself so he could pull the life right out of her. With a sick little squeak, like the kind heard through open windows at night when a cat killed a rabbit, Tricia...Whatever-Her-Name-Was, was dead, slumped over Jasmine's bed, and all done within minutes. He knew he had plenty of time, so he decided to set the stage for Jasmine's exit from the shower.

It has to be dramatic, memorable. He sucked in a breath. *Yes. Yes. Jasmine would find her nude.* He snatched his victim's clothes off and merely became a bit aroused, merely fondled the dead girl's breasts a moment or two. But then he'd realized it was a betrayal to Jasmine, and he scolded himself. He stuck the clothing under the bed; it simply didn't add anything to the scene, and he wanted everything to be perfect. So he posed her. It was hot, sweaty work, but well worth it in the end. He'd tied her neck to the bedpost with a neat bow and stepped away to admire his work. It was good...had the horror element... yet...lacked the gore somehow.

I need blood. He took his knife from his leg holster and quickly plunged it into the girl's heart, but was unimpressed by the amount of splatter. *I need more.* That was when he had the idea of writing Jazz's name in blood on the wall. *It will be just the right effect.* He set the knife on the bed and dipped his fingertips in the blood and began his twisted Picasso. When he'd completed his task, he stood in the doorway so he could see what Jasmine would see.

That's when he noticed the vase of roses on her dresser. On impulse he took a rose from the vase. He breathed in its fresh fragrance as he thought of Jasmine's body in the shower in the room behind him, of the water cascading all along those luscious curves of hers. He dipped the rose in the blood slowly seeping from the knife wound and placed it with care on the corner of the bed. *If only the blood were spread wider...*

He searched the room for anything that might provide a finishing touch. The lipstick. He did it carefully at first, surprised to find the girl's lips so warm and then smeared it all over for a more abstract, surreal effect. Then he heard the shower turn off. He wished he could see Jasmine's expression when she found her gift, but maybe next time.

There would be another time, he knew now. Killing Tricia had been too quick and hadn't quite satisfied his thirst for violence. He'd take more time on his second murder. Maybe Brody. After all, he had to be at least partially responsible for taking Jasmine from him. Yes, Brody would do. He'd simply have to wait for the right opportunity to present itself. He was a patient man, and Jasmine was worth it.

THE BOUNCE TO THE MIDSECTION woke Heath like gunfire.

"Daddy! Daddy!"

So much for cartoons.

"What's up, Squirt?" Heath said gruffly, ruffling his son's curly, blond hair. Before Jack could answer, he grabbed the boy by the arms and swung him onto the bed so he was on all fours above his wiggling son. Jack giggled with an expectant air. "You know what's going to happen, don't ya, Squirt?"

He nodded, staring gleefully into Heath's sleep-deprived face.

Heath stuck his mouth into Jack's neck-folds. He did his best imitation of the cartoon dog. "Scooby-dooby-doo."

The vibrations his voice made launched Jack into another laugh attack, which was followed by Heath inflicting the torturous form of raspberries known around the McGowan house as "belly blubbers." Finally, he collapsed, winded, on the mattress as Jack's peals of laughter bubbled down to shuddering gasps. He twisted to find himself eye-to-eye with his six-year-old. "That's paybacks for wakin' me, pal." He smiled into the face that happily mirrored his own, not his ex-wife's.

Jack crawled onto him, planting his small, sharp elbows on his chest and resting his head on bunched fists as he talked. He kicked his feet, Heath adjusting every so often to avoid potentially lethal blows below his waist.

"Uncle Luke said he's gonna take me to the zoo today. We didn't get to go last weekend 'cause it rained, remember?" He went on, not waiting for an answer. "And he said if it's okay with Timmy Wainwright's mom, maybe they can go with us too. Isn't that neat?"

"Sounds great, bud." He grinned. He was sure, even though he knew Luke would never admit it, the fact Timmy Wainwright's newly-divorced mom was cute had everything to do with his brother's invitation. He rolled and swung Jack onto his feet at the side of the bed then fell out himself. He crossed to an old, high-boy dresser to get a pair of jeans to cover his boxer-briefs. "Do you want me to make you some of my special chocolate chip pancakes?"

"Okay," Jack shrugged. "Are you going to burn them this time?"

Heath threw the t-shirt he had just pulled from the drawer at his son, watching it fall comically over his face. "No, I'm not going to burn them this time, wiseguy." He made a grab at his shirt, but Jack took off running. "Get back here, you little thief," he hollered, chasing his son along the lengthy hall to the curving front stairs. On a wider step that served as a ninety-degree angle for the stairs, he caught Jack and scooped him up. Holding him under his arm like a football, he proceeded downstairs and into the kitchen.

In the sunny kitchen, at the tiny wooden table, Luke sat, slightly over-dressed for his day at the zoo, in a crisp, freshly pressed shirt and khakis. He lowered his newspaper with a faux-frown as the pair entered.

"What is this ruckus for?" he growled sternly, but with a flicker of a smile.

Jack squealed as Heath flipped him upside down, then deposited him on the hardwood, retrieving his shirt and slipping it on. "Daddy's makin' pancakes."

"Oh, good Lord." Luke lifted the paper again. "Should I call the fire department?" A flying dish-towel bent his paper and he folded it resignedly. Luke rose to refill his coffee cup which he had saved, with quick reflexes, from crashing to the floor. "How did things go last night?" he asked casually.

"You got a new case, Daddy?" Jack asked, very businesslike, as he clambered into his seat.

"The kid has the ears of an elephant." Heath rolled his eyes as he drew a bowl from a glass-fronted cabinet. "Yes, son," he said more loudly. It was always a tough call deciding how much information to share with the boy. He didn't want to lie to him, so he kept things as simple as possible. Daddy caught the bad guys, all's right with the world.

"What's this one about?" he questioned with a serious expression.

"Well..." Heath stared into the depths of the refrigerator, hoping to find his answers in there with the eggs. He gathered the eggs and milk and then reached in again for the juice. "This one actually involves a lady who is a rock star, you wouldn't know her. Her name's Jasmine Barrett—"

"Jazz?" Jack's eyes grew wide. "You know Jazz?"

"How do you...?"

"Timmy's mom listens to her when she drives us places. Plus, I've seen her video on TV," he answered matter-of-factly.

"Is that so?" Raising a brow Heath glanced sideways at Luke, who shrugged innocently.

"She didn't get hurt, did she?" Jack asked with concern.

"Oh, no, pal. She's fine. Really fine," he added under his breath to his brother.

"I'll bet," Luke commented. "I was reading the story in the paper."

Heath scanned the headlines in bold on the paper Luke had set on the counter. He couldn't see all the words, but deciphered, "Murder a New Tune for Jasmine Barrett." What the hell was that supposed to mean? Who wrote that kind of crap anyway? "Shit. I mean, shoot. I thought we had flown under the radar. I didn't see any press last night."

"Well, apparently they heard." Luke swiped with a rag at the egg he had speckled all across the countertop.

"I'm gonna need to read that when you're finished, if that's okay?" Heath strained to read the pancake recipe on the box over again, for the third time, checking the ingredients he had in his bowl and what was still left on the counter with uncertainty.

"Sure." Luke leaned on the counter, eyeing his big brother. "So...what was she like?"

"Different than I expected," Heath mused, half to himself.

"In what way?"

"I don't know." He shrugged.

Luke frowned. He withdrew a skillet from the cabinet and put it on the stove to heat. "You are usually pretty succinct and unerringly accurate when it comes to summarizing people."

He shrugged again, but got an uneasy feeling in the pit of his stomach.

"Hey, Jackie-boy...why don't you scoot on upstairs and get dressed? It's gonna take your dad at least a half-hour to produce a pancake at the rate he's going anyway." Heath gave Luke a sharp thwack on top of his head. "Ouch." But Jack obediently scurried off to hunt for passably-clean clothes on his bedroom floor. "So...was she as hot in person as she is on TV?"

Heath smiled, remembering. "Yes. But in a different respect." He quickly elaborated before his unusually nosy brother could interrupt. "She wasn't as 'rock star' as I expected. More...classy, high-brow...." He frowned. "But, you have to remember, she'd just seen her best friend, and as far as I could tell, only friend, murdered." He stopped mixing the ingredients in the bowl and stared into space, recalling how her eyes sent a ripple of desire through him.

After a second he sensed Luke watching him and began to stir furiously. He needed to change the subject, and quick.

He exhaled. "So...you using my son to score with the divorcée?"

"Oh, you heard about that, huh? No, man. I'm using *her* son to occupy *Jack*, so I can score with the divorcée."

"What? Planning to find some dark corner of the reptile house to run your hand up her dress?"

"Now that's an idea..." Luke blanked out for a beat, then switched gears, smacking Heath's arm. "Don't be crude. Besides, I don't even know if she'll be wearing a dress. Hey, Jack, buddy...lookin' sharp."

Jack was sporting blue jeans and a white video game t-shirt with merely a small spot of chocolate ice cream on it. Heath debated whether to risk the headache of asking him to change or not and decided, since Jack was in a fairly good mood, he'd try for a clean shirt. "Any chance we could find another shirt with a little less dairy product on it?"

Jack rolled his eyes, but turned around and trudged out of the room.

"Did you see me put milk in?"

"Move," Luke snapped, irritated. He pried the wooden spoon from Heath's fingers and nudged him so he could get in front of the bowl.

Heath grinned and hiked himself onto the counter to observe the chef prepare breakfast. "I thought Kole had the hots for little Ms. Wainwright?"

"You mean Mr. 'Hi, my name is Kole, as in hot as a...'?"

"Ugh. I vomit in my mouth every time he says that."

"No kiddin'. What kind of woman falls for that trash?"

"Well, a lot, apparently 'cause he never seems to be minus one."

"Yeah, but their combined I.Q.s wouldn't equal a temperature at a pediatrician's office."

"Good point." Heath high-fived him, but then added. "Sadly, we're jealous."

"Yeah, I guess. And for the record, Kole didn't officially call dibs on Vanessa, so she's fair game."

"*Vanessa*, eh?"

Jack sauntered in with an Army-green video game shirt on that hid the food that had been spilled on it well.

"Muuuch better."

Luke slid a plate of pancakes in front of him. "Here ya go, Jacks."

Jack grinned. "You made 'em, Uncle Luke?"

He returned the grin. "You didn't hear any smoke alarms going off, did ya, son?"

Heath shook his head at the pair. They never gave him a break, but he guessed he wouldn't have it any other way.

CHAPTER FOUR

Heath jogged up the steps of The Lofts. The day was bright and sunny and he bit back the urge to whistle. His beige suit coat rustled in the breeze as he held the door open for an elderly man. He wore blue jeans, and a white shirt, unbuttoned at the neck. It was Saturday, after all; some casualness could be expected. Once in the door, he patted his blond, wavy hair, restoring order where the wind had disturbed it.

He knew he needed to tone it down some, although he couldn't help but be in a good mood. He'd been able to play some catch with Jack before he left, something they both enjoyed immensely. In addition, he got some final jabs in at Luke prior to the Wainwrights arriving. Luke had actually seemed nervous. It was good for his little brother to be with someone, he spent way too much time alone with that damn piano of his. Or maybe it was his excitement for Adam. He had called in the middle of the night to say his wife was in labor.

Whatever the reason, it was time to put his business face on. People were mourning upstairs. He understood that far too well. His mother had died of cancer when Luke was 14, he was 16, and Kohl was 18. His father had died a year later when he had driven drunk into oncoming traffic, killing himself and a family of three. The same people who had come to mourn when his mother died, who looked on them with pity and compassion and offered soft advice, came a year later without knowing what to say. Kole became their legal guardian, but it was Heath who held them all together. He was the one to go to the grocery store, to help Luke with his homework, to pay the bills. The guilt and shame that came with knowing his father took innocent people's lives drove him to become a policeman, to right wrongs, to keep others safe. Yes, he knew how blinding sorrow could be, how tempting it was to give in to it, and he knew how to survive after death left its calling card.

But today he was here for not only those mourning Tricia Norman's death, but for Tricia herself. He would discover who killed her and make sure they were brought to justice. He strode along the hall purposefully, checked in with the officer stationed at the door, and knocked.

JASMINE HAD BEEN LIVING in a daze. She couldn't absorb it. Her friend was dead, and all she wanted was to have Tricia's shoulder to cry on about it. They were supposed to watch a movie together. Trish had rented that old John Cusack flick, "Say Anything," the one where he held the radio above his head outside the girl's window to win her over. They had both loved John Cusack...

And then she walked into her room.

My God...who could have done that to Trish? She was yards away while a stranger had killed her best friend. Had Trish been scared? Had she been in pain? Did the killer do it because of something Jasmine had done, or said, or been to them? How could this have happened in her home? How could she not have stopped whoever it was from doing the awful things he did to her best friend? Her mind spun.

"Dammit, Jasmine. Get the damn door."

Someone had been knocking for a while. She knew that now. She unfolded herself from the couch, and went to answer it.

"Hi."

He stood there, the detective from the night before. She squinted at him for a second, unable to think of what came next. He waited expectantly.

Oh, my gosh. Where are my manners?

"Come in, please." Her voice sounded strange. She was detached. Was it the pills her uncle kept shoving down her throat? She would refuse to take them. She regarded the man vacantly. Small talk was out of the realm of possibilities.

JASMINE BARRETT HAD answered the door looking incredible in a less-than-incredible outfit. She wore tailored creamy-beige slacks and a lightweight, black V-neck sweater that rode elegantly over those tempting curves of hers. She was barefoot and he admired her dainty feet again. He watched her as she moved, couldn't help it. What the clothes did for the front, it did for the back, too. She held herself straight as she walked and he was grateful for the large room, and lengthy trip to the couch. He took in the gentle slope of her shoulders, which he yearned to caress, the inward curve of her tiny waist, and her seductive hips. That little stroll to the couch was enough to give him material to fantasize with for weeks.

Heath sat opposite of her in an oversized chair. He cleared his throat, trying to clear his mind of visions of her at the same time and opened a notebook.

"What can I do for you, officer?"

Her voice was cool, prim even. He glanced up, surprised by her tone, and her beautiful green eyes stared right through him as if he wasn't even there. This is what he had expected last night, the you're-a-lowly-civil-servant-and-I-am-so-far-above-you-I-won't-even-waste-the-effort-of-being-polite-on-you attitude. And even though he expected it, he experienced a moment of shock, an invisible slap in the face. The lust she stirred turned cold in him in a rolling wave and he hardened his features.

Just like Juliette. His Juliette. His ex-wife.

HEATH HAD MET HER AT the Policemen's Ball, of all places, a do-gooder socialite with legs that wouldn't quit. He still remembered the black dress she wore, with a slit along the side that ran from here to eternity, and rhinestones that followed the V-neckline between her breasts and sparkled there like a landing strip guiding a plane in. She had raven-black hair, twisted into some elaborate bun. He was wearing his dress blues. Their gazes met from across the room, and that was it. She traversed the dance floor and boldly asked him to dance, and he was captured by her spell from the instant she parted those red, sensuous lips to ask him. Juliette had told him he was her Romeo.

They dated for months, light playful dates, often followed by sweaty, heart-pounding sex. Juliette's parents hated him, which had been a bonus from her viewpoint, and when she became pregnant and he asked her to marry him, she said yes. The wedding was a grand affair, attended by everyone from the mayor, to Juliette's hair stylist. Heath thought they were happy and dreamed about the family they would have together, but they started to fight almost immediately. Juliette didn't like that Heath had to go to work all the time, which he found somewhat baffling, and she became bored. Boredom stoked her shopping urges and his wife spent outrageous amounts of money on dresses she would never have the opportunity to wear on a policeman's salary. His house, which she had found so quaint at the onset, became worn and dismal to her, a trap from which she had to escape. But when Jack was born, they again had a sense of euphoria similar to their first days of marriage.

That was, until Juliette wanted a nanny. Heath thought they should raise their son themselves and the arguing began all again. Responding to the stressful environment, Jack cried nonstop. Finally, fearing their discord was harming their child, Heath consented to a compromise by moving with Juliette and Jack into her parents' mammoth manor house. But, eventually, he felt like a kept man. Juliette was seldom home, leaving the baby with the housemaids, and Jack seemed more miserable than ever. Finally, waking at three-forty-five one morning to Jack's scream and no Juliette beside him, Heath packed his bags and the things that Jack needed, and drove, before the sun had even risen, back to his house, which luckily hadn't sold yet. The next day, he took the house off the market and Juliette flew to Paris. After that, they only spoke through their lawyers. Juliette hadn't seen Jack since. She had dismissed them both from her life like discarded playthings. The sad thing was, after all was said and done, Heath still loved her. It had taken him a long time to get Juliette out of his system, and even at the moment, some of her lingered.

HE COULD FEEL THE LASTING effects as his neck bristled, sitting near this woman whom he'd just decided was one cold, hard bitch, like Juliette.

"Ms. Barrett," he said evenly, "I need to ask you a couple of questions."

She waited, saying nothing.

"I found a camera in the ceiling fan in your bedroom."

She stared at him blankly. "A c-camera..."

"Listen, I'm not here to judge you. If you want to put a camera in your bedroom, it's your business. But if it was running last night, we could have the killer on film."

"...in my ceiling fan?" She dropped her chin, folding her arms over her chest, and rubbing them. "And you think I..." Her gaze came up to his again and he could see now she wasn't mortified, she was terrified. *She* hadn't installed the camera. Someone else had, without her knowing. "Oh, my God. I-I've got to get some air. I'm sorry." She jumped from the couch as her uncle and another man entered. "What is he doing here?" she screamed, nearly hysterical. She glared at the man as if he were a snake that crawled from the grass.

"Jasmine," her uncle said sharply, shocked by her rudeness.

"I've got to get some air," she said again, covering her stomach. She dashed from the room, opening a sliding door and stepping onto a wide balcony.

Brody Barrett peered after her for a beat, and then shook his head as if to shake off the behavior. He turned to Heath. "Detective, I didn't realize you were here. Let me introduce you to Lionel Parker. Lionel, Detective Heath Mc...McGarrett was it?"

"McGowan." Heath responded, extending his hand. He glanced at Jasmine on the balcony. The sun was still shining, but the wind buffeted her, pushing hair back into her face roughly. "I was asking Ms. Barrett a few follow-up questions. If you'll excuse me..."

"Of course. Of course. Please, don't let us interrupt."

Heath nodded to them and strode to the balcony. When he opened the door, Jasmine spun around, her eyes flashing. "You thought I...because I play rock, you think I'm...some kind of slut?"

"No, Ma'am. I'm sorry. I jumped to the wrong conclusion."

Her jaw remained clenched for a moment, but then she sighed and he watched the anger drain from her expression, replaced with a delayed astonishment. She sank onto a chaise lounge, and he sat on the edge of the one next to it. "Someone got into my apartment somehow and put a camera..."

"Actually, it appeared to me like the fan had been specially fitted for the camera. Do you remember who installed it for you?"

"Yes. My neighbor, Sam. He works for a lighting store. He said he'd gotten some new fans in that went with my bed—he saw it when the men delivered it—and Sam told me he would be happy to install it."

Even before she finished speaking, he was dialing his phone. "I'll call in and have Officer Davis check the report to see if they have any more information on your neighbor." He spoke into the receiver. "Franklin? This is Hawk. I'm in the field and I was wondering if you might have the time to find some information in the Barrett file for me? ...Great. Ms. Barrett's neighbor, a Sam..." He glanced at her for confirmation and she nodded. He waited.

"Sam Dobski...in 14A?"

Jasmine nodded. "That's him."

"Do you, by any chance, have written down there what he does for a living? ...Thank you," he said grimly. He disconnected. "Ms. Barrett," he said gently, "your neighbor does not work for a lighting company. He's an accountant for David and Hyde."

"But he said..." She digested this new information. "But, he's so nice." She paused. "Do you know...what he c-can see?"

He touched her shoulder, feeling guilty for having thought poorly of her. "No, ma'am. But I definitely need to have a talk with him."

"You don't think he...had anything to do with Trish?"

"I'm not sure. But I'll find out." He rose from his chair, and Jasmine cautiously got to her feet. "Ms. Barrett..."

She studied him appraisingly. "Please," she said, "call me Jasmine...or Jazz."

He felt horrible. "I'm so very sorry for assuming—"

"It's okay," she responded dismissively, staring at the floor, apparently too embarrassed to even keep eye contact.

She was so different from what Heath had expected, sweet, innocent, forgiving, trusting, perhaps too trusting. "I'm going next door to question him. Then I'll come back and let you know what I discover."

"Thank you," she said, finally meeting his gaze. "I'm sorry I yelled at you. My emotions are all over the place...or not even there... I guess I'm not handling this too well."

"You're handling this fine. And don't worry about me. I live with my brother. We yell at each other every day. I have thick skin." Heath had tried to lighten the mood a bit and was rewarded with a glimmer of an upturn at the corners of her lips. He held her arms and bent to get her to lift her chin again and look at him. "I'll investigate this guy. Don't worry."

"Thanks. You know, it's funny. This is the kind of thing I would discuss with Tricia. We'd go to the roof to get away from my uncle." A sad smile crept across her face. "She and I even moved one of her couches up there. Now she's gone."

"Are you okay? Do you want me to call your uncle out here?"

She shifted her focus to take in the men in the living room. She paused a long moment, a number of emotions shadowing her features. "No," she said tiredly. "I'm fine."

Heath left her, and giving no further explanation to her uncle, told him he'd return in a little while.

CHAPTER FIVE

Heath was ticked. At the very least Jasmine Barrett's neighbor had taken advantage of her, and it was possible he was even guilty of murder. The detective rapped on the door loudly, and then tried to settle his emotions. But every time he thought about the bastard spying on Jasmine, his teeth began to clench. When the door swung open, he made sure Sam Dobski saw a man smiling broadly on the doorstep.

"Mr. Dobski? My name is Lieutenant Heath McGowan." He showed the man his badge. "I have a few follow-up questions from your interview yesterday. Is now a good time?"

Tall and lean, the man opened the door further. "Of course, officer. Come in."

Heath casually searched the apartment, noting the same white carpeting and beige paint as Jasmine's. However, Dobski favored furniture with a modern design, and huge prints of black and white swirls and geometric figures on unframed canvas adorned the walls.

"Please, have a seat."

The amiable man indicated an armless couch that was firm when he sat on it. Dobski had a seat opposite him on a bright red chair of a similar design. He judged him to be in his mid-forties, with tightly curled, but thinning strawberry-blond hair. He wore a conservative, navy sweater atop a starched white shirt tucked into tan pants. Glasses sat neatly on the bridge of his nose. Heath thought he looked like a dentist.

Dobski crossed his legs and rubbed at a smudge on his expensive shoes. "What can I do for you?"

"Well, I'm sorry to bother you," Heath grinned to beat the band, "but..." He opened his notebook. "Hey, you wouldn't by chance be a Cardinals fan, would you?" He gestured to the TV set. "I'd love to try to catch the score."

"Sure, sure, no problem." Dobski rose and strolled to the TV to switch it on to the appropriate channel.

Heath took the opportunity to glance around. He didn't see any extra wires leading to the TV. He peered through the open door of a bedroom. He saw a bed that appeared tidy enough to bounce a quarter off and a dresser with two TVs. He could see wires intertwined as they ran along the floor and knew Jasmine's bedroom was on the other side of that very wall. Unable to stop himself, he stood. "Do you get good reception on those TVs?" He motioned toward the bedroom, his voice becoming edgy.

Dobski hurriedly slid over to pull the door to the bedroom shut. "Those TVs don't even work. Keep meaning to repair them one of these days."

His anxiety was enough confirmation for Heath. He advanced on Dobski.

"Do you get off watching her undress?" His voice had a low growl. He moved forward until he was inches from Dobski's face.

Dobski wet his lips, his gaze flying everywhere but to Heath. "I don't know what you're talking about."

"Do you get off spying on her when she..." he swallowed, uncomfortable with the thought, "...entertains guests?" He banged his fist behind the man's head, making the bedroom door vibrate, feeling an unusual slip in his control. "Is that how you get your jollies? Observing a girl who has no idea she's being observed as she engages in her personal, *private* business?" The more he thought of the pencil-necked geek getting a hard-on as he viewed...and listened to what went on in Jasmine's bedroom, the more pissed he became.

"I think I'd like you to leave," Dobski said, trying to sound like he was in charge, but unable to keep his voice from trembling.

"Is that what you want, Sammy?" Heath stepped closer, his arms rigid, his own muscular chest bumping against the sweater-wearing accountant's.

Dobski cleared his throat. "I don't believe you have a warrant, do you officer?" As he ended his sentence, he became a bit more defiant, his eyes picking up a little fire.

Heath hesitated. "No," he admitted. "No, I don't." He sighed, frustrated with himself. "But you damn well better believe I will when I come back. And if you had *anything* to do with that girl getting killed, I'll make sure you do some serious time. If you cooperate and give us evidence that helps us find the killer, then things will go easier. You mull over that." He stared at Dobski for a few more long seconds then turned around to storm out the door and slam it shut.

When he reappeared a couple of hours later with the warrant, Dobski was gone, as were all the wires and any tapes he might have had. Heath indulged himself by kicking the dresser. He'd blown it. He'd let his emotions get away from him and whatever evidence there may have been had probably been destroyed. It was so unlike him to make such a big mistake. And now he had to return to an already frightened Jasmine Barrett and tell her the man who had been spying on her was in the wind and, thanks to his ineptness, no evidence existed to tie Sam Dobski to the murder of Tricia Norman.

CHAPTER SIX

Heath knocked resignedly on the apartment door. Brody Barrett opened it. "Lieutenant McGowan, please come in."

"Is Ms. Barrett available?"

"As a matter of fact, she is. She hasn't said word one to me and has been exercising like a fiend since you left. What exactly took place on that balcony?" he asked with a suggestive leer.

"Nothing," he said defensively. "Where is Ms. Barrett?"

"I'm pretty sure you can call her Jasmine, officer." Brody eyed him speculatively, then turned and headed toward his section of the apartment. "She's down the hall on the right."

Heath lifted his voice. "Did you know your neighbor was spying on your niece?"

Brody froze and then turned on his heel. "What?"

"Sam Dobski planted a camera in the ceiling fan he installed for Jasmine."

Brody's face went from pale to two shades of red in less than three-point-five seconds. "What?" he roared. "Well, you're arresting him, aren't you?"

Heath considered his reaction; it seemed sincere. "Unfortunately, your neighbor destroyed all the evidence, but we are searching for him."

Brody Barrett still hadn't recovered from his shock. "That little bastard. That sick little bastard. You can bet if I find him, he'll have to do some explaining to me. That's for damn sure." Brody whirled again and stomped away without another word.

Heath kept his gaze on the man until he was gone then turned and proceeded along the hall in the opposite direction. As he got closer, he could see shadows flitting across the carpeting and could hear puffs and grunts as well as the sounds of impact. When he came to the rectangular spot on the carpet lit by an open door, he paused.

Jasmine was dressed in smooth, black spandex shorts with a white stripe on the side that reminded him of a highway he wished to God he could travel. The matching athletic bra was snug and revealed enough of her voluptuous breasts to make him want for more. She stood in a small makeshift boxing ring and danced in front of a punching bag that hung from the ceiling. She furiously jabbed and kicked at it, her hair and body dripping with sweat. Fascinated, he stood noiselessly, admiring her work, impressed by her form. Someone had obviously taught her well. Her concentration was intense and he got the sense the condo could burn to ashes around her and she'd still be swinging at that black bag.

JASMINE FELT BETTER than she had since...*it* had happened. Replacing the horror and fear with anger helped. She imagined the punching bag wearing a sweater vest, like her perverted neighbor seemed to prefer, and kicked the heck out of it. She was taking control back a bit, being less of a victim. Then she imagined the bag as her Uncle Brody.

She became aware she was being observed. She glanced over, startled, and saw him standing in the doorway. Tall, Blond, and Gorgeous. She steadied the punching bag, wishing it was as easy to still her heart. She watched him without speaking. Of course she had noticed how good looking he was the other night, but only in a peripheral sort of way, registering the fact but not really soaking it in, her mind wrapped in grief. Now, she decided to let her body feel, and to respond as a woman naturally would. Tricia would have flipped for him, she realized sadly.

Jasmine was glad she finally refused the little white pills her uncle kept forcing on her, as it was a pleasure to feel again, even the pain. She grabbed a towel and meandered toward Officer McGowan, wiping her neck where the sweat was dripping uncomfortably between her shoulder blades.

AS JASMINE ADVANCED, her focus trained on his, he couldn't help but think of a cat. Each movement she made contained a certain feline gracefulness and mystery. She stepped forward until she was within a foot of him, dabbing at the sweat on her throat. He struggled to steer his gaze away from the beads of moisture slowly gliding down her skin and into the shadow of her cleavage. How was it that a woman could get so sweaty and still smell fabulous, like a garden after the rain?

She was actually shorter than he thought at first. Her willowy figure gave the impression of height, but he noted her forehead was almost level with his lips. There seemed to be a shimmery, vibrating field between them. He contemplated the ease with which he could bend and touch his lips to her unequivocally inviting ones.

They stood for several moments like this, her chin tilted up to study him, her breathing gradually decreasing to its normal rate after her bout with the bag. Her eyes seemed clearer than he had seen them before. It was obvious the workout had the desired effect of relaxing her, as a slow, sexy smile spread over her face, mirroring the one that had worked its way onto his.

She broke the spell. "Detective."

She turned from him and he gave himself a minute to appreciate what spandex could do for a really tight tush. "Yes, Ms. Barrett...Jasmine," he said as she began to correct him. He cleared his throat, glancing at his feet and inhaling. "I talked to your neighbor." He thought about how to frame things in the most positive light.

"And?" She swiveled to peer at him, her expression wary, and he knew she was bracing herself for whatever it was he had to say.

"I'm afraid what we suspected was true. I saw two TV sets in his bedroom."

She winced and put her back to him again, her arms crossing in front as she stroked them in a gesture that seemed to be both an attempt to comfort, and a belated effort to cover herself from prying eyes. He debated running his own hands along her arms to offer warmth and reassurance.

Then he considered how inappropriate that would be. He realized he had come to like her.

"I'm sorry," Heath murmured.

She angled her head and bobbed it slightly in acknowledgement of his words. "Did he...did he have anything to do with Trish?"

"I don't know. By the time we returned with the warrant, he had disappeared, and all of the evidence was gone."

She nodded again, and then spun around. "I don't think he could have done that. I know I misjudged him...but I couldn't have misjudged him that much. Could I?"

Heath knew she needed him to reassure her that her radar was not totally askew. That, while her neighbor was not the man she thought, he wasn't a heinous monster either, one she had let into her house. "I don't think he killed Patricia Norman. I could be wrong, but not to sound too cocky or anything, I'm usually not on these kinds of things. He's not the type. He's a coward who hides in his bedroom and spies on—" She cringed and he chastised himself for not knowing better than to keep reiterating what Dobski did. "I don't think he could have done it. But, I'm not taking any chances either. Until he's found, I'm leaving a guard at your door."

She sat on a weight bench with a sigh. "I hate being trapped in here, where it happened. It's driving me insane," she said, more to herself than to him. "I wish I could escape, could get away for a little bit." She lifted her gaze. "I'm sorry. I shouldn't complain."

"How about I take you to dinner tonight?" Heath asked spontaneously.

"Oh, no. You don't need to. I shouldn't have said anything."

"No. Are you kidding? Who wouldn't want dinner with Jasmine Barrett?"

Her lips rose at the corners as she stood. "Anyone who knows me, I'm afraid."

"I doubt that."

She eyed him as if weighing the proposition. "I really would like to get out of here for a while. And you won't let me leave here with just my own bodyguard, will you?"

"Not a chance. It needs to be someone from the department. It needs to be me," he amended.

She smiled. "All right then. I appreciate it. What time?"

"Seven?"

"That will be perfect. I guess you'll have to drive since I can't leave on my own."

"That's the plan. We'll go somewhere nice. I'll charge it to the department. I'll be spending my time getting to know you, which will undoubtedly help in the investigation."

She grinned at him. "Undoubtedly."

"I hate to interrupt whatever is going on here," Brody Barrett said loudly, "but we have to get some studio work in, Jazz."

"Sir, if you are planning on leaving, I'd like to have someone from the department accompany you, if that's okay."

"If that's what you want, fine. You have fifteen minutes, so hit the shower Jazz."

She hurried off, peeking over her shoulder at Heath regretfully.

He stared after her retreating form, sliding his phone from his pocket then calling Luke to see if it was okay if he was gone for the rest of the day, taking a mental note to make the time up with Jack later.

CHAPTER SEVEN

True to her word, Jasmine came out fifteen minutes later. Heath sat with his arm stretched atop the back of the couch in a relaxed position, waiting for her. He had dismissed the officer at the door for the evening. When she entered the room with a surprised expression, he stood. She wore a pair of jeans that were faded just right, a snug white concert T-shirt from another band, and a cute, short-waisted, blue denim jacket.

"I thought you were leaving, detective."

"I was planning on tagging along with you to the studio, if that's okay? And it's Heath."

She beamed. "That would be great." She peered beyond his shoulder as someone entered the room, and her smile faded, her eyes becoming cool and hard.

"Lionel's coming with us," Brody Barrett said as if anticipating an argument on the point.

She stood frozen for a second. Then she abruptly headed toward the front door, grabbing her purse from a nearby chair. "Then you'll have to take your car Uncle, because I'm taking the convertible."

JASMINE SEEMED TO BE brooding about something on the way to the garage, so Heath didn't interrupt her thoughts. They crossed the concrete and he listened to the sound her heels made and noted how her legs looked especially lengthy in them. He decided to break the silence.

"Are you going to tell me why that man upsets you so much?"

She shot him a sideways glance, seeming shaken by his ability to read her. She contemplated her answer. "Because..." she said slowly, tucking her tiny purse into the center console of her sleek, black two-seater, "...Lionel Parker is...an ass," she said decisively. "You wanna drive?"

He sensed a delaying tactic in the smooth transition to a new subject. He decided to let it go, for the time being. "Sure."

She tossed him the keys, and conversation was soon whittled away by the wind to a few shouted directions. They zoomed over the interstate. After a time, Heath peeked at her from behind his sunglasses and could see she was grinning, enjoying the sunshine and the wind whipping her hair into a frenzy. He imagined carefree moments, such as the kind that she was experiencing now, were found few and far between with her domineering uncle constantly present. After roughly a quarter of an hour, he swung the car into a parking spot and killed the engine, still exhilarated from having guided the powerful machine to its destination. He hopped out and quickly went around so he could open Jasmine's door and help her to exit the vehicle.

"So—" he said, arching his brows, "—will the rest of the band be here?"

"Ah," she responded, knowingly. "You were hoping to meet Nick Jordan." She referred to her famous guitarist. "No, they already laid down their tracks. I'm here to add the vocals. I could make sure you meet him sometime, though. He's a great guy..." She trailed off as her uncle pulled into the lot with a squeal of tires. She regarded them with an air of contempt as the two men parked and left their car. Taking Heath's arm, she turned to enter the studio.

Jasmine was greeted warmly by all of the sound people and offered quiet condolences. No one seemed to dwell on Tricia's death, but he supposed that would be counter-productive to what they needed to accomplish. Still, they clearly wanted to express their sympathy to her. She went into the sound booth and donned a set of headphones while Heath hung back in a corner, watching what unfolded.

"It'll be a couple of minutes before we can get the tracks we recorded yesterday up, Jazz."

"No problem, Mike." Jasmine sat on a stool, strumming her guitar casually. Her uncle came in and immediately got into an argument with the engineer, but she seemed to tune it out. Perhaps not realizing her mike was hot, she started singing quietly to herself, but her voice filled the room where the men were crowded. The discussion was getting heated, so no one paid any attention to Jasmine except for Heath. The music she played was low and sad, not like anything he heard her play in the past. He listened to the lyrics.

Your leaving shook me to the core,
I don't know who I am anymore
I still remember your voice
Though I no longer hear it
And I'm sure I'd let you go
If I thought I could bear it.
I need you to tell me it's okay
Ooh, ooh, if only for today
The little girl who once held your hand
Now doesn't know if she can stand
All on her own, lost and alone.
God, how I wish you could come home,
Home to me.
I search everywhere for the warmth you gave me
And am blind to the things, the things that enslave me
But I can't let you go
You're all I know
If only you'd come back to save me
From these things that enslave me
Come back and set me free
And help me to find me
Cause I'm all on my own, lost and alone.
God, how I wish you could come home,
Home to me.
"Jasmine!"

She jumped and almost tumbled off the stool she was sitting on, her hand sliding across the guitar strings with a discordant twang.

"I told you not to waste your time with that shit. It won't sell. If you have to sing something, practice the damn music you came in here to sing."

She glared at him for a second, and then lowered her head. Heath's heart went out to her. He couldn't take his gaze from her, wondering what must be going through her mind. When she finally straightened, he could see she had buried her emotions into some deep, dark section of herself where she would keep them locked away indefinitely.

Within a short while, Brody Barrett finished his argument with the technicians, seemingly winning, as it appeared he always did. They began to run music for Jazz and she sang to a pulse-pounding rock song that showcased her raw energy and sexiness. Wearing headphones, she screamed the lyrics, closing her eyes and dancing to the music. Heath sat in the corner, riveted, barely breathing as her voice seemed to fill him, tease him, tempt, and seduce him. She didn't look at him, didn't seem to be performing for anyone but herself, but he bet every man in the booth was charged by her sensuality. Heath was so caught up in the music, he had a moment of self-consciousness where he quickly glanced around to see if anyone had noticed how fixated he was, but everyone else seemed to be as captivated by her performance as he was.

As he redirected his focus to her, he caught the reflection of Lionel Parker in the glass that separated them all from Jasmine. He had one arm crossed in front of him, the opposite elbow leaning on it and his chin resting on a fist, appearing relatively bored. But in his reflection, Heath noticed that Parker's eyes gleamed. He was honed in on her with a high intensity. Heath studied the man. He was tall and slender, probably six-one, six-two, flint-grey hair, a long pointy nose, and beady, dark grey eyes above which arched seemingly perpetually raised brows. When he spoke, his voice was sharp, almost metallic, and he reminded Heath of the Dr. Smith character from the old TV series Lost in Space, who was forever criticizing the robot and Will Robinson Shaking this image from his mind, he promised himself to run a background check on Parker and ask Jasmine some more about the man's relationship to her.

As he returned his attention to her, she brought her hands to the sides of her face as she belted out the words to the song. She slid them down her cheeks and over her body as she shimmied to the rhythm of the electric guitar on the prepared track. The song ended and she opened her eyes. Everyone sat, a little stunned by the dynamic performance.

When no one spoke, Jazz asked timidly, "Was that okay? What should I change?"

Brody Barrett twisted to confirm with the sound engineer, who wore a huge smile, then punched a button. "That was fantastic, Jasmine." He beamed at her and she exhaled. "Let us play it back to make sure we've got it all. We've got more work to do to synch some of the tracks, but I think we may have pretty much all we need from you. Don't we, Mike?"

"Oh, yeah," Mike murmured appreciatively.

Twenty minutes later, Jasmine and Heath were making their way to The Lofts. He pulled into the garage drive and she snatched an entry card from the sun visor so he could swipe it to let them in.

"Do you mind if I get changed for dinner upstairs?" he shouted, competing with the groaning garage door rising. "I have spare clothes in the trunk. As a cop, you never know when you might need them."

"Not at all."

They parked and he swung by his car, which seemed unbelievably normal after his ride in the sports car. "Not much of a vehicle," he acknowledged. It was unmarked, but may as well have had sirens announcing it was department issued.

"Gets you where you need to go. That's what's important, right?" They had become very relaxed in each other's company throughout the course of the afternoon.

When he straightened, he noticed she was focused on him. She ran her hand along his hair. He was surprised by the action.

"Sorry, lieutenant," she said with a hint of amusement, "a few hairs were delinquent, but I've subdued them." She gave him a mock salute.

He copied it with an easy grin. "Good work, cadet." As he let his gaze slide over her again, he fought the urge to swing her around and press her against the car and see what came naturally after that. *I am a professional,* he kept repeating to himself. He hung the bag on his shoulder, slammed the trunk shut and they crossed to pushed the button for the elevator.

"Thanks for letting me drive your car. It's a beautiful machine," Heath commented.

"My uncle gave me the convertible for my birthday. It's one of those birthday gifts that's really more for the giver than the receiver though, as he drives it more than I do." She smirked as they stepped into the elevator.

Once inside, the elevator was far too small, making her far too near and far too tempting. He watched the numbers, but he was really imagining himself bumping against all of the walls with her as they tore off each other's clothes in a mad attempt to get naked. He laughed. She sure had a talent for making his mind spin out of control. And that performance at the studio had his juices going too. He couldn't forget the way she had looked as he observed her now.

"What?" she said, peering at him with a furrowed brow.

He stared at her. "Did I say something?"

"You laughed."

He concentrated on the floor numbers, but his smile never dimmed. "Did I?" he responded innocently. After some time, he glanced at her. "I made reservations, while you were taking your shower earlier, for seven. So we could get changed and maybe have a drink. It's within walking distance."

"Sounds fantastic. Hey, any chance you would be interested in some concert tickets for Thursday night? I'd be happy to get you some if you'd like."

"Are you kidding? I'd love that."

"Good."

When they got to the condo, Jasmine offered, "You can change in the guest room. Tricia was staying there. It's down the hall to the right. I hope you don't mind if I don't show you. I haven't been in there since..." She couldn't go on. Grief was a funny thing, he remembered. In the days that followed his parents death, it would sneak up on him when he least expected. And in the middle of it all, moments existed in which he felt almost normal, then the pain would swamp him again.

"I think I can find it," he said gently. He started to turn away, but then he twisted to say something else. Right at that point, she lowered the barricades and released her tears. She covered her face with her hands and muffled her sobs. "Are you okay?"

She shook her head, and he dropped his bag on the floor so he could hold her. Her arms slipped under his jacket and she fell against his chest. She began to shake and really cry for her friend, perhaps for the first time. He held her close and let her cry, rubbing her back, or her hair, in an effort to comfort her.

TO EXPERIENCE THE TOUCH of another human alone was so comforting, it made Jasmine want to cry even more. Everything she had been holding in escaped past the prison walls she erected and she couldn't bring herself under control. Heath murmured soft, comforting words to her. Her uncle would have told her to stop making a fool of herself. Finally, it was as if the reservoir of tears had emptied. She was exhausted, but internally cleansed. "I'm sorry," she murmured into his chest, embarrassed by her reaction.

"Hey, hey," he said tenderly, putting a fist under her chin to lift it. "There's no reason to be sorry." He bent his knees to look at her with a smile. His thumbs brushed aside the final tears that clung stubbornly to her wet cheeks. He gazed at her strangely and his thumbs moved to brush her lips.

She watched him, trying to deaden the sudden hammering of her heart. They heard voices in the hall and jumped apart.

"I'll go get changed," he said, his voice thick.

"Me too," she responded hurriedly.

HEATH WALKED THROUGH the hall with a long sigh. He entered the bedroom, closing the door and leaning on it for a second. He tossed his things on the bed and sat on the end, running a hand down his face. Then with a huge, exasperated exhale he threw himself backward so he was lying on the bed staring at the ceiling. He crossed his arms behind his head to form a pillow.

There were so many reasons why he should not become involved with Jasmine Barrett. *A. I am the lead detective investigating the murder of her best friend. Very unprofessional, unprincipled, not to mention, unethical. B. She's very vulnerable right now. She said so herself, her feelings are all over the place. I can't take advantage of that. C. We lead very different lives. She's a rock star. I'm a cop. It would never work. D. I need to consider Jack.* He couldn't bring someone new into his life without a lot of forethought. *E. I'm in the middle of an investigation.* He couldn't let those bottomless sea-green eyes, which seemed to cry out every time he peered into them, distract him. Or her body, molded by the gods...or her legs, which were...geez...a living sin...or any other part of her...her siren's voice...curvy hips...her... All these things were bad and wrong and he was a professional. All, very bad. Very, very bad. He squeezed his eyes shut. This would never work.

CHAPTER EIGHT

When Heath returned to the living room, he was surprised to find a bottle of white wine on ice with a glass and a note lying nearby.

Please help yourself. I already have. –J

He smiled and poured a glass. As he raised it to drink, he was stunned when he caught the flutter of a green dress on the balcony. He was not used to this. Juliette would take nearly two full hours to get dressed for dinner. But whatever shortcuts Jazz was taking, they didn't leave her lacking, he thought appraisingly. Six-inch, emerald heels that could likely serve as a compass for some lucky sixth-grader's math, caught his eye at the end of her very shapely legs. The skirt part of her dress was pleated and airy, revealing more skin as the breeze blew. The straps came over her shoulders and almost to her waist, leaving a fine view of the interesting curves of her back. She was leaning on the railing, her wine glass nearly empty on a nearby table. Her hair was gathered up in some kind of large clip that let curls spill down.

Jasmine shifted positions and fidgeted with her dress. She seemed to sense him and rotated slowly. The picture from the front was equally stunning. God, she had this mysterious way of turning him to molten lava, not to mention what she was doing to the rest of his body. Heath took his time approaching her, noting how she reached behind her for the railing for support as he drew near. When he stepped out, she immediately began to speak. He guessed her words had been practiced while waiting for him.

"Heath, I want to say sorry for what happened earlier...I mean—" she stammered, "—for my falling apart on you. I'm sure that was very uncomfortable for—" She stopped as he took her hand and lifted it to his lips.

"You look...amazing." He loved how she blushed and glanced aside. *Professionalism is overrated. To hell with it.* "Jasmine," he said huskily.

And then he was pulling her to him, as he had fantasized about on the walk there, his palm gliding across her incredibly smooth, bare skin, drawing her in until their bodies touched. Her candy-apple red lips parted in astonishment and he dreamed of nibbling on, and then slowly possessing them. He tilted his head and bent close enough to feel her warm breath, when his phone vibrated in his breast pocket. He contemplated finishing the act of kissing her before answering, but decided while that was okay for a second or third kiss, the first kiss needed his full attention.

With a groan, he separated some to get the phone, though still holding onto her possessively. "What?" he growled. It was Luke.

"Did you tell Jack he doesn't need to wear a helmet when biking?"

"No." He released Jasmine's waist and retreated a foot. "Helmets are a must. He knows that."

"He says you said it was okay not to wear one if it was only for a short distance."

"What? I didn't say that." He spun away from her, running his fingers through his hair in frustration. "Put him on." He reeled in his irritation during the brief break.

"Hi, Dad."

"Hey, pal. Uncle Luke tells me you said I said you could go without a helmet if you weren't going far. Is that true?" Heath turned and noticed Jasmine's face had gone pale. He divided his attention between speaking to Jack and trying to determine what was going on in her mind.

"Uhh..."

"Jack...?"

"None of the other guys wear them."

"Well maybe their parents don't care whether they get a closed head injury, but, personally, I'd prefer you stay in one piece." He knew he shouldn't have said that, but he'd seen far too many accident scenes where people had become brain damaged. "Besides, we're not talking about them, we're talking about you, and you know what the rules are."

Jack sighed and Heath relished the small sense of victory. "Yes, Dad."

"You're grounded from your bike for three days."

"But that's not fair."

"It is too fair." He glanced at Jasmine again. "Listen, we'll discuss this when I get home. All right?" His voice softened, "You go in and hit the tub."

There was a pause on the other end of the line. "Okay, Dad. I love you."

"I love you too, buddy. Bye." He disconnected, leaning against the railing.

"I am so sorry," Jasmine blurted. "I should have realized you were married...and that in your line of business you wouldn't wear a wedding ring."

"What?" he asked confused, not sure what one had to do with the other. "Why is that?"

"Well...with chasing suspects and..." She was flustered. "I don't know...I..."

"What? A wedding band would get in the way of my trigger finger? Jasmine, I'm not married. I have a son, but I'm not married."

"Oh. What happ—no, that's none of my business."

"It's a perfectly reasonable question to ask." He plucked his wine glass up from the table where he had set it next to hers. He took a long drink before answering. The wine was pleasantly cold. He rested his elbows on the railing and looked out at the Arch as it glowed silver-hot in the rays of the setting sun. "It didn't work. We were too different, I guess. I came from a world where Sunday meant football games. She came from a world where Sunday meant charity dinners. I came from a world where people went to work every day. She came from a world where people hired others to do their work for them. I came from a world where bologna sandwiches are perfectly acceptable. She...well...you get the picture." He polished off his wine and then turned to peer at her.

She stared at her manicured nails. "I'm sorry. That must have been very difficult, for all of you."

"It was. At least it was for me. Jack doesn't remember her at all. 'Course, she left when he was only six-weeks-old, so I guess that would be expected," he added dryly.

Jasmine's eyes went wide and she brought her hand to her throat. "But...he was her son."

"We were both...not what she expected, I guess."

"But...she had a son."

"I know, and you know, but apparently *she* didn't know." He was surprised by the bitter taste of the words on his tongue. "I need some more wine. How about you?"

"Sure."

He went inside, taking her glass and feeling relieved when the door closed between them.

Shit. I carefully outline the reasons why I can't get involved with this woman, and then, the first chance I get, I practically jump her bones. What is wrong with me? Pro-fes-sion-al distance. That's the motto for tonight, Heath. Professional distance. He poured the wine and took another drink before returning to the balcony.

He passed Jasmine her glass, maintaining space between them. "Okay...if I'm charging this dinner to the department, I need to get some information from you. So...you and your uncle have lived here for how long?"

She took a drink of her wine. "I came to live with my uncle when I was ten. My parents died in a plane crash along with the pilot. I was the sole survivor. They were taking me to L.A. where my uncle had gotten me a part in a movie." She said it matter-of-factly, but the regret was etched on her face. "My Uncle Brody took me in when I had no one else." Her voice was laced with pain. "Heath, this wine is going straight to my head. I think I need to get something to eat. Do you think we can go?"

She was trying to evade questions, and he knew it. At the same time, he couldn't bear to make her delve up any more painful memories. He glanced at his watch. "Okay. Maybe we can get an appetizer at the bar." He held his elbow out to her and she took it gratefully. "Lucky for you, we don't have far to walk or those sweet little heels of yours would be putting you in a world of hurt." He held the door open for her.

"Dude, I've given entire concerts in higher heels than this. My feet are permanently numb."

He laughed.

"You know, Heath," she said, giving his arm a squeeze, "you're an excellent listener. I'm sure that's part of the reason you make such a good cop."

"That and I look good in my uniform," he replied with a wink.

"Umm," was her only response, but he caught the way her eyes shone and enjoyed the sensation that created. "What made you want to be a cop?" she asked as they entered the hall.

"My dad was a cop, so I guess I wanted to...follow in his footsteps, or something."

"He must be so proud of you."

Heath sighed as he pushed the button for the elevator. "I'd like to think so. He died when I was a teenager."

"Oh, Heath. I'm sorry. I know how hard that is." They entered the elevator and she was quiet for several minutes.

"What's on your mind?"

She shrugged. "I had this image of a young JFK, Jr., saluting at his father's funeral and then imagined you, vowing to wear the uniform your father did and to wear it well. No wonder you have risen in the ranks so fast."

Heath didn't comment. When they reached the pavement she twisted toward him. "I understand how what your parents want for you can become a part of who you are. It was the same reason I continued to pursue a life on stage. It was what my parents wanted for me, and they died trying to give it to me. I owed it to them."

"I'm sure your parents would be proud of you, too."

She stared vaguely up the street. "Yeah, I don't know..."

Noticing she'd sobered, Heath steered the conversation to lighter matters, talking about Jack and his brothers, giving her a funny little thumbnail sketch of all of them, on their way to the restaurant. They quickly arrived at their destination, Stephano's, an Italian restaurant near The Lofts.

"Jazz!" The owner, Sebastian Fezzari, grabbed her hands the moment she set foot through the door and kissed both of her cheeks. "I'm so sorry for what happened to Ms. Tricia. So awful. But I am glad your friend here is seeing to it that you eat. I've been worried for you, bella."

Heath felt foolish. He thought he had been pretty clever, thinking of a restaurant so close to her home. He hadn't considered the fact that she had probably eaten there a hundred times and he said as much after they were seated in a quiet corner together.

"Oh, no. This is great. I haven't been here in...gosh...at least a month. And I could probably eat Stephano's food every day of the week, if it wouldn't turn me into a fat cow."

"I don't think that could ever happen," he replied with a smirk. They read through the options on their menus until a waiter stopped by with a bottle of wine.

"Hello, Antonio. Good to see you."

"And you, Ms. Jazz. Sebastian sent this wine for you, and sir, we weren't sure...Ms. Jazz doesn't care for red wines, although most of our customers prefer it with pasta—"

"The white will be fine."

"Are you sure? Sebastian said to get you whatever you want."

"Really. This is great. Tell him thank you."

"Ms. Jazz...you want the Cannelloni, the Chicken Bianco, or do you want to try something new?"

"No, Antonio. The Cannelloni, please."

"I thought so." He smiled. "And you sir, have you had enough time?"

Heath passed him the menu. "Cannelloni sounds excellent."

"Good, good. Two Cannelloni, then."

Jazz laughed at Heath's exasperated face after the waiter left.

"They know your order?"

"I guess you could say I'm a regular. That is when I'm home, which is rare."

"How often do you eat here?"

"When I'm home, usually only—" she twirled her wine glass, stalling for dramatic effect, "—once a week." She finished quickly, taking a sip of her wine, her eyes dancing.

"Geeeezzz. Why didn't you say something?"

"No, Heath, really...this is great. I love the food. That's why I'm here all the time. Just because I'm not a Stephano's virgin—"

"I'd say not," he snorted with fake indignation.

She laughed and he couldn't resist the urge to lean forward and take her hand. "I like it when you laugh."

"Thanks for bringing me here and for going with me to the studio. I needed to get out."

"I liked that song you sang."

"'Rock My World'?"

"No. The one before that...it was pretty."

"Oh, that." She waved it off.

"No. That was a really nice song. You should sing it. No matter what your uncle says."

"Oh, no. I couldn't do that."

"Why the hell not? You don't have to listen to your uncle. You're an adult." The thought of Brody snapping at her still had a ball of fire knotted in his stomach.

"You think I'm not acting like an adult?" she asked evenly, looking at her fingers as they skimmed along the stem of her wine glass.

"I think you let your uncle intimidate you." Heath had been holding it in from the beginning and decided he wasn't sitting back any more.

"It's just that—"

"You feel an obligation to him because he raised you."

"Yes, and—"

"But the fact he raised you doesn't give him the right to treat you like dirt."

"I know but—"

"Jasmine. It's time you stop kowtowing—"

"You think I kowtow?" A fire was in her eyes, but Heath was too upset himself to heed it.

"Yes, I think you kowtow to him. You let him bully you constantly. You're not ten years old anymore. You don't have to take orders from him."

"So I'm acting like a ten-year-old?"

He could tell she was quickly on the road to becoming infuriated with him, but for some asinine reason, he couldn't let it go. "Yes. You simply let him criticize you and— "

"So," she said, her voice as cold as steel, "you want me to defend myself. Not let myself get pushed around."

"Damn straight."

Jasmine rose from the table, taking her purse. "Good night, then."

She stormed away from the table, leaving him flabbergasted. A quick re- view of the conversation showed Heath he was way out of line. He let his anger at Brody spill onto her. "Jasmine, wait." Heath hurriedly pulled some bills from his pocket and threw them on the table. But as he was going to rush through the door from which she fled, a large party entered and he was stuck on the wrong side.

When he finally hit the sidewalk, she was nowhere to be seen. He increased his pace as he climbed the stairs to the door of The Lofts. A bloodcurdling scream echoed from the parking garage to his left. Alarmed, he swung himself quickly over a railing, dropping the short distance onto the driveway of the garage. When he landed shockwaves radiate from his ankles to his calves, reminding him that he didn't have tennis shoes on to cushion the impact. He ignored the sting as he jerked on the doorknob to an entry to the right of the garage door. He tried several times, but the door was locked. He could hear more terrified screams from inside and now could easily identify Jasmine's voice. A tiny glass window showed him only parked cars as he beat on the door. "Jasmine!"

He ran down the drive, bounded up the stairs and into the building. When he reached the elevators, he punched the button, but when none of the doors opened immediately, he abandoned them. As he traversed a short hall, his coat flew behind him. He turned the corner, speeding to the end of another short hall and took the door to the staircase. He hurdled the steps two at a time and slid across the landing in his dress shoes. He barreled through the door and raced along the hall just as Jasmine ran around the corner in blind terror. He caught her by the waist as she tried to run past him and she began to flail at him like a demon, her hair covering her face.

"Let me go. Let me go!" The panic in her voice about undid him.

"Jazz. Jazz. It's me. It's okay, babe. It's me." He swept her hair away and kissed her temple. "Shhh. Shhh, It's okay."

Jasmine was crying hysterically.

"What's wrong? What happened? Are you okay?"

"Oh, my God. Oh, my God! This can't be happening. This can't be happening!"

"What can't, Jasmine? What happened?"

"He—in the garage—oh, my God!"

"Okay, okay," he said urgently. Whatever it was, it wasn't good. Thinking quickly, he walked her to the elevators and pushed the button. To his relief, one opened within seconds. "You go in here, and when the doors close, you hit the emergency button. Then you'll be locked in there, safe. Got it, Jasmine?"

She nodded and obediently got into the elevator. He watched her with his heart in his throat while the doors came together then drew his revolver. As the detective entered the garage, he heard the elevator alarm go off and a wave of relief hit him but was turned back at the sight of Jasmine's bloody footprints crossing the garage floor. Carefully, searching between vehicles, he made his way to his car. He opened the door and reached in for the radio. "This is Lieutenant Heath McGowan requesting backup and a bus to The Lofts condominiums on Market Street. Copy."

"We've got that Lieutenant McGowan. A squad car and an ambulance sent to your location. Over."

He threw the mike on the front seat and let the door shut. Carefully, he followed the tracks, continuing a constant surveillance of his surroundings. He saw the convertible, but the blood seemed to be coming from the SUV parked next to it. It was pooling underneath, dripping from the driver's side door. In the middle of the blood he saw a pair of mangled glasses, the lenses smashed to bits, but still, somehow, mostly intact. He edged closer, scanning for any sign of a suspect or movement of any kind. His heart was thumping with the force and rhythm of a freight train. He got near enough to chance a glance into the driver's window. What he saw there sickened him.

Sam Dobski was behind the wheel, head back, throat slit. His eyeballs had been carved out and someone had painted a "J" in blood on his forehead. "Holy shit!" Heath exclaimed, wiping his mouth. The wailing of a siren announced his reinforcements arriving. But one thing he knew for certain, Sam Dobski would not be in need of an ambulance tonight.

CHAPTER NINE

A s soon as officers had the crime scene secured, Heath took one uniform with him and went in search of Jasmine. The first thing he noticed was the elevator's alarm wasn't sounding anymore. He tried not to panic as the doors opened to an empty elevator and he and the officer entered and punched her floor.

Getting off the elevator, he ran down the hall, his fellow officer struggling to keep pace with him. Without bothering to knock, he burst in the front door. Brody Barrett sat on the couch, perusing a document with his reading glasses perched on the end of his nose.

Brody jumped, startled by his abrupt entrance. "Lieutenant McGowan, you—" He began to scold him, but catching sight of the uniformed officer trailing him, and the way the two were panting, he broke off in mid-sentence.

"Where's Jasmine?" Heath shouted between breaths.

"Huh?"

"Jasmine. Where is she?"

"I assumed she was with you." His face paled.

Heath hurried in the direction of her bedroom. "Jasmine!" He threw open doors as he raced about the condominium. He could hear Brody on the opposite half of the condominium doing the same thing.

"She's not here," he called.

Heath tried not to let his fear engulf him. Speaking to the other officer, he ordered, "I want men crawling all over this building, combing it for any sign of Jasmine Barrett. Anybody sees anything, they report to you. You're sticking with me."

"Got it, lieutenant." The officer relayed the message via his radio, following Heath as he went tearing around the building, knocking on doors. Five minutes had passed when an officer reported he talked to the building's superintendent who told him he released Ms. Barrett from the elevator a short while ago. The super said she was distraught, but unharmed. He sent her to her condo, telling her he would notify the police.

Within a quarter of an hour, policemen were reporting in from all floors, and were scattered in the neighboring vicinity. No one else had seen any sign of her. Heath stood in the hall outside of her condo, worried and perplexed. *Think, Heath. Where would she be? She was beside herself...she would go somewhere where she felt safe...* Then it came to him.

"Wait here!" he yelled to the uniform, and took off running for a second stairwell. He raced up the stairs, pulling himself forward with the banisters as he climbed to the top. He exploded through the door. Jasmine was lying on her side on a white, canvas couch, which seemed semi-surreal on the roof top. She bolted upright; then, recognizing him, flew to him. Overwhelmed with relief, he held her while she sobbed. When his heartrate had returned to near normal, he lifted her from her feet and carried her to the couch. He sat, holding her in his lap.

A few minutes later, Officer Davis burst in the door. Jasmine jumped in Heath's arms, and he instinctively wrapped them tighter. "I've got her," he said, his voice strained.

"Yes, sir," he pivoted, closing the door quietly behind him.

"You're shaking."

She stared at him, her eyes swollen and horrorstruck. "I keep seeing him. I can't stop seeing him!"

"I know, baby. But it's going to be okay. It will be okay." With his palms against her cheeks and, without thinking, Heath started kissing her everywhere, comforting, and being comforted, after his frenzied search, by the feel of holding Jasmine, the taste of her on his tongue, though she was salty with tears. Seeking the warmth of her skin, he caressed her. His lips accidentally brushed hers and the contact sparked something in them. It was suddenly as if he had to swallow her whole.

Heath shifted so that she was laying against the cushions and she surged against him. It was as if he couldn't get enough of her. He trailed kisses down her throat, sinking his teeth into her as she drew a shuddering breath. She moaned his name, and it incited him all the more. He tugged on her dress, ripping a strap on her shoulder but barely registered that in some far recess of his mind. He wanted Jasmine with an intensity he had never known before. She was as frantic as he, and as she whispered his name again on the crest of a moan, he lost all sense of reason. He ran his hand along her smooth thigh and underneath the dress, pressing between her legs, hard and desperate. Her desires became his. He wished to soothe her, to somehow make it all better for her. But greater than that was his craving to be needed by her, to be important to a woman, this woman, to be capable of making her happy, of easing the pain, if only for an instant. His senses swirled with her, the scent of the crisp night air mingled with her perfume, intoxicating him like a drug.

A single siren wailed in the distance, cutting through the blanket of lust that had cocooned Heath's brain. The sound slammed into him suddenly, and unalterably, the fact that he was a cop. He pulled away, rising with his arms outstretched on either side of her as she lay beneath him. He panted and tried to clear his vision, shaken by his own urgency. She peered at him, her expression questioning.

"Dammit. Dammit, Jasmine. I can't do this." He yanked the unbroken strap up and swung off the couch to stand with his back to her.

There was a loud knock on the door and someone yelled from the interior. "Lieutenant? We have Brody Barrett requesting he be able to see his niece, Ms. Barrett."

"Shit," Heath muttered, rubbing his chin.

He hadn't heard Jasmine rise behind him, but motion caught his attention. She stood by the door, posed to press its release bar, but hesitated, her head lowered. Another knock and call came. She inhaled deeply, straightening her spine and pushing to disengage the catch. The door flew open as she moved aside, and she slipped past the officer and her gaping uncle.

"Jasmine, are you hurt? Your dress is ripped. Did someone hurt you?"

She didn't answer Brody, but continued downward, his words hanging empty in her wake. He threw Heath a quizzical look. Setting his jaw, Heath turned in the opposite direction. After a second, rapid footsteps descended the stairs with Brody's repeated calls for Jasmine. The uniform apparently followed, as Heath heard the soft click of the door and then silence.

He stood alone in the deep dark that was not illuminated by the few stars that shone, his suit coat beating against him in the stiff breeze that battered the rooftop, his pulse still pounding her name.

JASMINE'S NEIGHBOR had deserved to have his eyes taken from him, the bastard. Watching his Jasmine. It was unthinkable. He had to suffer for it. And the fool had been so meek. Literally like a lamb being led to slaughter. Of course the whack on the skull helped to subdue him, and was somewhat satisfying at the same time.

He was so happy when the gag kept the noise low, but didn't eliminate the sound of the man's agony. It pleased him to hear the weak slob cry, to beg, and then to let his victim know there would be no mercy for him...none at all.

And when Jasmine finally heard it was he who had eliminated the creep who spied on her—who made her feel dirty and frightened in her own home—she would be so grateful. She would take him back and they could build their life together. How he couldn't wait to have her warm body next to his in bed. To touch her again...and to have her touch him. He became aroused just thinking of it.

He had been disappointed when the twisted little neighbor had passed out again, no more gurgling cries, no more pathetic moaning. He slapped his victim into consciousness once more and told him he was going to cut his throat so he would know the fear Jasmine had when she heard the pervert had been spying on her. And then he did it. Afterward, he used the plastic bag that had the hair in it to toss the bloody knife and gloves into; the rest of him had stayed pristine behind the car's seat. He walked away, his hand stuck in his pocket, whistling. It gave him such a glorious feeling of power.

Jasmine made him powerless when she left, but it wasn't her fault. A goddess such as she could never be blamed. And he was getting so much closer to having her. She would be his any day now. He would sense when the moment was right. He would have his Jasmine once again.

CHAPTER TEN

Heath listened to reports from people at the scene, but always, he kept searching for Jasmine. She filtered in and out of his vision, between the people who were milling around, sitting rigidly on the couch in the circle of the lamplight. Her uncle sat next to her, for a time. She finally talked to him in a soft voice, seeming to reassure Brody, from the snatches of conversation he overheard, that she was physically okay. They argued in subdued tones about her taking some pills. She gave in after a time, swallowing the half-dozen Brody pressed into her palm. Then her uncle disappeared. She didn't look at him, didn't cry, or shake, just sat stone still.

His mouth was dry. All he wanted was for the people to go away, so he could make things right with Jasmine. But he knew it was important for him to put aside personal feelings in order to get work done, so his professional nature took over.

"I want to speak to the coroner when she is finished," Heath ordered. Officer Davis nodded and went downstairs to the crime scene. Heath thanked officers who had scoured the vicinity for Jasmine, shook their hands, and dismissed them. He sent others to canvass the area, hunting for anyone who had seen or heard anything. Finally, the same Black crime-scene technician from the previous night appeared in the door.

"I didn't expect to be seeing you so soon," she said dryly.

Heath raised his brows. "Yeah." He chuckled ruthlessly, pushing the sides of his jacket back to grasp his hips, lost in thought temporarily. He looked up. "What did you discover?"

"As near as I can tell, the killer waited for the victim in the garage, or perhaps brought him there under duress, as there are no signs of a struggle or defensive wounds. Once seated in the car he then knocked him on the head with a blunt instrument, possibly the butt of the revolver. The size and shape of the wound is consistent with that theory, although there will be no way of telling for sure until tests are run. When he had the deceased subdued, he secured him with a rope and tied the gag hard enough to cause tearing at the corners of his lips. He then extracted his eyes with a small knife, while he was still alive. From the amount of blood from the eye sockets, I believe he sat there for several minutes while the victim was in pain, then finally slit his throat."

"If he was in the car for that length of time, there must be some trace evidence."

"Oh, I'm sure there is," she replied with a hint of irritation. "But our killer is clever. I've never seen this before. Apparently he had a bag of human hair and synthetic hair, which he spread throughout the car. His DNA's in there all right, along with that of at least twenty other individuals."

"Could he be a hairdresser?"

"Could be. Or he could have collected it from a salon floor. It's hard telling. One thing is for sure, whoever he is, he is very angry, very smart, and very bold. Anyone could have walked into that garage at any point." She frowned.

"Thanks. Let me know as soon as you have the whole report entered."

"It'll be awhile, lieutenant, with all that evidence to collect, but I'll get it to you all right. This guy is not done murdering. Oh, and lieutenant...the eyes being gouged out—"

"It was a punishment, I know. Thanks." It could only have been retribution for having seen Jasmine in her private moments. That's what the "J" on the face meant. That had to mean the killer knew about Dobski planting the camera. That limited the field some. The killer was murdering his victims then bringing her the bodies, like a cat brings corpses of its prey to its owner as gifts, leaving its dead moles on the front door step. He would need to delve into her background a lot more thoroughly. He couldn't take his time when the body count was escalating, and he knew Jasmine couldn't take much more. And maybe for his grand finale the killer meant to end her life, too.

Finally, when all of the policemen had finished canvassing and given Heath their reports, the condo was empty. No one had seen or heard anything, except for an elderly woman who saw Dobski arrive at roughly 5:30.

Heath had to check into the reason for this not being spotted by the police-men who were supposed to be on the lookout for Dobski.

Closing the door on the last uniform to leave, he pivoted to find the couch empty. He glanced up and could barely discern Jasmine's outline on the balcony. She had changed into jeans and a wine-colored turtleneck sweater. She was barefoot and had her hair pulled into a stubby ponytail. Leaning on the railing, she was gazing over the city, holding a glass of wine.

He opened the door to the balcony quietly. "Jazz, I—"

"I'm going to bed," she said hurriedly, and spun to rush by him.

"Wait a second." He grabbed her elbow as she passed, swinging her around roughly and spilling her wine.

During a long hesitation, they studied each other's eyes, trying to read what was there. Then she shrugged lose from his grip. "Get your hands off me," she said frostily, and left.

His jaw hung open briefly. Making an aggravated noise in his throat, he whirled to stare blindly at the view. He saw the wine bottle on the table, near-ly empty, and nabbed it, drinking straight from the bottle. The temperature had dropped and he left his sport coat inside, his shirt sleeves not much pro-tection against the breeze, but he'd be damned if he would go in there right now.

After some time, angry noises from the rooms behind him filtered into his thoughts. He swung and opened the door, the words and voices immedi-ately becoming clear.

"You *will* sleep in there, Jasmine, by God. If I have to drag you in there myself."

"No, I won't. You can't make me." Her voice was desperate and infuriat-ed.

"Jasmine," Brody growled. The sound of a struggle reached him.

"Get your hands off me. Get your damn hands off me!"

Heath rounded the corner quickly to catch Jasmine struggling with Brody Barrett, his fingers clamped around her biceps. They both froze when he stepped into view in the hall.

Several moments of awkward silence followed.

"Everything okay, Jasmine?" Heath asked through gritted teeth, scowling at Brody.

She whipped her arms free of her uncle's grasp. "Fine," she said, glaring at both of the men in turn. She marched past Heath without looking at him.

He observed Brody with loathing, his fists clenched, debating his course of action. Brody didn't give him the time to come to a decision on whether or not to pulverize him, opting instead to stride past him defiantly. He allowed himself a minute or two to regain his composure, and then reentered the living room, finding it empty. He sat on the couch and dialed his phone with a tired sigh.

"Luke, man, I'm sorry to wake you."

"That's all right. What's going on?"

"I'm sorry I didn't call you earlier, things got a bit crazy. The killer brought Jasmine Barrett another prize."

"Another body?" Luke sounded wide awake now.

"Yeah. And it wasn't pretty." He rubbed his face, adding wearily, "This guy's eyes were removed...while he was still alive. Then his throat was slit."

"Shit, man," Luke answered squeamishly. "Did you not want me to sleep at all tonight?"

Heath couldn't help but grin. "Maybe you should try fantasizing about little Ms. Wainright."

"Well, you ruined that for me." Luke became serious. "How's Jazz dealing everything?"

"Well, she hasn't totally snapped yet, so I'd say she's doing pretty good, under the circumstances. She was pretty shaken, though. Hell, I was pretty shaken."

"Hmm. So—" Luke yawned "—you staying there tonight?"

"Yeah. Sorry, bro. I'll pay this back to you, I swear."

"There's no need to. You keep righting the world's wrongs and I'll be the one in the shadow, silently supporting you."

"Yeah," Heath said with a grimace, "you're the friggin' wind beneath my wings. And don't you start singing."

Luke belted the first lines to the Bette Midler tune in his baritone.

"I'm hanging up."

He continued, unabashed.

Heath laughed and hit the end button. He kicked off his shoes and lay on the couch, using his jacket as a blanket. The image of Dobski appeared again in his mind. He gave a small shiver as he flipped and burrowed further into the cushions, wondering how Jasmine would ever sleep tonight.

HEATH WOKE FROM A NIGHTMARE. Had he heard something? After listening for several seconds, he thought with a wry laugh, "Must have been my own screaming." In his dream, an eyeless Sam Dobski had been discussing the Cardinal's lineup with him in the adjacent apartment. Heath rose to get a glass of water from the kitchen. When he returned, his gaze lit on a figure on the balcony. A single moonbeam spotlighted Jasmine lying on a chaise lounge on her side, one arm curled up to her temple, the other draped across her stomach.

Shit. It's supposed to get down to the mid-forties tonight. Heath scrambled and jerked on the door to open it, but found it locked. *The bastard locked her out.* He unlocked the door and stepped onto the balcony. The wind had increased considerably and the chill almost took his breath away. Cursing roundly he squatted by Jasmine to try to wake her. *Poor baby.* Heath skimmed his fingers along her hair. She didn't stir. He laid his palm against her cheek. She was ice cold. "Jasmine." He shook her gently and she groaned, swiveling her head in the opposite direction. The pills Brody gave her had her under deep.

Slipping his hands under her, he cradled her against his body. He rose with her, turning toward the door. After a struggle with opening the door, he finally got her inside and gently laid her on the couch.

She moaned, her expression troubled in her sleep. Again Heath squatted near her and swept her hair off her face, framing it for a moment. His heart was heavy in his chest, so full of feelings for her it gained weight. He sighed and, leaning in, brushed his lips tenderly over hers. With this, she finally stirred, opening her eyes slowly.

"Heath."

He sat on the floor next to her. "Yeah, baby." He continued to smooth her hair. Her eyes blinked closed again.

"Why...? Why is this happening?" she murmured. "I don't understand. It hurts so much." A small sob escaped.

It broke Heath's heart. "I know, honey. I'm sorry." He paused. "I don't know why this is happening, but I'll find out."

"You'll find out for me?" she mumbled sleepily.

"Yeah, Jazz. I'll find out." She drifted off. He pushed the coffee table to give him room to lay on the floor by the couch. He touched her hand, it was still cold. He held it in his and fell asleep.

He woke around 5 a.m. and rose to watch as the sky started to lighten above the horizon. He gazed through the French doors that led to the balcony and stretched his sore back. Occasionally, he would spin and peer at Jasmine from his place by the window. When dawn broke, he saw her magically bathed in soft pink light, glowing like a fairy princess. How was he to keep a professional distance from a woman who moved him so deeply?

CHAPTER ELEVEN

At six, a uniform came to relieve him. Jasmine was still crashed out on the couch. He drove home and was on his second cup of coffee when Luke came shuffling into the kitchen. Luke gave him the once-over in his wrinkled shirt and pants, slumped against the counter.

"You look like hell."

"Good morning to you, too, asshole."

"Did you get any sleep?"

Heath shrugged, staring out the window at nothing. "Some."

Luke tilted his chin and scrutinized him.

Catching his expression Heath commented, "You look like a dog when you do that."

Luke poured himself coffee and sat at the small, rectangular kitchen table, pulling a chair out for Heath. "Want to talk about it?"

"About what? The murder?" He sat in the chair. "It was bad, man. Most of them generally are." He drummed his fingers on the table and avoided eye contact.

Luke sipped his coffee, peering over the rim at his older brother. "And Jazz?"

Heath's gaze snapped up. Something about his brother using her familiar name set him on edge, even though it was the name most of her fans knew her by. "I told you. She was pretty damned upset, as most people would be." He drummed louder and started some off-key whistling, his attention darting around the room. Noting Luke was still surveying him, he glanced in his direction again. "What?"

He took another long drink of his coffee, studying Heath, perhaps deciding from which angle to pounce. "You were gone for a while yesterday. So what did you do there all day?"

"Well...she was much more put together when I arrived. Actually, she was kind of acting cool and standoffish towards me, which pissed me off. Then I told her I had found a camera in her ceiling fan—all this is confidential by the way..."

Luke mimed zipping his lips shut.

"I thought she put the camera there to...you know...film her sexual conquests or whatever. Some people do that kind of thing. Who am I to judge?" He tried to lose the defensive tone in his voice. "So I asked her if she might have had the camera on and filmed the murder."

"And you didn't think insinuating she was some kind of nympho, who liked having reminders of her crazed lovemaking, might be the tiniest bit insulting?"

He frowned at Luke, then, sat back with a half laugh/half grimace, putting his hands behind his head in a gesture that was part incredulity, part annoyance. "I didn't think, okay?"

"So how did Ms. Barrett respond to this line of questioning?"

"She was pissed." Heath got to his feet and pushed his chair under the table with a loud scraping sound, then stood behind it, holding on to the top. "And freaked out. Turns out her neighbor is running his own peep show next door. She thought he was a nice guy. Had him pegged plenty wrong on that count." He let out an exasperated breath. "So, I go and have a little discussion with the asshole—"

"After you got a warrant?"

Heath gave him a hard stare. Obviously he'd shared too much with his brother if he knew he hadn't exactly followed sound procedure on that one. "No. We were just gonna have a brief discussion is all."

"Umm."

"What does that mean?"

"Nothing. So the neighbor...?"

He hesitated, wondering if he should go on, as Luke was really getting under his skin with the way he was sitting there, kitchen-chair analyzing him like some freaking shrink. But finally he broke. He wanted to discuss it. "Is a pencil-necked, sweater-wearing pervert who no doubt whacks off while watching Jasmine get undressed or does—" he gestured widely, "—whatever it is she does, in her bedroom."

Luke raised an eyebrow, the steam rolling from his coffee as he took a sip. He leaned forward, his elbows on the table.

"Why are you looking at me like that?"

"I'm not looking at you like anything. Go on."

"So, I go back to Jasmine's—"

"After, no doubt, threatening the pencil-necked...what was it? Oh yeah, sweater-wearing pervert—"

"Are you telling the story or am I?"

"All right, all right." Luke held out his hands defensively, amused. "Go on."

"I will, if you'd keep your yap shut."

"Yap's shut."

"All right. So I go back to Jasmine's—" his lips curved involuntarily as he brought it to mind "—and she'd been working out."

"Looks pretty good working out, does she?"

"Oh, yeah," he exclaimed enthusiastically. Then, realizing he'd made a mistake, he glanced over quickly. But Luke was the picture of ignorance. "Long story short, I accompanied her to a music studio, in her sweet little convertible sports car, and got to see her record a song."

"That must have been pretty cool."

"It was. Then we went to dinner—" Heath recalled their near-kiss in the hall, but edited out that tidbit, "—and, at dinner I said something to make her mad again."

"Such as...?"

"Such as, I told her she shouldn't let her uncle bully her so much." He got so infuriated when he thought about it he began to pace behind his chair. "Guy insults her every chance he gets, bosses her around, is basically a jerk on all fronts when it comes to her."

"Which you don't like."

"No. I don't. Wouldn't like it if someone did that to you, either."

"But I don't look good when I workout."

A slow smile crept across Heath's face. "O-ho-ho. I'm done talkin' here."

"No, you're not. Come on, Heath. I'll be good."

He squinted at Luke sideways, trying to size him up, but deciding it felt good to discuss it, he continued. "So...she gets angry at me and leaves."

"Good for her. Sorry. I'll reserve comment."

"I go after her and that's when I hear her screamin', man. In the parking garage. Her voice echoed hellishly. And I've got no idea what's going on in there. So I enter the building to take the steps down, and she comes running out of nowhere, hysterical. I can't figure out what she's saying, but I know it can't be good, so I put her in the elevator, tell her to push the alarm to lock it, and I go into the garage. That's when I find the pencil-necked geek with his eyes carved out."

"No shit?"

Heath took a seat again. "No shit." They both sat for a while in silence.

"And then what happened?"

"Well, I had called for backup, so we secured the scene, and I went to find Jasmine, and she wasn't in the elevator."

"You must have been out of your mind."

"I was. I finally found her—it must have been twenty minutes later—on the roof. I remembered that's where she used to go with her friend, Tricia Norman, the one who got killed."

"Was she more composed?"

"No, she was still pretty shaken." He stopped talking, staring into Luke's abandoned cup of coffee.

Luke waited, but when Heath clammed up, he prompted. "And then what happened?"

"Well...she was pretty upset, you know. And I was trying to calm her and...well... I kissed her." He paused. "All right," he said, aggravated. "I did more than kiss her. I practically ripped her dress off. In fact, I did rip her dress."

"You ripped her dress?"

"She's just so...gorgeous. And...she's...sweet, and innocent...and sexy and compassionate. Damn." He raked through his thick hair. "I know I shouldn't have done it. I'm a cop. She's a victim."

"You're a man. She's a woman."

"Yeah, but—"

"Were you the only one involved in this kiss?"

"No. Hell, no! But the timing wasn't right. She was so shaken, grieving, scared... So, I pulled back. And...I guess she took it the wrong way."

"Ahh."

"Man. This is nuts." Heath ran his fingers through his hair again, although he knew it was now totally disheveled. He rose from his seat and trudged to the sink, with his coffee cup. Hearing something, he peeked out of the window above the sink. Strolling along the walk, his hands tucked into the pockets of his leather bomber jacket, whistling as he came, was their brother, Kole.

"Oh, shit. It's Kole," He spun around. "You aren't saying anything."

"Dude, relax," Luke replied, his eyes twinkling. "My lips are sealed, remember?"

"Your lips are sealed about what?" Kole asked, leaning against the door frame casually. His hair was wavy like his brothers', but it was jet black, contrasting with his gleaming white teeth. He wore his devilish good looks with an ease marginally short of arrogance. Luke and Heath exchange a glance, amused on one side, anxious on the other.

Heath sat at the table, resigned. "You're going to squeal."

"Not me. I know how to keep a secret."

Kole snorted. "Since when? 'Mom, did you know Kole uprooted your flowers so he could bury Hopper?'" he simpered in a high voice, mocking Luke.

"Shit, man. I was five years old. Get over it. In any case, you should have known better than to bury your pet frog in her flower garden."

Kole laughed, and let his gaze shift to his next victim. "Nice outfit. Is that blood on your sleeve?"

Heath yanked on his sleeve to check his elbow. "Shit."

Kole rose and walked to his chair, gripping his shoulders and massaging him in a none-too-soothing manner. "So, what's little brother wanting to keep on the down low? Must be banging someone new." He paused. "Pay dirt. Your muscles tightened. Jacky told me you were working a new case...with Jasmine Barrett." Kole's hands stilled, and he studied Luke's eyes across the table. "Oh, my God. That's it. You're banging the rock star!"

"Thanks, Luke."

He laughed. "What? I didn't say anything."

"You didn't have to say anything. That shit-eating grin said it all." Heath stood and stormed away from the table in disgust. "And, for your information, I'm not 'banging' anyone."

Kole peeked at Luke again. "Ahh. You'd like to though," he concluded. "I thought she was dating that Michael Veritek guy."

"Who?"

"The actor," Luke explained patiently. "No, they broke up before the summer even started. He's dating Simone LaTeur."

"The Olympic swimmer?"

Luke nodded.

"Geez, *girls*," Heath said, his voice dripping with sarcasm. "How do you know all this?"

"Maybe if you went to the grocery store...but I guess that would be too much to ask from the guy who doesn't know what salad oil is."

Heath appealed to Kole. "Do you know salad oil and vegetable oil is the same thing?"

Kole shook his head in wonder, turning to Luke. "He didn't know salad oil and vegetable oil is the same thing?"

"No. He was searching for it with the salad dressing." They both roared.

"That's why I pay you to go to the store for me. What are you doing here anyway, Kole?" Heath added, desperate to change the subject "It's a work day and it's early enough Jack isn't even out of bed yet."

"Well, I was en route to the gym—" he flexed his muscles and his brothers exchanged looks behind him "—so I thought I'd stop by and satisfy my curiosity on a certain subject." He took a drink from Luke's coffee cup and grimaced. "It's cold."

"Satisfy your curiosity about what?"

Kole focused on Luke steadily. "Jacky tells me you were swapping spit with Mrs. Wainright in the Primate House."

"I was not 'swapping spit' as you so elegantly put it, with Vanessa—"

"Ooh! *Vannessa*," his brothers said simultaneously.

"—in the Primate House." He said, glaring at them balefully. He took a sip of his coffee. "It was the Reptile House."

They hooted. "How freakin' Freudian is that?" Heath said between laughs.

"Shut up."

"Geez, what's going on with you guys?" Kole added. "Heath here is putting the squeeze on a rock star, and little bro is getting it on hot and heavy with Little Miss Divorcee—"

"I'm not putting the squeeze on—"

"Her name's Vanessa," the brothers protested simultaneously.

"Next thing I know Jacky-boy is gonna be scorin' with an eighth-grader. Still...I wouldn't mind playing a song or two with Little Miss 'Rock My World.'"

"You'd never get past her keyboard," Heath retorted. "Now—" he said dismissively "—I have to take a shower."

Luke followed. "Me too."

As they left the kitchen, Heath glanced over his shoulder. Kole was pushing back from the table—presumably to warm Luke's coffee for himself—his smile glowing. "My work here is done."

CHAPTER TWELVE

Heath got his son to school. Feeling bad about having been away so much, he promised to take him to the baseball game Wednesday afternoon. Jack would miss some school, but Heath figured skipping one afternoon of kindergarten wouldn't put him off the college-bound track. He climbed into his old Mustang and pulled onto the road, leaving his police-issued sedan behind. The sun hadn't quite taken the chill from the air yet. They had reached the days when the heat had to be turned on in the car in the morning and switched over to the air-conditioner in the afternoon. Today the forecasters predicted temperatures would get into the mid-seventies.

The shower and fresh clothes went a long way to compensate for lack of sleep, and by the time he scrambled up the steps of the precinct building he was almost chipper. From his desk he called The Lofts. Brody Barrett answered. "This is Lieutenant Heath McGowan. I was wondering if I could speak to Jasmine Barrett." He didn't know why he asked so formally. He guessed it was out of the habit born from working from his desk.

Jasmine was on the other extension. "Yes, *lieutenant*." Her voice sounded as cool as the October frosts coming around the corner. So much for starting on a better foot with her this morning. His attempt to create professional space may have, instead, created professional distance.

"I was wondering if you would be available to answer some background questions so we can get information we need to further the investigation. I could come down whenever it is convenient for you."

He could practically hear her bristle at his polished, and perhaps even bureaucratic tone. "I'll come to you. I'll be there in twenty minutes."

"Jasmine," he said quickly, before she could end the call. The use of her first name may have been what made her pause. "Please make sure you are accompanied by an officer. I'll send another one to guard your place while you're gone."

"Okay," Jasmine responded simply, and then she was gone.

JASMINE HAD AWAKENED on the couch that morning having no idea how she had gotten there. The last thing she remembered was watching her uncle turn the lock on her and leave, and then seeing Heath come in and sit on the couch. She was going to knock on the window for him to let her in, had raised her fist, even, but she let it fall to her side. He made it pretty clear he thought she was a tramp. A tramp who brought men into her bedroom to seduce and then, film them. One who flung herself at unsuspecting police-men on rooftops. What was worse was she felt like a tramp. Had felt like that for quite some time, even though she had let very few men touch her since that night when she was twelve.

It frightened her that she didn't know how she had gotten to the couch. She hated the pills her uncle gave her, but at times the pain was unbearable. She wished there was a means to take the edge off and still be able to feel, but not too much. She wished things were normal again. But then again, they had never really been normal. At least not since the plane crash. Previous to that her life had been great. Okay, maybe she idealized it in thinking back, but she knew for a fact it had been really good.

Her memories were vivid. She remembered walking through the St. Louis Botanical Gardens with her father, holding his big, soft hand in the warm sunshine and mild breezes, surrounded by well-kept paths and flowers, and ponds with scenic bridges—just her and her dad. He would buy those overpriced juices in the plastic oranges or apples, with the straws that poked out. They were the best thing she had ever tasted, cool and comforting.

She remembered walking with her dad on the bridges over Highway 44 to "The Checker Dome," where the St. Louis Blues played hockey, named af-ter the classic symbol of their sponsor, Ralston-Purina. She had been terri-fied, up so high, with cars whizzing past below like dragonflies darting across the sky, but he held her hand and talked to her gently and it was so wonderful. He explained the game to her patiently and got so excited when they scored and so upset when a poor call was made, or an unfair penalty assessed.

Times with her mom had been different...making cookies and hot chocolate, kissing away hurts, snuggling in bed, even when she was a big girl. Her mom had possessed the best voice for reading stories and would even create her own. They were wildly imaginative and creative, but she made them seem real to her. She acted silly with Jasmine and her daddy and they loved to laugh and play games together. Jasmine had loved them so much.

Then in a flash, her world had changed. Changed from a world full of love and laughter, to a surreal world of expectant audiences, bright lights, wild parties, and pretense. She had been exposed to too much, too soon, while simultaneously being kept isolated by her uncle, preventing her from forming any meaningful relationships.

That was, until she met Tricia. She had accepted Jasmine for who she was, had not set expectations for her, but had truly understood and enjoyed her. And now she was gone.

Jazz had thought Heath was like Tricia. He had seemed so compassionate at first. He cared enough for her to argue with her, she admitted. And then her thoughts drifted to the rooftop. Having been so unbearably alone for so long, she found herself letting go within his embrace. The heat of his kisses was so damn good. A blinding desire filled her, ridding her mind of everything else and she lost herself to him completely. Only Heath had the power to make it all disappear with the taste of his wine-kissed breath and strong arms. If she lost herself to the sensations that he was creating in her body, he could make the faces go away, the blood go away, the terror and revulsion go away, the sense of being invaded. She wanted only his invasion, only him, the only one she could trust with herself. She yielded to him, melting into him, at the same time, pushing against him, needing him surrounding her to block out the pain.

And then he pulled back, gaping at her with...what...in his expression? Shock? Disapproval? He had kissed her first, she knew he had. Or maybe it was her? Clearly he had expectations of her, preconceived ideas. Or maybe he had just seen right through her.

Whatever the case, he had left and she was alone again.

She spent most of the morning standing by the French doors to the balcony staring at the nothingness outside that seemed to match the nothingness inside of her.

Then, Heath called...Lieutenant Heath McGowan. He sounded so detached and unfeeling. It infuriated her. Well, if he intended to dismiss her, she wasn't about to make it easy for him.

CHAPTER THIRTEEN

Heads whirled when Jasmine Barrett walked into the squad room. Her outfit was designed for that. She wore a short, black mini-skirt and stilettos, but still managed to appear attractive, rather than trampy. Her snug, red tank drew the eye like a stop sign to her tempting curves and the soft, golden skin of her upper chest. The short-waisted, black jacket she wore was accented with rhinestones that sparkled in the squad room's fluorescent lights.

When Heath glanced over from the report he was engrossed in, he kept moving his gaze up and up, lingering so he could devour every last inch of her. Her hair was bigger than before, her makeup bolder, her lips, an invitation to self-destruction. The pen dropped from his fingers, landing loudly on the floor, breaking his trance. As he bent to retrieve it, the sharp click of heels rang on dirty linoleum as she came around his desk. He stole another peek at the legs as he rose, from ankle, to calf, to thigh, to heaven. Yes, an outfit designed to put professional space on a back burner. If only it weren't for those frigid green icicles glaring at him from that stellar face of hers. She was irresistibly hot, and undeniably cold, all at the same time, a little microcosm of their relationship, hot, then cold...or heatedly cool, and then frigidly hot.

"You wanted to talk to me?" Her voice was velvety smooth and seductive.

She balanced on the corner of his desk, crossing her legs and all he could think of was, *Ouch!* He was keenly aware everyone in the squad room was focused on them, or at least on her. He was equally certain dozens of voices inside of dozens of minds right now were saying, "*I* want to talk to you."

"Not here," he muttered under his breath.

She tipped forward and her fragrance swept over him reminding him of the couch on the roof and how much he wanted her then. He was having trouble taking in air. "I'm sure there's an interrogation room open," she said edgily.

He had been thinking of taking her to a private lounge...thinking of begging her for forgiveness and locking the door so he could fulfill his every fantasy with her. But at the moment, her smart-assed attitude had him more than hot, it had him hot under the collar. He snagged a pen and tablet and grabbed her arm, pulling her off the desk and dragging her with him. "An interrogation room, then."

As they weaved through desks, Heath sent dark looks to all those who were wolfishly leering at her, dreaming about what *they* would do with her in an interrogation room. He took her into a room and slammed the door on prying eyes. She sauntered to the long metal table and slid out a chair, plopping into it and folding her hands on the table so she could stare at them. He rested against the door, furious, exhausted, turned on, and most of all, confused. He threw the tablet on the table, and she jumped, but then leaned backward in her chair as if perfectly relaxed. He slowly sat on the other side, doodling on the paper while he thought of what to say, drawing tight, concentric circles that became blacker and blacker as seconds ticked away.

"Where was I on the night of September fourteenth?" Jasmine said with a sense of irony. Their gazes met, searing with emotions. He remembered where they had been yesterday, on the fourteenth, and what they had done and almost done together. "Isn't this when you use all the big lamps and put the heat on me?"

Finally Heath had to smile and shake his head. *Dammit.* She was so cute sitting there, defiant, like so many others who had sat across from him at this same table. She slouched down in the seat, hunching her shoulders and trying to act disinterested. "Unfortunately they'll be plenty of heat soon. This room always gets hot," Heath replied, loosening the tie he chose to wear that morning.

She moved her chair closer. "I can take the heat. Can you?"

I doubt it, Heath thought weakly. He cleared his throat and attempted to regain control. "In order for me to proceed further with the investigation into Tricia Norman's death, I'll need to get more information from you...concerning various relationships in your life." He noted a spark of curiosity in the rebellious eyes. "First, and foremost, do you believe you might have any enemies, anyone who might hold a grudge against you for any reason, something like that?"

She sat forward, seeming more willing to help. "I've been concentrating on that, but I can't think of anything. We might dip into a party here and there, but besides Tricia and my uncle, I'm essentially a loner. The next most solid relationship I have is with Sebastian and the boys at the restaurant."

He sat straighter, clearing his throat again, and paging through his notes, stalling for some reason. "What about—" he pretended to read from his notes "—a Michael Veritek."

Jasmine's gaze narrowed. "I'm not sure what my relationship with Michael—"

"I have to verify he is not a threat to you. You went out, did you not?"

"I guess."

"And you broke up."

"Yes."

"Was it a mutual parting of ways?" Heath couldn't stand the thought of the man being with Jasmine, seeing her in that hot outfit she had on, laughing with her, touching her.

"I don't see why—"

"Dammit, Jasmine. Answer the question."

She glared at him. "All right. I guess you would call it a mutual decision. Michael and I are still friends."

Heath ground his teeth, pretending again to look at his notes. After a time, he sighed. "And your relationship with Lionel Parker?"

She paled. "My relationship?"

"Yeah. You know...how you met, how long you've known each other, that kind of stuff."

"Oh."

She recovered her equilibrium, but not before he saw something in her expression. There was more to this than she was saying. Had she been a normal suspect he would have pressed her, but he knew he had to take his time with her or she would go silent immediately. "When did you meet?"

"When I was t-twelve."

This time he was sure he saw a shadow of pain pass over her face, but she swallowed and went on, sticking to the facts.

"He was producing films then. I did a few...a few commercials...and Lionel either produced or directed them. Now he's switched to the music industry. Produces sound tracks and videos. He's working with my uncle." She rose abruptly and stood behind her chair, grasping the top of it. "God, it's hot in here."

"Then take off your jacket," Heath said, concentrating on his notes. After a moment, he glanced at her and saw beads of sweat forming on her upper lip and forehead. "Take off your jacket, Jasmine." She shook her head a little, and he noticed her eyes had gotten wide. Then, in a flash, his mind returned to last night's scene outside her bedroom door. Brody Barrett had been trying to force her to sleep in the bedroom where she had found her friend's murdered body... and he grabbed her. Heath stood and slid around the table toward her. "Take off your damn jacket, Jasmine."

"I'm not feeling well. I have to go." She made an attempt to slip past him, but he blocked her way.

"Take off the jacket." His voice was low and commanding.

"I don't have to—" Before she could finish her sentence, he got hold of the collar of her jacket and yanked it down from her shoulders. As he suspected, bruises, the color of an overripe banana, covered both biceps.

"He did this to you, didn't he? Brody did this."

"H-he was upset. He...he didn't mean to—"

"Why the hell are you making excuses for him, Jasmine? He was trying to drag you into a room where you found your best friend's nude body, strangled and stabbed—"

"I know!" she screamed hysterically. "My God, I know!" Her voice trembled and she took a shaky step back. Her gaze searched the room frantically like a caged animal. "I can't do this anymore." She reached for the door knob again, and he captured her arm.

"Don't—"

What happened next shocked them both. As he swung her about, she slapped him, hard. They both stood frozen, mouths hanging open in surprise. Jasmine's eyes were huge. He watched as her face crumbled like a house of cards hit by a fan. Without another word she ran out the door. Heath didn't move at first, still astounded by what happened. He entered the hall as she bolted toward a staircase.

"Davis!"

Officer Franklin Davis knew immediately what he was being asked to do and flew after her. Heath stood rubbing the heat from his cheek. Others who had heard their raised voices quickly tried to appear busy when he cast a look in their direction.

Heath strode over to his desk and leafed through some files, pretending to be busy, but his mind was on anything but the papers on his desk.

CHAPTER FOURTEEN

When Heath came back later with his fourth cup of coffee, the phone records he had requested were on his desk. Brody Barrett's phone had indeed been in use at the time of the murder, two long phone calls. But, to be certain he hadn't just kept the line open and then left to commit his murder, Heath decided to verify they were legitimate phone conversations.

"Gloria, here."

"Yes. This is Lieutenant Heath McGowan of the St. Louis City Police Department. I'm calling in regards to the murder of Tricia Norman."

"Who? Oh, oh. The girl who was killed at Brody's place, sure." Her New Jersey accent was so thick he could almost smell the Delaware River.

"I was wondering if you could confirm for me you were on the phone with Brody Barrett on Friday night?"

"Sure. Sure. I was speakin' to Brody. And I don't mind telling you, it sort of gave me the creeps, when I heard later, that, while we were on the phone, having an intimate like conversation, that girl was killed."

"Yes...well, the phone records say here you were on the phone for forty-five minutes. Could you tell me what you were discussing for that length of time?"

"Well...I told ya. We were having an intimate conversation." She paused. "You know, I was getting Brody's rocks off."

"Excuse me?"

"You know. Talkin' dirty to him."

This wasn't what he'd expected. "You were having phone sex?"

"Well, it was more like phone making love, 'cause Brody has the hots for me," she answered defensively. "It's not all about the sex, although I'm no slacker in the sack, if ya know what I mean?"

He cleared his throat. "So this...conversation...was going on for, roughly, forty-five minutes?"

"Yeah," she breathed. "I can make it painfully slow, but well worth the wait. You sound like you have a nice voice, officer. How big are you?"

Heath suddenly wanted nothing to do with the conversation. "Thank you, Miss."

"No problem, officer. You know, I like a man in uniform and I bet you have one *large* pistol, don't you?" she added suggestively.

Heath didn't know how to respond to that. Right before he hung up the phone Gloria Cohen said, "Ah, well. I gave it a shot."

He blew out a huff of air. *You meet all sorts in this business.* He peeked down at the phone log again. Brody's next call was to a one-nine-hundred number. Apparently Gloria wasn't as good on the phone as she thought she was. He knew it was somewhat pointless, but he called the number anyway.

"Hello, handsome," a low, sultry voice answered. "This is Jasmine, how can I pleasure you?"

Heath blinked. Had the throaty voice really said Jasmine, or was his imagination supplying details for him?

"Uhh...yes. This is Lieutenant Heath McGowan of the St. Louis City Police Department. Could you spare a minute for some questions?"

"It's your dime, sweetie," the voice answered blandly.

"Yes, well...I know this isn't likely, but do you remember having a rather lengthy conversation last Friday night?"

There was a long pause. "As a matter of fact, I do. One of my regulars called in. He told me he wanted me to do all the talking—"

"Is that unusual?"

"Not so much. Sometimes they need their hands free, if you know what I mean. But the reason I remember was because he asked me to keep going until he told me to stop and he had me on there forever. I was beginning to think I was losing my touch. So I used the big guns, you know, stuff that really gets them all hot and bothered. And when I'd run through most of my material and needed to pee on top of that, I told my regular I was done, but he didn't answer, so I ended the call."

"So it's possible he wasn't even listening to you?"

"I guess. But honey, at ten bucks a minute, wouldn't you be listening?"

Not if the only reason you called was to supply an alibi for yourself. "Yeah...I guess so. Thank you for your time."

"No problem. And officer...I'd be willing to give you a freebie, seeing as you're a cop and all."

"Thanks, but I'm at work."

"That usually doesn't prevent anyone, but okay." The line went dead.

So Barrett had an alibi, but not one that would hold up well in court. Heath couldn't rule him out as a suspect, and it didn't break his heart. He made a few more calls.

HEATH FOUND IT HIGHLY suspicious Michael Veritek happened to be in St. Louis right now, filming a movie at the Art Museum in Forrest Park, minutes from The Lofts. He decided to pay the actor a personal visit. Since Adam was gone on paternity leave with a brand new baby boy, he was on his own until another officer was assigned to him. Heath knocked on the door of Veritek's trailer on the set, shouting his name gruffly. A big guy, who he fingered for a bodyguard, answered the door. He had his badge waiting.

"Just a moment," the guard said cautiously. A few seconds later, he returned and opened the door. "Michael said you could come in."

Heath entered and located the star to his left, the blazing lights circling a dressing table mirror alerting him like a beacon.

"What can I do for you, officer?" Michael Veritek gave him a smile he was almost sure must be insured by Lloyd's of London. He sat in an untucked blousy white shirt with neon colored swirls on it. His thick, brown hair was worn in one of those trendy gelled, tousled styles Heath thought was stupid on a guy, but he knew women found appealing. After all, Veritek had been named "World's Sexiest Man" by some magazine the previous year. A thin, attractive brunette was working with his hair, comb at the ready, scissors in her apron pocket, a crescent of hair around the base of the chair. She raised a curious brow as he introduced himself.

"I had a few questions to ask you concerning Jasmine Barrett."

"Jazz is okay, isn't she?" The actor spun in alarm toward Heath, seeming to annoy his hairstylist who looked like she was nearly finished perfecting her client. His concerned demeanor was equally aggravating to Heath.

"Yes, sir. She's fine."

"Thank God. Janet, hon?" He squeezed one of the hands she had dropped to his shoulders. "Can we be done for now? I think it'll be awhile before they call me for a scene, anyway."

"Sure, Michael. I'll sweep later." The hairdresser bent and kissed his cheek, then strutted past Heath, giving him a suggestive wink as she passed.

"I read of Trish's death in the papers, of course, and I've been concerned for Jazz. I'm not sure how I can help you, though."

"Well, we have reason to believe the killer is actually targeting Jazz...I mean, Ms. Barrett. As a matter of routine, in cases such as this, we need to question anyone who might have been close to her, and your name was mentioned."

"Jazz mentioned me?" he asked quickly.

Veritek's eyes were almost as green as Jazz's, the fact this probably would have made them a cute couple made him want to yack. "Actually, no." He supposed it must be wrong for him to take pleasure in the fleeting disappointment he saw fly through the green eyes he had just been envying. But, if it was wrong, that didn't seem bother him. "I'm sorry I have to pry like this—" *No, I'm not.* "—but, could you please tell me about your relationship with Jasmine? Barrett," he added belatedly.

Michael sighed and sat on a couch, while Heath continued to stand, tapping his pen against his notebook, though listening with rapt attention. "We met at a party. The minute I saw her, I knew I wanted her. But, to be frank, I was solely interested in getting into her pants...at that time. I had to get past her uncle—you've probably met him. He's a real bulldog. But we managed." He grinned, remembering. Heath's gut clutched. "She was incredible." Veritek stared off, silently reminiscing and making him uncomfortable.

"And how did things end?" Heath asked, wanting to emphasize they had, indeed, ended.

"She—" Veritek hung his head for a minute "—I think her uncle finally got to her. I don't know. But it made me realize she was more to me than another mattress tango. She meant much more to me than that."

Someone rapped on the door sharply. "Michael, it's John."

"That's my director. This should only take a second."

The actor went to the door and Heath took the opportunity to observe the area. His focus landed on a picture frame on the dressing table. Glancing over his shoulder to check on Veritek, he took a step nearer. It was a picture of Jasmine with the actor. He picked it up to study it. Veritek had his arms around Jasmine, their cheeks were together, their faces shone, and they were smiling brightly. Heath honed in on her expression. She looked so happy. He'd never seen her happy like that. *But then again, all the time I have known her, she's been dealing with death and terror.* Still, strangely, it hurt to think she could have been happy with Veritek.

Michael finished his discussion with the director and turned from the door. "Detective!" he said sharply.

Like a kid caught with his dad's *Playboys*, Heath half twisted, still holding the frame. In the dressing table mirror their gazes connected. Veritek strode angrily across the trailer, snatching the picture from Heath's hands. "May I ask *you* a question, detective?" he sneered. "What, exactly, is *your* relationship with Jasmine Barrett?" Probably seeing Heath's blink of surprise, and knowing he hit the nail on the head, he added. "Have you kissed her yet?"

He blustered, "I'm the lead detective on—"

"Um-hum. Let me assure you, it will be a very pleasurable experience. It certainly was for me." He seemed to purposefully leave the idea dangling so he could observe what must be the brilliant shades morphing his features. "But I must warn you, detective, Jasmine Barrett is a very complicated woman."

Regaining his composure, Heath barked, "With all due respect, Mr. Veritek—" he had just decided very little respect was due "—I believe *I* am the one who is supposed to be making the inquiries here. So, where were you Friday night?"

"Are you accusing me of something, detective? Should I get my lawyer?" His eyes flashed with anger.

He wanted to say, *Yeah, get your fucking lawyer,* but he sensed that would be somewhat counterproductive. He sighed, "It's the same thing I'll be asking anyone who had anything to do with Jasmine Barrett."

Veritek hesitated, no doubt debating whether it would be worthwhile to ruffle his feathers further, and finally, chose not to. "Friday..." he said, considering, "...we were here late. I went home at 9:15 or 9:30, zipped up 40 and was in bed by 10. I watched the news and fell asleep. I was exhausted."

"Is there anyone who could verify that?"

"No," he said, flashing that million-dollar smile. "I guess you'll have to trust me."

Not a chance. "And last night?"

"What about last night?"

"Where were you from four to seven?"

"Why? What happened last night?"

"Haven't you read the paper?'

"Detective, I hardly have enough time to read my lines, let alone the newspaper."

He mulled over his response. He seemed sincere, but after all, he was an actor. "Jasmine's neighbor was found by her with his throat slit."

"Holy shit. She must be going out of her mind. I have to call her."

"And you were...where...last night?"

Veritek stared at him darkly. "Your questions are becoming insulting. I was here until 5:00, then at a dinner party at my director's. He can confirm that for you."

"Good. He'll need to," Heath answered, grumpily. "You have an address for where you are staying?"

"I don't know it offhand." Veritek pulled his wallet from his pocket, thumbing through it, then gave him a card. "You can call my agent. He booked it for me. He'll have the location. Now, if that's all?" He turned toward the mirror and began to preen the hair his hairdresser had finished styling moments before.

Heath scowled in disgust and started to walk toward the door but then spun back. "How long did you and Jasmine date?"

"Five months."

Heath's brows rose in surprise, and then he shook his head, wishing he could shake the information off as easily. "And, after those five months, what would your opinion of Brody Barrett be? Do you think he would hurt Jasmine?"

"Do I think...hell, yeah I do. He hurts her every day. Maybe he doesn't hit her, he wouldn't because her face is one of the things that pays for his gambling, but he does physically bully her and constantly demeans her. You must have seen that yourself. I hate that bastard. If *he* ever winds up dead, you better come arrest me."

He nodded. At least they agreed on something.

CHAPTER FIFTEEN

Jazz pulled the convertible to a smooth stop in front of the house. It was gorgeous. A huge screened-in porch, with wide steps that she decided were made strictly for lounging on, and a green lawn gently sloping to the sidewalk. Her gaze was drawn to an interesting trio of windows on the second floor with a sunburst design over the middle one. It added interest to an already charming house. She glanced down at the business card Heath had given her after having quickly scribbled his personal information on the back. This was it, all right.

She exited the car, closing the door and leaning against it, engrossed enough she forgot the police car had trailed after her from the condo. Though not far distant from busier thoroughfares, the street he lived on was surprisingly calm. *The city is like the man,* Jasmine reflected, *big and tough, with unexpected quiet spots.* She took a deep breath and headed up to the door. She raised the quaint, wrought-iron knocker and let it fall. Almost immediately the door was opened by a little boy in a Cardinals hat. He wore a mitt that sheltered a ball.

"Hey, you're Jazz!"

He was adorable. Thick, wavy blond hair, his eyes a lighter grey, but basically a miniature Heath. She fell in love with him at once. "That's right." She squatted and tugged on the bill of his cap. "And *you* must be Jack."

"How'd you know?" he asked, a brow cocked in suspicion.

"Because your dad told me about you."

"Jack, you know not to open the door to a stranger without—" A tall, slender man opened the door wider from behind the boy. He had longer, curly brown hair and the most gorgeous brown eyes Jasmine had ever seen, surrounded by lashes that shouldn't have been wasted on a man, she noted enviously. His mouth, with strong, full lips, hung open.

"It's not a stranger. It's Jazz." The boy blew a huge bubble, which popped, but was sucked in expertly. "Wanna play catch?"

"Sure. But I didn't bring my glove—"

"That's okay. You can use my dad's."

Jack rotated and disappeared into the house, leaving her with the man she presumed was his Uncle Luke, who was still gaping at her.

"Hi." She offered her hand. "I'm Jasmine Barrett."

"I know," he replied stupidly, but then seemed to come to his senses, clearing his throat and taking her hand in his. "Luke McGowan. Please, come in."

"Well, if it's okay with you, I'll stay here until Jack returns. I'm not sure Heath would want me in his house right now. I was kind of...I don't know...not very nice to him, this morning. To tell you the truth, I feel simply awful over it."

"Whatever you did, I'm sure he deserved it. Heath can be a putz."

Jasmine laughed. "You're a pianist, aren't you?"

"Yes."

"Heath mentioned you. He said you were extremely talented. He also said you helped babysit Jack the other night so he could...well, babysit me." She grimaced. "Thank you."

His answer was interrupted by Jack tearing out the door and throwing a mitt haphazardly at Jasmine, who caught it, although surprised by the toss. Jack didn't stop and let the screen door slam behind him. "Come on!"

"I guess I'm playing ball."

Luke followed the pair and sat sprawled on the steps while watching them.

HEATH SAW HER CAR EVEN before he saw the house. His heart leapt, but then he remembered it could be Brody. Hopeful, he leaned forward so he could see around the gigantic fir tree in his neighbor's yard. Maybe she had just arrived and was on the porch. First, he caught sight of Jack, beaming while squawking excitedly and lobbing the ball to someone. Then he spotted Jasmine, her sweet little buns sticking out as she pretended to go through a full motion, including an exaggerated leg kick, as she was pitching to Jack. Heath pulled up and parked opposite from her car, noting the patrol car near it. He could hear Jack's shouts even prior to his hitting the pavement.

"Hey, Dad. Jazz is here."

He exited the car, twisting to rest his arms on top of the roof, getting a long hard look at her, his foot on the bottom of the door frame. A grin split his face and the warmth it gave spread over him. "I can see that."

His cheerful demeanor seemed to unnerve her some. Her expression brightened when she saw him, but then she bit her lip. He closed the door of the Mustang and walked in front of it, slinging his suit coat over his shoulder.

After giving his fellow officer a nod, he signaled and Jack threw him the ball which he caught with his free hand. She sauntered toward him until she was right by his side, never taking her focus from him, which he found incredibly sexy.

Jack followed her. "She throws pretty good too. For a girl."

Heath bent his head toward her. "He got his sense of tact from me," he said in lieu of an apology, his voice low and husky.

"I'm sorry, Heath." She shaded her eyes from the sun and searched him, squinting a tad, though her gaze was spellbinding. "Really sorry."

As he stared into those green orbs, he found himself temporarily lost. He could see the depths of her regret and her desire to be forgiven. But his heart was in his throat, and he couldn't find his voice.

"Dad, can Jazz stay for Pizza Night?"

His son's voice registered somewhere on the periphery of his awareness.

When he didn't respond, Jasmine addressed Jack. "That's nice of you to ask, Jack, but your daddy is probably tired from his day at work and not in the mood for guests. Thanks for asking me to play ball with you. It was fun." She gave Jack the glove with a small, sad smile and spun to leave.

As if he didn't hear her, he said, "I don't see why she couldn't stay for Pizza Night. That is, if she wants to."

She whirled, beaming at him, seeming relieved. "Oh, I'd love to."

They turned to go into the house.

"Oh, I forgot my bag." She ran back to the spot where she had been pitching, and grabbed the sling-bag. As Heath watched her, he spied Kole ambling up the sidewalk. His upbeat mood wavered. Kole, who could wind women around his finger with a flash of his whiter than white teeth and a wink.

Kole had zeroed in on Jasmine, as she bent to retrieve her purse. He made a bee-line for her. "Well hello, gorgeous." He gave her a grin that could melt a Popsicle in sixty seconds.

Heath evaluated the exchange, his good cheer fading all the more.

"Hello," she replied, her voice friendly. But she appraised him warily.

"I'm Kole McGowan." He took her hand, kissing it. "As in, 'hot as a coal.'"

"Uh-huh," she replied, though her face showed skepticism.

"Jasmine," Heath's voice seemed to startle her as he came up from behind them, "this is my other brother, Kole. Kole, Jasmine Barrett."

"Ahh. Yes. I didn't recognize you at first. I'm a huge fan."

She studied him. "I don't think so," she said slowly, with a sexy smirk. Kole sputtered and seemed about ready to protest but she swiveled and walked away from him.

Heath breathed a sigh of relief then chuckled. Luke nearly fell off the steps, he was laughing so hard. Kole observed his brothers' antics with nonchalance, unperturbed by their laughter, but shaking his head a little. Luke recovered, somewhat, and stumbled to Jasmine's side, still choking on his amusement. He put his arm over Jasmine's shoulder. "I love this woman," he announced loudly. "Come on, darlin'. Anyone who can put Kole in his place, with such ease, is all right by me." She followed him, throwing an amused look at Heath and Kole, who were staring after them.

CHAPTER SIXTEEN

While Jack gave Jasmine the grand tour of the house, Heath pretended not to listen. When she walked in, Jasmine immediately commented on how beautiful the oak floors were. He assessed them with new eyes.

They are. I never really considered that.

They climbed the staircase to the left. He followed, but paused midway to scan the living room area, trying to see it as Jasmine would. The spacious room was sectioned off with a couch, coffee table, and two chairs around a throw rug. The alcove area under the steps held a small wooden table and chairs with a simple white wrought-iron chandelier hanging above it. Along the far wall was a large white ornate fireplace and to the left a swinging door led into the kitchen. The room was bright, airy, and comfortable with loads of light slanting in from a line of tall windows on the right. Heath grinned, hearing more exclamations from Jasmine on the upper level. He was lucky Luke was a neat freak.

Pizza arrived in a fairly short time, and within minutes of its appearance, they were all sliding thick, hot slices from the cardboard boxes on the kitchen counter. Heath winced when Jack produced paper plates to eat on, remembering an argument he had with Juliette, who thought paper plates were "gauche." At the time he hadn't even known what the word meant, but Jasmine didn't seem to care. Jack was pleased to be allowed to eat his pizza on the front porch, while the four grown-ups ate at the tiny kitchen table, which Heath was also suddenly embarrassed of, since they were practically bumping knees under the table. But he didn't mind so much when, during the meal, Jazz ran her hand quickly up and down the top of his thigh.

"So," Luke asked between bites, "you were raised in St. Louis, right?"

"Yes." Jazz drew another slice out of the box and returned to the table. "We lived in Kirkwood. I was finally able to convince my uncle to let me buy a place here last spring. But, truthfully, we're not here as much as I'd like to be. A lot of my work has to be done on the West Coast."

"Is that where you met Michael Veritek?" Kole asked, oblivious to the dark look Luke was shooting him.

"Uh, yes," she answered uneasily. "We met at a party."

Heath cringed, remembering how Veritek mentioned wanting her so badly when they'd met. Although he knew it was illogical, a smoldering fire was fanned inside of him.

"You've probably met a bunch of famous people," Kole added, wiping sauce from the corners of his mouth with a section of paper towel.

"Not as many as you'd think. The life of a female rock singer is a lot different than the life of a male rock singer, at least in my experience. We women seem to have no qualms about screaming for a guy or throwing undergarments at them while they're performing. But, I never once had a pair of boxers tossed my way. But maybe that's me. Maybe other female singers have men trying to maul them after shows."

"Oh, no. You're definitely maul worthy," Kole said with a winning smile.

"Why, thank you," she replied with a laugh. She glanced at Heath who wasn't smiling and hadn't since Kole mentioned Michael Veritek's name.

Luke redirected the conversation to more neutral topics, like asking which singer/songwriters had the most influence on her music. Throughout the discussion, Heath remained quiet and after a time it became harder and harder to draw Jasmine in. After several minutes, she rose from the table, picking up her plate. "I want to thank you gentlemen for dinner. It was lovely, but I guess I should be going."

"Why?" Heath said quickly, with an edge to his voice. "Would your uncle not approve?" He drummed on the table without raising his head, trying to look relaxed though internally seething.

Jasmine flinched, seeming disconcerted. "No. As a matter of fact, he wouldn't." She took her plate to the trash can and dumped the remainder of her food hurriedly. "Good night," she called over her shoulder and then all they heard was the swishing of the swinging door.

Luke slammed his fist on the table. "What the hell's the matter with you?"

Heath sat staring at his plate for several seconds, then hopped to his feet and went after her, sending the door swinging crazily. He caught her on the third porch step. Jack was nowhere in sight. Night had begun to fall and the welcoming lights from people's homes shown in the neighboring windows, but they barely took notice.

"Jazz, wait."

"Why, Heath? I shouldn't have even come in the first place." She padded down the stairs.

Desperate to stop her, he cried, "Is this how you solve all of your problems? By running away?"

That brought her up short. She whirled, eyes shooting sparks. "Who the hell do you think you are?" she raged, her voice thick with restrained violence. "Do you realize what I've been through lately? Do you have any idea?" Her voice cracked and she came close to losing it. She gulped in air, blinking back tears. "I don't need this, Heath. I just don't." Her voice was dangerously calm now.

A whistling man and his dog walked by and they both stood stone-still, as if caught in an intimate embrace. Despite his casual demeanor, the man sent several sidelong glances their direction in the gathering dark. Heath watched the man for a minute, but then returned his gaze to Jazz's, keeping it there until the dog walker was beyond earshot.

"Jazz, we need to talk. We need to clear the air between us."

She combed her hair with her fingers. In the lamplight, he noticed she was shaking and was swamped with guilt.

"I-I don't know." She squeezed her temples. "My brain hurts and I'm so tired. So damn tired."

"Please," Heath said simply, holding a hand out to her.

Jasmine studied him with an exhausted air. Then she walked past him without taking his hand. He swung around and caught up with her, opening the porch door. "We can speak on the porch. It's more private. I need a beer. Do you want anything?"

"A glass of water, please."

When he reentered, she was leaning uneasily against a vertical porch post. He set her drink on a horizontal rail next to her while they took measure of each other, like prizefighters in a ring. Heath lowered himself onto the porch swing, taking a swig of his beer.

"I should leave. You've got your family to take care of and—"

"Jasmine, I don't want you to leave." He peered at her earnestly. A current ran between them, almost pulsing in the air. They were silent again. "I paid a visit to Michael Veritek today," he said carefully.

"You did?"

"Did you know he was in St. Louis right now?"

"Yes," she responded quietly.

"But you didn't mention it to me?"

She exhaled, staring at her feet which were crossed in front of her, her arms behind her, grasping the two-by-four her glass was set on. "I didn't want Michael to get into any trouble. I know he doesn't have this in him. He couldn't have killed anyone." She considered him. "And I wasn't completely honest with you concerning our breakup either. I knew it would look bad for Michael if I told you the whole story."

"You understand I am an officer of the law. Not revealing this kind of information could make you liable for criminal prosecution for hindering an investigation and, let's not forget, could make you appear suspicious yourself. You were the one to discover the body after all. Some would say that makes you automatically suspect."

"Do you really think...?" she started, aghast.

"No. No. Of course not. Not for one minute. I pride myself in knowing people, Jasmine, and I know you wouldn't hurt anyone."

"I slapped you today."

"And you felt so bad about it you had to come here to apologize to me, which, incidentally, I appreciate."

"That wasn't the sole reason I came here. I wanted to see you." Again there was a long pause. Heath was well aware others were in the house only a short distance from them, but the pull between them was there none the less.

"I have to admit, I was glad to see you." He smiled, but then turned serious again. "But, if you want me to catch this guy, and I know you do, you can't pussyfoot around with me. You have to tell me everything."

"All right. I'm sorry. I'll tell you every last horrible detail." She sat on the swing beside him and sighed. "Michael was always a much bigger partier than

I was. It didn't bother me at first. Drugs are so prevalent at Hollywood parties, they're like after-dinner mints. He kept urging me to try it. I told him, no way, not my scene." She reflected. "One night, we went to this party. Michael disappeared for hours in one of the back rooms of this mansion we were in. I was getting ticked, when he materialized from nowhere. When I got on him for leaving me alone with a bunch of people I didn't know, he apologized and kissed me. He took me to a room upstairs, kissing me again and...touching me."

Heath was beginning to think maybe he didn't need to know all the details.

"But then he got really rough. I told him to slow down, he was hurting me, and he got really angry. He dragged me out of the house in front of everyone, cursing at me, and shoved me into the seat of his SUV. I told him I wasn't going anywhere with him, he was too stoned to drive, but he closed the door and locked it with a remote key, keeping it locked. Some guy made an attempt to help me and Michael almost ran him over. I can still remember the guy's terrified face in the SUV's headlights. It was awful." She shivered and got up to take a drink of her water.

Heath wished he could have been there. He would have loved to knock out a few of those pearly whites Veritek was so proud of.

"Then Michael left, squealing his tires. He drove into the hills surrounding L.A. He was driving like a wild man and it had started to rain. I was crying, begging him to lower his speed and pull to the side. So finally he said, 'You want me to stop. Okay, I'll stop,' and he locked the brakes and skidded onto the edge of the pavement, with a huge drop-off below. I was terrified. I tried to jump from the SUV, but he caught hold of me."

The calm she had displayed during the whole narration seemed to leave her, and she became upset, reliving what had been a traumatic night. He held her hand and squeezed it reassuringly, but didn't interrupt her.

"He said I was going to try some heroin, whether I liked it or not. He had some rubber tubing, which he tied around my biceps so tight I thought it would be severed. I fought him, I pleaded with him, but he was determined. I remember feeling powerless."

She shook her head. "Finally, when he reached for the syringe, I saw my chance. I got out of the SUV. I ran and stood in the lights, the rain drenching me. I ripped the tubing off and threw it on the ground. He got out, his tux getting wet. He was so angry. I'd never seen him like that. He said, 'Okay, you bitch. Have it your way.' He got in his SUV again and screamed away, leaving me there. I had to scramble to keep from getting run over. And then it was absolutely silent, except for the sound of the rain beating on the asphalt and my sobbing. And I realized I had no idea where I was."

He could imagine her there, alone and frightened. Merely the thought of it made him sick.

"I could see the lights of the city below, so I turned and went downhill, following the road. After a while, a pickup truck pulled in front of me on the shoulder. Two guys got out. The rain had slowed to a drizzle, but I was soaking wet. I don't know how, but somehow they still recognized me. I could tell they were drunk and I was afraid of the how they were leering at me. They offered me a ride, but I told them I'd had a fight with my boyfriend and I wanted to walk to clear my mind. They were smiling, sneering at me, then one of them grabbed me and pinned my arms behind me. The other guy began to remove his belt, said he was gonna show 'Little Miss Hollywood' what it was like to slum it. I thought they were going to rape me." Heath could feel her go clammy.

"Oh, babe. Come here." He coaxed her onto the swing with him, wanting to relief her distress.

She leaned against him, and continued quietly. "When he came close, I braced myself against his friend and brought both legs up to kick him solidly in the gut. His friend was laughing so hard he loosened his grip. I ran and they chased me, howling like crazed animals. I was looking back as they were overtaking me and I stepped off the cliff, right into space. I landed on a patch of loose rock and then skidded and tumbled several hundred feet. I lay there, bruised and bleeding, and I could hear them laughing from above, telling me they'd come and find me. They told me to just wait there. I guess I lost consciousness because when I woke, it was daylight and some old man was standing next to me. He saw the party dress and thought I had stumbled there, drunk. He took me to the hospital. Somehow my uncle managed to keep it out of the papers. Uncle Brody blamed it all on me."

Her voice was lifeless. She stood, her mood restless. "The next day, Michael came to apologize. I didn't even let him in. And that," she ended, "was the last of Michael and me."

She finished the rest of her water and clinked the ice around in the glass. "I saw him a year later at some function," she added thoughtfully. "I think it was a kickoff party my uncle had thrown together for one of my album releases. How Michael got in, I haven't the foggiest; my uncle had always hated him. Michael told me he hadn't taken a single drug since that night, not even an aspirin and I guess I was drunk enough to believe him. I told him we'd let bygones be bygones, but made it clear I wasn't interested in anything more than friendship. He wanted a romantic relationship, but he said he understood." She peered at him finally. "So you can see why I didn't tell you. Michael's a jerk, but he's not a killer."

He didn't want to tell her he'd come to that same assessment. "Sometimes people can amaze you by doing things you never thought they would do. Like, I bet you never thought he would leave you stranded in the rain in the hills in the middle of the night."

"That's true. But that's a far cry from murder."

He felt like pointing out injecting someone against their will was pretty heinous, too, but he didn't want to dredge it up any more than it had been. But, for the record, he had to ask her a few more questions. "Have you seen him since he came to St. Louis?"

She nodded solemnly. "The night before Tricia died."

"The night before the murder?"

She nodded her head again.

"And you didn't think this was important to mention?" He fought to control his temper. His chest was tight and his right temple throbbed.

She sat beside him again. "Heath, the last several days, it's like I can't even complete a sentence. My heart, my brain, feels fried. And those pills my uncle keeps insisting I take, I've quit taking them, but they weren't helping matters either."

He sighed. "I know, Jazz, you're right. You did the best you could." He paused. "So, when he came to your place, what did Veritek want?"

"Me. I mean...he wanted me back. And part of me wished for that too. I loved him at one time. When he came into my life I was so damned lonely.

He didn't seem like the others, like he was only hitting on me, although I discovered later he was." She smiled. "But I couldn't forget that night he left me alongside the road. I was afraid he would do something like that to me again. I just couldn't do it."

Heath put his arm around Jasmine and drew her in, kissing her hair. "Poor baby. You've been through so much." He caressed her skin, thinking she had given Veritek a motive for murder. He would have wanted to get revenge on her; his ego was too big to lie down and take that kind of rejection. "I know it's been difficult to tell me about all of this, and I appreciate your doing so. Do you think you would be able to answer more questions, or should we stop for tonight?" He pulled away a little so he could stare into her face.

Her body seemed to have shrunken in on itself, and her weariness was written in every breath she took. "May as well finish it."

"Okay," he said softly. "Then I need you to tell me why you have such animosity for Lionel Parker."

At his name, her head snapped up, her eyes at first were wide, but then became set with grim determination. "Okay, but I'll need a stronger drink for this."

CHAPTER SEVENTEEN

H eath went to the kitchen for a glass of wine. When he returned to the porch, he didn't see Jasmine, and thought she had cut and run. Then he saw her, a few feet out on the sidewalk, gazing at the moon. With the *bam* of the screen door, she pivoted.

"Can we go on the porch?"

Heath nodded and held the door open for her, guessing the porch offered a veil of privacy for the story she had to tell. He sat on the swing again, but she didn't join him, standing approximately five feet away. She took a large, bracing drink of her wine, and began her story.

"Well, I told you about my uncle taking me in after the plane crash. He had lived in L.A. for as long as I could remember, having gone there with hopes of doing some acting or performing musically. When I came, he seemed to transfer those hopes to me. I wanted to please him, so I agreed with whatever he suggested." As Jasmine spoke, she roamed around, in what appeared to be a leisurely manner. She grasped one of the porch's support posts and let her gaze wander upward to where it met with the ceiling. Then she tapped her nails on the intersecting railing. But every so often, she would focus on Heath with an intensity that would belie her casual actions, and his heart squeezed more tightly in his chest with each passing second, the dread hollowing his stomach.

She took another drink, seeming to bolster herself for what she would say next. "Shortly prior to my turning twelve, he landed me a small part in a film Lionel Parker was producing." She paused, setting the glass on a low wicker table and lacing her fingers together. "I've never told anyone this story before." She shook her head with an odd, strained smile. "When Lionel materialized yesterday, it brought everything flooding back. I was going to tell Tricia the night...the night she was killed."

She hesitated, looking over the lawn. When she resumed, it was as if she was reading from a cue card held by someone beyond the screens of the porch. "From the outset, Lionel's actions toward me were strange. He bought me dresses, but the kind that were meant for women, not little girls, which I still *was*," she emphasized. "He sent me flowers and jewelry..." She gestured wearily, but then her voice trailed off.

Taking another gulp of wine, she examined him above the rim of her glass, eyes wide, but unreadable. He didn't speak, didn't feel as if he could. He leaned forward, forearms on his knees, legs slightly apart, hands clasped between them. He peered at her. She was lit by the soft glow stealing from the living room, and he was spellbound by her story and actions, waiting to catch the bomb he knew she would drop. Jasmine set the wine glass down again, her expression now cast in shadow. She dropped her chin, but the light caught her sliding the ring she was wearing in and out rapidly. Then she inhaled deeply and became still. When she started again, her voice hung in the air with a haunting quality.

"Then, on the night of my twelfth birthday, we went to his house for dinner. A beautiful table cloth was on the table, candles lit and fresh flowers. I noticed it was only set for two. My Uncle Brody left. Left me alone with him. Lionel, that is." She stared at the wine glass on the table between them. "Lionel gave me wine. I'd never had wine. My head was spinning. And then he took me into a bedroom. He wanted to make love to me."

She closed her eyes as if the ugly words that came from her mouth were too much for her. "He got angry when I refused, but then the next minute, he acted as if everything was fine...like I was pretending not to want it, like his forcing me was okay. I remember being smothered by his scent and his weight. I wanted to scream, but there was no one to hear me. And then I screamed anyway."

She rubbed her arms, although the night was mild. Heath wanted to make it stop, to cross to where she was and scoop her up, and somehow erase it all from her memory, but he was frozen in shock.

"He took me home afterward, walked me to the door like nothing was wrong, and gave me a passionate kiss good night, like I was his date or something. Right there at our door. Twelve years old." She shook her head, as if still in disbelief. "He told me, at one of the points in the evening when he was ranting and raving at me, he had given my Uncle Brody six 'damn fine' pounds of California weed so he could do with me what he wanted, so I better not cause any trouble." She lifted her wine glass and swirled the contents a couple of times. "My innocence for six pounds of weed. Quite a steal, don't you think?" The bitterness was palpable in her voice.

She raised her glass to her lips, and drank the rest of it. "And *that*," she enunciated distinctly, "is why I can't stand Lionel Parker." She peered at him, her eyes murky with emotion. She seemed to be trying to read his reaction.

"He raped you," he said, still shocked. His mind fumbled around dully. "I can arrest him."

She gave a snort. "I think the statute of limitations has run out on a rape that occurred thirteen years ago. And even if it hadn't, there's no evidence..." Her voice faded, and she stared into space, twirling the ring now, appearing emptied.

He observed her. She looked so small and vulnerable in the porch light. Should he embrace her? He knew he wanted to comfort her, but would that unnerve her, after all she had relived, to have a man touch her? He rose slowly and came to her. She gazed at him and did the one thing he was afraid she would do, she burst into tears. She turned from him and covered her face, weeping quietly, her back shaking.

"Jasmine." He made a move to clasp her shoulders but she took a step forward, shirking him off. He stood, confused, sticking his hands finally into his pockets.

She took a few deep breaths, trying to calm herself. "So, you were right about me. A rock and roll whore who lost her virginity at twelve."

"Hey, I didn't say anything like that. And as far as I'm concerned, people can't *lose* what is taken from them by force."

She whirled, and looked at him fully, her features molded with rage, and shame, and pain. "But you still don't want anything to do with me. That's why you pulled away from me on the roof. You thought I was the kind of girl who planted cameras to secretly film my revolving door of lovers. And after tonight, you're sure I'm that kind of girl." she shouted. Both of them heard the door creak open. Jasmine spun in the other direction and wiped desperately at her tears.

"Hey, Dad."

Heath gaped down at his son and then watched as his little footie-pajamas shuffled over to stand in front of Jasmine.

"Jazz? I thought you left." He studied her. "You've been crying."

"No. No, buddy." She squatted to speak to him. "Well, actually, I have," she confessed, forcing a smile. "I'm very tired. I haven't been sleeping well lately, and when I get tired, I get cranky." She ruffled Jack's hair, still damp from his bath. He smelled of soap and innocence.

"Oh, is that all? That happens to me, too. Will you stay for ice cream?"

"I don't know. I think I may have to—"

"Dad, you'll make her stay, won't you?"

Heath tried to hide his emotion. He squatted next to Jack. "I'll do my best, son. Why don't you run in and hunt for your flash cards and I'll be in after a minute."

Jack spontaneously threw his arms around him, almost knocking him on his ass. "Okay, Dad," he said, in his bubbly voice. Then he ran off.

Heath couldn't help but chuckle as he rose. He glanced at Jasmine, and was surprised to see her smiling.

When she realized he was observing her, she blushed, and lowered her head. "He's wonderful, Heath."

"Yeah, I'm lucky." He took a step forward. "You're pretty wonderful yourself, you know?"

She took a step backward, waving her hands desperately. "Don't do that. Don't feel sorry for me."

Frustrated, he closed the gap between them and took Jasmine by the hips, startling her. "Jazz, I've been listening to what you had to tell me this evening. Now it's my turn to talk." Her mouth, that had been open in astonishment, shut, reminding him, comically, of a goldfish.

He stroked her clumsily as he decided what words to use. "I'm not very good at expressing myself. I know I've been sending you mixed messages. The fact is, I shouldn't be getting involved with you. I'm a cop, you're a victim. I'm supposed to be investigating a murder." He released her to gesture, palms up. "The list goes on and on. But every time I'm near you..." He looked down, watching as one of his thumbs brushed over her biceps. He drew in a long breath, raising his face again. "Every time I'm near you, I get this overwhelming urge to kiss you."

Her features changed, her eyes becoming unfocussed. She wiped her forehead and murmured something about being hot.

It was fortunate Heath still had hold of her, because she collapsed, her knees going out from under her. He spun her quickly, alarmed she was limp, then lifted her and cradled her against him.

"Jazz? Oh, shit." He hustled to bring her inside, nervous sweat beading on his skin. "Luke! Kole!" He managed to get the door open just as his brothers hit the foyer.

"What the hell did you do?"

"I didn't do anything, you idiot. She fainted." He rushed her to the couch.

"Well, why'd she faint?" Kole insisted.

"Oh, I don't know," Heath answered sarcastically. "Maybe, because she's kinda been under a lot of stress lately. People killed in her bed and all." He took a copy of a sports magazine from the coffee table and fanned her. "Luke, get a glass of water." Luke rushed to the kitchen.

She started coming around. "Heath...I..." She tried to sit, seeming disoriented.

"No, you don't, champ. You stay there for a minute."

"Wh-what happened?"

"We were talking one minute, and then you fell into my arms the next." He moved a stray hair into place, relief flooding him. "You know," he joked, to lighten the situation, "you don't have to lose consciousness to get me to hold you." He winked and was rewarded with a weak smile. He passed his hand along her cheek again. "Shit, Jazz, you scared me. You sure you're okay?"

"What's wrong with Jazz?" Jack's worried voice sounded from the stairwell as Luke bustled in, spilling a trail of water in his hurry.

Jasmine's eyes became big at the sound of his voice. "Nothing, buddy," she called in her most reassuring voice, instinctively wanting to protect him from anything that might scare him. "I'm okay," she said to Heath in a low voice, sitting.

Jack's small pajamaed feet created a scratchy, scuffing noise as he galloped across the wooden floor to her. "But why are you laying on the couch? And why are Daddy and Uncle Luke and Uncle Kole sitting by you? Are you sick?"

"No. Remember I told you I'm tired? I wanted to rest on the couch for a bit, and your daddy helped me to stretch out, is all. What are those?" she asked to distract him. She pointed to a pile of cards, drawn together by a red rubber band, Jack held in his chubby little fist. She accepted the glass of water from Luke.

"Oh. These are my flashcards," he replied proudly. "Do you want to see how good I do them?"

"Yes, I certainly do." She sat behind him, taking a drink of the water. Heath was glad to see the color come back into her face. "Thanks for the water, Luke," she added, with an air of embarrassment.

"Okay. Dad made up this game. "It's really cool." He laid the cards down on the coffee table in a predetermined pattern.

Now that Heath knew Jasmine was okay, he relaxed, allowing himself a brief moment of pleasure as he thought about how it was his mention of kissing her that sent her over the edge. He drew her in, nuzzling an ear. "Are you sure you're okay?" he said, his voice rippling with amusement.

Only he could hear her soft moan of pleasure. She twisted so her lips were inches from his. "Not if you continue to do that."

He gave a self-satisfied smirk, then slid to the floor next to Jack to play the game. Jasmine sat with her legs folded at the opposite side of the table where she followed Heath's interactions with his son.

"Well," Kole said, rising from his chair where he had been busy checking his text messages, "it's time for the Kolester to be going. Got a hot date." Jack rolled his eyes and Jasmine covered her mouth, snickering. "It was lovely meeting you, Jasmine." He bent to kiss her hand as she straightened and strove to be serious.

"Nice to meet you, too, Kole."

Jack watched her and when she was sure Kole wasn't looking, she rolled her eyes, sending him off on peals of laughter. Kole turned with a quizzical expression as he slipped into his jacket. "What's so funny, Squirt?"

Jack couldn't stop laughing, so Jasmine responded for him. "Oh, nothing. He's laughing because I was being silly. Right, Jack?"

He regained his composure and nodded then burst into laughter again, rolling onto his back and hooting. Jasmine started giggling, too, and Kole shifted his gaze to Heath, who shrugged.

Kole shook his head good-naturedly. "See ya." He left without further comment, perhaps thinking of the beautiful woman he would be meeting downtown.

"Okay, sport," Heath said, helping Jack to a sitting position. "One more game, and then you've earned your ice cream." Jack was taking deep breaths, trying to calm himself. He glanced over at Jasmine, her eyes still twinkling, and they both cracked up again, folding their arms on the table and laying their chins on top of them and roaring.

"O-o-okay. Maybe it's ice cream time now." He rose to go to the kitchen and Luke joined him. "You two behave."

Used to working as a team, Heath went to the freezer and Luke to the cupboard to get bowls. As Luke hunted for clean spoons, and he rifled among all the utensils for an ice cream scoop, Luke commented, "I like her."

"H-m-m-m?"

"Jasmine. I really like her, Heath."

"Oh. Yeah." Not elaborating on his viewpoint, he muscled his way through the hard ice cream and plopped scoops into the bowls handed to him.

"So?"

"So what?" Heath replied, frowning.

"So, what are your feelings for her?"

He stopped mid-scoop. "What are you, her friggin' dad, asking me what my intentions are?"

"No, Heath. She doesn't have a dad, remember? Someone has to look out for her. And from what you've told me, her uncle certainly doesn't."

He returned to scooping. "You don't know the half of it."

"So fill me in."

"I can't."

"You can't, or you won't?"

Setting his scoop on the counter, he faced Luke, ignoring the pool of ice cream that began to collect and eventually made a trail down the cabinet door.

"Tell me again why this is any of your concern?"

Luke sighed. "Listen, let me tell you what I see. You've dated a lot of women. Most of these women were either shallow, or brainless. Jasmine is different."

"Hey, hey, hey. Wait a minute here—"

"Brook?"

"So she asked a couple if their twins were identical and they weren't, so?"

"They were a boy and a girl."

Heath laughed, remembering. "Anyone could have made that mistake."

"Yeah. There are some parts I know for certain weren't identical. And Brenna?"

"Brenna was..." he searched for an adjective.

"A ditz. Need I remind you she woke her neighbor at 2 a.m. to tell him he left his 'snow blower' running on the sidewalk, during a power outage?"

"A common mistake."

Luke chuckled. "For Brenna, maybe. Most people would have taken into account the fact that no snow was on the ground and determined it was a gen-er-a-tor. And wasn't she the one who is infamous for saying, 'I know all about bees. I saw *The Bee Movie*?'"

"No," he snickered. "That was Claire. Or was it Lea?" He thought. "Yeah. It was Lea."

"And then there was Janet."

"Okay, Janet did attend way too many rock concerts." Heath paused, contemplating, then grabbed his scoop and shoveled again. "But, then again, so does Jasmine."

"Oh, come on!" Luke exclaimed. "It's hardly the same thing. Janet paid thousands to attend concerts. Jasmine *gets* paid thousands to attend concerts. Besides which, it's not solely that Jasmine is different. You're different when you're around her."

"Like how?" Heath asked, stopping the progress of his dishing out ice cream once again to gawk at his brother with irritation and concern.

"Well..." he pondered it. "For one thing, you were jealous of Michael Veritek."

"Jealous? Jealous?" he retorted, trying to sound incredulous but coming off shrill. Luke crossed his arms and pinned him with a come-clean stare. He knew it was useless to try to deceive his sharp-eyed brother. "Why would I be jealous of Mr. Sexiest Man of the Year? A guy who makes millions of dollars to do one film, when I could offer her all of this?" He gestured wildly, flinging drops of ice cream everywhere. Luke wiped at a spot on his shirt. "Oh, sorry."

"Heath, you have a hell of a lot to offer her. That's not why I'm worried. She seems like a nice girl who—"

"You've known her for like, two hours."

"You're not the only McGowan with a talent for reading people. Now shut up and listen to me."

Heath closed his mouth. Luke seldom got mad, but when he did, even the bravest ran for cover.

"That girl has been hurt in the past. She's lost her parents, has an uncle who treats her like shit, and I don't want to see her get hurt again."

Heath was incensed. "You think I'll hurt her?"

Luke took a minute to reign in his emotions. "I think—" he said carefully, "—you have been hurt previously too and...hell Heath, you picked a fight with her tonight and she almost left." Heath had no pithy retort for that. "Then, you run after her and come back fifteen minutes later carrying her limp body. What the hell happened on that porch, man?"

"What the hell happened? She told me she lied to me in regards to her relationship with Veritek, that's what the hell happened." Luke waited for more. "She told me things that are private, that I can't share with you. Let me just say that Veritek is an even bigger asshole than I pegged him for." He exhaled, leaning against the counter on his knuckles, creating a new line of ice cream dripping along the cabinet door. "And then, she told me about a man who was even worse to her. That should be fucking arrested for what he did. Could be, if we had any proof."

Luke sighed. "Okay. So she's been hurt, as I suspected. And what you went through with Juliette was no walk in the park, either. I'm saying, be easy on her, and be sure this is what you want before things go too far."

"Are you finished?"

"Yeah. I guess so." They looked at each other evenly for a minute.

"Good, then here." Heath shoved two bowls into Luke's hands and picked up the other two. "The ice cream's melting."

As he passed, Luke rolled his eyes as Jack had done. "Why doesn't anyone ever take my obviously stellar advice?"

CHAPTER EIGHTEEN

Heath was halfway through the swinging doors when he drew up short. Jasmine and Jack had their heads together over the coffee table. He heard Jasmine say, "So I've got one, two...ten cards."

"You won!" Jack cried excitedly.

"I did?" she responded gleefully. "I couldn't have done it without your help."

"No sweat," Jack replied, sounding like Heath.

The picture of the two together stopped him dead in his tracks. It hit him full force. This is what he wanted for his son, someone to love and nurture Jack as a mother would. Pain seared him and at the same time an ache to hold them both. Not noticing he halted so suddenly, Luke ran into him. Jack and Jasmine spun at the noise.

"Yippee! Ice cream." Jack went to accept a bowl from Heath. He took it to Jasmine.

"Thanks, Jack."

He retraced his steps and accepted the bowl Luke offered as Heath went to sit with Jasmine.

He spoke softly, lowering himself to the floor. "I've never seen him lose and not throw himself on the floor with the melodrama of a bad Shakespearian actor. How'd you do it?"

She shrugged with a pretty smile. "I don't know." She stuck her spoon in her mouth.

"I think he has a small crush on you," he whispered to her, taking a bite of his ice cream, too.

"I know I have a huge one on him. He's so open and giving. You've done an amazing job with him."

"It's been a team effort." He watched Jack and Luke at the small dining room table, the light hanging from the ceiling bathing them in a comforting glow. The pair was chattering away about the game and Luke said something then ruffled Jack's hair. Jack grinned like the Cheshire cat and then must have said something funny, as Luke threw back his head and laughed.

She followed his gaze. "I hope you realize how lucky you are."

Heath turned, catching the longing in her eyes, before they shifted to meet his. "I do," he murmured. He brushed her face with his thumb.

"I should let you go so you can be with your family."

He put an arm on her leg to keep her from standing. "Don't go. Let me get Jack to bed and we can talk some more."

She hesitated. "Okay. Give me your bowl, and I'll clean while you do that."

"All right. It'll only be a minute." They stood. "Come on, Jackrabbit. Bedtime." He squatted and Jack barreled across the room and high jumped onto him, a nighttime routine. "Can you say good night to Jasmine?"

"Good night, Jazz." Jack laid his cheek on Heath's shoulder, his first sign of weariness.

"Good night, Jack." She gave one of his little PJ'ed-feet a squeeze. "Thanks for teaching me how to play that game."

"Anytime."

JAZZ CHUCKLED QUIETLY as they climbed the stairs, enamored by Jack's speaking like a forty-year-old while wearing Spider-Man on his chest. She wheeled around with her dishes and moved into the kitchen with Luke following behind with the other two bowls. She could hear the dishwasher running and noticed a dish strainer already with a pot in it, so she decided while she was waiting she would do the few dishes in the sink. She rinsed the dishes off and reached for Luke's.

"So, Luke, I saw the piano in the living room. Do you do most of your work from here?"

"Yes. That way I'm available to look after Jack when he gets back from school."

She gave him a smile, her hands buried in suds. "It's really great that you are willing to help your brother in that manner."

Luke stared at her for a second with his mouth open. "It works well for all of us. And I'm grateful for the opportunity to see Jack grow up."

"Man..." Jasmine sighed. "...you guys are so lucky. And this house is incredible. I've been in a lot of multi-million dollar homes and let me tell you, you can't buy the wonderful warm, comfortable charm this house has. Those houses are all showpieces, not homes." He watched her face as she chatted. "That's one thing I really miss, a home, a family. Of course, I have my uncle, and I'm grateful for that. But we don't have the close relationship all of you share, that easy, gentle teasing, the flow of working together in harmony. I noticed that sort of cohesion when we were getting the pizza ready to eat. Everyone seems to know what their job is. It's virtually a ballet."

"I've never really thought of it like that. I guess you sort of take those things for granted when you have them." He located a towel and thoughtfully began to dry the dishes she washed.

She nodded. "It's been so long, I'd almost forgotten." She gazed absentmindedly into the bowl of a spoon she been wiping over and over. She gave a little shake of her head, and then continued wistfully. "I guess I've been letting people make decisions for me for so many years, I forgot I could make choices of my own. It's easier, you know. Comforting, letting someone else be in charge." She exhaled. "But I guess it's time for me to act mature and take responsibility for my own life. To decide what I really want in life and go for it. And I want this, what you have here." Then, realizing how her words could be misread, she hurriedly backtracked. "I mean, I want *a* home, *a* family. Not your home, or your family. Not that that would be bad." She became flustered and her cheeks became hot. "I'll quit speaking now." She lowered her chin, embarrassed.

He laughed. "Boy, you throw it right out there, don't you? No small talk for you."

"I'm sorry. Being here tonight has made me stop to think."

"No. No. That's okay. I like someone who says what's on her mind."

They both turned as they heard the swinging door creak open. "Uncle Luke, your services are requested."

"Ah. I guess I need to go then." He gave Jasmine's hand a squeeze as he set his towel down. "We'll have to finish our discussion sometime."

She grinned at him. "I'd like that."

Heath held the door open for Luke as he passed. Jasmine admired him. He looked so good standing in the entrance, grasping the door frame wide and high, sleeves rolled, carelessly displaying the muscular arms she wished, for a minute, she could feel around her.

As those interesting gray eyes zeroed in on her, Jasmine flushed, but she allowed her lips to curve slowly into a smile. As he walked unhurriedly toward her, she grabbed Luke's abandoned towel and carefully dried off. Neither spoke aloud, but they were having a conversation all the same. He halted mere inches from her and gripped the edge of the counter on either side of her. The heat of their thighs meeting made her inhale sharply. Her gaze danced over him, pleasant shivers running through her.

"I want to kiss you," he said solemnly, despite the teasing undertone.

Her pulse pounded in her ears. "I want," she said, enunciating her words carefully, and watching how that affected him, "what you want."

He brought his lips to hers, stealing both her breath and her heart. It took her a few seconds to react but then her fingers, which had been clasping the sink next to his, dove into his hair. After a moment though, she switched to tracing his firm shoulders then drew herself closer to him. She gave as well as she received, emotions guiding her with each heartfelt touch of her lips to his.

THIS TIME IT WAS HEATH who was weak-kneed. Jasmine had looked so good when he opened the door, standing in his kitchen, soap suds climbing her arms. It reminded him of what their house was missing, that special, mysterious something a female brought to the mix. And now everything she did was making his blood surge. The sharp sensation of her nails on his scalp, the way her body both melted into his and remained firm, substantial, real, there...

The creak of the door gave them less than a second to separate.

In that short amount of time, Luke's expression went from surprised to laughing. Heath inwardly groaned as their mouths parted and would have cursed his brother if his mind could have retrieved the words and his lips, still warm from hers, could have formed them. If he could, he would have yelled at Luke to get the hell out, he had things he wanted to do to her, things he needed to do, desperately. Jasmine gave him a little shove, but he remained immovable. He was trying to return from orbit.

"Uhh, Luke," Jasmine said awkwardly, "how was story-time?"

"Not half as interesting as things seemed to have gotten downstairs." Heath grabbed the towel from where Jasmine had dropped it on the counter and threw it at him, but he caught it with ease. "Jasmine, Jack was wondering if you might read him a story, too."

Jasmine responded like she'd just won the lottery; her face glowed and she sprung forward, all but running from the room. "I'll be right back."

As the door swung shut behind her, Luke immediately questioned. "So, that appeared to be some kiss."

"Is that what it was?" Heath said, chuckling low, and still happily dazed. "I've *never* been kissed like that." He slid into a chair, grinning.

Luke studied him for a beat. "I'm calling Vanessa."

He left to hunt for his phone in the living room, leaving Heath to sort through the strong feelings the kiss had stirred up.

CHAPTER NINETEEN

Jasmine was gone for so long, Heath eventually went to search for her. As he approached his son's door, he heard her soothing voice softly singing a song he didn't recognize. He slowed his pace, straining his ears to listen, an invisible force pulling him toward Jack's room. As he came into the lamplight shining from Jack's door, he stilled, his heart suddenly too big for his chest. She sat with her back against the headboard, her legs under the covers, Jack curled asleep on her lap. She raked his sun-bleached hair as she sang. The book, *Where the Wild Things Are*, was open beside her, three or four more spread haphazardly across the bed. The song ended, and she kissed the top of his head.

It wasn't until she twisted to place a cheek on the tousled tresses in front of her that she saw Heath, giving her a start.

"I'm sorry," he said quietly, entering the room. "I didn't mean to scare you."

"That's okay," she whispered. "I'm sorry I didn't reappear...he was so comfortable."

"That's fine." He stood, hands in his pockets, near the bed, looking at the pair. "I can help you move him."

"Okay." Regret accompanied her response. She glanced at her dozing listener, seeming unable to resist one last gambol through his hair. Heath gently held Jack forward and she slid, somewhat clumsily, off the bed, bumping her shin and almost knocking over the night stand. Once she was successfully freed from behind him, he laid Jack onto the pillows.

"Are you okay?" he whispered hoarsely, a chuckle choking his words.

"Ouch." She laughed and grabbed her leg, rolling for a moment on the floor.

He helped her to her feet, where they both stood gazing on Jack's sleeping form. His miniature mouth hung open a little as he breathed, his cheeks were rosy from his too-warm jammies and his long, black lashes contrasted sharply with his ivory-colored skin. Jasmine let a small, envious sigh escape. Heath flipped the switch on the Winnie-the-Pooh lamp and they tiptoed out the door. They watched as the door closed and the pie-shaped glow of light grew smaller, and smaller, finally ending their view entirely as the door clicked shut.

They crept down the stairs occasionally hitting a squeaky step, Jasmine trailing after Heath, clasping his fingers. When they reached the first floor, they heard the low sound of Luke speaking on the phone as he stretched on the couch. Heath led the way to the porch. After the door swung to, he jerked her in like a yo-yo, his arms coming around to squeeze her trim body against his, his lips claiming hers again, this time in a tender kiss filled with a different sort of yearning. When he parted from her, her eyes opened slowly in the porch light and remain sexily unfocused, his kiss still swamping her senses. He smiled, reveling in his power to stir her.

She kissed him again. "Mmm. I should go." She frowned. "It's a school night and you have to work tomorrow. And I have a funeral to attend." The thought made her instantly sober.

He restrained her. "I don't want you to go."

"Heath," she said with a warning tone.

"You can stay in my room. I'll take the couch. I don't think you should drive after fainting like that."

There were other solutions. He could drive her home and they could make arrangements for the car later or she could take a cab.

She sighed. "I'd need to call my uncle."

FROM THE OPEN WINDOWS Heath could hear her talking to her uncle on the porch.

"No. You can send a cab if you want to, but I won't get in it. Uncle Brody, please, I haven't been able to get any sleep there. Please try to understand." Her voice drew to an edge. "Of course I'm not sleeping with him, and if I were it wouldn't be any of your business. ...Don't be crude. ...Listen Uncle Brody, I didn't call to get your permission. I called to let you know. So now you know."

He could see her in the window, fists on her hips, one still holding the phone. She exhaled, then she walked through the front door, across the porch and outside again. When he joined her, she was sitting at the bottom of the stoop, holding her knees.

He descended and plopped down next to her. "You thinking of calling him back?"

"No. I've said all I have to say to him." Her voice sounded sad and tired. She set the phone on the stairs.

"Hey," he murmured softly. She spun her head to look at him, her eyes listless. He brushed his hand along her cheek. "I'm sorry."

She leaned into him. He wrapped an arm around her and reclined on his elbows, supporting her against the steps. Her body let go of its tension, melting to his like candle wax on a Chianti bottle. He was lazily playing with her hair.

"Jazz, there's something I've been wondering. Did your uncle know what happened between you and Lionel Parker?" She stiffened a little, and he wished he hadn't asked.

"He knew. I...bled, a lot. But he was afraid to take me to the doctor's." Her voice was low. "The next day, I refused to return to the set or to be anywhere near Lionel Parker. My uncle was furious and tried to drag me to the car, and I threw up on him. He didn't make me go after that."

Heath didn't say anything. What could he say? In his mind, he believed Brody Barrett was as guilty of rape as Lionel Parker was. He also knew, for some reason, Jasmine loved her uncle and he didn't want to make that error again. They sat in the stillness of the evening, the locusts hanging on, knowing their time was at an end, continuing what sounded to him like a never-ending verbal argument. "No, you didn't. Yes, I did. No, you didn't. Yes, I did." He rubbed Jasmine's skin thoughtfully. Her breathing became more rhythmic and he was afraid she would fall asleep. He nudged her.

"Jazz, honey?"

She inhaled deeply and stirred. "Hmm?" she mumbled sleepily.

"How about I take you to bed?" She twisted to stare at him. "To my bed. To sleep, by yourself. You're exhausted."

She smiled at him lazily. "Thank you, Heath. For dinner and for inviting me to stay here."

"It's been our pleasure entirely. Come on," he said, shifting to stand, "let's get you to bed."

When they went in, Luke was nowhere to be seen. They climbed the stairs, Jazz behind Heath, holding onto a finger or two. They got to the middle of three white, paneled wood doors, and he paused. "Time for the disclaimer," he said solemnly. "Keep in mind I did not know you were coming over, so my room's probably—" he swept the door open, his face tightening in apprehension. To his utter shock and amazement, the room was tidy as a pin. The bed was made with the quilt that had been their parents', the soft light of a lamp glowed from a bedside table, and the floor was bare of dirty clothes. "—a mess." *I love you, Luke.*

She gazed at the gleaming oak floors, the highboy dresser and wooden trunk at the end of the bed. A breeze blew filmy white curtains into an area with three window seats angled slightly to project above the grounds below. She meandered to the bed and ran a hand across the quilt.

"It was my mom's," Heath explained. He usually hid it on the rare occasions he had company, thinking it added an unwanted feminine touch to his bedroom.

"It's lovely," she said in a dreamy voice. "I love your house, Heath. It's everything a home should be. You may have to kick me out of it in the morning." She blinked and then stammered, "Wh-what I mean is...I mean...I don't mean to suggest that—"

He took hold of her arms. "I know what you mean. And I'm glad you like it. Sometimes I look at this place and think it's such a dump."

"Oh, no. Don't say that. It's utterly charming."

Charming? It's that damned quilt!

His thoughts were interrupted by her bending her neck to peer up at him. "You're utterly charming."

For a minute, staring down into those deep green, fathomless depths, he thought of seducing her. He thought of caressing those beautiful legs of hers and feasting on her fresh, dewy skin. He thought of hearing her moan and call his name on a sigh, of seeing her wrapped in nothing but that quilt afterward. Even now he could smell her, that highly-charged, siren's fragrance that was, at the same time, simple and pure, much like the woman. She was capable of making his heart dance with lust and simultaneously squeeze with sympathy for her hurts and sorrows. They stood frozen.

"I guess you better go," she said finally, stepping away.

"Yeah," he murmured, the word was slightly strangled. But he didn't move.

"Would you have a T-shirt?"

"Huh?" he muttered, still done in by her closeness.

"A T-shirt I can borrow, to sleep in?"

"Oh. Yeah." He strode over to the highboy and began rifling through the drawers. "I have to find a decent one."

"Any old t-shirt will do. I'm not going anywhere in public."

"Okay, then. I will allow you the privilege of wearing my Mark McGuire homerun number 62 T-shirt. It has a small hole, but it's extremely soft."

"That was so cool when he broke Roger Maris' record." She accepted the T-shirt, and examined the picture of the front page of the newspaper imprinted on it.

"Were you there?"

"No. I've never been to a game. My uncle loathes baseball and Trish was kind of a homebody. We watched it on TV, though."

"Excuse me, did you say you've never been to a baseball game?" He was stunned.

"Yes. I'd love to go to one, but I've never had anyone to go with."

"Never?"

"Okay, you don't need to make me feel like an even bigger loser than I already am."

"No, it's just... How would you like to go to the game with Jack and me on Wednesday?"

"You're joking. I'm not sure if my uncle will... You know what, I'd love to go."

He grabbed her hips. "It's a date, then." He kissed her on the nose happily. "You go ahead and get ready for bed and I'll get my work clothes together so I don't bother you in the morning."

"No, I'll get up."

"No, you need your sleep. Go." He shooed her into the bathroom.

Heath gathered his clothes while Jasmine changed. As he bent to get his shoes from the bottom of the closet floor, the sound of water running got louder and he swung around. The door never latched well and she may have bumped it in the tight confines of his small bathroom as it now was swinging open. He saw her framed in the door with her back to him. As he rose, his gaze climbed slowly along Jasmine's bare legs to the hem of his worn T-shirt. The shirt barely covered her, hinting at what lay beneath and outlining her curvy figure deliciously as he continued to take her in. His mouth was dry and his mind became completely blank. He lost his grip and desperately juggled the shoes, but, unable to stop their descent, he froze as they landed one after the other with a loud thump on the hardwood.

Jasmine jumped and whirled in time to see him peek from the culprits on the floor to her with alarm. He looked at her sheepishly. A slow grin spread over her face perhaps recognizing the glint of desire in his eyes he was trying so hard to disguise. She pushed the door open wider and placing one foot carefully in front of the other, came toward him, her hips swinging tantalizingly and her legs exposed with each purposeful stride.

His jaw fell open and he nearly dropped the shoes again, but managed, after a series of awkward bobbles, to keep possession of them. She giggled and turned from him, abandoning her teasing walk, to move toward the bed. In one swift motion he tossed the clothes and shoes on the mattress and grabbed her, spinning her enough to bring his lips down, crushingly on hers. When he stepped away a few minutes later he saw, once again, she was dazed by both pleasure and yearning and he reassured himself he did, indeed, still have it. Her fluttering hand flying to her heart confirmed it for him. She reached for the bed gingerly and lowered herself to the edge, still seeming a bit dazed. She, who had been so in control of him a few mere minutes before, weakened by his kiss. He had never felt so powerful. With a smug smile he gathered his belongings again.

"Y-you're going?" she mumbled, her voice throaty.

"I'm sleeping on the couch, remember?" he answered with amusement.

"Oh, yeah. And that's downstairs." After a few seconds, she giggled then murmured a soft, "Good night, Heath."

"Good night, Jazz." He closed the door behind him with a subdued click.

Heath stood for a while, leaning on the broken door knob, gathering his wits with a shake of his head and thinking how great it was she was in his bed, even if he wasn't.

Once on the couch, Heath twisted onto his side, tucking the fleece Missouri Tigers blanket under his shoulder. His feet pushed against the arm of the couch, and he thought about her sleeping above him, of crawling in to the warm sheets to lie next to her, to feel the soft skin as his leg came in contact with hers, to be enveloped in her scent. He lay awake for a quite some time, wishing he could take his revolver and shoot out the street light that managed to shine in, over the top of the curtain rod, straight into his eye, and wishing more he were sleeping in the same bed as Jasmine.

CHAPTER TWENTY

Heath's eyes popped open as he recognized the sound of the loud thud, disproportionally created somehow by the small feet belonging to his son.

"Oh, shit." He climbed the stairs as quickly as he could to try to catch the boy as he barreled down the hall toward Heath's bedroom. Turning the corner of the landing, he saw Jack's small frame disappearing beyond his door. "Shit," he moaned again, wiping his face. The bed springs gave an exaggerated creak as the bed and its occupant were trounced upon. Resigned, he trudged in the same direction like a man being led to the dentist's chair for a root canal. Pushing the door open slightly, he heard a second thump as the opposite side of the broken doorknob he held fell and rolled toward the bed. He found Jack snuggled in under the covers next to Jazz, both grinning from ear to ear. As he clung to the doorjamb, Heath struggled to catch his breath. "I'm so sorry—" he began.

"Nonsense. He's the best alarm clock I've ever had," Jazz said, tickling Jack's rib cage as he squirmed, and no doubt planted a foot in hers. "Ouch. You little bugger." She laughed and tickled him harder, his laughter escalating to shrieks. "Oh. Shh-shh-shhh. Your Uncle Luke might still be asleep," she said regretfully.

Heath was pleasantly surprised by her reaction to Jack's entrance. "Not if the smells emanating from the kitchen are any indication. I think Luke is awake and cooking."

"Ooh," Jack said happily. "I hope he's making his crepes," He bounced out of the bed and ran past Heath without a glance.

"Be careful," Heath called belatedly as Jack slid across the landing and ricocheted off the wall. Heath spun to find Jasmine standing, wrapped in the quilt, as he had fantasized about seeing her. She retrieved the doorknob. As she stretched to grab it, the quilt split open and he got a shot of one of her fabulous, bare legs. She walked the doorknob to him, rocking it in her palm reflectively. He inspected it with a grimace. "Piece of shit."

"Oh, no, Heath, Don't say that. It's exquisite." She felt the smooth facets of the clear, crystal doorknob. "You don't see knobs like this anymore. It's a shame." She gave it to him, then her attention wandered to his bare chest as he stood, leaning against the door frame. He wore only Levis. "Good morning." She smiled.

He set the doorknob on top of the highboy. When he looked at her, he caught her eyeing his abs before hurriedly elevating her gaze to his.

"Good morning," he said, low and sexy, shifting to run his hand up the door's trim as she watched him. Her rumpled hair did nothing to detract from her beauty. "So much for sleeping in," he said, with a slight shrug.

She slipped her arms around his waist, letting the quilt drop to the floor. "Sleeping in is overrated."

"You're not kiddin'," he replied, chuckling nervously, turned on to the extreme as she drew him into the room, closed the door behind them and pressed him against it. His touch glided along the back of her smooth thighs, teasing them both. "You got anything on under there?"

She grinned but didn't answer.

He searched higher, under her T-shirt, and buried his face in her hair with a groan. "I want to get you in this bedroom alone."

She separated slightly, peering at him. "What about your rules, lieutenant? No dating people involved in one of your cases."

"To hell with rules." He smashed his mouth to hers, his tongue probing skillfully, demanding a response from hers, which he was not disappointed in. He lifted Jasmine from her feet and walked to the bed, heaving her onto it smoothly. She bounced, rising onto her elbows, breathlessly, her focus made keen by her passion.

He held her gaze steadily for a moment. "I have to go to work," he said with a smirk, and spun abruptly to leave. The pillow flew over his shoulder and hit the door as he went to reattach the door knob and let himself out.

"You're a tease, Heath McGowan."

He smiled and revolved slowly. She had knelt to get off her ill-fated shot, and now she remained, knees spread apart, a pretty pout formed on her lips.

Heath regarded Jasmine so intently she sat on her heels. He strode to her purposefully until he stood against the bed, inches from her. He grabbed her chin and stared fixedly into her eyes. "I'm no tease, Jazz," he said steadily. "I *firmly* intend to make good on every promise that kiss made." He tilted his head and moved painstakingly toward her. She closed her eyes and his lips lightly brushed hers, but before he took the kiss deeper, he released her and left swiftly, giving a low chuckle.

Heath laughed when he heard the cry of outrage and the sound of the second pillow hitting the door.

WHEN JASMINE CAME DOWN twenty minutes later, makeup fresh and hair damp, she seemed decidedly more sober. Heath guessed contemplating the day ahead of her as she showered might have changed her mood. She was appreciative of the apple-cinnamon crepes Luke made, and discussed what might happen in school that day with Jack, but a shadow of sadness haunted her eyes when she thought no one was watching, and it could be heard in the edges of her voice.

When she was finished, Jazz rose to rinse her dish in the sink. Luke took it from her, placed it in the dishwasher rack, shut the door, and started the wash cycle. "Thank you again, so much, for the crepes, Luke. They were fabulous."

He shrugged. "No biggie."

She squeezed his hand. "Yes, it was. And I appreciate it."

Luke must have noticed her more subdued demeanor as he exchanged a look with Heath when she swung away from him, his brow furrowed.

"Well..." She exhaled. "I guess I should get going."

"I'll walk you to your car. After I get Jack to school, I'll call and have an officer waiting to escort you when you get to The Lofts. Jack, get your stuff together and I'll take you to the bus stop in a few minutes."

As he whizzed up the stairs, Heath embraced her lightly. "Are you okay?"

"Yeah," she said, but she didn't raise her gaze. He held the door for her as they went on the porch, and out to the sidewalk. She sighed. "It's so hard."

They were silent as they walked to her car. He turned her so he could scrutinize her. She leaned against the car, absentmindedly flipping the key in her palm. "I'll try to make it on time, but sometimes the commander's meetings go long."

"No, that's okay. You don't have to."

"No, no, no. Not at all. I want to be there for you."

She studied him. "Thanks," she said quietly, and he knew she had more to say, but she couldn't find the words.

He gathered her in, kissing the top of her head, breathing in the scent of her sun-washed hair. "Come back and stay here again tonight," he pleaded.

"I can't. It wouldn't look right." She withdrew from him when Jack came pounding down the porch steps. She took Heath's arms before he could spin, peering meaningfully into his face. "I'd like to, though." They stood for a few seconds, not breaking eye contact as they heard Jack's squeaky tennis shoes approaching.

"Jazz, I wanna give you a hug goodbye, too."

She smiled, checking both directions exaggeratedly prior to crossing the street and bending to welcome his squeeze. "Thanks for letting me stay last night, Jack."

"No problem." He parted from her, holding onto her shoulders. "It was cool. I like it when you're here."

"All right, Jack," Heath interrupted. "Why don't you hop in the car, and make sure to buckle up. You did brush your teeth, didn't you?"

Jack hesitated long enough to put his answer in question. "Yes."

"Jack?" Heath said in his best Daddy-warning-voice.

"Okay, okay. Geez." He plopped his backpack and lunch box on the sidewalk and trotted inside.

Jasmine chuckled as she rose. Heath's hands took the place of his son's as he spun her. "You're sure you're okay to drive?"

She squinted at him. "I'll be fine."

He bent to kiss her softly. "I'll see you later."

"Thanks."

They strolled to the convertible and Heath opened the door for her. After she was in, he gave her room and watched her drive off. When she was out of sight, he peeked at his phone. "Come on, Jackeroo. We're going to be late," he called, as the boy exited the house. He hefted Jack's gear and chucked it into the Mustang's trunk then opened the rear door for his rambunctious kindergartener as he began to mentally organize his workday.

CHAPTER TWENTY-ONE

Jasmine did a fair job of keeping herself together, despite her refusal to take the pills her uncle tried to coerce her into swallowing. But when the boys from Stephano's came through the receiving line, she lost it. The fact that Sebastian chose to close down the restaurant for a few hours so they could all come offer their condolences touched her deeply. Since, like her, Tricia had been an only child whose parents died when she was young, there weren't many family members, an aunt she had lived with, and a couple of cousins. Even so, the place was packed with the curious, those who came to see the mega-star in mourning, and Jasmine was terrified she'd throw up her crepes.

She was so overwhelmed with strangers filing past her, she didn't notice Luke approach. When she turned from the heavyset woman who had forced all of the blood from her fingers and saw him standing there, dressed in a dark grey suit and tie, she nearly lost it again. She embraced him and held on to him without speaking, knowing, if she did, she'd become a babbling idiot. With a shuddering breath, she finally whispered in his ear, "You came."

"Yeah, Jazz, I'm here. I wasn't sure if Heath would be able to make it. Is he here?" He separated from her.

"Not yet."

"Is there anything you need? Anything I can do for you?"

"Well, how long can you stay?"

"As long as you need me to. I don't have any plans."

She didn't release him. "Do you think you could possibly drive me to the grave site? I'm not feeling exactly...well."

"Of course. I'll be in the back until you need me."

She kissed him on the cheek. "Thanks."

After the brief ceremony was finished, Jasmine searched the crowd for Luke. He stepped forward. Her tension eased some when he took her elbow. "Are you ready?"

She nodded and he tucked her arm through his to escort her to the car. Once outside, she donned a pair of large, dark sunglasses to cover her swollen eyes. He opened her door, and then slid confidently behind the wheel of the convertible. As they pulled onto the highway, Jasmine stared out her window. She was grateful for the roar of the wind as it whipped her hair, preventing conversation. She was glad Luke was there, but she couldn't talk to one more person. She was still, going deep inside herself to try to wrap her mind around the idea she was saying final goodbyes to the woman she shared all of her secrets with, all of her joys and sorrows.

Luke grabbed her hand and gave it a gentle squeeze. She twisted and faked a smile. He looked at her briefly then concentrated on the road. She laid her head on the headrest then rotated it to watch the scenery flying by.

"HEY, HAWK."

"How's it going, Danny?"

"Not bad, not bad. How's the Barrett case going?"

"It's comin' along. Uncle's alibi is sketchy. Have to follow up on Veritek's this morning."

"Ahh. Good luck." The slightly pudgy cop sat across from Heath. They had known each other since he joined the force.

In his opinion, Danny Ruphart was an okay guy. They played ball together on the Police and Firefighter's League and he could be pretty funny in a crowd. But one-on-one, he sometimes grated on Heath; so they were friendly, but not close. He had been assigned to partially fill in for Adam while he was at home with his wife, toddler, and new baby.

As Heath talked with Veritek's agent now, Danny listened in on the conversation, and strained his eyes to catch what Heath was jotting in his notes.

"Thank you for your time," Heath finished.

"So, what'd he have to say?"

"He gave me Veritek's address. He was supposed to be home Friday night when Patricia Norman was killed."

"Where was he staying?"

"He was renting a condo in Chesterfield."

"Friday night? I was out there myself. A horrible rollover accident occurred with a tanker truck. We had to shut Highway 40 while the road was hosed down. Tank was carrying petroleum. One spark and the place would have exploded like a Roman candle. Made me a little nervous, I don't mind telling you."

"What time was that?"

"Oh, we had it closed from...nine to ten-fifteen, or thereabouts. Fire Department took their sweet time, so traffic was backed up for miles."

Heath sat straighter. "You said no one was getting past the accident scene?"

"Yeah, man. It was a real mess. The shit was everywhere. We had all—what is it there between 270 and Chesterfield Parkway—five or six lanes? All of it blocked off for half the night. And no one could move until the Fire Chief and his buddies gave us the green light."

He checked his notebook. 'That's exactly the time Veritek told us he was going home. Said he got there at ten."

"Not goin' 40 he didn't."

"Thanks, Danny." He glanced at his watch. "Whoa. If we don't hurry we'll be late for our Squad Meeting." He swung his jacket on as he and Officer Ruphart raced to the conference room.

Less than an hour later, Heath was congratulating himself for dodging the meeting in time to attend the services at the funeral home, when the chief flagged him over. "Give me an update on the Barrett case."

"But chief, the services for Tricia Norman start shortly."

"I won't keep you but a moment." Gary Larson walked away, expecting Heath to follow him.

He sighed, knowing it would be a good half-hour before he left Larson's office. And, as predicted, twenty-five minutes had passed, and he was still giving details to his boss. First Larson pored through his notes, while Heath fought to sit with his legs still. Then he launched into his questions.

"So, Brody's alibi is weak. What would his motive be to kill Tricia Norman?"

"I'm not sure, exactly. My guess is Jasmine Barrett was beginning to become more independent, maybe because of her relationship with Tricia Norman, and Brody didn't like it. I still need to investigate financials."

"Hmm. And killing Dobski?"

"Brody told me himself he wanted to kill him for spying on Jasmine."

"Okay. And this Michael Veritek fellow?"

"Like I said, he lied to me concerning where he was Friday night. I'll be inquiring into that."

"And his motive?"

"He wanted Jasmine. She refused him."

"And he would want Dobski dead for the same reason as Brody did. Didn't like him peeping in on Ms. Barrett."

"Exactly."

"The bodyguard?"

"Alibi checks. He was with six other guys playing poker. According to several of them, robbing them blind."

"Any other suspects?"

"Lionel Parker."

"Alibi?"

"Haven't talked to him yet."

"Well, see to it that you do. And report to me. Any chance there could be some other connection between the two murders? Could Norman and Dobski been having an illicit affair that an ex found out about or something?"

"We're sticking with our other theory right now—that this has to do with Jasmine Barrett, since the killer wrote her name in blood on the wall."

"Good. I've been riding the crime scene folks, but we don't have much as far as physical evidence yet. I'll let you know when we do." Larson straightened the papers in front of him. "Oh, and Heath, word around the squad room has it you and Ms. Barrett have...become close." He looked at Heath meaningfully. "Be careful there. You don't want to lose your objectivity."

"Yes, sir," Heath answered, his throat tight.

Larson nodded and handed him his file. "You're dismissed."

CHAPTER TWENTY-TWO

When they arrived at the cemetery, Luke pulled next to Heath's car. Heath stood leaning against the door of the Mustang, his legs crossed in front of him, hands in his pockets. Recognizing them, he stood, breathing a sigh of relief when seeing Luke with Jasmine. He hurried to open her door.

"How are you doing?"

"I'm okay," she said, but Heath knew she was lying. "Luke's taken good care of me," she added as he came around the car.

"You're not makin' the moves on my lady-friend here, are ya, bro'?" Heath said with a smile, clutching her to his hip.

"No. No," Luke replied, waving as a sign of innocent denial.

Heath gave his hand a strong shake, holding on to it briefly. "Thanks, Luke," he said sincerely.

Luke took Jasmine's arm on her left and the trio walked forward. Heath noticed Brody Barrett whispering something in the ear of a large man who had detached himself from the limo with him. The dark-skinned man, who must have been at least six foot five, three hundred pounds, walked a few paces to their rear, observant and alert. *The bodyguard.* Brody seemed miffed to be replaced at Jasmine's side by them, but he, thankfully, had enough good taste to not make a scene.

The minister said only a few words, but the whole time he talked, tears ran down Jasmine's cheeks from underneath the sunglasses. Tricia's aunt put a rose on the casket, and then it was her opportunity to do the same. She set the long-stemmed flower on the mahogany lid leaning on it for a second as if steadying herself. After a moment, she straightened her back and returned to Heath. But as they lowered the casket into the hole, she wheeled and buried her face in his shoulder, sobbing quietly.

Brody Barrett was shooting him dark looks. He matched the glares with equal vehemence, thinking, *If you did this to her, I'll make you sorry.*

As they walked to Jasmine's car, Michael Veritek hailed him from a distance.

Heath eyed him. "Luke—" he began without shifting his gaze.

"Yeah. We'll wait for you. Come on, Jazz." He took an elbow and led her to the car.

Heath strolled over, taking his time as he registered the tension in Veritek's jaw and how he paced, grasping his hips underneath his Italian suit jacket. He stopped five feet away from the actor.

"Yeah?" he drawled, intentionally injecting a hint of insolence.

"You phoned me?" Veritek spat, implying a line had been crossed.

"Yeah. I phoned you."

"Well?"

"Well, what?"

A vein bulged near the actor's temple. "Why did you call me?" he shouted. As if suddenly realizing he had lost his cool, Veritek glanced in Jazz's direction.

"Oh..." Heath kicked at some dirt. "I was curious..." He rolled a pinecone with his shoe. "Curious about why—" he abandoned his relaxed attitude and scrutinized the man opposite him "—you lied to me," he ended precisely.

"Lied to you? Lied to you in regards to what?"

He shook his head in a condescending fashion, as if chastising him for not coming clean immediately. "For your information, there was a huge accident on Highway 40 Friday night. It was closed at the time you said you were going home. So that got me to wondering." He dragged things out, hoping to irritate Veritek more, but this time the actor bit his tongue. "Wondering why, Michael. Why would you have lied to me?" As he spoke, he kept remembering what Veritek had done to Jasmine on that rain-slick road years ago and his temperature came to a boiling point. He advanced until he was in Veritek's face.

Finally, the other man took the bait. "Listen. Just because you're getting it on with Jasmine doesn't give you the right to throw around accusations."

"What did you say?" Heath hissed through clenched teeth.

"Not that I don't understand how great it is between those fabulous legs of hers, because as you remember, I've been there, too—"

He didn't get a chance to finish his vile sentence as Heath pushed him and the next instant the two were grappling with each other on the ground. They rolled, jockeying for position. Heath was barely able to get a few good punches in before someone was pulling him from his opponent. Veritek struggled to his feet moments later. Like Heath, he was rumpled and dusted with dry dirt, and he, in addition, sported a bloody lip.

"What the hell are you doing? You're at a funeral, for God' sake!" Luke screamed at them.

The pair twisted as one to look at Jasmine. Heath was jabbed by regret. She stood in the shadow of a massive oak tree, shades in her hand, green eyes wide with shock. He glanced toward the grave. The people who'd been lingering now stood gawking in their direction. His focus returned to Michael Veritek and they both strain against Luke's arms, which were braced to hold them apart.

"If we weren't where we are, Veritek—"

"You'd do what, officer?" Michael replied snidely. "Take Jazz, right here, against this gravestone?"

In a flash, Luke had released Heath and pinned Veritek against a tree, his forearm pressing into his chest. "Listen, asshole, I don't know what your beef is with my brother, but you're not allowed to talk about Jazz like that, got it?"

Veritek didn't seem to like what he saw in the second McGowan's features, a fierceness he wasn't ready to tangle with. He wisely kept his mouth shut.

Luke pushed away from him. "Let's go, Heath," he said in disgust.

"You better come up with one hell of a story to cover your ass, Veritek. 'Cause if the crime scene techs find even a strand of your over-gelled hair from the scene of the murder, I'll be bringing you in personally." He spun to leave, but Veritek yelled after him.

"You do that, detective. And be sure to bring your brother."

Heath swung, but Luke grabbed him by his suit coat. "Forget him. He's not worth your energy."

Heath turned his back to Veritek but grumbled, "I wish you would have given me a few more minutes with that asshole. I would have liked to take another shot or two at those perfect friggin' teeth of his."

Luke gave him a sidelong smile, and they both laughed.

"You're hurt," Jasmine cried when they got close, touching his swollen lip.

"It's nothing." He shrugged her off.

"What was that all about?"

"Nothing for you to be concerned with." He rubbed along her arms as she leaned against her car. "What are you going to do now?" he added in an effort to redirect the course of the conversation.

She gazed at him for a spell, as if deciding whether to pursue her questioning further, but eventually chose to let it go. She seemed too tired. She sighed, pulling her hair away from her face. "I think I'll go to the condo and sleep. Even though I slept better last night than I have in days, I suddenly feel like I haven't slept at all."

"That's understandable," Luke said sympathetically. "Do you want me to drive you home?"

"No," she said, squeezing him. "Thanks Luke, but it's not far from here and I'm calmer than before. So calm I think I could sleep for the rest of the afternoon. Can I give you a ride to the funeral home?"

"Nah. Heath'll give me a ride." He scowled at him. "We need to talk anyway."

Heath hung his head, knowing exactly what Luke wanted to discuss. He shouldn't have lost his temper with Veritek here, at the funeral, and he knew it.

Jazz shifted to get into her car. Michael's Maserati burned rubber out of the cemetery's lot, the engine whining in protest.

Heath bent resting one hand on the windshield, one on the top of the window frame. "You have somebody to walk you in?"

"Yeah. Bociefus there will protect me." She indicated the large man who had been shadowing her all day. "That's Bociefus Jones. But we call him Bo."

Heath sized him up. "I bet people call him pretty much whatever the hell he wants them to call him," he joked, and was happy to see a small smile from her. He gave her a soft kiss. "Call me when you're awake."

"Okay." She gave him another wan smile, and then spoke to Luke. "Thank you again for being here for me."

"Sure thing, babe," he said with a wink. They stood back as she exited the parking lot. Luke seemed to be chewing something over in his mind.

"You think Veritek had something to do with the murder?" he asked, not turning.

"It's a possibility," Heath commented, watching as the light changed to green and the convertible accelerated, imbedded in its line of cars.

"Then I hope to God you nail him," Luke pronounced. He walked to Heath's car without another word.

CHAPTER TWENTY-THREE

Heath drove the Mustang down the lengthy, curved drive in front of Lionel Parker's swank home in Ladue. The neighborhood was for the rich and elite of St. Louis, doctors, lawyers, and professional sports figures, among others. Heath admired the design of the home, partly brick, with stone accents around the door and at the corners. It was meticulously landscaped, with a wide lawn that ended in a grove of trees keeping the house hidden from the road.

Danny Ruphart sat in the seat beside him. Heath had decided it might be a good idea to have a buffer with him when he went to see Parker. Ruphart whistled. "Nice place."

"Yeah, I guess it's all right." Heath shrugged and got out.

While Danny stood appreciating the view of the grounds, Heath marched purposefully to the door and lifted the heavy iron knocker.

Parker answered the arched door himself, appearing relaxed in trim gray slacks and a soft-looking, darker grey sweater. He held a cocktail glass, gripping it from the top with one long finger extended over the rim, a golden-brown liquid glittering within its depths.

"Detective McGowan, come in. Come in," he said, with a gaiety his cooly-appraising eyes belied.

"This is Officer Daniel Ruphart."

The director quickly offered his hand. "Officer Ruphart, a pleasure."

To Parker's rear, a winding staircase with a wrought-iron railing led upstairs. He guided the two policemen to the left, into a sitting room with deep maroon carpeting and larger-than-life framed movie posters dominating the wall that ran below the base of the staircase. The director gestured to a pair of wrought-iron backed chairs with maroon cushions by the windows, while he became ensconced behind a short wet bar. He dug with tongs into an ice bucket and retrieved another cube to plunk into his glass. "Drinks, gentlemen?"

"No, thank you," Danny responded, while unabashedly marveling at his surroundings.

Heath took a seat. "If I could get a glass of water, please."

"Of course," replied Parker, but he sat studying Heath for a minute then reached for a glass. "What can I do for you today?"

Heath opened his notebook slowly, hoping to focus his thoughts. He found it surreal to be sitting in the same room sharing drinks with a man who had seduced and raped Jasmine before she was even a teen.

I may not be able to arrest him for that, but if he had anything to do with the death of Tricia Norman, I will damn well be sure he pays for that, at the very least. But to get the information he needed, he'd have to play things a lot cooler than he had been lately.

He cleared his throat. "As you know, I am investigating the death of Patricia Norman, which seems to be tied in some way to Jasmine Barrett. Because of that connection, it is important I get to know as much as I can about the people in Ms. Barrett's life, and that is why I am here talking to you today."

Parker nodded but said nothing, his expression bland.

"To begin with—" he took a deep breath to steady his already seething emotions "—I understand you met Ms. Barrett while working on a film together."

"That's right." The grey-haired man padded gracefully around the bar and gave him the water, but remained standing.

"But, isn't it true she did not finish the film with you?"

"Yes, that's true. Else Burks ended up playing the role—" he smiled at Ruphart engagingly, "—although she was never as talented as Jasmine was."

"I see. And do you recall why Ms. Barrett was unable to complete the picture?" He knew damned well why, but he wanted to see how Lionel Parker would spin it.

"Yes. Unfortunately she was sick at the time. Or so her uncle told me."

"Oh? She went through nothing serious, I hope."

"I don't think so. I don't recall the whole story." He waved dismissively.

"Uh-hum," Heath mumbled, taking notes. "And, you are working with Ms. Barrett currently?"

"That's right. I'm helping with Jazz's new video."

"But you've never done any music videos before, have you? Your history is mostly in film."

"Yes, that's true," he responded with a thin sneer. "You've done your research, detective." He raised his glass to him in mock salute. "But there's always a first for everything," he continued, addressing Ruphart this time. "Music videos are a lot like movies, actually. They often tell a story. Only it's a lot shorter format."

"So, you would describe your relationship with Jasmine Barrett as close, say like a father-figure." Heath found it hard not to keep the edge out of his voice, although keenly desiring to emphasize the age difference between the two.

Lionel Parker's gaze narrowed a fraction, and his voice took on a distant quality. "Jasmine and I *are* close."

"Hmm. Despite the fact you just did this one film together? And even that, she quit on you." Danny's attention shifted curiously from Heath, to Parker, perhaps beginning to understand something was going on here.

"*Some* relationships detective are not the sum total of the hours you've spent together, but *how* you've spent those hours."

Heat infused Heath's cheeks.

Lionel Parker appeared amused. Danny followed the conversation, swiveling from one man to another like he was watching a very interesting and competitive table tennis match.

Heath wanted to vomit. Parker was practically admitting to his intimate relationship with a preadolescent girl. *The idea of this leech touching Jasmine...!* He fantasized briefly about ramming his head into Parker's midsection and riding him over the top of the wet bar, even gloried in the imagined sound of breaking glass as they crashed to the floor, his hands around the pompous man's neck.

Heath pronounced his words distinctly. "I couldn't agree more," he retorted pleasantly. "It's more important how you spend your time together, not how much time you spend together." He emphasized in turn, *his* new-found relationship with Jasmine. Now it was his opportunity to see Parker's face redden. If it was a table tennis match, he was certain he'd scored a point.

"Detective," Parker snapped, "is there anything more? I suddenly have an awful migraine."

"Oh, well, I won't keep you then." Heath rose. "Oh...there's one more thing I need to ask. Where were you on Friday night during the time Patricia Norman was murdered?" Before Parker could begin sputtering indignantly, he added, "It is a standard question I need to ask everyone, for the records." He shot him a hard look which contradicted the ease of his spoken words.

Lionel Parker lifted his glass to his lips, sipping without taking his gaze from Heath's. After draining it, he set the empty tumbler on a glass coffee table with a resounding ring. "I was here. In my home, alone. Anything else?" he said flatly.

Heath made a tsking noise that sent a vein visibly pulsing along Lionel Parker's thin neck. "And Saturday when Dobski was killed?"

"Saturday, as you well know, detective, I was with *Jasmine*." He lengthened the sound of her name, probably as another dig. "And afterward, I wasn't feeling well, so I came home. By myself."

Parker seemed totally unconcerned that he lacked an alibi. In fact, he seemed to be flaunting it.

"No one saw you? No one at all?"

"Not...a soul." Parker gave a self-satisfied smirk that made Heath's jaw tighten as he took a step forward.

"Is there anything else, lieutenant?" Danny asked, jumping to his feet. Both men turned to gawk at him as if surprised he was in the room.

"Huh?"

"Anymore questions for Mr. Parker?"

Heath twisted to glare at Lionel Parker one last time, coldly. "No. I think I'm finished here."

As they left, Ruphart added, "If you think of anyone who could vouch for your whereabouts on both nights, please call us. It would certainly help clear you if we had some sort of witness." He gave the director his card.

"Next time someone is going to be murdered, I'll make sure I have more of an airtight alibi. But, since I didn't murder anyone, and it's hard to tell when someone else might do it, I may come up short."

His dry tone seemed to irritate even Danny. "We'll show ourselves out," he said curtly.

When the door closed behind them, he exclaimed, "What the hell was going on in there? It was like the two of you were speaking your own language and I couldn't understand a damn thing that was being said." When Heath didn't answer, just kept stalking toward the car, he added, "It almost seemed like male posturing. Like two men arguing over a woman. Any validity in that, lieutenant?"

"Put a sock in it and get in the car, Ruphart. I don't want to discuss it."

"Ooh. Touchy. Touchy."

CHAPTER TWENTY-FOUR

Heath was playing submarine war when the phone rang. Jack continued to splash and Heath made loud, "periscope up" pinging noises and dove his submarine at impossible angles while keeping half an ear open for Luke. But after a few minutes, he determined it was Vanessa who had called and Luke was talking to her in his bedroom. He sat on his heels, absentmindedly letting the suds drop from his elbows onto the bath mat.

Jack made noisy swooshing sounds as his submarine seemed to be spiraling out of control, somehow, in midair, before crashing into the depths of the tub with a foot-long green dinosaur, two gnarled on sailboats, and various-sized pieces of Tupperware.

"Dad, did your submarine spring a leak?"

"Springing a leak" was a common downfall among the McGowan bath-time boating vessels.

But Heath was lost in thoughts of Jasmine. "Huh? No, no. Ya know, sport? I think it's time to dry off," he said, rising from his knees to grab a towel. "The water's getting cold and you've turned into a king-sized prune." He grabbed his son under the armpits and lifted him while at the same time wrapping him in a towel. As soon as Jack's feet hit the ground, he was gone, leaving copious puddles of water trailing him all across the ancient hardwood floors. Heath sighed and released the rest of the bath water, watching it swirl down the drain, mountains of suds left behind to cling to the sides of the tub, as his mind wandered.

Why hadn't she called him? He had acted like kind of an ass at the cemetery, he reflected. While fisticuffs at funeral homes were not unheard of, emotions generally running high and all, it was never in good form. Should he call and apologize, or wait until morning?

He began mopping the floor, surmising more water had escaped onto the tile than had eventually gone into the drain. Seeing his half-naked son running along the hall draped in a towel made him flashback to Jasmine that morning, sporting his T-shirt and his mother's quilt. He smiled, thinking of how he'd teased her, while not letting on he was teasing himself as well. He had wanted nothing more than to follow up on his kiss. But of course, that had been out of the question with Jack in the house, and school and work waiting for them. Maybe he could get her to return tonight and seduce her back into and out of that T-shirt.

He scooped toys from the bathtub, holding them at angles and shaking them to drain the water before plunking them one-by-one into the suction cupped pocket made of netting hanging on the wall. He spun and impulsively took a hand towel from where it was draped over the lip of the sink and wiped the rest of the fading steam from the mirror. He studied his face in the aged glass. What was happening to him? He'd never felt like this about a woman before.

With Juliette, it was an exhausting show of trying to meet all of her demands. He realized in retrospect that he had always been acting with her. He never experienced the ease or comfort of being himself like he did with Jasmine. Add to that, Jazz was fantastic with Jack. His brother, who also happened to be his best friend, adored her. And she made his heart beat with something other than lust, although the lust was certainly there, he conceded. After Juliette, he thought he would never get involved with another woman again, on more than a surface level, at least. But now he believed he was like one of those McGowan vessels, springing a leak and going under fast.

"Dad?"

Heath grinned into the mirror, hung the towel on its bar, and followed his son's voice to his bedroom. The beloved superhero p.j.s were on again and Jack had already gathered a small stack of books next to him on the mattress.

"Is Jazz reading to me tonight?"

Heath picked up a comb. "Not tonight."

"I like her. She's cool. You kissed her this morning."

His hand stopped its motion, the comb midway down Jack's head, then resumed. "Yes, I did."

"You like her, too," Jack said slyly.

"Yes, I do."

"She's coming to the game with us?"

"Uh-huh."

"Good." Jack said decisively, and then he opened *Go, Dog, Go.* Heath beamed and shifted into a comfortable reading position.

HEATH'S MIND WAS TROUBLED as he straightened his tie in the bathroom mirror. He had opted for a tie, knowing he had to teach a defensive maneuvers class this afternoon, and wanting to appear more professional, and perhaps a bit older, than those taking the class. But his mind was again on Jasmine. The night before he'd read a Tom Clancy novel until well past midnight, willing the phone to ring. Finally he'd thrown in the towel and gone to bed. He woke at 3:17 a.m., staring at the throbbing red alarm clock's numbers, and then, bleary-eyed, at the phone on the bedside table wishing he could hear her voice.

He knew she was safe. The uniform at the door had assured him "Ms. Barrett" had returned home at 8:30 the night before and all had been quiet throughout the rest of the evening and the night. Heath had decided an apology was in order, but figured he should wait at least until ten before calling in case she was getting some much needed rest.

His mind kept traveling back. Back to the dizzying kiss she had given him when he'd pinned her against the kitchen sink. Back to her tortured face in the porch light when she had discussed her past. Back to her terror after discovering Dobski's body. Back to the sight of her head, joined with Jack's over a set of flashcards. Back to the rooftop, when he'd cupped her soft flesh as she trembled against him and let her moans shake his resolve to be a professional.

He knew he was long past professionalism when it came to his feelings for her, but he was determined to use it on her case, at the very least. He would have to confront Michael Veritek today, but he would do it coolly, calmly, and rationally. The sooner Patricia Norman's killer was behind bars, the sooner he could express his emotions and see where all of this was taking the two of them. He couldn't forget, either, the killer could also be after Jasmine, and he needed to protect her.

HEATH CHECKED AT HIS desk to see if he'd received any messages, hoping maybe Jazz tried to contact him there. Seeing no messages, he was about to leave, when his phone rang.

"Lieutenant Heath McGowan."

"Yes, lieutenant," came a sultry voice. "I need to report a crime."

His lips rose in the corners as he plopped into his chair. "Yes, ma'am," he returned, his good humor coloring his words, "what can I help you with?"

He could hear her grin through the phone. "Oh, I'm sure you could help me with any *number* of things, lieutenant—"

Her voice was low and sexy, and he found himself glancing around the squad room to see if anyone was listening, but everyone was busy with their own work.

"—but the crime I needed to report was...waking up alone this morning."

Heath swallowed his tongue, her voice sending pleasant tingles everywhere. He cleared his throat to try to regain his ability to speak. "I see. That *is* a crime. Maybe I should rush right down to make a report."

"Umm, that sounds wonderful, Heath," she purred dreamily, but then laughed.

He laughed, too. "How come you didn't call me last night?"

"I'm sorry. After I left the cemetery my uncle dragged me out to the studio. He couldn't understand why I wasn't 'into my work' so he made me stay until 8:30 before he finally ended our session in a fit of temper. I was starved. No lunch, no dinner."

"Poor baby." He sympathized, unable to take the smile from his face as he listened to her talk.

"No kidding. So, I came home, put a meal in the microwave and plopped on the couch while waiting for it to cook. I was going to call you after I ate, but I never made it off the couch. My chicken parmesan was still in the microwave this morning. It reeked."

"Well, I'm glad you're not mad at me. I acted like sort of a jerk yesterday."

"Oh, Heath, whatever you did, I'm sure Michael deserved it."

"Actually, I may have egged him on a little."

"Hmm. Why did you do that?"

"Because I don't like him."

"Why? It's not because of what I told you, is it? Because that was years ago."

"Maybe for you, but I heard it last night and then I saw him and the thought of anyone treating you like that makes me sick. And it wasn't just that, either."

"Well then, what was it?"

"He made a comment," Heath grumbled.

"About what?"

"About you and him," he burst forth with, causing several people's gazes to shift in his direction.

"You were jealous," she said teasingly.

He rotated, shielding them from prying eyes and lowered his voice. "Damn right I was."

"Well, there's nothing to be jealous of. Whatever was between Michael and me is *completely* over. I don't feel a thing for him, other than friendship. You're the one I was thinking of this morning when I awoke..." She slipped back into her seductive tone. "...officer, when I awoke alone, all by myself."

"You better stop, ma'am," he said, tempting her in return, "before I'm forced to come and cuff you."

"Ooooohh!" She laughed again. "Really, I'm sorry I didn't call you like I said I would. Would you let me make it up to you and take you and Jack and Luke out to dinner tonight?"

"That sounds great. But I know Luke won't be able to make it. He and Vanessa have a hot date tonight. Got a sitter for Timmy and Jenna and everything. In fact, I was sort of supposed to make myself scarce for a couple of hours anyway. Oh, wait. I forgot. I have batting practice tonight," he muttered, disappointed. But then he had an idea. "You want to come with us? Jack'll be there."

"Sure. It sounds like fun. What time?"

"Can you be at the house by four-thirty?"

"You got it, babe. And hey, will you have those cuffs?"

"Don't tempt me, Barrett. Don't tempt me."

She chuckled. "Goodbye, lieutenant."

He got off the phone feeling ten times better than he had all morning. *Now I'm ready to face Veritek.*

CHAPTER TWENTY-FIVE

M ichael Veritek was less than thrilled to see him.

"Ugh. Detective, it is way too early in the morning for me to have to deal with your crap."

"Listen," Heath said, drawing on reserves of patience he didn't even know he had. "I'm sorry I was being...less than pleasant...at the cemetery yesterday. That being said, I do still need to ask you your whereabouts on Friday night."

"Oh, come on, man. Get off it!" Veritek shouted, but Heath noticed his leg beginning to tap nervously as he sat across the table from him in the actor's trailer. "Maybe I took another route home that night. Yeah. I went on surface streets, that's what happened, and I forgot that."

Heath sighed. "Is that your story?"

"Yes. That's my story."

"Michael, you have no alibi for Friday night, and we both know you have a motive for the crime. You wanted to punish Jasmine for rejecting you again, so you killed her best friend."

Despite Veritek's years of acting, it was still easy for Heath to see the hurt the other man couldn't hide. "Is that what she told you? She told you we were over?" He managed to sneer, but not convincingly.

"She told me you came to her, and she rejected you. She told me *everything*. How you tried to force her to take drugs, and how you left her on a rainy road that night to nearly be raped again by two men." He choked back his anger. This wasn't how this interview was supposed to go.

Color drained from Veritek's face. "Raped again? What are you talking about? Did Jasmine tell you I *raped* her?"

Heath bit the inside of his cheek. *That's right. She said she'd never told anyone else.* He was stung by guilt for sharing information she'd entrusted to him and, at the same time, proud. She told him, but not Veritek. "No, sorry, I misspoke."

Veritek's mouth hung open a second. "She never told me she met anyone on that road, only that she...fell." His guilt was palpable. "I left her in the dark, and she fell from a cliff and needed to be hospitalized." He jumped up. Turning from Heath, he seemed to grapple with his feelings.

"Dammit." He whirled. "I'm a different man now. I swear. If I had been in my right mind, I would have never done that to her. I loved her. I still do." He ran his hands through his hair with an exasperated groan.

"Look. A jury hears that story, your poor excuse for an alibi, and, God help you if they find any physical evidence in that bedroom..."

Veritek glared at him darkly for a minute. "Of course if Jasmine and I made love in that bedroom earlier in the day, there would be some...evidence...of that."

Heath stared at him in shock.

"That's one thing Jasmine and I never had a problem with. We were always good in bed."

Heath flew to his feet, all but toppling the table, and Veritek involuntarily took a step in the opposite direction. A red wave of anger washed over him, but he held his ground and didn't act on it. Unsure of what would happen if he actually spoke again, he swallowed his retort and slowly spun to leave.

"What?" Veritek taunted. "Not so brave without your brother around to protect you?"

Heath froze. For the second time in as many days, he imagined himself beating the living daylights out of someone. He could practically taste the salty blood from a crack Veritek slipped in—although it would be well worth it—hear the sound of his body knocking into hairspray cans and gel bottles, light bulbs breaking as they crashed into his dressing table. He could almost feel the soreness of knuckles battered by crashing into his perfect teeth and face... He froze, and then—his legs like lead weights—left the trailer knowing Michael Veritek was probably staring daggers into his back.

HEATH WAS PLAYING CATCH with Jack when the convertible pulled up.

Jack screamed, "Jazz! Jazz!" and took off at a gallop. Before Heath shouted a warning, his son halted at the curb and waited for her. She made a show of checking the traffic then crossing the street and scooping Jack into her arms.

"Hey, bud," she said with genuine warmth. "How's it going? Playing ball with your dad?" She glanced at him.

Moments earlier, the idea of seeing her had made him unsure. All day long his thoughts turned to Jazz even though he'd told himself not to dwell on her. He reviewed the things Veritek said, and told himself not to dwell on them. He'd convinced himself Michael Veritek was a liar and he was trying to get his goat. Then he found himself wondering if, since he'd known Jasmine only a short while, maybe everything he thought he knew concerning her was all wrong. Hell, maybe *she* was the murderer.

But now, as she gazed at him with a sparkle in her eyes, he knew, in his heart-of-hearts, that could not be right.

The problem was, ever since Juliette, he didn't trust his heart. He'd convinced himself to keep it all free and easy. Fun, easy girls. No feelings, no strings. Maybe he needed to return to that. With Jasmine he was like a kid learning to drive a stick shift. His heart started, his heart stopped, and he found himself leapfrogging through his time with her. When she was there, he was perfectly at ease one minute and had his heart in his throat the next. He didn't want to care, because caring made him vulnerable, but when she was with him, he couldn't help it. And when she wasn't with him, he drove himself crazy thinking about her.

Thinking. That was what he was doing wrong. He needed to not think. He was a guy. Guys didn't think.

And then, there she was in front of him, and he couldn't help but grin. She was so cute in her jeans and white baseball jersey-type shirt that buttoned a third of the way down, with pink sleeves. She wore a pink Cardinals hat and her hair was in two ponytails. He didn't even know they made pink Cardinals hats.

"Hey." The smile was slow, smooth, and easy and seemed to belong exclusively to him.

"Hey, yourself." He tugged on the bill of her hat. Her makeup was fresh and light; she wore clear lip gloss and he wanted so much to taste her. Then he thought, Jack's seen us anyhow, and he drew her in to kiss her. Her brows rose in surprise and she laughed.

"Lasting effects from our phone conversation earlier?" she murmured, loud enough for just him to hear.

"Something like that," he growled. "You ready to go?"

"Sure. You ready to go, Jack?"

"You betcha." He grabbed her hand and dragged her toward the Mustang.

"Take it easy on her, buddy. She's not an action figure. That arm's attached."

Enroute to the batting cages, Jack and Jasmine chattered together like a pair of squirrels with Heath inserting a comment here and there. He was content enough to share a couple of meaningful looks with her. At one point, she leaned in to give him a peck on the cheek and he sighed with contentment.

When they got to the mini-amusement park where the batting cages were located, he retrieved the bats from the trunk while Jack filled her in on every fun-filled option available to them.

Danny Ruphart was also getting equipment out of the rear of his car a few spots down.

"Hey, Hawk."

"Hey, Danny. Ready to smash a few?"

"You bet. Isn't that Jasmine Barrett?"

"Yeah. She decided to join us for dinner tonight, so I thought I'd drag her with us."

"Great idea," Ruphart replied, his gaze skimming over her as she squatted to hear something Jack was saying.

Heath lugged his bat bag and the two of them caught up with Jazz and Jack. "Jasmine Barrett, I'd like you to meet Danny Ruphart. He's on the police department's baseball team with me."

"Nice to meet you, Danny."

He shifted his bag so he could clasp her hand. "The pleasure's all mine."

Heath thought Danny held her hand a beat too long, but he managed to shrug it off.

As they rounded the first set of cages, a chorus of greetings rose from a group of men who stood watching another batter in a cage, offering advice and insults in equal measure. Heath introduced his guests and got approving looks behind Jazz's back. He shook his head with a grin. *What a bunch of goofs.* Still, he was warmed by the ego strokes and enjoyed her nearness until it was his turn in the cage.

"Yeah, you go on in there, Hawk. We'll take care of Jazz here for you." Tony Fitzgerald looped his arm easily across her shoulders. She continued to smile, but he could feel his fading. He pushed the button to the pitching machine and stepped uneasily to the plate.

Gideon Manahan cleared his throat. "So, Jasmine...I saw your video for 'Rock My World.' And if you don't mind my saying, it was seriously *hot.*"

Her laugh sounded like bells tinkling. "Thank you."

FWAP. A ball whizzed past him and hit the backdrop with a *thrupp.*

"Hey, Hawk. You sleepin' in there?"

Heath chuckled with the others, but his gut began to clench.

"Come on, Dad," Jack encouraged.

Another pitch went by and he swung late.

"What's the matter there, Hawk? Having trouble concentrating?" one of his friends shouted.

He twirled and gave the jokester a glare, but then settled in and refocused.

"Why do they call him Hawk?" he heard Jasmine ask, seeming to speak more to herself than to anyone else.

"'Cause he's got a hawk's eye," Juan Alvaro explained.

"Ahh," she murmured.

With a crack, Heath's bat connected solidly with the ball, sending it rocketing into the nets that captured them.

"Wow."

"Nice hit, lieutenant," Alvaro called.

He grinned and tightened his grip. He finished the rest of his pitches going eight for ten.

"Your turn, Jazz," Danny offered. Brows rose in interest accompanied by statements of agreement.

Heath opened the door and crossed over the threshold, peering at her and asking quietly, "What do you think? Do you want to? You don't have to," he quickly reassured her.

"I'll give it a try," she responded gamely.

She took the batting helmet from his head, and placed it on her own. It was obviously a couple of sizes too big, but she still managed to look good enough to eat.

"Do you want some batting gloves?" He peeled back the loud Velcro straps. "I'm afraid they're sweaty."

She wrinkled her nose. "I'll pass." She took the bat and stepped into the cage.

"You get settled in there and tell me when. I'll push the button for you."

She toed the plate and wiggled her ass. The men jostled each other and rolled their eyes as if in pain. Jeans had never fit a body so well.

"Okay," she said tentatively. She watched the mechanical arm rise and the pitch came out. She swung loosely, falling off balance. The men chuckled softly.

"That's okay, darlin'. You'll get the next one," Danny Ruphart said condescendingly, then chortled.

Heath frowned at him.

In the cage, Jasmine pushed the helmet up, probably to see better, and then wasn't ready for the next pitch.

"Raise your bat, sugar," Danny suggested.

Heath noticed her shift, balancing her weight between her two feet as she did when kick boxing. She fouled the next pitch, but she was getting the timing down.

"Jazz," Heath said tentatively, "do you want me to give you a tip or two?"

She wheeled without hesitating, "Sure."

He quickly paused the machine and entered the cage. He moved behind her. "First, I'd scoot away from the plate a tad. Your form is good and you're swinging pretty level, but you need to hold your bat like this." He wrapped his arms around her small frame and adjusted her hands a little. "Lift your elbow some more." He gently nudged it higher. "There."

While he helped Jasmine, Danny Ruphart bent to talk to Jack. "So, Jackie-boy, what's it like to have your dad date a rock star?"

Jack beamed, happy he was finally getting some attention. "He kisses her," he whispered loudly.

"Jack," Heath scolded. He caught Jasmine's blush. "I'm sorry about that."

"That's okay, it's true, you do kiss me." She stared straight ahead, as if concentrating, but then added, "But not enough."

"Huh?" he asked, not sure if he heard her right.

"Nothing," she responded sweetly, a smile dancing on her lips.

"Uh-huh." He grinned and made a few unnecessary changes in her positioning. As he did so, their cheeks brushing, he growled in her ear, 'I can certainly make up for lost time, Barrett. Just say the word."

"Promises, promises," she replied, then twisted her head to steal a kiss. The crowd emitted an "Ooh."

"Enough comments from the peanut gallery," he admonished halfheartedly.

Jasmine modified her stance, seeming to intentionally shimmy her backside closer to him. "Jazz," he hummed in her ear, "you wiggle that cute tush of yours any nearer and I'll have to stay in this cage a while." She giggled, and moved away. He checked his handiwork and then sighed. "Just swing level."

He stepped out and pushed the button. She seemed to focus and crushed the first ball that emerged from the slot. "Whoaa."

"Lucky shot," Danny teased. But he had to swallow the rest of his comment as Jazz zinged another one into the netting. "Hey," he stated thoughtfully as she hit the third ball solidly, "she's not bad."

"Who are you kidding?" Heath laughed. "She's great."

Jazz clocked the next one and waited for more. When the arm remained motionless, she released a groan. "Oh, it's over." She started towards the door.

"You don't have to leave, sweetheart," Danny suggested. "We can put more money in for you."

"Yeah. Yeah." came several agreeable voices.

"No. It's somebody else's turn, then I'll try it again. What about Jack?"

Jack switched places with her and Jazz cheered him on wildly. Heath instructed him until he was able to get a few strong whacks in. When Jack was finished, she lifted him onto the railing, standing behind him to support him and keep him from falling as they chatted animatedly. After several batters, an enthusiastic cry arose for Jasmine to take another crack at it.

"Really?" she said eagerly. She took her spot, but then spun. "Jack?" She looked to where he was standing on the bottom rung of the fence, clinging to the top rail so he could watch her. "Can I borrow your batting gloves?"

"Sure thing." He hopped down and sped to the door.

She sidled up to the fencing. "It really burns," she said quietly to Heath, no doubt knowing there'd be no end to the ribbing if the guys heard that.

"Let me see." He examined her palms. They were painfully red. "Ouch," he said sympathetically.

She slid Jack's gloves on and was reentering the cage when Jesse Lee rushed forward with a batting helmet. "Here. This one's smaller, and it's purple."

"Ooh," Danny said snidely. "Pretty."

"I'll show you pretty," Jazz challenged, finding her position by the plate again. She hit eight of the last ten, two going foul and six hit well. She left the cage to hoots and back slaps.

"You can play on my team any day, sweetheart," Ruphart acknowledged. "Why don't you come in and let us buy you a beer?"

"Sorry, guys. I promised to buy dinner for my two favorite fellas here." She put her arms around Heath and Jack. "Maybe some other time."

"We'll hold you to that," Jesse Lee stated. Then they took turns shaking her hand, all sincerely telling her it had been nice to meet her.

"That was fun." Chin held high, a smile at the corner of her lips, she was clearly pleased with herself.

"You looked like you were having fun." Heath gave her a lopsided grin.

She addressed Jack. "So, where do you want to eat?"

"Mouse-A-Rama!" he shouted with gusto, sprinting toward the Mustang.

"Mouse-A-Rama?" she repeated, sounding confused.

"You've never been to a Mouse-A-Rama?" Heath chuckled. "Oh, are you in for a treat."

CHAPTER TWENTY-SIX

Forty-five minutes later, Heath sat with his arm around Jasmine in a booth. Children ran everywhere, like Indians on a warpath, and twice as loud. Parents either chased after them, or—like he and Jazz—slouched at a table, weary from chasing. In front of them sat a large silver disk with crumbs and a few pieces of pizza crust, and they each hefted a plastic mug of brew from a half-full pitcher on the table.

"Man, I'm not usually much of a beer drinker," she confessed, "but I was so thirsty. This tastes awesome."

"Ahh. We *have* turned you into one of us. Crushing balls and swilling beer. Next thing you know, you'll be packing heat." He pulled back his jacket a little to reveal his holster.

She walked her fingers along his chest. "I have to tell you, I find the fact that you carry a gun very sexy." She slipped her hand beneath the fabric and caressed him.

He peered at her and bent to nibble on her lip. "You have a naughty side, don't you? I like that about you." He took the kiss deeper and she closed her eyes. They were lost in the moment until Jack appeared at the table, pizza sauce still smeared on his cheek. He was tugging on Jazz's sleeve.

"Wanna play Whack-a-Mole with me?"

"Ooh. Sounds violent." She let him drag her forward, twisting to give Heath an apologetic smile. "Sorry, Whack-a-Rat calls."

"It's Whack-a-*Mole*, Jazz," Jack repeated patiently.

"Oh, Whack-a-Mole. Whack-a-Mole. Are you sure that's humane?" she asked as she followed Jack.

"They're not real," Jack assured her.

HOURS LATER THEY ARRIVED home to find a very relaxed and happy Luke who offered to put Jack to bed so they could have some time together. It was decided Heath would drive the convertible to The Lofts and take a return cab, as Jazz was slightly tipsy. When they neared her condo, she tilted her head to look up at her windows, her face tense. "Do you want to take a walk on the waterfront?"

"Sure." He steered the sports car toward the waiting Mississippi.

They got out and strolled hip to hip, carefully picking their way across the uneven, cobblestone levee. The moon rose above the Eades Bridge, providing a magical glow that made the old bridge seem somehow beautiful as the light dripped down into the water below like silver confetti streamers.

"Heath," Jazz said lazily, "I don't remember when I've had more fun."

"I'm beginning to think you are the only girl in the world that would think getting blisters on your hands—" He brought them to his lips to kiss them. "—not to mention, being serenaded by a man dressed in an over-sized mouse suit—was one romantic evening."

"Oh," she countered, "romance is what you make of it, and I had a wonderful time. And this is plenty romantic. Beautiful breeze, moonlight..." She stopped and her expression clouded.

"What is it?"

"Nothing...I..." She swiveled away from him, but he caught the glint of a tear drop that clung to her lashes as she turned.

He dragged her into his embrace, gently cupping her chin and raising it to scrutinize her. "Come on, Jazz. I can tell something is bothering you."

"It's just..." She pivoted to keep walking, sliding an arm behind his back. "I feel so damn guilty. Here I am enjoying myself and, Trish will never—" Her voice failed her. He remained silent, giving her room to gather herself. The sole sounds were their footsteps and the sounds of the highway whirring over them and the water lapping against moorings below the levee. She sat on the cold cobblestone. Finding a piece of grass growing among the sand between the stones of the levee, she plucked it, running her fingers along it as she spoke. "You would have liked her. She was funny. Sarcastic. I mean, she had a *real* deadpan sense of humor. My God, could she make me laugh." Her lips curved into a trembling smile as she reflected on it.

"She loved to play little jokes on my Uncle Brody. Stupid stuff. Like taking his reading glasses and stashing them somewhere, and then replacing them. Or stealing his briefcase, which is his constant companion, and leaving a ransom note. We used to get into so much trouble." Her voice broke, and she shook her head. "I'm sorry. I'm ruining everything. Maybe it's the beer making me so morose."

"No, Jazz. I want you to discuss this, discuss everything, the laughter *and* the tears." He drew her closer, squeezing her shoulder.

They sat for several minutes without speaking. "Do you know you're incredible?" she said suddenly. "You never try to pressure me into being something I'm not."

"I don't know if that's true. What about when I got onto you for letting your uncle be bossy with you?"

"Even then, you were only looking out for my welfare. You didn't have some hidden agenda."

"Well," he said in a hushed tone, kissing her. "I think you are pretty special too." His lips parted her softly yielding ones.

The whoosh of the blood leaving his brain that came on whenever his lips touched hers had become familiar. The kiss stirred something within him and he hungered for more of her, the need suddenly sharp and fierce. He was quickly losing control. He brought his hand to her throat, slipping it under the flap of her t-shirt, pressing it flat against her cool skin, feeling her heart racing against his palm. She trembled and his yearning became an undeniable need. But she abruptly separated from him, leaving him grasping for breath and clarity, seeing the glint of his jagged, hot-blooded desire reflected in her irises. She clenched the lapels of his jacket and shut her eyes. "Oh, God. I want to make love to you so badly. But I can't. Not there. I want to buy a new place, move away—"

"I know." He pulled her into him so she couldn't see his disappointment. "It's okay. We have plenty of time."

"It's just—" She seemed to struggle to make him understand. "—there's nothing good there anymore. And when we make love, I want it to be somewhere right. I know that sounds silly."

"No. I want that for us too." Heath hadn't recognized the truth of it until he said it. He did want that. He wanted it to be right for them, the first time and every time. That's what she had changed in him, he realized, she made him want things for himself again. He didn't want to pass through life anymore, getting along, being with women who meant nothing more to him than a pleasant distraction. He wanted to build a future and he wanted it to be with her. He knew she was too tender at the moment to plan that future with him, but he could wait. "I should get you home to bed. You've got a big day tomorrow. Your first Cards game and all." He helped her to her feet.

"You're right. I'm so excited."

"And then Thursday's your concert."

"I already have a half dozen tickets waiting for you at Will Call. I asked my uncle if I could tone it down some, so Jack could come if he wanted to, but Brody said plenty of kids his age would be there and we shouldn't have to change the act." She sighed, obviously angered by the decision. "I don't think a boy that age should be exposed to...I mean, I'm not that bad, but there are a few cuss words in the lyrics and it can definitely be suggestive."

"It's okay. I wouldn't want you to change anything. I was planning on bringing Luke and Kole, though."

"Really?" she said, clearly pleased. "Now I'm nervous."

He laughed. "Nervous? Why?"

"Well, I want to perform well for you and your brothers."

"You've got thousands of adoring fans, have sold millions of records. Why would you be nervous?"

"Because," she said, squirming, "it's you guys." She shrugged, appearing a little embarrassed.

He raised her hand to kiss it again as they strolled back to the car. "I've no doubt we will enjoy your show. Don't worry about us."

"Okay. I'm thrilled you're coming."

"Me, too."

When they got to The Lofts, he stole his goodnight kisses in the elevator, as he knew there would be someone posted at her door. He whistled as he waited on the street for his cab afterward. He had the baseball game tomorrow, Jazz's concert Thursday night, and he had plans to wrangle a sleepover for Jack out of Vanessa Wainright so he could cook dinner for Jazz Friday night. And, with any luck, Crime Scene would have the evidence he needed to put someone behind bars soon and they could begin to build that future together. He hadn't been so hopeful in a long time.

CHAPTER TWENTY-SEVEN

Jasmine's enthusiasm for the game was almost comical. In fact, Heath found it highly amusing. She was like a kid. She loved it when fireworks burst over the stadium when the Cardinals scored a home run. While she watched them, he noticed the way her pupils contracted and dilated, the sky-blasts of color reflected in her beautiful eyes. She wanted a hot dog, and a pretzel...and peanuts and beer. And while the ballpark experience was new to her, it was obvious she knew her baseball. She knew all the player's names and most of their stats, and, unlike a few of the girls he had brought to a game previously, she did not harbor the misconception the shortstop was, by definition, the shortest player on the team. He had found it extremely difficult in the past to explain the infield fly rule to someone who believed it was wrong for players to try to "steal" bases. And even though she knew the importance of putting in a relief pitcher when the starter was getting shelled, she still could enjoy the attendance quiz and acted embarrassed when the loudspeaker blared one of her songs.

He spun and caught her observing Jack, who was getting frustrated as he tried to follow Fred Bird in doing "The Macarena".

"Here, Jack." She swept him up to stand him on the empty seat in front of them. Reaching from behind, she helped him do the motions while a big grin split his face. Heath stepped to her rear and encircled them too, bringing his hands to her hips at the appropriate time to feel them wriggle to the beat. She sank against him happily and when she twisted for a kiss, he took her lips gladly and wished things could stay like that.

A young woman with a camera around her neck and a Cardinals shirt on approached them. "Can I take your picture? It'll be available for purchase after the fifth inning."

Heath glanced at Jazz. "Sure." She shrugged and leaned toward him.

The flash went off and the girl gave them a card. "You can see the pictures in Section 5, across from the first-aid station."

"Thanks."

With her hair in a ponytail stuck through the back of her Cardinals cap, she wasn't recognized or disturbed by anyone; she was just another baseball fan. She reveled in this newfound anonymity when they went to get some food, and she could simply walk arm-in-arm with Heath, as Jack ran before them, like any other girlfriend and boyfriend. Since she had never had "Dippin' Dots", he treated the three of them.

"This is delicious!" she exclaimed, turning to him. He lay crumbled in half in his seat, rubbing his temples. "What's wrong?"

"C-cold h-headache."

Jack rolled his eyes, "He *always* gets them."

"Is that true?" she asked, stifling a laugh.

Heath nodded miserably. "Feels like someone rammed a steel girder into my brain," he muttered with clenched teeth.

"Every time," Jack commented with a sad shake of his head.

"Well, I'm glad you told me," she whispered to Jack loudly. "I'd hate to have gotten seriously involved with someone who was so cold-headache impaired."

"Dad, stick your thumb on the roof of your mouth. I'm telling you, it works."

"I'm not doing that. I'll look like an idiot." He groaned and squeezed his temples in between his palms.

"Oh, 'cause that looks so much better," she quipped and then dodged when he tried to grab her. "Is Mr. Big-Bad-Police-Officer being done in by the little Dippin' Dots?" she cooed.

Heath gripped her knee tightly, laughing even as tears gathered and he whimpered. "As soon as I can...f-function enough to...r-reach for my gun...y-you're in trouble. Aghh!"

She giggled, trying to squirm free of his grasp. Later, when she wasn't expecting it, he dropped a piece of ice in her cleavage then pulled her close so she couldn't remove it.

"Pay back's hell, isn't it, Barrett?"

"You are sooo dead." She struggled against him uselessly until he swallowed her protests in kisses, making her forget the quickly melting piece of ice between their bodies.

When the game was complete, they took turns walking with Jack on their shoulders to the parking lot. When she got into the car, Jasmine took off her ball cap and shook her hair out. He sat frozen, with the key in the ignition, watching her. It was an unconsciously, insanely sexy thing to do, and as she fluffed it, the sunlight danced in her hair playfully. He entertained a fantasy of her hair splayed on his pillow as the sun caressed each strand, shining in his bedroom windows.

Jack fell asleep on the short jaunt to her place. When Heath parked on the street and killed the engine, the pair peeked into the rear seat.

"Oh," she gushed. "He's so cute." She swung to Heath. "Thank you so much for taking me to the game. I had a blast."

Heath ran his hand along her cheek. "I did, too." She became flushed and he maneuvered to gently cradle her chin. His gaze drank in her face as he leaned slowly forward to kiss her. He glanced in the rear seat again. "Jack?"

"Oh, no. Don't wake him," she whispered. "I'll call Bo and he'll walk me in." She cut off his protest by opening her phone. "I'll see you at the concert then. There will be backstage passes for you if you have time to come and say hello."

"We'll come for sure."

When Bo arrived, Heath and Jazz were outside the car, while Jack snoozed with the windows open, letting in some fresh air on the warm Indian summer day. He gave her arms one last rub and brushed his lips over hers quickly. "See you tomorrow then."

JASMINE DIDN'T EVEN have a chance to set her purse down and her uncle was hauling her through the door, shoving a hanging bag at her. "We have to check and make sure everything is arranged properly at The Dome."

She secretly believed the only reason her uncle wanted to go was so he could strut around and act important before the concert. If it had been her choice, she would have left it all in the control of the very competent people who worked for her, most of whom had been doing so for more than four years now. But she had long ago come to the realization not much was worth arguing about with her uncle. It was easier to let him have his way. In the elevator, he commenced to map out his plans like a general. "You'll ride with Bo. I'll take the convertible. Then if I need to stay later, you can leave with Bo." She was glad to hear an escape plan was already in place for her. She listened with half an ear as her uncle continued to dictate his plan of action to her, asserting an "um-hum" every so often to keep him happy.

When they reached the parking garage, Jazz and Bo went to the sedan she'd purchased for the bodyguard a few short months ago, Brody to the convertible. She searched the shadows nervously. Ever since discovering her neighbor's body, the garage sent shivers down her spine. She tried to ignore the cold zigzagging along her skin and breathe around the knot in her gut.

She swung the garment bag with costume pieces in it into Bo's trunk, but as she shut it and began to walk toward the front of the vehicle, a huge explosion propelled her onto the trunk of the car. Her momentum sent her over the side, where she fell hard onto her right hip and elbow, hitting the concrete floor full force, without time to break her fall. Dazed, and in pain, Jasmine rolled onto her back, trying to identify the noises she was hearing.

She'd hit her head against the rear window, and her vision kept coming into and out of focus like some sort of twisted kaleidoscope. She rotated her head carefully to peer beneath the car, and saw Bo laying on his stomach, moaning and cursing quietly, his eyes squeezed shut, his face contorted. Smoke filled her nostrils, making her choke. A warning sounded in her mind, which seemed to be working at half speed. *Something is wrong,* it said, asininely. She sat quickly, popping up like a child's punching bag, causing her stomach to pitch. Flames were shooting from under the engine compartment of the convertible opposite her.

"Uncle Brody," she murmured slowly, trying to get to her feet. And then, with more panic, "Uncle Brody!" She stumbled against the car next to her, ironically setting off its alarm, and sending a wave of agony through the arm that sought to steady her, the same arm she landed on. Heedless of the pain, she rushed to the convertible. Her Uncle Brody was in the driver's seat, his chin lying on his chest. She banged on the window then screamed and withdrew quickly. The glass had already turned searing hot. She yanked on the door handle, but the automatic locks were engaged. Fearfully, she scanned the area near the sedan for her purse, which she thought she remembered having. To her relief, she saw it almost immediately, its contents strewn far and wide across the garage floor. Luckily, the keys landed only feet from where she stood. She retrieved them, pressing the remote entry, and was relieved to hear the lock's pop, despite the other loud noises surrounding her.

Having opened the door, she grasped her uncle underneath his armpits, coughing as the black smoke rolling from underneath the car's hood overwhelmed her lungs. Her uncle fell against her, and for a moment, she thought she would drop him onto the concrete, but a pair of strong, dark hands helped her to grab Brody and pull him free of the car. She and Bo dragged the unconscious figure as far as the sedan, and then she fell weakly to her knees. Above the crinkle of metal contracting, the lick of the flames, and the car alarm blaring right next to her ear, she caught the *whirr* of an emergency vehicle approaching.

Jasmine looked toward the convertible and her vision was filled with a blinding white light. The next minute, her mind was bombarded with messages from every part of her body, and like the sky behind the fireworks at the baseball stadium, the blackness of her mind reflected the explosions of pain.

She didn't know how much time passed before she began to sense people moving about her. They asked her questions, but her mind couldn't formulate any answers. An oxygen mask was stretched over her face, which panicked her briefly until she realized what it was. She let herself slip back under into the calming blackness. She woke again under the blazing ambulance's lights. She asked for her uncle, but no one seemed to be listening to her. She drifted off again.

CHAPTER TWENTY-EIGHT

"Heath, it's for you," Luke said, passing him the phone. "It's work."

"Lieutenant Heath McGowan speaking."

"Lieutenant, this is Franklin Davis."

"Yes, Franklin, what can I do for you?"

"I was calling to update you on a situation we have here at The Lofts."

Heath's stomach tightened. "Yes?" He watched Jack, who was busy playing a video game. Probably hearing the tension in his voice, Luke glanced over from his piano bench.

"It seems there was an explosion in the garage. Ms. Barrett's vehicle—"

He whirled away from his son and barreled through the kitchen door. "Is Jazz okay?" he asked, worriedly.

"Well, Ms. Barrett, along with Brody Barrett, and the bodyguard, a Bociefus Jones, were all injured. I don't know the severity of the injuries, but they were taken to—" Luke entered the kitchen behind him.

"Which hospital?" Heath asked impatiently.

"Saint Louis University Hospital."

"I'm on my way." He disconnected and grabbed his keys from a basket on the counter.

"What's wrong?"

"Jazz," was all Heath could manage. "Would you mind...?"

"Go," Luke ordered.

Heath was out the door like a shot.

WHEN HEATH WALKED INTO the hospital room, the first thing he noticed was how wide with worry her eyes were.

"Heath."

"Hey, babe." He walked toward her, but she held up a hand.

"Wait. Can you please go check on Uncle Brody for me? I need to know he's okay."

"Can't I ask about you first?"

"No."

"All righty, then," he said slowly, smiling with relief. "You must not be feeling too bad if you can be so bossy." He reversed, leaving the room to find Brody.

Not seeing any hospital personnel, he began peeking in doors. He found Brody three rooms down. He was gazing in the direction of the window, tapping on his bedrail nervously. He appeared drained and had several small cuts on his face. When Heath entered, he turned.

"Oh, lieutenant. Thank God. How's Jasmine? No one will tell me a damn thing."

Heath was stunned by his uncharacteristic concern. But was it genuine, or was he a man anxious about his meal ticket? One thing was certain: Brody Barrett could be removed from the suspect list. Unless he'd blown himself up to throw off suspicion, the man was innocent.

"I really didn't get a chance to determine her status, to tell you the truth, because the minute I walked into the room, she sent me to check on you."

Brody sighed loudly, the relief taking years from his features. "She must not be hurt that badly then. Do me a favor, would you? Go and ask her and let me know how she's doing."

"Sure. But what should I tell her in regards to you? You okay?"

"Yeah. I'm a tough ol' dog. A few scrapes and bruises, a concussion, but the doc says I should be released by tomorrow."

"Good. Well, I'll be back."

He barely finished relaying the information to Jasmine when she sent him to see how Bo was doing.

"Bo is fine," he told her after returning for the second time. "In fact, he's already been discharged. Some cuts and scrapes, had the wind knocked out of him, but apparently he's fine. Now," he exhaled, "how are you?"

"I'm fine."

He approached the bed, focusing on her bandaged hand lying on top of the sheets as he neared. "What happened to your hand?" He brought it gently to his mouth and kissed the fingertips visible under the gauze.

"Oh, nothing. I was stupid. The car was on fire, and I didn't think to take any precautions before touching the glass."

"Ouch. And this?" He swept some hair away to peek at a bandage on her forehead.

"Just a cut I got." She coughed, grimacing.

"Does that hurt?"

"My throat's a little sore from all of the smoke."

He nodded. "You know, from what they tell me, you probably saved your uncle's life."

She shrugged, uncomfortable with the thought. "He certainly saved mine. I guess we're even." She changed the subject. "My Cardinals T-shirt got ripped," she told him, pouting.

He grinned. "We'll get you a new one."

"Promise?" she asked teasingly.

"I promise," he answered, bending to kiss her cheek. "You had me scared, Jazz," he said seriously.

"I'm sorry."

"It's hardly your fault." He looked down at his fingers as they played with hers. "Do you remember anything?"

"All I remember is opening the trunk of the sedan."

"You don't remember any noises, any smells..."

"No. I'm sorry, Heath. I was going over what I needed to do at The Dome."

"That's okay. I thought I'd give it a try. Don't worry about it. We'll be able to determine what happened." He patted her arm in an attempt to reassure her.

A doctor entered the room. "How are we doing, Ms. Barrett?"

"Fine, doctor."

The doctor was reading her chart, but glanced at Heath. "The best thing for that concussion, Ms. Barrett, is rest."

Heath took his cue. "I'll go, then." He bent to kiss her. "You didn't mention a concussion," he whispered to her, raising an eyebrow.

"A tiny one." She smiled weakly, but now that he examined her up close, he could tell she was tired.

"I'll see you tomorrow. Try to stay out of trouble. Geez, I leave you for five minutes..." He clucked his tongue.

She laughed softly.

He reported to Brody on her condition, answering as best as he could his many questions, and then couldn't resist one last peek at her before leaving. The lights had been dimmed in the room, and she was sleeping, but one lamp was still left on that came from behind her right shoulder, illuminating the figure in the bed. He was reminded of the night of the murder, when he'd come upon her asleep on the couch and thought of her as being caught in a spotlight on stage. He stood inside the door for a bit, hands in his pockets, watching her. Then he crept forward and smoothed the hair away from her face as he bent to sweep his lips over hers faintly. He imagined her stirring and calling his name, but she remained motionless.

He paused, hovering near her. What was she dreaming of? She'd had so little good to dream about in her life, he reflected. Lost her parents, lost her innocence, lost her best friend. But maybe she was remembering the Cardinals game, or her success at the batting cages. He suddenly realized he wanted to provide a lot of those types of memories for her, so many they would erase all of the bad ones.

Overhearing Franklin Davis in the hall inquiring after the location of Jasmine's room, Heath went to talk with him.

"Oh, lieutenant. How's Ms. Barrett?"

"She's doing okay."

"Good, good."

"What do you have for me, Franklin?"

"Not much. Crime scene found no prints. We do know the device was detonated by remote control. The explosives used weren't, I guess, the typical kind. The Bomb Squad will get back to you on that. We had a man on the garage door, so the perp must have entered through the building. So that narrows it down to all of the tenants and their guests, which would be, what, hundreds of people?" It was obvious Officer Davis was as frustrated as he was that an explosive had been set right under their noses. "We already have people working on the tapes from the security camera we installed and you should have a list on your desk by seven a.m."

"Good work, Davis." Heath sighed. "We've got to get this guy."

"I'm going to the house now to work on those tapes. I'll see you in the morning."

"Thanks again, Franklin."

"You're welcome, Hawk," the officer returned, using the nickname as he so rarely did.

After Davis left, Heath stood contemplating the situation. With Brody off his list, only Michael Veritek and Lionel Parker remained as suspects. He was certain it was one of them. He decided to stop by the lab first thing in the morning to see if they had come up with anything yet. Unable to do much that night, he went home to get some sleep.

CHAPTER TWENTY-NINE

"How's my girl this morning?" Heath said cheerily as he stuck his head in Jasmine's room.

She turned from where she was staring idly out the window, her face brightening at the sight of him. "Hey."

He crossed the room and grabbed both of her hands, giving her a quick kiss, in deference to the doctor who was busily scribbling notes at the foot of the bed.

"I'm getting sprung from here within the hour," she said happily.

"No kidding?" He checked with the doctor for confirmation.

The doctor nodded without looking away from his notes. "Against doctor's advice, Ms. Barrett here is bound and determined to play a little rock and roll tonight."

She winked. "I bribed him with a pair of concert tickets."

The doctor smiled at her. "I should have held out for backstage passes." Heath raised an eyebrow. "Hey, somebody needs to be there in case Ms. Barrett was to need further medical assistance. I happen to be the poor slob on call for the hottest concert of the season." He tapped her arm with his chart. "I'll be back in a couple of minutes with discharge papers."

Heath frowned. "Are you sure this is a good idea?"

"I'm feeling fine. I don't even have much of a headache, really."

"Until those amplifiers start pumping guitar chords."

"Baby, that's like breathing for me."

"So you've played with a concussion before?"

"Geez. Now you're sounding like Uncle Brody."

"Brody wants to call the concert off?"

"Yeah. Mostly because he won't be there to call the shots, though. He's trying to wheedle his release by concert time."

"Hmm..." he murmured, still unconvinced.

"I'll be fine."

"You going home to rest until concert time?"

"Pretty much," she answered evasively. "Bo is giving me a ride. I know you have work to do. But, Heath," she continued thoughtfully, "lying here I've had a lot of time to think, and I don't know if this is appropriate or not...if, with us...*seeing* each other and all, it would be okay for me to ask you...a few questions in regards to the case. I don't want to put you in an awkward position or anything—"

"No, Jazz. Go ahead and ask. If something's confidential, I'll let you know."

"Okay," she said more confidently. "I was wondering if you have any ideas yet about who can be doing these things, and why. This may sound strange to you, but I've sort of been caught up in grieving Trish's loss, and been in such shock with Sam Dobski's murder—actually, first over discovering he had been spying on me, then his murder—I have never really let myself focus on who could be doing these things, and why. But...someone put a bomb in my car. They were trying to kill me, and my uncle got hurt instead." Her guilt was evident in her speech and in the shadows haunting her face. "Who would want me dead?"

"I don't think they necessarily want you dead, at least not yet," he answered slowly.

"Why do you say that?"

He half sat, resting one hip on the bed. "Because, for one thing, that bomb was set off by remote control. Whoever it was knew it wasn't you behind the wheel of that car."

She rubbed the hairs down on her arms that had begun to rise. "You mean, the person who killed Trish, who killed Sam Dobski, was in the parking garage watching us?"

"I think so."

She shuddered. "Why?"

He sighed. "I keep going back to your name on the wall. It's like they're wanting to get your attention."

"Someone I didn't listen to? A fan I overlooked on the street somewhere?"

"I think with the level of violence with which these crimes were committed, we're searching for someone with a much more personal reason. Someone who is closer to you," he said softly.

She looked toward the window, though he was sure she was seeing nothing.

"Hey." Taking the hand that lay on top of the sheet, he held it in his own. "Are you okay?" She nodded slightly, but didn't turn to him. "Jazz?" He gently grasped her chin and made her face him. Her expression was a mirror of pain. "Tell me what you're feeling."

Her mouth opened but nothing came out at first. She shut her eyes, unable to keep the tears from sliding from beneath her lashes and swallowed. Her voice was barely a whisper. "Whoever's doing this killed her because of *me*. It's all because of *me*. And my uncle—" She choked on her words and covered her trembling lips. "Heath, he could have died." She clenched her hand above her heart. "This is killing me inside. It's like my stomach has been emptied then filled with lead. I don't understand why this is happening. I can't take this." She sobbed as he pulled her into his chest. "I can't take this." She gave in and wept, the sobs ripping through her like a storm.

Her cries sounded so pitiful, like a wounded animal, and then, like a child. It tore at him until he was crying with her, "I can't take this." Seeing her in such pain put his heart in a vise. "I know, I know," he murmured, running his palm over her silky hair.

He needed to find answers for her. He needed to do what he could to put an end to her pain. He knew, however, nothing really could do that, though time would help. But finding the murderer would go a long ways to helping her to heal. And he was determined to do just that.

HEATH SPENT THE MORNING doing research on his two top suspects.

He discovered Michael Veritek was the son of Mikael Veritov, C.E.O. of Titan Industries. The business man had married a young debutante when he was in his fifties and Michael was their sole child. The actor had been arrested for possession twice; once when he was in his teens, and the other time, a month prior to the murder. So much for staying clean. He was worth a mint on paper, but his bank accounts didn't reflect it. Heath surmised most of his money must be going up his nose. None of this seemed to be hurting his career any, however, as he had been signed to his current project for several million dollars. He was a notorious womanizer. The only woman he had ever spent much time with at all was Jasmine.

In contrast, Lionel Parker was not as easy to find information on. He was also an only child, raised by his father. Beyond the marriage license, the birth certificate, and the divorce papers served a few years later, no evidence existed to show he had a mother at all. His work had received numerous awards, but, unlike Veritek, he was rarely caught in the tabloids. He attended major events alone. For all intents and purposes, he was, as he had told Heath, a loner.

His eyes bleary from reading information from the computer screen, and feeling like he was no closer to uncovering the murderer, he decided to take a stroll.

CHAPTER THIRTY

Anastasia Lorne was drilling holes into a man's skull. Luckily, he was dead. She pushed the plastic visor covering her entire face back and grinned at Lieutenant McGowan.

"Hey, Hawk. I was wondering how long it would be before you came down here to rattle my cage."

He gazed at the coroner in wonder as she chewed off a corner of her half-finished tuna fish sandwich. Her two-toned, short grey hair stuck out at all angles, which seemed to suit her, her appearance made even wilder by the visor wedged onto her head.

"You need results on Patricia Norman. I know." She took a sip from the can of soda that sat on top of the chest of the victim she was working on. "We're swamped. As you can see," she said, waving around the large, open room. Indeed, several corpses were laid on exam beds throughout the lab. "I'm so busy I can't even have a friggin' lunch break—excuse my French—and I'm afraid some of the cases I'm currently working on involve some even bigger V.I.P.s than Jasmine Barrett, or at least V.I.P.s who are a lot more vocal and persistent than she is. You know, the whole squeaky wheel thing."

"I know it can get crazy, and I know you're not finished with the report yet, but I was wondering if you could share with me what you already know concerning Tricia's murderer."

"Sure." She turned to her laptop, which was open on a rolling stand next to her where she had been taking notes. "Let's see here…" She pulled up a file. "Okay." She hummed as she scanned the screen. "Patricia Norman was killed by someone who was left-handed, we can tell by the angle of the knife wound."

He jotted the information into his own notebook.

"We also know he is likely between six-one and six-three by the angle of the ligature marks. The killer would also be very strong, or very angry, or both. Her neck was actually broken during the course of the strangulation. It all would have been very quick. She wouldn't have known what hit her."

He nodded. So far, he wasn't getting much more than he had already determined on his own.

"The only thing the killer seemed to leave at the scene was the knife, which was a standard, six-inch hunting knife. It could have been purchased anywhere." Anastasia hummed again, and scrolled. "The rose found on the bed and the scarf were simply instruments of opportunity. Like I said, the death happened in a matter of minutes, no DNA under the girl's nails or on the bed."

She continued to scroll over the notes, but something she said jarred Heath's memory.

He cleared his throat. "You found no evidence of a sexual nature?" He couldn't get rid of the image Michael Veritek put in his mind.

The coroner didn't look away from the screen. "No. She wasn't sexually abused."

"And if some sort of sexual encounter happened in say, the previous twenty-four hours in that room, you would have detected that."

Anastasia peered at him curiously, and for an instant it was as if she was seeing right through him and knew he was not asking her the question on a professional basis. But the next moment he realized she was debating the issue internally. "Yes, I think we would have discovered that, even if there had been a condom used. There wasn't *any* evidence of anyone being in that bed other than Jasmine Barrett, and the victim, which, considering she is a rock star and all, I found surprising. I thought we'd find all sorts of things."

He exhaled.

"Of course, if the sheets had been changed before the murder occurred, then it's a whole different ball game."

He frowned. "What else can you tell me? Anything from the Sam Dobski scene?"

"Not much more than you already know. That one's a real mess. From the hair samples your boy could be red-headed, blond, brunette, grey, or raven black. He could be of Asian descent, Caucasian, or black. In fact, he could be a she. Again, the victim did not seem to have the opportunity to struggle with his attacker, no DNA. Sorry, Hawk. I know this isn't what you were hoping to hear."

"That's okay, Anastasia. I'll keep working things from my end and if I get some sort of proof, maybe I can subpoena some hair samples from somebody that we can match with those at the crime scene. Good luck with...this," he said, grimacing and indicating the plethora of corpses strewn about.

Anastasia laughed as she returned the visor to its place and grasped her drill. "Yeah, thanks, Hawk."

AFTER HEATH READ THE Bomb Squad's report, he immediately called Gary Pottokin.

"Gary, Heath McGowan. English, please."

Gary chuckled. "Okay, Heath. Here's the gist of it. This explosion was made by a device called a "squib". Squibs are used in movies and in live theatre for special effects. It looks like a piece of dynamite, but with less explosive force. But, attached to a tank full of gasoline, then you've got something. Coupled with that, we found some gel explosives, an item that's also used in special effects. The reason this is significant is because it's not really commonly used. We more often see Molotov cocktails or some other homemade device, or some elaborate, more professional, military-type explosive."

"So why can't you simply say that in your report?"

"'Cause I gotta throw in those big-ticket words to justify my overinflated salary."

He snorted. "Yeah. Exactly as I thought. Seriously, Gary, thanks for getting me this info so fast."

"No problem, Hawk. Hope it helps."

Heath ended the call and pushed away from his desk, turning to stare blindly out the window at the office building across the street. Special effects explosives. Could have been picked up on the set by Michael Veritek. Or by Lionel Parker, he supposed. Although Veritek would have had easier access. The singular new thing he got from the autopsy was the killer was left-handed. Since approximately only ten percent of the population was left-handed, it could help him narrow down his choices, but would hardly be evidence, and evidence was what he needed.

He swung his suit coat over his shoulder, grabbed a pair of binoculars from his bottom drawer, and headed to Ladue.

CHAPTER THIRTY-ONE

From the tree line, Heath watched through the binoculars as the undercover cop, posing as a delivery man, gave Lionel Parker an electronic pad to sign. Parker signed with his left, as he suspected he would. Now all he needed to do was eliminate Michael Veritek, and he'd have his main suspect. Parker ripped open the delivered envelope and read the one word message he'd withdrawn.

Gotcha.

Lionel Parker scanned the grounds, searching for an explanation for the strange message, then angrily stormed inside, slamming the door behind him.

"Temper. Temper," Heath said aloud. He whipped his cell phone from his pocket as he sauntered back to his car, which he'd parked along the street. Scanning his recent call list, he placed the call to Veritek's agent.

"Brian Kingsley."

"Yeah. This is Thad from the props department." He pitched his voice a bit higher than usual. "We need to know if Michael Veritek is right or left-handed."

"Left."

"Thank you."

He banged his fists on the steering wheel. What were the freakin' odds?

HEATH WAS ENJOYING himself. The two opening bands were entertaining and the beer was going down easy. Kole and Luke were having a good time too. It had been way too long since the brothers had all done something together. In the break before Jasmine appeared on stage, they argued loudly over the odds of the University of Missouri's quarterback getting The Heisman, but they were suddenly crowned out by the roar of the crowd as the lights dimmed. The adrenaline rush and enthusiasm were wildly contagious as whistles and shouts filled the auditorium. He shot a grin at Jazz's doctor, who he had been kibitzing with throughout the evening, and the light focused on Jazz. She wore a tight-fitting, fire-engine red, strapless dress that rode up high on her well-shaped thighs. She shimmied to "Rock My World," meandering across a strip of stage jutting into the middle of the audience, so close to them they could almost untie her strappy red heels. She had every man in the auditorium's heart throbbing in their chest and other body parts responding as well.

After a particularly enticing dip of her hips, Heath heard Kole whisper hoarsely, "Holy shit, man."

Beside him, Luke's head bobbed and all three men's mouths hung open in shock and amazement.

Recovering first, Kole shot Heath an elbow to the ribs. "You can't handle that, brother."

He was having his doubts too, but he knew he'd love to try. He would have made some sort of comment, but his throat had gone dry, and it didn't seem important at the moment in any case. It seemed far more important to fantasize about what those hips could do to him in bed than to crush Kole.

A good-looking teenager in front of them turned to his companion and said, "Man, if I could have fifteen minutes alone with her, I'd die a happy man."

His friend nodded. "No doubt."

Heath stared at the pair incredulously and Kole burst with laughter, slapping his little brother on the shoulder. Heath found himself unreasonably upset by the teens' comments, but then came to the realization they were only sharing the same thoughts he'd had himself.

After the song ended, Jazz addressed the audience. "Hellllo, St. Louis!" The applause was deafening. "Man. It's good to be here tonight. There is some definite energy in this place. I want to thank you all for coming tonight to listen to us. Didn't "Even Man Out" and "Too Fried to Rock" do an awesome job tonight? Let's hear it for them one more time." She paused so the audience could show their appreciation. "This next song, I'd like to dedicate to my dear friend, Tricia. It was her favorite." Her voice broke slightly, but she pulled it together. "So let's rock it for Trish."

The lights went down again, and she disappeared. An extended, complicated guitar rift introduced the next song and a spotlight landed on her on an upper platform with the drummer. She had somehow changed into a one-piece black velvet number that clung to her like a second skin. She leapt from her perch, gracefully landing center stage like a cat as she began one of her bigger hits, "Just Cattin' Around." She moved stealthily across the stage, every bit the feline the song portrayed, practically sliding on her stomach at one point, and then flipping on her back to kick her legs. Two male dancers appeared from the wings, dressed in black leather pants and vests, their bare chests glistening in the footlights as they helped Jazz to stand. She leaned against one and ran her fingers through the other's hair as she gyrated and lowered herself along him, trailing her arm like a cat's tail. When she rose again, the dancer bent in for a kiss, her mouth open and ready, but she pushed him aside at the last moment playfully. The other dancer grabbed her waist, urging her in for a similar, sizzling dance. When she ended that song with a slow backbend that led into the splits, Heath got another jab in the ribs.

"Oh, yeah, man. You're in trouble."

His stupid grin made it clear he didn't wish to be anywhere else.

WHEN THEY FINALLY MADE it to the dressing room, Jazz was fighting off her stage makeup. "Heath," she cried, rushing into his embrace the minute she saw him in the doorway.

He lifted her and swung her in a circle, nuzzling her nose. "You were fantastic." He set her on her feet, kissing her passionately, like a lover returning home after months at sea.

"A-ahem." His brothers simultaneously cleared their throats in a loud and exaggerated manner.

"Go *away*," he murmured against her lips, but she squirmed.

"Luke. Kole," she said, trying to escape from him. "I hope—you enjoyed—the show," she stuttered, slapping at Heath's hands. He finally shifted behind her, not releasing his grip on her waist as he pressed her warm body to his and smiled smugly at his brothers.

"Yes, we did. But apparently not as much as Heath did," Luke joked.

"Don't get us wrong, if we didn't think he would draw his weapon on us, we'd be jumping you too," Kole countered, a little drunk.

"Nobody's jumping my patient," the young doctor stated as he nudged past Luke and Kole, having finagled a backstage pass from Jazz prior to discharging her. "In all seriousness Ms. Barrett, after an exhaustingly physical show like we saw—which was terrific, by the way—you should go straight home and get some rest." He looked knowingly at Heath.

He grudgingly relinquished his grip on her and walked over to whisper in the good doctor's ear, "Spoilsport."

"Well, everyone needs to stay long enough to help me drink this champagne. It was sent to me and I never drink it because it gives me a huge headache, and I don't really like the stuff either."

"Don't mind if I do." Kole quickly and expertly popped the cork.

After a few minutes of conversation, as the rush of performing in front of a wildly cheering audience had worn off, it did become fairly evident Jazz was, indeed, very fatigued. Heath roamed the room restlessly while she entertained her guests, but suddenly his focus was caught by a dozen cream-colored roses on her dressing table.

"Jazz, who sent these flowers?"

"Hmm?" she replied, caught in midsentence. "Oh, um, I'm not sure."

Dozens of roses were scattered about the room, but only these grabbed his attention. Jazz left the group at the door to learn why they interested him. Amidst the cream roses were three, slightly taller, red roses.

"Do you mind if I read the card?"

"No, of course not."

He pulled the small card from its envelope.

With all my love —Apollos.

He extended the card to her. "Do you know this Apollos character?"

"No, Heath, I swear."

He nodded. "Ever received flowers from him before?"

She shook her head. "Not that I know of."

"Who sent the flowers that were on your dresser the night Trish was killed?"

Her face became flushed. "Michael did."

"Veritek?" he queried, his voice suddenly brittle.

"Yes," she responded quietly. "I told you, he was trying to make up with me, but I told him I didn't want that sort of relationship anymore."

"So, why'd you keep the flowers?"

"He told me to. And besides, it would be such a waste to discard perfectly good flowers, so I stuck them in the bedroom, so I wouldn't have to answer any of my uncle's questions." She shrugged, her cheeks flushed. Her gaze darted around. "They were pretty," she murmured.

The childlike excuse she offered cut right to his heart. It wasn't her fault Veritek sent her flowers, or that he was baiting Heath by implying there was more to his and Jazz's relationship than he knew. She simply kept the flowers because she liked them. "I'm sorry," he said, caressing her. "But the reason I'm so interested is because I think these may be from the killer."

Her eyes went wide. "You think the killer sent me flowers? Why?"

He ran a finger along a red velvety petal contemplatively. "I think it's his way of bragging. Why are there three red roses in here?"

"That does seem rather odd..."

"I think, to the killer, they represent the three attacks, Tricia, Sam Dobski, and your uncle." He pointed to each one in turn. "What about this 'Apollos'? Does the name mean anything to you?"

"Not a thing. It's the name of a Greek God. But what does that mean?"

"That's exactly what I intend to discover," he answered. Luke and Kole approached them.

"Everyone else is gone, if you two lovebirds haven't noticed. We'll give you guys a moment to do—" Luke cleared his throat "—whatever it is you want to do." He gave the classic McGowan roll of the eyes. "I don't want to know."

"I do," Kole whispered loudly, having generously helped himself to the champagne.

"Get out of here," Heath ordered, pushing them through the door. As the tumbler fell to on the handle, he grabbed Jasmine and pressed her against the door. He tilted her head and claimed her lips. Without saying a word, the message was clear. *You belong to me now. There's no room for Michael Veritek.* One of her arms lay trapped by her body, the other lay limply on his shoulder as he changed tactics, coming to the front of her neck, exploring the collarbone and the hollow of her throat, the soft skin beneath her chin, feeling her racing pulse.

She was just so beautiful. He pulled back, watching her eyes open slowly, the hazy desire sliding away in their depths. He skimmed his fingertips across her cheek, staring into the fire-green eyes which concentrated on one of his eyes then the other, observing him warily. He held her heart and they both knew it. She trembled with need, but she lifted her chin defiantly even as his hand slowly left her neck, resting on the door beside her ear. When he brought his lips to hers this time she simply melted into the kiss. Grasping her hips, Heath hitched her a little higher to align their bodies better, wanting her to know the heat of his need for her fully.

A knock interrupted them. "Mmm," Heath groaned, laying his forehead against Jasmine's. "Lady, all I want is fifteen minutes alone with you."

Her smile was tinged with triumph. "Anytime, McGowan."

"How about tomorrow night?"

She laughed. "You work quickly."

"Jack is spending the night at Timmy's and Luke said he'd sleep at Kole's place."

"I don't know," she said coyly, "you and me alone in that big house of yours...?"

"Yeah." He grinned wickedly. "We could get into all kinds of trouble." He kissed her neck.

"I guess I can give you your fifteen minutes, in any event."

"After you've had fifteen minutes of me, you'll be begging for more."

"Is that so?" She nibbled on his chin lightly.

"Um-hmm," he mumbled.

"Then I guess it would be in my best interest to show."

"I'll even make dinner for you."

"You will? Jack said you couldn't cook."

His head came up. "I can cook," he replied defensively, then switched gears, nuzzling her ear and growling. "Only not so much in the kitchen."

"Umm...what time do you want me there?"

"Now. But I'll settle for five tomorrow." He trailed two fingers along the side of her face. "You get plenty of rest," he said suggestively.

"Yes, sir, Lieutenant McGowan." She gave him a salute as he took his weight off her reluctantly. Another simultaneous rap on the door vibrated against her back and she moved away from the entrance.

Heath yanked the door open. "What's wrong with you guys? Don't you have an ounce of patience?" he scolded, grabbing Kole in a headlock and digging his knuckles into his scalp as the trio trouped down the hall. He glanced over his shoulder to see Jasmine sigh with a smile and lean against the door frame, her hands grasping the edge.

CHAPTER THIRTY-TWO

Heath threw the pot of burnt marinara sauce into the sink with a sigh. He tried. Luckily, Luke agreed to get some sauce for him and deliver it to the door at the rear of the house so Jazz wouldn't be aware of his culinary failure. As he sat impatiently waiting for Luke and watching the window for a glimpse of his car, he reviewed his day.

He had hoped the killer had erred. Become too cocky in sending the flowers, but whoever the killer was, they even covered their bases at the florist's. It would appear they paid a homeless man to order the flowers, from the description the clerk gave him. But at least he was certain the flowers came from the killer now. Who else would hire someone to send flowers from them to Jasmine? *It had to be Veritek,* he thought as he took the florist's gift card from his jeans pocket again. *'Apollos.' It must be a clue.* He had checked his Greek mythology and found he remembered correctly, Apollo was the sun god who drove his chariot over the skies each day toting the sun behind it. If one of his suspects had a last name of Sundiver, maybe that could be a clue, but what was the connection in this case? He read further and discovered Apollo fell in love with a nymph, Daphne, and was scorned by her. Scorned lover was the role Michael Veritek was playing. Maybe the pieces were fitting together after all.

He then began to call and reinterview Jasmine's neighbors, the superintendent of her building, and anyone who could have seen Veritek on the evening of Tricia's murder, or perhaps seen his vehicle. No luck. He tried to place the fact that Veritek had a pretty solid alibi for the evening of Sam Dobski's murder at the back of his mind. It wouldn't be the first time someone had bought an alibi, even if it was from a dozen dinner guests. He was continually pounding his head against a brick wall. He'd have to wait for Veritek to make a mistake. But would it be too late? Would Jasmine be his next victim?

These were the ideas haunting him when he was supposed to be stirring his sauce. That and images of Jazz from the concert the night before, which had been pushing their way into his thoughts all day. At least the smoke from his ruined sauce had thinned to a sort of ethereal haze. He went to inspect the table for the fourth time. Luke had insisted on ironing a table cloth. It did look a lot less...lumpy. Wine, his and Juliette's wedding china—which he was hoping wasn't a bad omen of some sort—wine glasses, candles. Things seemed in order. When he returned to the kitchen and glanced at the window, he could see Luke strolling up the sidewalk with a bag. At the same time, he spotted Jasmine pulling to the curb. "Oh, shit. Shit. Shit!" He rushed to the door, getting to it at the moment Luke did. He reached out and yanked the surprised Luke in by his jacket.

"What the—"

"Get in here, you moron. She's coming."

"Hey, this *moron* just went downtown to get you a red sauce—"

"Oh, no. You didn't go to Stephano's did you?" He grabbed the bag from him and recognized the familiar logo. "You went to Stephano's." The despair was thick in his voice.

"What's the big deal? Stephano's has one of the best—"

The doorbell rang and Heath seized Luke by the lapels again.

"I'll distract her." He pushed Luke hurriedly toward the door. "You sneak out and keep low when you pass the windows."

"Keep low? What the hell for?"

Heath gave Luke a sharp rap on the noggin.

"Ouch."

"Stay, low!" he hissed.

"You're a nut," Luke mumbled as the door was slammed in his face.

Heath scrambled to answer the front door. "Hey, come on in. How's it going? Do you want some wine?" he said without taking a breath. He extended a glass he had already poured.

"Hi. Is Luke here?"

"Luke? Luke?" he stated like a parrot, his eyes betraying his alarm.

"Your brother...Luke?" Jasmine repeated slowly, her brow furrowed.

"Oh, Luke. No, Luke's not here. Remember, he's going to Kole's."

"Yes, I know that was the plan—" Her sentence was lost in a sudden kiss. He had seen Luke walking by, brazenly holding himself tall and waving as he passed the windows. In order to distract her, Heath threw her into an unexpected lip lock. The awkward kiss was finished before it had even begun. He made an attempt to inconspicuously scan the windows. When he spun around, Jazz was staring beyond his shoulder with a puzzled expression. He twisted to peek at the window but didn't see anything.

Jazz nudged his chin so that he would focus on her and not continue to gawk at the windows. "Heath—" She kissed him tenderly. "—whatever is bothering you, don't let it worry you anymore." She kissed him again. "All I need is right here—" She feathered a kiss on his lips, then looked him directly in the eyes "—with you." She planted a kiss on him so wonderful it did make him forget about his annoying brother.

"Okay, then," he said, "let's get this dinner over with so we can have sex." He whirled and marched through the swinging door.

As the door swung back and forth he heard her mumble, "That was some of the strangest foreplay I've ever had." In seconds he returned with steaming spaghetti and meatballs.

"I thought you told me you were making marinara sauce?"

I did, but Luke got the wrong thing. "I decided to throw together some meatballs."

She sat at the little alcove table. "Very nice. You know, you didn't have to go to all this effort." She took a bite of the pasta, chewing it thoughtfully. "We could have gone *down* to Stephano's." She glanced up at him with a sexy smile, holding his gaze.

"Okay," he caved. "I tried to make dinner, I really did. But I burnt the sauce and—"

He stopped because she was laughing. Laughing so hard she was practically falling out of her chair. Unable to resist her infectious attitude, he laughed at himself too.

"I would have gotten away with it, too, if Luke hadn't chosen Stephano's. Of all the Italian joints in all the world." He shook his head in wonderment.

"Was he supposed to be hiding outside?"

"You saw him?"

She nodded, still stifling a giggle. "He waved at me."

"I told him to duck," Heath fumed.

"You must have made him pretty mad. What did you do?"

Heath considered. "I may have called him a moron...and *thwapped* him a few times," he added hurriedly. "But he deserved it."

"I'm sure he did. You are so sweet."

"Ahh. I'm sweet and charming. I may as well be a Basset hound."

"No, really, this is the most wonderful meal I've ever had—"

"Who are you kidding?" he said, rising and taking the plates. "This stuff is horrible. The noodles are cold and stuck together. I may as well trash it."

"No, wait. It can be salvaged. You can't wash Stephano's red sauce down the drain." She took the plates. "Come on. Grab the wine."

She led him into the kitchen and hunted for some noodles. Heath had used all of the spaghetti noodles, but she found some bow-tie pasta and got a pan boiling on the stove. While Jasmine bustled around the kitchen, she talked to him about the concert, and discussed Missouri football. He relaxed and leaned on the counter, watching her with utter admiration. Of course, Stephano's had sent far too much sauce, so she was able to heat it and add it to the noodles when they were done. For the first time, he noticed her dress. It was a simple black dress that scooped low in the back, the fabric lying in loopy folds. She wore a couple of strands of white and black crystals that draped between her shoulder blades tantalizingly. She had a short-cut jacket over it, but had removed it as she cooked. They sat at the kitchen table with their feast.

When he was finished eating, Heath pushed away, stretching his legs under the table with a well-satisfied sigh. Fingers laced behind his neck, he listened to her speak, noting how the setting sun sparked in her eyes, like tiny emeralds that twirled to catch the light. She got to her feet and cleared the plates. He helped her to rinse and put them in the dishwasher.

"Do you want to go on the porch now?"

She shook her head solemnly, laying her glass on the counter and taking his hand. "I want you to take me upstairs and make love to me."

"Well, gosh. I'm really feeling pressured here. We've known each other for such a short time..."

She stomped her foot, but before she could form the indignant words bubbling up inside of her, he finished his statement.

"...but I think I can live with it. Race you." In a split second he was out the door and she followed in hot pursuit, giggling as she ran. On the stairs they bounced off walls and railings alike, Jasmine losing her heels in the process. They finally burst through his bedroom door. Jazz flopped on the bed, laughing and inhaling raggedly. He rested against the closed door, clutching the doorknob. His mood became serious.

Jazz studied him uneasily as she caught her breath. He slowly walked to her and cupped her face. "Jasmine," he murmured, his voice rough with emotion. He sensed her fear even as he kissed her tenderly, drawing her to him. Each kiss was a loving statement, each trembling touch a testimony to his feelings for her.

JASMINE HAD NEVER BEEN loved like this in the past and it frightened her. This was not the whirlwind passion that often ignited between them. She understood desire and heart-stopping heat, but the seriousness in his expression was terrifying. She shivered.

"Are you cold?"

She shook her head. He found the zipper at the back of her dress. Slowly he parted the fabric that kept him from her. She wished he would kiss her, throw her down on the mattress and take her. He brought his hands underneath the fabric and slipped the dress from her shoulders, letting it drop in a heap. She leaned toward him, but he put a finger to her lips. He parted from her, giving himself space to peer at her. Self-conscious, she reflexively put an arm across her chest.

"Don't do that," he said softly.

"I don't...feel comfortable." Panic rose in her. "I'm scared...I...." Her attention darted everywhere, but she wouldn't look at him.

"Jazz..." He waited until she lifted her gaze to his. "It's okay. I won't hurt you. I'm not like the others."

"I know. I know." She wanted to weep.

"Oh, baby. Don't cry." He embraced her.

"I'm sorry. Oh, my gosh!" she cried in anguish. She was ashamed and wished she were someplace else. When she raised her face to his, he kissed her gently. She pushed into him, trying to recreate the fire that was safe, and she nearly did. She nearly sent him over the edge, she could feel it.

"Jazz," he said, withdrawing a few inches. He held her wrists, and gulped in air, seeming to steady his resolve. "This isn't how I want it. I fantasized all day about being with you that way—tearing each other's clothes off, going at it until we were hot and sweaty and satisfied—but now I have you in my room, I want more. I want to show you how much you have come to mean to me." He focused on her wrist, where he still clasped her, and then on her. "I want to make love to you. Let me love you, Jazz," he said it with such need in his voice, even he seemed surprised.

She could see in his eyes how much it meant to him. She nodded slightly.

He scooped her up and set her gently on the bed. He laid next to her, surveying her in the streetlight shining through the windows. "You're so beautiful." She started to protest, but he put a finger on her lips again. "You are beautiful, inside and out. And I love you, Jazz."

She gasped, stunned. "No, don't—"

"I love you, Jazz," he said firmly, bringing her wrist to his mouth. He began to kiss her, and caress her, with painstaking care. She slid under, giving in, letting go, trusting in him. She permitted herself to relish in the sensations he was creating throughout her body, as she allowed him to fill her heart.

When he was ready, he came to her and it had never been so right. He moved slowly, sensually within her, watching her until she called his name in ecstasy and gratitude.

She fell asleep in his arms and woke in the same position. As she opened her eyes to the warmth of the sun and a single bird chirping happily on a branch by the window, she could hear him snoring gently in her ear. She giggled, twisting toward him and sighing contentedly. She couldn't remember a time when she was happier.

He jolted awake and caught her observing him. "Hey, gorgeous."

"Hey," she replied, stroking his stubbly cheek.

"Have you been awake for a while?"

"No. Only a few moments, really."

"Good. 'Cause I wouldn't want to miss a second with you." He kissed the top of her head then rolled out of bed. "Why don't I make us some breakfast? I'm starved." She admired his cute little butt as he walked to the highboy to find something to wear.

"I'll help."

He glanced over his shoulder with a wry expression. "Last night's dinner give you a lack of confidence in my cooking ability?"

"Not exactly," she answered diplomatically, sitting in bed and clutching the quilt to her breasts.

He turned and froze. "You look as good as I thought you would in that old quilt. Even better, really." She noted the fire in his gaze. "After I get my tank refilled, I'm going to ravish you shamelessly."

She grinned. "Let's go then."

WHEN SHE CAME DOWN wearing one of his dress shirts, he didn't think he would make it through breakfast. All that luscious leg. At one point, she rubbed her foot against his leg under the table playfully. He caught it and explored the smooth curve of her calves.

"Finished with breakfast?" he said tensely.

She leaned across the table with a wicked twinkle in her eyes. "Uh-huh." She kissed him and he pulled her to her feet.

"Whatever restraint I showed last night, I'm not gonna show it now."

She gave him a devil-may-care smirk. "Restraint is for wussies."

"Well nobody's ever called me a wussie." He took a hold of both sides of his shirt and ripped it open, listening with satisfaction as buttons ricocheted off crockery and landed in distant corners of the kitchen. He immediately cupped her breasts with a guttural moan of pleasure. He swept the dishes from the kitchen table with the back of his arm, and as they crashed to the floor, he was already lifting her onto the table. The hands that had been calm and loving last night were reckless and demanding, cruising along her body and plundering her.

Afterward he lay on top of her, spent and trying to bring his breathing under control. She clung to him. They broke into laughter.

"I think I have syrup in my hair."

"Oh. Sorry about that."

"No you're not," she said with a smile.

"You're right. I'm not." He kissed her and then helped her to stand. "You okay?"

She held onto his waist. "I'm better than okay." She inspected the damage surrounding them. "But we better clean this mess before Jack gets home." She bent to collect the pieces.

"No. I'll get that. You go take a shower."

"Are you sure?"

"Yeah. Go." He shooed her away. When he was alone in the kitchen, carefully gathering the shards of glass, he did a mental replay and chuckled. There had been no woman who made him as crazy as she had, on many different levels.

When she returned a short while later, he asked her, "So, what are your plans for the rest of the day?"

"Well, I need to go visit my uncle. He's getting released tomorrow, hopefully. Other than that, I didn't have much planned. Maybe fiddle with a song or two I've been working on. What are you guys doing?"

"Well, the reason I asked was, I was wondering if you might want to join Jack and me for a Missouri Tigers game?"

Her face lit up. "In Columbia?" she asked excitedly.

"Yeah. But we'd need to leave in an hour and a half."

"I'll see you soon," she said, whirling and rushing from the room.

He laughed, hurrying to follow after her. "I'll pick you up then?"

"Yeah." She found her purse hanging on a chair, slung it over her shoulder, then ran to give him a kiss goodbye. "This is gonna be so cool!" she squealed.

He stuck his hands in the back of her jean's pockets. "Let me guess. Never been to a Tiger's game?"

"Never." She rushed out the door, clapping and exclaiming, "Yes!"

"She is so damn cute," he said to the empty living room.

CHAPTER THIRTY-THREE

It was a beautiful fall day, fifty-five degrees, sun shining, and thousands of enthusiastic fans packed into a stadium to root their team on to victory. Heath looked at Jazz and laughed, "You've never been to a game, yet you have all this Tiger-wear?"

"That's why. My uncle wouldn't let me go, so I satisfied myself with going on-line and purchasing stuff, and charging it to his credit card." She wore a black and gold knit cap and a matching, fluffy scarf. Over her thin, gold Missouri sweater she wore a black quilted vest. Gold and black beads hung from her neck and to top it off, she had a Tigers stadium seat. A Tigers stadium seat, but had never been in the stadium.

"He paid in the long run, huh?"

"Damn straight."

Heath held onto Jack's legs as his son straddled his shoulders taking in all the action around him, which included wildly screaming, black-and-gold-wearing fans, band members with big, shiny instruments, cheerleaders, full of energy, doing a routine at mid-field, and vendors, winding amongst the crowd and hawking their wares.

Jazz's smile was brilliant, cheeks rosy, and eyes glowing with anticipation. He bent, being careful to balance Jack's weight and gave her a quick kiss. "What was that for?"

"Because you're so damned irresistible, I can't help myself."

She slipped her hand in his as the announcer began the introductions. The loudspeakers blared Guns and Roses' "Welcome to the Jungle," and the Tigers ran through a paper MU symbol and loads of smoke. Jazz jumped and screamed, as did Jack, and both clapped to the alma mater.

Hours later, when the alternating chants of "M-I-Z" and "Z-O-U" —which spelled the school's nickname—had died down, when the warmth of a cup of cocoa restoring her heat was a memory, and the peanut shells had all but been annihilated beneath their feet, Jazz and Jack crashed in the warm car, as the miles zipped by beneath the Mustang's wheels. Heath glanced at her serene face turned toward him and wondered why it was so easy for them both to forget someone could be, at this very moment, planning her murder.

JAZZ PHONED AHEAD ON her way back from the game so Bo would be there to walk her up. She greeted him as he opened the car door for her. She had taken to parking on the street, despite her uncle's warning that something bad would happen to the convertible. As far as she was concerned, something bad had already happened in the garage and she wasn't about to go in there. Besides, the convertible was ruined and she had been stuck driving Brody's sedan.

"Miss Jazz...you have a visitor," Bo warned. Instinctively, she followed the line of the building to the penthouse window. She could see him in silhouette, holding a glass. "Mr. Veritek."

"Michael?" she said in surprise.

The big man nodded. "He's been here for an hour. I told him I wasn't sure when you'd be here, but he insisted on waiting. I can throw him out, if you'd like," he added, enthusiastically. She sensed he had never liked Michael.

"No, Bo," she said with a smile. "I'll hear what he has to say, *then* you can get rid of him, if necessary." She sighed, muttering under her breath, "I guess I owe him that much."

When she got to the condo, Michael was sitting on the couch like he owned the place. He wore a white tuxedo shirt and black pants, but had apparently abandoned his tie. His arms were stretched on the top of the couch and he held a tumbler, newly filled with the scotch her uncle kept stocked.

"Jazz," he said, his voice steely.

She noted the tone. This wouldn't be a pleasant encounter. "Hello, Michael," she responded evenly. "I see you've helped yourself to my uncle's scotch." She snatched her knit cap off and dropped it on a chair, fluffing her hair.

Michael took another giant swig, making no comment but watching her with a gaze that seemed to snap in the subdued light of the condo.

Bo hovered near her, taking in the exchange with skepticism.

"We need to talk."

"Do we?" she said, exhaling. "I thought we'd said everything already."

He stood, taking a firm hold of her elbow and glaring at Bo. "Outside."

"Okay," she said, surprised by his insistence. She could see he was jumpy, agitated. She wondered how much he injected into his system and how much alcohol he had poured down his throat while he waited for her. She peeked and was relieved to find Bo still keeping his focus on the pair. When the door closed behind them, Michael released her. She crossed to lean on the railing, taking in the beautiful St. Louis skyline twinkling beneath and around them.

Michael seemed oblivious to the charms of the city. He rested his back against the railing and observed her. "So, what's he like in bed?" She twisted to stare at him in shock. "Your boyfriend cop?" His hazy green eyes flickered all over her. He stroked her skin and she retreated. He advanced on her. "Does he make you feel like I used to?" She didn't answer or even glance at him. He began to pace, running a hand through his hair roughly. "You need to get him off my case, Jazz. I can't work with him showing up every other day to accuse me of things."

"He told me you lied to him," she said coldly.

He stopped pacing.

She turned to face him. "You didn't have anything to do with—"

"Damn, Jazz. Do you really...? Is that what you think of me? You think I'm a murderer?" He grabbed her and gave her a little shake. Bo took a few steps toward the door, but seemed to wait for a signal from Jazz.

She stuck out her chin defiantly. "You lied to him."

He let her go. "I friggin' lied to him because I couldn't tell him the truth. I couldn't let him know...I was with my dealer."

She shook her head, tears building. She believed him when he'd told her he'd quit. What a fool she was.

"Don't look at me that way. Not everybody's got it all together like your friggin' boyfriend, okay? Mr. High-and-Mighty. You know, I'm guessing he wouldn't be so all-fired high-and-mighty if some scandal involving him sur-faced at work. I'm guessing that police chief of his would be mighty unhappy if he discovered one of his men was boinking someone involved in one of his murder cases."

"Michael...no."

"A scandal like that...he'd likely lose his job."

"Michael, you can't do that, he has a little boy." The minute she said it, Jasmine knew she made a mistake. This man in front of her had no sympathy for children, or anyone other than himself.

"Does he now?" He ran a hand along her arm again but she moved further from him. Holding her gaze, he enunciated his next sentence carefully, "I'm sure you wouldn't want anything to happen to that boy or his father, would you, Jazz?" This time when he stepped toward her she bumped into the wall, effectively cornered.

Bo chose this point to open the door. "Ms. Jazz, you okay?"

For a beat, they all stood there, waiting for Jazz's response. Michael gave her a hard stare. A warning. Her voice sounded strangled. "Yes, Bo. I'll be fine."

Reluctantly, the bodyguard turned to go inside.

On the balcony, Michael played with her hair, "Good girl, Jazz," he said condescendingly.

"What do you want, Michael?" The middle of her forehead ached.

He peered at her for a moment. "You. It's all I've ever wanted."

"What does that mean?" She was gripped by fear. *He can't be serious. I can't be with him.* But the more she thought about it, the more she realized she had no other option. *I can't let him hurt Heath or Jack. Heath's job is everything to him. It's what he is.* Her mind was reeling. *Maybe I can stall until the case is closed. Then Michael would have no grounds for blackmail.*

"It means that tomorrow you'll tell your cop friend goodbye." He traced her lips with his finger. "Then, you'll give me a fresh start." He leaned in, and before she knew it, he was forcing himself on her.

As his tongue pried its way between her teeth, a revulsion hit her so strongly she was actually queasy. When he separated from her, she involuntarily wiped her palm across her mouth.

"You're accompanying me to a charity event tomorrow night at The Millennium Hotel and I'm booking a suite for us—" he bent to whisper the rest in her ear, still gripping her "—so we can consummate this dirty deal of ours."

She stiffened. His eyes flashed. "You know what, the more you are repulsed by me—you're tightening up, wiping your face after I kiss you—the more I'm getting off on this. I can make you do all kinds of things to me you won't like. What a fucking kick." He pushed against her and ran his tongue over her ear and nibbled hard on her earlobe. She twisted away with a look of disgust, but he grabbed her chin and yanked it back, squeezing as he smashed her harder against the wall. "I'll be here tomorrow at three to get you. Wear something slutty under your dress. And you damn well better satisfy all my needs, or I'll go to the press." He left her, waltzing passed Bo with a triumphant grin.

Bo assessed her through the window. She was still rigid, against the wall, her hands shaking.

He shook his head.

CHAPTER THIRTY-FOUR

"**G**ood morning, sunshine."

"Heath." The sound of his cheerful voice ripped into her.

"Are you sure you really want to make chili for us and help us rake today? Doesn't sound like the life of a superstar to me?"

Tears rolled down her cheeks, but she tried to sound normal. "Umm, actually...I'm not feeling well today. I don't think I can make it." It wasn't a lie, her stomach was churning and she was lightheaded.

"Oh." His disappointment was obvious. "Do you need someone to come and take care of you?" he asked, suggestively.

Yesterday it would have made her laugh. *God, yes*! *I need you to take care of me.* "No," she said more forcefully than she intended. She made an attempt to lighten her voice, "I don't want you to see me like this."

"Don't be silly, Jazz. That's not important to me. I hope you know that."

Her hand flew to her stomach and she swallowed a sob. "I..." She knew she couldn't hold on much longer. Her voice was strained as she added, "I'm sorry. I think I've got to go."

"Okay, babe. You do sound awful. Get some rest." He paused. "Call me when you're feeling better."

She disconnected the phone and sat with her back against the couch, hugging her legs as the tears came harder. Finally she laid her head on her knees and bawled like she hadn't in ages, except when she was in Heath's arms and thinking of Tricia. But now, she wasn't in Heath's arms and she may never be again.

HEATH PULLED UP TO the curb and reached into the passenger seat for the Tupperware bowl of chicken soup. He chuckled to himself as he got out of the car, ready with a joke about Luke cooking it, so it was safe. As he turned to cross the street, he saw a couple exit the door of The Lofts.

Michael Veritek had on a tux and Jasmine was wearing an ankle-length dress. He couldn't have reported the color of the dress, only that Michael was touching her as he opened the door of a Porsche and helped her in. Veritek glanced in his direction and he instinctively spun around and acted busy with the lock of his car. He hesitated a second and then climbed behind the wheel, throwing the soup on the floorboard without caring if it spilled.

He followed the Porsche a few blocks to The Millennium Hotel, where Veritek escorted Jazz in, giving his keys to some lucky valet. Heath quickly found a place to park on the street and hustled into the lobby. No telling where they had gone to. He was going to try the hotel's five-star restaurant, when he saw a sign near a conference room door.

The Arch Supports the Arts
Fundraiser for the St. Louis Alliance for the Performing Arts
Keynote Speaker: Michael Veritek

So, she had to go to a charity event. Why would she lie to him in regards to that? From inside the room he could hear Veritek speaking, but couldn't distinguish the words. He contemplated trying to sneak in, but decided since he didn't know the layout of the room, not to chance it. He could be walking right into the front of the room with all gazes upon him. So, he would wait.

After a time, applause carried to him and he surmised Veritek was done. From a chair in the corner, hidden by a plant stand, he focused in on the door. After roughly a half hour, Veritek and Jazz appeared together. He was holding her hand and leading her, but not back to the car, as he had expected, but to a bank of elevators. He watched as they waited. Jasmine looked so beautiful, he thought with longing. He noticed the dress had an old-fashioned air to it, an antique white lace bodice, with wide, lace straps. The skirt was a vibrant, red silk. As soon as the door closed on them, he made a beeline for the desk. He flashed his badge. "Lieutenant McGowan. I need to know if Michael Veritek has a room here."

The young hotel clerk nervously typed in the name. "Yes sir, he has suite number 1301."

"Thanks," he called on the way to the elevator.

Once at the suite, he paced.

What are they doing here?

Another voice answered. *What do you think, you idiot? She lied to you, and she's in a hotel suite, dressed to kill, with a former boyfriend. What the hell do you think they're doing?"*

The real question became, what was he doing there? The elevator doors opened and a uniformed man carrying a bucket of ice that had a champagne bottle sticking out of it approached. With lightning speed, he hurriedly withdrew his ID.

JASMINE WAS ILL AGAIN. Michael was waltzing about the suite blabbering as if this was any normal day while putting her through hell. He actually expected her to make love to him in exchange for his silence. She'd do anything for Heath, but why did it have to be this? She felt so dirty, as she had from the first day Lionel Parker touched her. And now, to hop into bed with a man she was not in love with, it turned her stomach.

She stood on wobbly legs, "Michael, I can't do this."

He walked to her slowly, his shirt unbuttoned and untucked, cuffs open. "Jazz," he chided, then seemed to switch courses. "Okay." He shook his head. "If that's what you want. But I hope the officer's little boy won't get beat up at school when the newspapers carry stories zeroing in on his dad, the dirty cop."

She gaped at him. Could this be for real? "*Please,* Michael," she begged, her voice a whisper, "don't do this to me."

Someone knocked on the door. "Come in," Michael barked, irritated. "It's really not that bad, Jazz," he said, grabbing her wrists and jerking her into an embrace. The quick movement made the straps fall off her shoulders until they encircled her upper arms. He buried his face in her bosom and began to kiss her. She glanced at the room service attendant with embarrassment, and nearly fainted.

She staggered backward. "Heath!"

Michael whirled, a pleased sneer stealing over him when he saw Heath. "Oh, officer. Good to see you." He reached behind Jasmine and grabbed her wrist, squeezing it.

Heath's steely blue stare seemed to cut right into her. "Here's your cham-pagne, madam." He glared at her steadily, setting the bottle on a table with a violent clang. "But I thought you didn't like champagne, Jazz. Or was that another one of your lies?"

"Heath...I..." She almost yelped as Michael dug his fingers into her wrist.

"I'm sure she doesn't know what you're referring to, *Heath*," he added sar-donically.

"I'm referring to the lie she made when she slept with me yesterday."

"Oh, that," Veritek laughed, but his expression was hard. "She was doing that as a favor to me, so I could go and do my dastardly deeds."

"Is that it, Jasmine?"

She dropped her gaze. She couldn't bear to see the hurt in his eyes. It was killing her.

"You two have been playing me for a fool this whole time?" He turned his back to her angrily, clasping his hips. "Maybe the two of you committed the murders, too. I never considered you as a suspect, but I was wrong about you. Maybe I was wrong about that, too." He wheeled around. "It all makes complete sense," he said, gesturing wildly. "You seduced me after you killed your best friend."

Her head whipped up and her jaw tensed. "How could you?"

"How could *I*? How could *I*? Oh, that's rich, Jazz." He laughed humor-lessly. "You know what the really pathetic part is? I bought it all. I really thought you had feelings for me. But now I find you'll spread your legs for anybody."

She jolted as if he had physically struck her.

"All right, that's enough." Michael stepped toward Heath. "Unless you've got some proof we're guilty of a crime, I don't want you coming here any-more."

Heath's voice became icy. "Well that's fine, because I have no desire to see either of you anymore."

She couldn't bear to watch him walk away. She waited, braced herself for the slam of the door, but all she heard was a soft click, and still, it was a bullet shot through her heart.

"Jazz, I'm sorry that happened."

Her voice was a choked whisper. "Don't waste your breath when we both know you're not." She walked wearily across the room and into the bathroom, closing the door behind her.

Thirty minutes later, Michael waltzed into the bathroom. Jazz sat on the lid of the toilet, her legs carelessly apart, her forearms resting on her knees, her hands folded. Her mind was in a stupor.

"You didn't even have it locked?" He swung the half empty bottle of champagne in the direction of the bathroom door. He crouched in front of her and slid a finger underneath the lacy straps of her dress, running it along her skin. "I've been waiting for you."

She raised her gaze slowly, tears glistening on her cheeks. "I loved you at one time, you know," she said in wonder. "If you make me do this—" She stood and walked a few feet before spinning to plead with him. "I love him, Michael. This will kill me. I know it's over between Heath and I—" To say his name cost her, and she trembled as she covered her mouth briefly. "But I can't sleep with him one day, and sleep with you the next. I'm not made like that. I know some people do it, but I just can't."

He dropped his backside to the floor, and rested his arm on the toilet lid and glared at her.

"If you force me to have sex with you, I'll only be thinking of him." She didn't say it to hurt him, merely to make him understand. She had little hope he would.

Michael got to his feet slowly. He stood grasping his hips, duplicating Heath's stance earlier, his eyes staring, unseeing, into the corner of the ceiling. "Geez, Jazz. It's quite a blow to a man's ego to beg him not to have sex with you." He sighed. "If I let you off the hook tonight, you'll still have to pay to keep me from spilling the beans."

"*Anything.* I'll give you anything."

"And you can't see him."

"I think that's a moot point," she whispered miserably.

"If I don't get to sleep with you tonight, Jazz, you're gonna have to pay a pretty penny."

"I'll go to the bank in the morning."

CHAPTER THIRTY-FIVE

Heath knew he was far too agitated to get behind the wheel, so he headed across the street to a bar, perhaps not a wiser choice, but at least a more satisfying one. Thoughts were whirling dervishes in his mind, but the one he kept coming back to over and over again was, *how could I have done it a second time? How could I have let another woman play me?*

For God's sake, I'm a detective, paid to get inside people's minds, determine their motives, uncover their secrets...and I was a blind idiot when it came to Jasmine Barrett.

And this wound hurt much more than Juliette's leaving had. Even though they'd known each other for a much shorter period of time, he'd believed he knew Jazz, had connected with her on a deeper level than he'd ever connected with Juliette.

I guess I wasn't nearly as 'connected' as I thought.

He had consumed a great number of shots when he had the brilliant idea of confronting Jazz again. As he was rising from his bar stool to do so, his cell phone rang. After fumbling it several times, he finally managed to get it to his ear.

"Hello? Hello? Heath?"

"Hey, baby brother."

"I was getting worried something happened to you. How's Jazz feeling?"

He twirled one of his empty shot glasses around and then raised it to the bartender to ask for one more. "Oh, she's probably feeling fine now, drunk on champagne and doing the deed with Michael Veritek." He pounded down the shot that had arrived and signaled for one more. Maybe he wasn't ready to leave yet.

"What? What did you say? Where are you? It sounds like you've been drinking."

"Whoo. Very good, Luke. Maybe you shoulda been the friggin' detective. Is it too late for me to learn piano?"

"What the hell are you talking about? Where are you? Kole's here. I'll come to get you."

"In a bar on the opposite side of the street from The Millennium," he said begrudgingly. He ended the call. Ten minutes later, forgetting entirely Luke was on his way, he staggered across the street.

Michael Veritek opened the door and ran his hand up the frame, with a hip cocked. He held a mostly empty champagne bottle, but no glass was in sight. His gaze was unfocussed. "Well, well. To what do I owe the pleasure? Twice in one night, couldn't that be considered police harassment, officer?"

Heath grabbed him by his still unbuttoned shirt and exploded into the room. He quickly scanned the suite. "Listen, you prick. You're telling me where Jasmine is so she and I can speak, or I'm gonna beat the crap out of you. And even if you do, I still might beat the crap out of you." His voice was slurred, but his fists were sure.

Veritek shrugged. "I'm finished with her, man. We had our bit of fun—" He gestured to the bed. "—and she left. And if you lay a finger on me, I'll press charges so fast you won't even have time to make it to the lobby."

Heath shook him off. "I don't have time to waste on you." He stumbled to the door. "But I'll be back, you can count on it."

Luke was leaning against the Mustang with his arms crossed when he exited the building.

"Oh, shit," Heath muttered under his breath.

"'In a bar *across* from The Millennium.'"

"Sorry. I forgot."

"You forgot. ...Where have you been?"

He waved his hand in the general direction of the hotel. "Having a discussion with Michael Veritek."

That got Luke's attention. He stood quickly. "You didn't beat the crap out of him, did you?"

"No. I wanted to, but no."

He released a sigh of relief. "Where's Jazz?"

"How the hell should I know," he responded heatedly. "She and Veritek got done screwin' and she went home, I guess."

"What? Wait. Wait, wait, wait. Are you trying to tell me Jazz and Michael Veritek...?"

"Were getting it on. Sweatin' up the sheets. Doin' the horizontal tango. Do I have to draw you a friggin' picture?"

"No, no. Those colorful phrases will suffice. ...How do you know this?"

"How do I know this?" He paced a tiny circle in the street behind his car. "You know, you're a real pain in the ass sometimes, bro."

"I do my best. Well?"

"They've got a suite. I delivered champagne. He was half-dressed with his lips on her tits."

Luke paled. "She was...naked?"

"No. But things were definitely going that direction."

"Well, what did she say when she saw you?"

"Nothing."

"Nothing?"

"Nothing."

Luke thought about this, and then asked accusatorily, "What did *you* say?"

"Well, I was mad." Luke stared at him with that annoying look he had that made Heath want to punch him. "I was mad. I had a right to be." When Luke continued to glare at him, he added, sheepishly, "I may have implied...she was a whore."

"You what? You didn't. Tell me you didn't."

"Not in so many words...maybe."

"You didn't wait for an explanation, you just assumed."

"If it walks like a duck, and talks like a duck, it's probably a duck. They were in a hotel room with champagne and he was *kissing her*."

"Shit." Luke did his own little stroll back and forth. "I can't believe this." He paused. "So what happened next?"

"Well, basically I told them to go screw each other, which they were on the way to doing as it was, and left."

"So, you called her a whore, didn't wait for an explanation, and left. Basically, you've treated her like every other man in her life by assuming you know her and what she wants without even asking her."

"Oh, hell." Heath rolled his eyes. "I'm leaving." He hauled his keys from his pocket but Luke snatched them from his hands. "Hey!"

Luke grabbed him by his jacket and dragged him toward the bar. "We're getting some food into you, and then you'll go to Jazz's and apologize to her."

"Why are you always on her side?"

He hustled Heath through the door. "I'm not always on her side. I'm on the side that wants to see you two stay together. Jazz is the best thing that's ever happened to you and I'm not sitting by and watching you blow it. There must be some explanation. The Jazz I know wouldn't do something like that to you."

Heath wanted to say, "You don't know the real Jazz," but he knew his brother was the eternal optimist and he really didn't want to discuss it with him anymore. Luke was making him feel confused, and he didn't need any help in that department.

So, when Luke went to the bathroom, Heath snuck out.

CHAPTER THIRTY-SIX

The ten block walk sobered him a little, but did nothing for his temperament. As much as he endeavored to hate her, he couldn't quite pull it off. He kept seeing her face. There had been no trace of defiance in it. No attempt to deny. Something was wrong. He couldn't quite put his finger on it.

Then he remembered Vertek's expression, so smug. And his hands on her. And by the time he made it to the condo, he was furious again.

He pounded his fists on the door. "Jasmine. Open up!"

Brody Barrett opened the door, freshly home from the hospital, flanked by Bo. "Detective," he said coolly, "I don't think you are welcome anymore."

"Where's Jasmine?" Heath rocked unsteadily on his feet and panted, exhausted from beating on the door. "We need to talk."

"On the contrary," the older man snapped. "I think you've said quite enough. My niece, who is normally not an excitable person, has been crying for the last hour and the most I can get from her is your name. So whatever it was you said to her, and it must have been pretty bad to make her this upset, you're done speaking with her. In fact, I'm calling the police station in the morning and having you dismissed from the case. I don't want you darkening my doorstep again." Brody tried to close the door, but Heath slipped in. Bo immediately grabbed him.

"Jasmine. Jasmine!" Heath struggled to get past, but Bo had his jacket in a vise and was giving no advantage.

JASMINE WAS ON THE balcony, still wearing her dress, but now with her uncle's suit coat. She was shivering from the cold, but she was too numb to move, and there was no longer any safe haven for her to retreat to. The killer had invaded her home and stolen her best friend and her sense of security. She was also too full of self-loathing to consider her own discomfort.

But after a bit, she became aware of the disturbance. She sought to open the door, but found it locked. Peering between the slats of the vertical blinds, she saw Heath fighting against Bo like a man possessed.

"Throw him out," Brody said precisely.

Jasmine began banging her fists on the window. "Don't. Let go of him! Heath!" She cried urgently, but wasn't heard above their arguing.

AS BO PUSHED HIM THROUGH the door, Heath fought to stay, grabbing hold of the door frame and trying desperately to gain access to the condo. "This isn't over, Jazz. *We're* not over. I won't give up on us." As he said it, he realized it was true. He wasn't about to let what they had together die.

With one final surge, Bo got him beyond the door and slammed it in his face. Heath laid his forehead against the cool door in frustration. Unable to devise an alternate way in, he turned and left.

"HANGOVERS HURT," HEATH muttered, rubbing his temples.

"Really?" Luke responded, sarcastically shocked at the news.

"Why didn't you stop me?"

"Why didn't I stop you?" Luke screamed at a level Heath thought was likely to split his head wide open. "If you weren't already in a miserable condition, I'd smack you upside that stubborn head of yours."

He wasn't really mad at Luke. He was grateful to his little brother for driving him home the night before. When he got back to his car, Luke was waiting, sitting on the ground, leaning against the Mustang. Seeing how dejected Heath was, he didn't ask any questions, simply opened the passenger-side door for him and got in to drive.

"Are you going to her place?" Luke asked now, eager to see Heath and Jasmine reunited.

"As soon as my head ceases to roll around of its own accord, yes," Heath snapped.

Luke rose and silently left the room. Heath felt bad for barking at him. He was actually proud of Luke. After their parents had died, Heath had tried hard to keep him on the straight and narrow, and in the end, Luke turned out to be a better man than he was. He had a generous nature, was fiercely loyal and never went off half-cocked, like Heath tended to do.

I could learn a thing or two from him. And as soon as the tiny jack-hammers in my brain quit their banging, I'll let him know that.

He moped for the rest of the day, half-hoping Jazz would call, yet knowing she wouldn't. When his eyes opened that morning, he found himself on the pillow she had used and he could smell her there. He flipped to seek her, and the movement sent cymbals crashing in his skull, reminding him of his personal shot war, and the reason for it.

But try as he might, he couldn't quit thinking of her. His mind would drift to her, particularly to the way she looked last night when he walked in on them. Her straps were on her upper arms leaving her shoulders bare and the skin was so invitingly creamy. Her beautiful jade green eyes opened wide in shock, her gorgeous mouth gaping with surprise. But it was another man she let touch that skin, he reminded himself, another man who gazed into those eyes and kissed those lips, and then he would find himself fuming all over again.

At three o'clock, when the battlefield in his cranium had gone silent and his stomach had quit lurching at any reference to food, he decided to go to her.

LIKE A SCENE FROM *Groundhog's Day*, Brody Barrett slowly opened the door to him. "Well, well, well. What do we have here? Detective, I wasn't expecting you." He gave Heath a hard glare, his jaw set.

He had been so focused on Jasmine, it hadn't even occurred to him Brody might open the door. He stood awkwardly, trying to come up with something to say. "I'm sorry about last night."

Brody studied him coolly, then retreated and let the door swing open. "Come on in."

He instinctively searched the room for Jasmine.

"She's not here," Brody noted, taking his drink from the table. "Want some scotch?"

Heath winced.

"Ooh. I forgot. That was thoughtless of me." His sneer told Heath he had mentioned the alcohol on purpose, guessing he would have the mother of all hangovers. Brody took a drink from his glass, eying him appraisingly. "You don't think much of me, do you?"

He cast around in his mind for a diplomatic answer to that question. "I know Jasmine thinks the world of you, and I respect her."

He smiled, "What a disappointingly safe answer." He stood, gazing through the window with his back to Heath. Heath began to feel extremely uncomfortable. He was licking his lips to say something benign to break the awkward silence, when Brody spoke.

"You think I am too tough on Jasmine." He sighed, staring into his drink. "And you are right. I'm controlling, insensitive..." He turned to Heath. "You're right. I don't deserve her and I know that." It was as if he was pleading his case. "But I lived as a single man for a number of years before my brother and his wife died. I didn't know how to take care of a little girl, especially a little girl who was so broken," he added thoughtfully. "I was selfish. I made mistakes. But there was not one second I didn't love her, in my own warped sort of way. She's been nothing but good to me since the day I first came to see her in the hospital, after the accident." He stopped, unsure of what to say next.

"I'm sure you did your best. I am raising a son myself, and I know it's not easy."

"Yes, I did my best. But it wasn't enough, was it?" This kind of soul-searching seemed like unchartered territory for Brody, and Heath wasn't surprised when he slipped into the more familiar act of placing the blame on others. "And then you come along and fill her head with your pretty ideas about being independent, and off she goes." He made birdlike movements with his hands.

Heath absorbed this for a minute, but then abruptly sat forward. "You mean she's not here?"

"Packed her bags this morning. She told me it was her idea, but it was you, wasn't it?"

Heath ignored the question. "Where is she?"

"How the hell would I know? She told me she'd contact me after she'd had 'some time to think.'"

"Is Bo with her?" he asked in alarm.

"No. She told Bociefus to go home."

"But she could be in grave danger. The killer's still out there."

"Well why do you think I've been ripping the hair from my scalp all morning?"

He jumped up and strode toward the door not glancing back.

"You'll call me when you find her? ...Detective?"

Heath didn't even bother to shut the door behind him.

CHAPTER THIRTY-SEVEN

Michael Veritek opened the door to the trailer himself.
"Damn. Do I need to get you your own friggin' parking space, detective?"

"Where's Jazz?"

"Haven't seen her."

Heath growled, stepping toward him. He hadn't noticed the bodyguard feet away, but he took notice when the big man pinned him against the wall. "Where's Jazz?" he spat while struggling with the bigger man.

"Too bad I can't hit you because you're a cop," the guard sniped. "Then again, you didn't announce yourself as a cop." He landed a few square punches to Heath's midsection.

Veritek turned, as if bored with the scene, "I told you. I don't know."

Since he was no longer fighting, the brute quit pounding on him. Though breathing heavily, he managed to get out, "Have you seen her since last night?"

"No. And it's a shame really. I would have loved to have another spin on the Jazzie-Go-Round this morning. Mmm."

"You give me another chance, when this behemoth isn't around to defend you, and—"

"I don't feel the need to prove my manhood and I'm not about to risk marring this face," he answered, inspecting his skin in the mirror. "The director wouldn't like it."

He debated over whether to tell Veritek of Jazz's disappearance or not. If he were the killer, Heath would be letting him know Jazz was totally unprotected and he might make his move on her. He made a decision. "Jazz is gone. As in, alone, without security... that kind of gone."

Michael spun. "W-well, you've got to find her," he stammered, his concern showing in his features. He gestured, irritated, for the bodyguard to let him go.

Heath straightened his coat. "That's the plan. You have any ideas where to search for her?"

"No." He sat in a chair slowly. "None whatsoever." He sighed. "You can track her though, right? Through her credit card purchases or something."

"Unfortunately, she seems to be paying in cash. She made a large withdrawal earlier." Did he see a flicker of something in Veritek's expression? He found one of his cards and laid it on the table across from Veritek, sliding it in front of him. "If you remember anything, *anything*, give me a call." He stalked off. As soon as he was outside the trailer, he dialed his cell phone. "Davis, I need a tail put on someone." Even if Veritek wasn't the killer, he still knew more than he was saying, and he might be able to lead Heath right to Jazz. Or, if he were the killer, he wanted to have him followed to protect her.

HEATH HAD PUSHED AWAY from his desk and was staring blankly at the computer screen. Jasmine withdrew a hundred thousand dollars from her banking account and closed all of her credit card accounts. She didn't want to be found. His sole consolation was, if he couldn't find her, then it was likely the killer couldn't find her either. His singular hope was a fellow cop would see her somewhere. He could go to the press and have all of America looking for her, but that would alert the murderer to her disappearance. He would save that as his last card. As long as they were the only ones who knew she was missing, they would be one step ahead of the killer.

Where would she go? She had no friends to target and millions of acquaintances. She hadn't taken a plane, train, or bus to flee the city, that he could tell, but if she had paid cash, they may not have asked for an ID and she could have given them any name. The more he spun his wheels on how he could find her, the more frustrated he became.

If the killer doesn't get to her first, I'm going to kill her when I find her.

But then again, he couldn't really blame her for wanting to disappear. He'd acted like a jerk. Luke's words kept floating through his mind.

"...So...you called her a whore, didn't wait for an explanation and left. Basically, you've treated her like every other man in her life by assuming you know her and what she wants, without even asking her." God, how he hated it when Luke was right.

Despair crept over him. She was out there somewhere, on her own, and he was at least partially to blame. Try as he might, he couldn't come up with a way to find her so he could protect her from a man who may want her dead. How could a woman who had once made him feel so powerful now leave him feeling so powerless? What good was it to be a cop, if you couldn't protect the woman you loved? And he did love her, he knew that. No matter what her relationship with Michael Veritek was, he would fight for her. His head was filled with a dull roar. He decided to go home to be with his family. Maybe some distance could clear his thoughts and then he would be able to find a solution.

CHAPTER THIRTY-EIGHT

Three weeks had passed since Heath and Jazz's argument at the hotel. She hadn't been sighted, in paper, or in person, and he was beyond frazzled. He wandered outside after putting Jack to bed and gazed at the moon with his hands in his pocket.

"You really miss her, don't you?"

He hadn't even heard Luke approach. He didn't bother to answer at first, but accepted the beer his brother passed him. "I'm really worried for her. He's out there—somewhere—and I can't do anything to protect her."

"She'll call you eventually. She's just cooling off."

"Nah, man. I don't think so. She's doing what I told her to do, making a life for herself. Only, the way I'd imagined it, I'd be a part of it. But I ruined that." He took a long pull on his beer.

"Somehow, I believe you guys will make it past this."

He gave his brother a sideways look. "My God, you are painfully optimistic."

He shrugged with a grin. "Can't help it."

Heath snorted, taking another drink. "Thanks for the beer."

Luke turned to go in. "You coming?"

"Yeah. In a second."

He lay awake that night, as he had so many nights before, watching the car lights zoom around his bedroom ceiling, and the dancing shadows of tree branches, thinking of her, wondering if she were safe, wondering if she were thinking about him. A thousand images of her played in his mind. He saw her again as he had the first night he met her, in her robe, paralyzed with fear and shock. Or he imagined her as she was at the Tigers game, cheeks chilled, eyes sparkling, her enthusiasm practically making her vibrate. Or he envisioned the cat-like creature that had crawled across the stage to him. Or her laughter as she felt the syrup stuck in her hair after their risqué breakfast.

The phone sliced into his personal slide show. He twisted to stare at it for a moment in disbelief, and its ring cut through the house again. He dove for it, lying on his stomach, on his elbows. "Jazz?"

"Uh...Detective McGowan, please?"

He sat, chagrined. "Franklin, this is Heath. What's up?"

"Oh. Heath, I'm calling you from St. Luke's in Chesterfield." Heath's heart beat faster. "Michael Veritek was brought in a little while ago with multiple stab wounds."

"Thanks, Franklin. I'll be right there."

He released a breath as he sat on the edge of the mattress. He thought for a minute he would hear Jasmine was hurt...or worse. He reached for his shoes. Maybe now he'd get some answers.

THE SUN HAD RISEN BY the time they wheeled Michael Veritek from surgery to the intensive care unit. Heath paced the halls, drinking cup after cup of stale hospital coffee, making him both jittery and tired. A doctor exited Veritek's room.

"You can ask him a few questions. Only a few."

When he opened the door, Veritek didn't move. He was deathly pale and seemed fragile, but when he saw Heath, he lifted a finger to call him to the bed.

"Michael, do you know who did this to you?"

He shook his head almost imperceptibly. Heath had to get closer to hear him whisper. "Jazz...you have to save her."

"What are you talking about? Did your attacker say something?"

"No, no." He shut his eyes as if gathering strength. "I didn't see anybody. The lights were off and when I tried to switch them on, they didn't work. It all happened so fast. The whole thing took maybe ten seconds. All I remember is pain ripping into me over and over again. I have to tell you...I have to tell you..." His voice drifted away.

"What, Michael? What do you have to tell me?" he asked desperately.

"I shouldn't have done it."

"Shouldn't have done what?"

"I made Jazz come with me...told her I would call the police chief, tell him that the two of you were getting cozy...call the press...she didn't want to...but I made her."

A chill ran up Heath's spine. "What are you saying?"

Veritek grabbed his wrist harder than the detective thought he could in such a weak condition. "I b-blackmailed her. She wanted to protect you from the publicity. I told her you could lose your job. Shit. I even brought your damn kid into it. But she couldn't bring herself to sleep with me." He could see how much this pained him. "...so I took fifty thousand from her. I was wrong. I still love her—" He opened his brilliant green eyes to tell him "—but she loves you, man. She loves you."

Heath lowered his chin and squeezed his eyes shut. How could he have been so wrong?

"Detective," the doctor said from behind him, "I think that's enough."

Heath wanted to thank Veritek, but he had fallen asleep.

HEATH HAD CHECKED MICHAEL Veritek's bank accounts. A fifty thousand dollar deposit had been made the day Jazz had disappeared. He was telling the truth. Heath knew he had to find her, but he'd exhausted all of his ideas. Then he remembered something an old sergeant told him. "When you run out of answers, start again from the beginning and maybe you'll discover you've missed something."

He reopened her file and read from the top. Five minutes into it, his gaze narrowed in on a single sentence:

Born and raised in Kirkwood.

It was the only place, outside of L.A., she had ever lived. He proceeded to call realtors. On the third one he sensed a hesitation.

"Listen. Ms. Barrett is in danger. If you know something you have to tell me."

"If I were to have seen Jasmine Barrett...how could I know you are a cop for sure?"

"I'll come to you. Show you my badge and ID."

After a long pause, she gave him directions to her office.

He borrowed a squad car to give him more credence. To her credit, the realtor was very thorough. She took his badge number and phoned head-quarters herself.

She returned to the front of the office with a slip of paper. "I wanted to make sure. Ms. Barrett was very clear we were not to give her address to any-one, but she did rent from us. This is the address."

"Thank you," he said with relief, rising from his chair.

"She asked us not to tell anyone...but I don't want anything to happen to her. She was very nice. Really sweet. Down-to-earth." The woman looked at him worriedly.

"You did the right thing." He shook her hand and then left, following the directions written for him.

On the way over to the house, he called Luke. Without any introduction he said, "I found her."

Luke blew out a sigh of relief. "Thank God! Go make this right, Heath, make things right with her. I'll stay here with Jack until you get back, when-ever that is."

"You're the best, bro."

Luke swallowed his usual retort and simply said, "Good luck."

CHAPTER THIRTY-NINE

When Heath pulled to the curb in front of her place, he had to smile. It had Jazz written all over it. On a relatively busy street in a quiet, older, tree-shaded neighborhood, the pretty bungalow was set deep on the lot. Large stepping stones ran from her door to the street's sidewalk and flower beds flocked the edges in straight lines. Dark, cedar shingle siding was lightened by the white dainty trim and shutters. A small, ground level shaded porch had enough room for two rockers and a small table. He waited for a car to pass, and then jogged across the street to knock on her door. After waiting several minutes, he shaded his eyes to peer in the large, paned windows to the right and left of the door. The interior was as homey as he expected it to be, and immaculate. The wood floors were polished to a high gleam, and he could see her sheet music spread out on the coffee table. Impatient, he decided to try another door. It had been three weeks and his heart beat in anticipation of seeing her.

He walked around the home, following another series of stones to a white, arched gate. He unlatched it, swinging it in. He took a moment to examine the area, sticking his hands in his pockets and grinning appreciatively. The yard wasn't very large, but was nicely landscaped with shady spots under two huge oaks in the corners, one with a bench, one with a hammock. Lights were strung in the trees and a little fountain flowed, creating pleasant background music. A small patio had a couple of Adirondack chairs separated by a matching table, all painted white.

He moved toward the house and approached the French doors of the patio. He knocked and then again shaded his eyes to survey the inside. Luckily she left the shades on the doors up. Her bedroom was largely occupied by a king-sized bed with a simple white comforter. On a table near it, he recognized the picture from the baseball game, unframed, but tilted against the lamp so she could see it. She hadn't forgotten him then. Opposite the foot of the bed was a long dresser with a mirror. He caught sight of her purse on top of the dresser. She was probably home then. Why wasn't she answering the door?

He was about to knock again when his gaze fell on a bright red droplet on the floor. He looked further into the room and noticed a trail of what he assumed was blood. His heart pounding, he reached into his holster and drew his revolver. Had he found her, only to be too late? He tried the door and found it locked. Desperately he rattled it, hoping to somehow jar it loose. He kept searching for a sign of her, but seeing none, he switched his grip on his gun, clicked on the safety, and took hold of the muzzle, turning his face away to hit the glass with the butt. With a loud crash, the pane by the handle shattered.

JASMINE RELAXED IN the tub, indulging herself with hot bath water, cold wine, and candles surrounding her during the middle of the day, just because she could. She had found she liked living on her own, being independent, and able to choose what she wanted to do at any time. She could go to bed at nine if she wanted, or wake at three a.m. to eat a bowl of chocolate chip ice cream. She could walk to the grocery store or take a nap in her hammock.

She tried to forget how much she missed Heath, and Jack, and Luke, and even Kole and her uncle. She wondered if Heath was giving Jack a bath now, or if it was "Pizza Night." Night time was the worst, when she had nothing to occupy her thoughts except images of him. She craved the taste of his lips and the warmth of his smile. She remembered how softly he could caress her, even with his big hands. She was haunted by the thought of how good it was to simply put her arm through his, to walk next to him, to talk about everything and about nothing.

Yesterday she'd seen the neighbor boy playing catch with his dad and her heart stopped. They'd looked at her once and she lowered her gaze so they wouldn't see the tears in her eyes. Shaking, she'd dropped the mail she'd gotten from her box and hurriedly bent to gather it and head into the house before anyone could approach her. On the other side of the door, she wept, leaning against the curtained glass. Her stomach was raw and she wondered how long she would go on hurting. She pushed her way through it because she knew she had no choice. Still, she'd be flipping channels and hear the sound of a baseball game and it would begin all over again, thoughts of Heath and Jack at the ball park, or of the sound of his deep voice in her ear, teasing her as he corrected her batting stance.

She slipped into one of these memories while she bathed and spoiled the mood. She climbed from the tub feeling soggy, not refreshed. She extinguished the candles angrily and that's when she heard the knock on the door. It startled her so much she dropped her wine glass and it shattered as it nicked the edge of the sink. She was so unused to visitors the sound was entirely out of place. She chided herself.

It's probably only the neighbor kids playing Ding and Ditch.

Regardless, she decided not to answer it; she would at least take that precaution. She hurriedly scrambled into her bra and panties and tried to collect at least the bigger pieces of glass. The shards shifted as she moved to get a sliver from behind the toilet and she sliced her finger open. Sucking on it in irritation, she dumped the rest of the glass into the trash can. She had stowed the first aid kit in the kitchen, since there was so little storage in the bathroom. She pulled her white robe on, being careful not to get any blood on it, and decided to grab her slippers by the bed so she wouldn't cut her feet too.

Dang these tiny cuts hurt.

When she picked up her slippers, she accidentally lessened the pressure on her cut and it dripped. "Agh!" she cried in frustration. She retrieved the first aid kit and returned to the bathroom.

That's when she heard the crash. Someone had broken into her house. She heard footsteps and panicked. She was trapped.

How ironic. How many times have I watched a horror movie and told the victim to never go in the shower. Now I'll get killed in the shower. What am I going to do?

HEATH GUIDED HIS HAND between the jagged fragments of the glass and opened the door. Cautiously, he crept into the room. Late afternoon shadows made it difficult to see, but he made an attempt to follow the trail of blood while still keeping his head high in case of attack. A large drop of blood shone on the white tile threshold under the bathroom door. He gripped the door knob and inhaled. He twisted the handle, and let the door open of its own accord, prudently keeping his gun at the ready. But the bathroom was bare. He was about to spin and leave when he noticed a smear of blood on the shower curtain. He took a step and heard the crunch of glass. Knowing whoever was behind the curtain knew of his presence, he hurriedly whipped the curtain back.

Jasmine screamed, cringing in the corner of the tub.

"Holy shit, Jazz. You scared the crap out of me."

"Heath!" Hysterical, she threw her arms around him.

"Come here, babe. It's all right." He holstered his gun, and with one arm circling her waist, drew her from the tub. "You're bleeding."

"I-I cut myself on the glass," she stammered, still trying to slow her breathing. He turned on the tap and held her injury under the stream. Belatedly, he noticed the first-aid kit on the toilet.

Watching the water run red down the drain he exclaimed, "Shit. Do you think you need stitches?"

"No. It's not deep," she responded, examining it. "It's just bleeding a lot."

"Here. Let me wrap it." He grabbed a towel from a holder and offered it to her.

Jazz laughed, relief making her a little giddy. "That's a guest towel."

"Oh," he said with a reciprocal grin, "well, we can't have that. Where are the towels you use when you're bleeding all over the place?"

"Under the sink."

She had to maneuver in the tight space so he could reach into the cabinet. He was so close to her he could smell her familiar scent and it was making him salivate. He wrapped her wound in the towel and applied pressure. He smiled at her hesitantly. "I've gotten pretty good at this with Jack."

Heath saw it in her eyes, the memory of all the hurtful things he'd said to her in that hotel room. "Jazz, I'm sorry."

She backed away, pulling free from the towel and bumping into the door with an expression of stark fear. "Don't, Heath. Don't." She shook her head, the tears threatening to spill.

Noticing the slit in her skin was gushing again, he mumbled, "Okay. Okay. Let me fix your finger." Gently, he cared for her while neither said a word. Jazz first regarded him warily, but then seemed to erect a wall between them, retreating inward, like he had seen her do with her uncle. When he was finished bandaging it, he rubbed his thumbs on the heel of her palm. No one else would have realized she was cringing, but he had come to know even the most subtle changes in her features. "There. I think it should quit bleeding. Can we talk?"

She hesitated, but then nodded dumbly, and led him into the living room. She sat in the corner of the couch, and he sat on the coffee table across from her, unconsciously mimicking their positioning the first time they met. He took her hands and she didn't retreat, which he took as a good sign, but she lowered her gaze, unable to look at him. "I've missed you, Jazz. More than I ever thought I could miss anybody."

Her head bobbed slightly, but then she shook it. "I can't do this," she said, her voice barely a whisper. She jumped to her feet and started to flee from the room then froze, suddenly, with her back to him. "I'm sorry," she said, clearly struggling for composure. She turned to him. "You accused me once of running from my problems. I don't want to do that anymore. I've wanted to see you so badly. Dreamed of you in my life again, both waking and sleeping. But now you are here, actually here, I'm afraid." She stared at her bandage. "This can't work."

When he stood and moved toward her, he noted the pain shielded in her eyes. "Jazz, you don't understand how sorry I am."

She took a step away from him, waving in front of her. "No, please, I can't." Her chin quivered. "Heath, you don't understand. We can't."

"What, because of what Michael Veritek threatened to do?"

She paled. "He told you?"

"Yeah, he told me. He told me what you were willing to do for me and I-I—" This time it was he who stammered. "—can't believe it. You would have..."

She covering her face in shame. "I didn't want to. I didn't want to."

He grabbed her biceps. "Jazz honey, I know it. I know you wouldn't have done something like that unless forced to. I was wrong to say the things I said, to believe things about you I shouldn't have. It's just...when I saw him touch you in that hotel room, I went ballistic. I wanted to be the one man to touch you. But I didn't even stop to ask you. If only you could know how terribly sorry I am for having hurt you." Her sobs shook her so hard he thought she would fall apart. He took her cheeks, slick with tears, and lifted her head. "I love you, babe. And I don't want to be without you anymore. Please say you'll forgive me."

She seemed confused and stunned for a second. "I can't...lose you again. It hurt too much."

"You won't have to. I'm here. And I'm not going anywhere."

She slipped her arms around him and put her head on his chest. He clutched her to him, his whole body giving a sigh of relief until she spoke again. "I don't know. I'm so confused. Michael could still cause trouble for you."

"No, Jazz. He won't anymore. He said he was sorry."

"He did?" For the first time, her voice contained hope, but she frowned. "But how can we trust him?"

He raised her face again. "Even if he did, you mean more to me than any job. Don't you understand?"

"Oh, Heath," she said, relaxing in his embrace. "I've missed you so much."

Before she could say anything else, he kissed her, tenderly at first, but his lips became searing with his suppressed desire. He'd dreamed of this for weeks, of holding her, her body pressed against him, her lips warm and sensuous under his. His hands slid slowly along the column of her perfect neck and under the thick fabric of her robe. Something was unbelievably erotic in her being almost entirely nude underneath such a thick barrier. He separated the sides to find the silky core beneath and the pulsing beat of her passion.

He changed angles on the kiss so he could swoop her up. She clung more tightly, and her breasts pressing against him, the tantalizing fragrance of her skin, the quickening of her breath in response to him, it all heightened his urgency. His heart pounded with a nearly animal need to have her. He kicked the partially-opened door to the bedroom wider so he could fit through with her and laid her on the bed.

Her robe fell completely open and she lay there, looking both innocent and insanely sexy at the same time. Her cheetah-spotted bra and panties contrasted boldly with the white of the robe and comforter and his lone thought was,

Of course. It had to be a cheetah print.

He often imagined her lithe body encapsulating the stealthy grace of the big cat. She was observing him carefully now, with her cat-like eyes, waiting for his next move.

He shrugged out of his holster, setting it gently on the dresser and then fought open the buttons on his shirt, all the while focusing on her and the unprecedentedly intense desire she stirred in him. Then, unable to wait any more, he touched her, merely her foot, and begged himself to be patient. He climbed onto the bed, peering at her. "Is this what you want?"

She caressed his face. He hadn't shaved. Then, with the mildest pressure, she pulled him down. "I love you. This has always been what I wanted." She closed her eyes and let him take her to bliss. Neither had shared themselves so completely, so magnetically, with anyone before. He watched her, witnessed what his love did to her, and what their love did to him, he knew nothing would ever be the same for him. She had truly rocked his world, and created something new and brilliant with him, something he could no longer live without.

WHEN THE MORNING LIGHT broke through the French doors and nudged Heath awake, he turned to find Jasmine. Their legs were still tangled together and the sheet was stretched diagonally across her stomach, leaving her chest exposed and he thought he had never seen a more beautiful sight. "Jazz, wake up," he said softly.

She stirred and then opened her eyes. "Good morning," she said sleepily.

He gathered her in until her back melded with him, his arms hooked under her breasts, his mouth to her ear. He kissed her neck then whispered, "I want to wake every morning like this. I've made mistakes in the past, but I know I can get this right with you. You have changed everything in my life and it will never be the same." He paused. "I know this isn't how I should ask you, but I have to know. I can't wait another minute."

He hesitated until she flipped over to look at him curiously.

"Will you build a life with me? Let me be the one to hold you when you're sad, to tease you, to make your heart beat faster?" He gazed into her eyes which had gone from sleepily content to wide-open and awake. "Marry me. Be my wife. I can't stand another day with you not in it. Please, say you will."

Her lips quivered and the vibrant green of her eyes swam with tears. "Oh, my God." He held his breath. She put her bandaged hand on his cheek. "Nothing would make me happier."

He kissed her joyfully, but separated from her after only a few seconds. "I'll do this better later, I promise. With the whole ring and everything and some big, romantic lead-up—"

She laid a finger on his lips. "Nothing you could do could beat this." She confirmed it with a mind-numbing kiss.

CHAPTER FORTY

They lay in bed for hours making plans, and when it was time, finally, for Heath to leave, Jasmine had a hard time parting with him. They kissed in her front doorway, he in his suit coat, she still in her robe. "We'll talk to Jack first, and then we'll swear him to secrecy and go to dinner tonight and tell the whole family."

"I can't wait."

He had decided to get his mother's wedding ring from the safety deposit box and surprise Jazz with it in advance of their leaving for the restaurant. "You lock this door behind me, and don't let anybody in. I'll call a glass repair man as soon as I get to the squad room."

SHE WATCHED FROM THE window and waved until he disappeared. She sighed with something deeper than contentment, with happiness, and hope, and anticipation of all the sweet times ahead. She dawdled on her way to the bedroom, already thinking about what she should wear to dinner.

She came to an abrupt halt. The door was open, and he was sitting in the chair, a gun in his lap.

"Jazz, darling. At long last."

She bolted for the door, reached it, and got the top lock twisted before he grabbed her by the hair. She shrieked as he retraced their steps, dragging her to the bedroom.

"Not a very polite method of greeting your guest," Lionel hissed in her ear.

She clutched at her robe as he threw her roughly to the floor where she lay sprawled, stunned briefly. After recovering, she scrambled to a seated position with her back to the bed.

"Did you sleep with him?" he said coolly, gesturing to the rumpled bed with his gun.

"Wh-what?"

"It's a pretty straightforward question, Jazz. *Did you sleep with him?* he screamed, advancing toward her.

"Y-yes. Yes!" Her hands shook as she extended them to shield herself from him.

He moved quickly to get around her defenses, striking her with full force. "WHORE! I knew you were nothing but a tramp the first time I touched you. And yet, I've never been able to rid you from my system," he finished with a tenderness that contrasted drastically with his statements of the previous seconds. He squatted next to her, and stroked the cheek where he'd struck her, even as she cringed. "Get up," he said, his mood changing in a flash again. "Get up, dammit. Up on your feet." Grabbing her elbow, he forced her to her feet. "Now it's my turn. And you will do to me, everything you did to him, and then some. Take off your robe."

"Wait!" she screamed, startling them both. "Wait. Y-you...killed Trish?" her voice rose in pitch, as if to deny it even as she questioned it.

"Oh, yes. Popped her neck like a chicken and squeezed the life out of her."

Her eyes widened and vomit rose in her throat. She fought to keep it down. "Why?" she said weakly. "Why would you do that?"

"Oh, golly," he said sarcastically, "let's see, why? Hmm." He laid a finger against his chin as if contemplating, then barked, "To repay you for the hell you put me through the last thirteen years."

"The hell *I* put *you* through?" she answered, incredulous.

"That's right. You didn't think it hurt me when you left me without so much as a goodbye? I was in love with you."

"I was twelve years old," she said, her anger seething. "I was a child. You raped me."

She didn't expect the blow that came, knocking her against the bed frame.

"Don't you ever say anything so vile again. We were in love, Jazz. In love! And you left me."

To her utter amazement, his voice broke. She stood in stunned silence for a minute, then asked quietly. "And Sam Dobski?"

"Oh. You really should thank me for that one. Sneaky little bastard," Lionel quipped proudly, his voice whipping from one extreme to another like a prize-winning roller coaster. "And I would have killed that creature you call your uncle if you hadn't stepped in and saved him." He moved closer to her. "I'll never understand your misguided loyalties." He ran his knuckles along her face, letting his focus wander to the edges of her robe. She drew them together. His gaze snapped to hers and hardened, but then he spun on his heel and walked several feet away. Jasmine quickly scanned the room, searching for a weapon. Her attention was drawn to a heavy lamp as he pivoted. "And I killed Michael Veritek, too," he added blandly.

"What?" she asked breathlessly, all thoughts of a weapon abandoned.

"Stabbed him. Repeatedly. Damn boy even bleeds pretty."

"No," she said weakly. Trembling, she lowered herself onto the bed. "Oh, God, no."

"Oh, Jazz, really," he scolded, coming to sit by her on the bed. He clamped onto her knee. In her shock, she didn't even take notice initially. "Don't waste any tears on him, honey. He wasn't worth it. He was never worthy of you. Of course, your cop boyfriend will be the next to go," he stated matter-of-factly.

"Heath? No, Lionel, no. You'll have to kill me first."

"Oh, I have no problem with a change in the order," he said brightly. He ran the tip of the gun down her cheek pointedly. "But first, we'll have some fun. For old time's sake. Take that robe off, Jazz," he commanded, his voice now brittle.

"No. I won't let you do it to me."

He grabbed her by the hair again, and she involuntarily shrieked as he yanked her to her feet. She clawed at the fingers buried in her hair, but he did not release her. Instead the director forced her to her knees at the side of the bed, the hardwood ripping the skin open on both knees. He knelt by her solemnly, inches from her as he hissed, "Then say your prayers, Jazzie, 'cause I'm going to kill you."

The cold muzzle pressed against her temple and she squeezed her eyes shut. "Oh, God. Oh, God," she said, shaking.

"Fold your hands. Fold your damn hands!" he shouted insanely.

Desperate, she did as she was told.

"That's it, Jazz. Good girl," he murmured in her ear, still jerking on her hair. He pushed her head forward and relinquished his hold on her, withdrawing the gun a bit and standing to gloat over her. "You're pitiful. One pitiful bitch. Take off—"

He didn't really get a chance to finish his command as she swung her arms as hard as she could, from her kneeling posture, at the gun. It clattered from his grasp and she sprang across the bed, trying to make it to the French doors. His nails dug into her calves, and he drag her backward. Screaming, she grabbed for the edge of the bed, desperately trying to pull herself away from him.

"You little bitch!" he screamed, his voice hysterically shrill. He straddled her and pried her grip from the mattress. She was surprised by how strong he still was, considering his age. He rose on his knees, giving her room to flip, which she did, in order to get in a better position to fight him, but he seized her neck, strangling her. Her breath left in a whoosh. Panicked, she tried to dislodge him, digging her nails into his flesh, but he tightened his grip all the more. "Well, it would have been fun to fuck you alive, but I'll fuck you dead if I have to," he sneered bitterly.

Jasmine saw their reflection in the ceiling fan above, the ceiling fan she had dismantled by herself so that she could search for cameras. Foolish, she thought now, and paranoid. Sam Dobski was dead, and no one else even knew where she was. As the oxygen became scarce, she felt inebriated. Strangely she thought about how she was marrying Heath. He would look so handsome in his tux, and they'd get Jack a matching tux.

Those were her last thoughts as she went into the blackness.

CHAPTER FORTY-ONE

Heath whistled happily and tapped the console in time to The Police's "Don't Stand So Close to Me," but his mind was on Jack, anticipating how excited he would be to hear Jazz would soon be coming to live with them. They had already decided on something fairly low-key, only the family and a few good friends, and he knew it would be one of the best days of his life. His wedding to Juliette was not high on that list. Then he was a novelty showpiece to be introduced to the guests, but he was never quite enough. At the end of the evening, instead of being excited to be with his new wife, he was exhausted, and relieved to have the whole thing over with. Perhaps that should have been an omen of things to come.

Heath flipped open his cell. "Officer Juan Alvaro."

"Juan. Hey, it's Hawk. Where's Davis?"

"Umm...I don't know, man. He's not at his desk."

"Well, do me a favor then would ya?"

"Sure, Hawk."

"Do you see a pen there?"

"Got it."

"Could you have Davis pick up Lionel Parker at his home in Ladue to bring him in for questioning in the Michael Veritek stabbing?"

"Lionel Parker? *The* Lionel Parker? The director?"

"That's right." Heath smiled with satisfaction. The suspect had narrowed the field for himself by stabbing his other prime suspect. "You know him?"

"Know him? Sure. I've seen all his stuff, *Sunset at Normandy*, *The Tale of the Tiger*, *Apollos*, *The Tad Hunter Story*... I'm kind of a movie buff."

Heath's grip on the steering wheel tightened. "Did you say *Apollos*?"

"Sure, man. That's one of his best. I think he won an Academy Award or something for that."

He veered sharply into a convenient store parking lot to turn around. "Change that, Alavaro, Parker's our man. Issue an APB on him and have him brought in immediately. Oh, and please send a car to 12 North Taylor in Kirkwood to the new home of Jasmine Barrett."

"You got it, lieutenant."

Heath negotiated lanes of traffic, directed toward Jasmine's. Now he knew who the killer was for certain, he wasn't taking any chances with her safety. He'd stay at her place with her until the uniform got there, then go into the station.

He walked along the stepping stones to her house and watched a cardinal fly from one tree to the next, its sweet, clear song grabbing his attention as much as the flash of red against the leaves. He knocked on the door and waited for her to answer.

She's probably in the shower. He grinned. *I wonder how much time we have before that uniform gets here...*

The gate was open in the side yard. He closed it and tested the latch; it seemed to be working all right. Shaking his head, he walked to the rear of the property. He raised his hand to knock, but froze.

Jazz was lying across the width of the bed. Had she fallen back asleep in that strange position? He reached in the glass and grasped the handle so he could enter. He approached the bed quietly so as not to wake her, but a loud crack exploded and fire ripped through his shoulder as he was propelled into the bed. He landed, his face inches from hers, and that's when he saw the ugly purple swelling on her neck. Her eyes were shut and she was perfectly still.

No. I'm too late.

But like in a dream, his shout wouldn't leave him.

"Detective Friggin' McGowan. How nice of you to join us." Lionel Parker shuffled over so he could see Heath as he lay panting. "Oh, yes. I like the way the blood is fanning out symmetrically on the comforter. It's quite pretty actually, like a flower growing in time lapse photograph." He sighed dramatically. "She's nearly as beautiful in death as she was in life, isn't she?" He paused and moved his gaze from Jasmine to him. "I said isn't she, detective?" he raged.

Heath stared at him in disbelief.

"You'll be happy to know, she didn't give it up easily." He sniffed. "I had to fight to do her one last time. But it was worth it." He smiled wickedly.

He was struck dumb. How could he have let this happen to her? Why did he abandon her for even one minute? He should have never had the chance to touch her again. He struggled to push off the bed and to standing, but the pain was excruciating. He fell to one knee, trying to desperately claw at the comforter with his good arm to haul himself to his feet.

"Look. You ruined my pretty blood pattern," the director sniped petulantly. "You're right, though. You shouldn't have the right to die here, next to my Jasmine." Parker grabbed his injured limb, yanking him so it twisted, the weight of his own body pulling on it as the maniac dragged him around the corner of the bed. Nausea hit him unexpectedly, and the pain was so intense, he thought he would lose consciousness. As it was, he could only see things murkily, like he was peering at it from under the bottom of a fish bowl. He howled in agony. Parker was talking on and on to him in a chit-chatty manner but he couldn't make sense of it.

Lionel Parker was huffing and puffing now. "Too bad you'll never get a chance to rid yourself of those extra ten pounds, 'cause dragging you is a real pain." Heath's feet got hooked on the threshold and his progress stopped. Visibly annoyed, Parker set his gun on the dresser and jerked on his shoulder with both hands, finally able to get his prisoner through, though leaving a shoe on the other side.

This time he hurt so badly he couldn't even make a sound. As the wave of pain crested, he slid under.

TO JASMINE THE GUNSHOT sounded like it had come from under water. But it was enough to register in her brain, albeit dimly. After several seconds her sluggish mind responded with a call to her lungs to inflate. She gasped air in, her head coming to life all at once, like some automaton in a horror house, bouncing from the bed several inches as oxygen exploded into her cerebellum.

Her breathing reverberated loudly in her own ears, rasping as it traveled over her abused windpipe, which ached unmercifully. Lionel Parker was screaming in the next room.

Who is he screaming at?

Befuddled, she half-dragged, half-rolled her way off the bed. Something propelled her forward, some urgency she didn't understand. Incredibly dizzy, she fell against the dresser, knocking some perfume bottles down. As she righted herself, her fingers discovered the cold metal of the abandoned gun and curled around it. Using the dresser to for stability, she put one weak foot in front of the other. When she reached the door, she clung to its frame, to keep upright. Her vision was distorted.

Swirly.

She was hazy, but after blinking a few times, the picture became all too clear. Heath lay slumped against the couch, blood forming a pool on the hardwood from where his shoulder dripped horribly. Parker stood near him, with Heath's gun. The coffee table was overturned and lay at an angle by the fireplace. The director kept slapping his victim awake into the horrifying reality of the moment so he could continue to taunt him.

Jasmine staggered into the room. Parker's jaw dropped. Heath's bleary eyes tried to focus in her direction.

"Well. Jazz. Back from the dead. I couldn't have written it any better." He grinned then motioned to her. "Well come in my dear, join me so you can watch me shoot this filthy bastard, the man who had the audacity to touch you knowing that you were mine."

"Y-you..." Jazz croaked, crossing haphazardly to the couch, the gun pointed at him.

"What? What dear? I couldn't hear you? You should never have stolen your mother's money for singing lessons." He laughed, bemused by his own twisted joke. "Maybe you'll entertain us with a little song, Miss Barrett."

She pointed the gun at him, having used the couch to get on the floor with Heath. "I won't let you kill him. I won't let you kill another person, Lionel." She sounded determined, but her grip was unsteady.

IN HEATH'S BESIEGED brain, where nerves were sending thousands of pain messages pinging about, a flutter of hope arose. Jazz was alive. The thought repeated itself until he understood it.

"Oh, really, Jazz." Parker sneered. He tossed his gun into a chair. "Go for it, then. Kill me."

Tears clung to her lashes and she held the gun with both hands. "I'll do it, Lionel. I won't let you hurt him again." But she shrank against Heath.

"You were never that strong, Jazz. Never strong enough to defend yourself against that overbearing uncle of yours. And you weren't able to defend yourself against my advances all those years ago. You gave in. You enjoyed it."

"No!" she screamed, her voice finally finding some volume. "I'm not that girl anymore. You've made a mistake."

He narrowed his gaze. "I don't think so," he said, definitively.

He took another step toward them and she closed her eyes. "Please, Lionel. Don't." He moved again and, hearing him, she squeezed the trigger. She screamed as two shots rang out, dropping the gun with a clatter to the floor. Heath, though hampered by his injury, managed to alertly scoop it up. When she opened her eyes, Parker stumbled and fell to his knees in front of her. His eyes were wide with shock and staring at her, uncomprehending. He collapsed face forward and lay still. With a loud crack the door shook, and after two more, the frame gave and two policemen barreled into the room, their guns drawn, one still smoking.

CHAPTER FORTY-TWO

The priest walked from the grave, brushing the dirt off his palms. Usually these mournerless funerals left him depressed.

How sad, really, to have no one even recognize your passing.

No one even there to listen to him speak the rites. As far as that was concerned, who was to know if he said them at all? But, he was a priest, he said the vows, he guessed it wouldn't hurt him any to speak the words over the grave one more time. But if anyone deserved to be left without final rites, it was this man. He walked away from the new grave. The sun filtered through the leaves on the old oak beside the tombstone, highlighting Lionel Parker's name.

HEATH CROUCHED TO STRAIGHTEN Jack's tie and smooth his shirt. "You look handsome, little man." They were in Forest Park. The sky was a perfect blue with a light dusting of wispy clouds and folding chairs were arranged under a sprawling oak tree ribboned in white.

Jack grinned at him, "So do you, Dad." He lifted his chin. "Ooh! Jazz. You look beautiful." He ran to her and buried his face in the layers of tulle and beadwork covering her skirt. She pulled him in with one arm, holding a slender bouquet of orchids in the other, the long ribbon tying them together trailing almost to the ground.

Heath straightened slowly, taking in every gorgeous inch of his bride-to-be. Her skin was dewy and her eyes luminous as she returned his gaze.

IT WAS AS SHE HAD IMAGINED, only better, Heath in a white shirt, vest, and tuxedo jacket with a black tie, Jack in a scaled down version, his curls tamed for the occasion by a bit of gel. He strode about with his chest puffed out, feeling quite grown up and important.

"Are you ready?" Heath said softly to Jazz, a smile that seemed to have been created just for her brightening his features.

She nodded, too happy to speak.

Heath took his place by Luke and Kole and all three turned to peer at her as the music began, with Jack in front of his dad, Heath clasping his shoulder.

Brody Barrett appeared even taller and thinner in his tux. He took both of Jasmine's hands in his. "You look pretty as a picture, Jasmine Barrett. Your parents would have been so proud and pleased for you. Heath is a great guy." He stared at his feet, then back at her, cocking his head. "This is a crossroads for us. I hope you'll still let your old uncle come see you from time to time."

"Of course, Uncle Brody. Nothing's changed except my address. You're welcome anytime."

His eyes misted and he got choked up then whispered, "Are you ready now, honey?"

She wondered at the change in her uncle. Had he ever called her honey before? But then she focused on her new family awaiting her near a makeshift altar. "I'm ready," she answered with a sunny expression. She was ready to start life again, standing on her own two feet, with the man she loved by her side and a real, warm family to love and cherish surrounding them. She had found her home at last and no one was ever taking that from her again.

NOTE FROM THE AUTHOR

Thank you for reading BETWEEN ROCK AND A HARD PLACE, part of the ROCKING ROMANCE COLLECTION. I hope you enjoyed it. Now that you've read the book, won't you please consider writing a review? Reviews are one of the best ways readers discover great new books. They don't need to be fancy or long, just a sentence or two honestly describing your opinion of/experience with the book. I would sincerely appreciate it.

Want more from M.J. Schiller?
Page forward for an excerpt from ~
MIDNIGHT MELODY

PROLOGUE

Tyler Remkus lifted the faux sheepskin collar of his denim jacket and shrugged farther into its depths. He didn't do it because he thought someone might recognize him here, but because the wind was whistling in the dark Texas night with nothing to block it except the odd tumbleweed. The jacket was worn to a perfect comfortableness. The cotton fabric snuggled his cheek and bathed his neck with warmth. It reminded him of who he used to be.

The bells above the door of the roadside diner jingled as he entered. Every person in the room turned to stare at him, including the cook and two waitresses. Conversation stopped, and a dozen or more pairs of eyes sized him up. He shifted in his boots. After what seemed like an eternity, as if responding to a signal only they heard, the diner's patrons began to move again, voices restarted where they'd left off, silverware clanged on plates. Ty released a breath he didn't even realize he was holding.

He didn't mind being recognized most of the time, but this trip was for getting away from all of that. Escaping the office, where everyone straightened and tried to appear busy when he came by, their smiles evaporating, the jovial talk concerning the local team's newest recruit stifled. This jaunt across familiar Texas territory was about dodging his wife, who had grown so icy toward him her edges cut. It was to avoid people who asked him to autograph everything from their concert stubs, to their bras, to their babies. He didn't want to be Ty Remkus right now. He wanted to be the guy at table five who ordered a double bacon cheeseburger and fries.

Ty slid into a booth and snagged a menu from a metal stand. He inadvertently chose a table by the window into the kitchen, and so caught the conversation there as he paged through the menu to make sure a burger was available.

"In any case," a female voice was saying, "If one more guy touches my ass or calls me honey, they are either drawing back a nub or rubbing gravy from their eyes."

Someone snickered.

A bell sang out several times as it was pounded on. "Mel. Your order's ready. All that ringing ain't for making angels."

"I've got it, Chuck. Give me a break, would ya?" Plates dinged together. "Who eats collard greens anyway?" she muttered.

"Table number six, that's who. So get your sweet little ass over there."

"Okay, okay."

Bored with the menu, and having found what he wanted as well, Ty looked around. Two waitresses passed each other. One with plates balanced in every conceivable fashion on her arms, the other rushing the opposite direction with an empty coffee pot. The first leaned into the second and said, "What crawled up his ass tonight?"

He chuckled at that, then his lips twitched as she came near. Long, straight, blonde hair, gathered into a sleek ponytail. Their gazes connected. Her eyes were midnight blue and intelligent. He sat straighter, his palms sticking to the booth's seat where apparently some syrup remained from an earlier customer.

"I'll be right with you, sir."

He cleared his throat. "No problem, hon—" he remembered the overheard conversation and swallowed the last. As she passed, he took in the rest of her. White peasant blouse, the elastic at the top pulled below her shoulders to reveal creamy skin. Short, red, pleated skirt accenting her legs. *Outstanding.* Black heels. Those had to be killing her about now, but they sure added to the ensemble.

"No problem at all," he added to himself. She was probably half his age, likely closer to his oldest son's twenty-two, but man, was she beautiful.

Plates thudded on the table behind him, to his left. He twisted slightly to observe her.

"Country fried steak and collard greens. Ham and eggs. And a tuna sandwich. Can I get you gentlemen anything else?"

The guy sitting on the end, a hulking thug, ran his hand over the back of her leg. "Yeah. You can get me something else."

She swatted at him as he tried to yank her into his lap. "Knock it off, Jimmy."

"Come on, baby. I wanna see if you're as good as my old man says your momma is."

She squirmed, trying to work her way free from his club-like arms. "I said knock it off!" Finally getting her feet under her, she shoved him and broke from his hold. His friends laughed. "Eat your damn collard greens, you ass."

"Hey. Watch it or you ain't getting' no tip," he called after her as she marched toward the kitchen. Again his cronies roared.

Ty looked on with interest as she left their table and entered a bussing station. She took a drink of water. His heart tugged when she shook as she placed her glass on the counter. The other waitress drew near and said something to the blonde, who murmured a reply, her lips tight. Her gaze flicked to the table beyond him, eyes snapping fire. She dropped her chin, and the other waitress patted her as she spoke to her. The blonde bobbed her head. She gripped the counter for a second then took a deep breath and picked up the scoop in the ice bin in front of her to fill a glass. Ty pretended to be reading an advertisement on his table for a brownie fudge sundae when she approached.

"I'm sorry it took so long. Can I get you something to drink?"

He surveyed her, leaning into the seat's cushioning. He tried not to smile, but he couldn't help it. He stroked the side of the water glass she'd brought him.

"Nah. This'll do."

Her attention flitted to the table of assholes by the window again, then she refocused. "Do you need some more time to decide what you want to eat, or—"

"I'll take a double bacon cheeseburger with some fries. Oh, wait. Do you have collard greens?"

She was writing his order but lifted her face and frowned, really scrutinizing him for the first time. "Yes, *sir*. We do," she said crisply. "Would you like *collard greens* instead?"

God, that fire was sexy. He chuckled. "No. Fries'll do."

"Fine." She slapped her notepad against her palm. "I'll get your food going."

She spun to leave, and as he followed the sashaying of her sassy hips, he dragged in air between his teeth. She was something.

While he waited for his burger, he strategized things to say to her when she returned. As she approached, he searched for her name tag. M-E-L was spelled out with spaces between the letters to make it occupy more room. "Mel?"

She nodded, setting the plate down before him.

He sat forward. "You probably never heard of it, but there was this show called Mel's Diner—"

"It was called Alice," she snapped. "Yes. Kiss my grits. The whole thing. I get it."

"Hey," he said softly. "No need to get hostile. I only thought—well, it struck me as funny. The Mel character was a big, grumpy, balding guy—and you, sweetheart, are *nothing* like him."

She at least smirked at that. "Thank you. I'm not like a big, grumpy, balding guy. I'll take that as a compliment."

He chuckled, happy she'd warmed some. "You should. You should."

She shifted into a more relaxed pose. "Maybe the grumpy part wasn't too far off. Listen, I'm sorry I barked at you." Her focus darted to the left and back. "It's been a bad night."

Ty tilted his head in the direction of the offending table. "Don't let those assholes get to you, darlin'." He peered over his shoulder. The trio was watching them. He raised his voice. "They obviously weren't taught any manners."

She studied him then glanced toward the parking lot, trying to see through the dark windows. "You're not from around here. Trucker?"

She didn't recognize him. Hadn't a clue. He weighed his answer. "I'm Ty Remkus."

She offered her hand, and he shook it. Soft as a pigeon. "Nice to meet you, Ty. Well, you know my name. We already established that. My folks named me Melody, but most people just call me Mel." She straightened, scanning the table. "Can I get you anything else? There's mustard and ketchup on the table..."

Ty gave her a wide grin. "Nah. Looks like I got everything I need. Thank you."

She dipped her chin, her smile a bit looser. "Well, let me know if you need anything." And then she was gone.

Melody, huh? Maybe it's destiny that brought me to you, because you're one melody I'd love to play.

Ty dug into his burger. He'd eaten less tasty plates in some five-star restaurants. As he was finishing, he heard the guys behind him rise, scraping chair legs against the vinyl flooring. He eyed them as they passed his table. The one she called Jimmy stopped in front of Mel as she was moving to a table. She tried to sidestep him, but he shifted, stretching his arms and holding on to the half walls of the booths she was walking between, blocking her completely.

She lifted her gaze. "Come on, Jimmy. I have a table to get to."

He leaned into her, all swagger and misplaced confidence. "What time you get off, Mel? Maybe we can meet at the dumpster and—"

Her voice held a tremor. "Get out of my way."

His jaw tightened. "Now you're being rude. Don't act like you're not the whore your mother is."

Ty couldn't tell where he touched her, because the wall was partially obstructing his view, but he heard the slap of skin-to-skin contact.

"Don't."

She was jerked against him. "Come on. Relax."

Ty threw his napkin on the table and rose, a muscle twitching near his right temple.

"Get your hands *off* me!" The two briefly struggled and then she escaped from his grasp. The server bell called angrily.

"Mel. Order up."

"You know what?" She worked furiously behind her at the knot in her apron strings and finally snatched it free. "I'm done." She whipped it onto the floor. And then stomped on it as she moved toward the door.

"Mel," the other waitress said weakly.

"No, Ginny. I'm sorry. I'm done."

"You walk out, you're fired," some idiot by the cash register counting the till called. A string bean of a kid in glasses, with curly hair. He was wearing a denim shirt and one of those stupid lariat things. Must be the manager.

"I think if she walks out she quits, Stan," the other waitress said dryly.

He shrugged. "Whatever."

Mel reached the door and tore it open, the bells above it crashing in protest.

Ty whirled to catch the reaction. The boss slapped the counter. "Great."

The Jimmy guy shrugged. "Let's hit the john." He and his crew strode toward the far end of the diner.

Spinning, Ty caught Melody plopping on the curb in front of door. She laid her head on top of her knees. He plucked a twenty from his money clip and threw it on the table. The other waitress raised a brow as he came to the exit.

"I paid."

Mel lifted her face at the bells' tingling and then jumped to her feet, rubbing at her eyes. She twisted slightly to look at him from under her lashes.

"Oh, it's you."

He worked his jaw, not sure how to approach her. Her arms were crossed over her chest, but the wind whipped her hair and snapped at her uniform.

"You got a jacket?"

She shrugged. "A sweater. But it's inside. And I ain't goin' back in there." She clutched herself tighter. "Forgot my damn ride won't show for another forty-five minutes. Might as well start walking."

Ty glanced in the diner. A black sweater hung from a chrome coat rack by the exit. He jerked his chin in that direction.

"That it?"

She checked too. "Yeah, but—"

The gravel crunched under his boots as he proceeded to the entrance. People peered up again at the door's jangle. He grabbed the sweater from the hook and nodded to his audience before leaving.

"Here." He held it open for her.

She hesitated, then turned and let him help her into it. Her reply was so soft the Texas wind almost carried it away. "*Thank* you."

He dropped his hands on her shoulders and gave them a squeeze. "No problem. Now, about that ride..." He pointed to his truck. It was a black monstrosity of a thing with gold stripes, but he loved it. "I could take you—"

"Oh, no. I can't ask you to do that."

"You're not asking, darlin'. I'm offering."

She twisted to stare at the diner and he followed her gaze. The other waitress was facing them, at a table by the window, her pen posed as if taking an elderly couple's order, but she was watching them.

"If it makes you feel any better, I think that girlfriend of yours wrote down my license plate number. If I kidnap you, the law is bound to find us."

She considered him and smiled. "Okay. If you don't mind. It's not far."

He bowed. "It'd be my pleasure." They started to walk toward his truck and the diner door opened again.

"Hey, Mel. Where you goin' with that old man? Don't tell me you're gonna do him instead of me?"

"Oh, God," she muttered. "Ignore him," she added from the corner of her mouth, walking faster.

"Hey." Jimmy reached them and grabbed her, swinging her around. "I was talking to you."

Ty stepped between them. "Get your hands off her."

"Ty, please. I—"

The kid hesitated, then released her. "What? Lookin' for a father figure since your old man be—"

"Shut up!"

Whatever he was about to say, it hit the mark because she was spitting mad, and tears built again. *Why won't this punk drop it?*

"I think the lady has made it pretty clear she isn't interested in you."

"Is that so?" He advanced forward. "What's it to you, old man?"

Mel grabbed Ty's elbow. "Come on, Ty. Let's just go."

"Oh. You ain't goin' anywheres with him."

Jimmy made a move to grab her again, and Ty closed the gap between them and seized the sides of his jacket.

"I said *leave her alone.*"

"What the hell?" In a flash, Jimmy broke Ty's hold then shoved him hard enough to knock him on his ass. Latching on to Mel, he dragged her toward a red pickup. She tried to dig her heels in, but only slid in the loose gravel. An ankle buckled, and she almost fell. Jimmy whirled with a growl. "Come on." He took her by both biceps and shook her. She yelped.

Ty sprung to his feet and crossed to them in two large strides. He grabbed Jimmy, jerked him away from her, then shoved him. Jimmy charged at him, so he threw a punch, putting his weight with it to give it momentum as he shifted and followed through. Next thing he knew, his knuckles hurt like hell, and Jimmy was laying at his feet, out cold. His arms were spread wide as if he was making some weird sort of gravel angel. Ty checked Mel.

Her mouth was set in a wide O. "Oh, my gosh," she breathed. Jimmy's friends appeared to be equally shocked, and...sort of amused.

"We better go." Ty swung toward his truck.

"Oh, my gosh!" she said again.

"Melody?"

"I'm coming. I'm coming." She hurried after him. He opened the door of his truck and she climbed in.

He walked around the tailgate, keeping his focus on the two friends who had pulled Jimmy to a seated position and were slapping his cheeks to try to get him to come to. Ty hopped into his cab.

"You knocked him out."

"Yeah." He watched in his side view mirror as he slid his cowboy hat off the dash and put it on.

"How'd you do that?"

He shrugged, twisting to check behind them. "Damn lucky, I guess. I never hit anyone in my life." He threw the truck in reverse. "And since his pals are waking him, I'd rather not be here when the three of them are otherwise unoccupied." He screeched to the parking lot entrance, his heart striking at his ribcage like a bronco in a stall. "So, where to?"

"Oh. Left."

As he exited the lot, he turned to peek back again. He half-expected them to be chasing after them, but Jimmy still wasn't on his feet.

"You like...cold-cocked him." She was grinning now.

"I did," he said, a wave of pride replacing the adrenaline in his blood.

They raced along the road. After several minutes of quiet, Ty sensed movement and glanced over. Melody was shaking her leg. She was looking straight forward, a fist against her mouth. He would have to ask her for directions in a moment, but he let her have time to absorb what had happened. He flexed his fingers on the steering wheel. They hurt like a son of a bitch, like tiny wasps were stinging him repeatedly across his knuckles. He concentrated on the dark road, not wanting to miss any curves. The more the tires ate the asphalt, the more the dark seemed oppressive. It was heavy, pushing down on them. Melody's wiggling increased in speed and intensity. She clapped a hand to her forehead.

"Oh, my God. I quit my job."

Ty didn't know what to say to that, so he kept quiet. When he cast his gaze at her next, she had shifted and was staring out the window. In the reflection of the glass, her face was pale. She chewed on her nails. "He's going to kill me," she murmured.

He gave her leg a pat, but she didn't seem to notice. "Mel? Do I keep going straight?"

"Hmm. Oh. Yeah. My place is about a mile up the road, on the left. I'll let you know."

He smiled at her. "Got it. You okay?"

She rotated to again look at the window. Her brow was furrowed. After a beat she said, "Yeah."

It started to drizzle. Ty switched on the wipers and studied her again.

Her eyes were squeezed shut. "He's going to kill me."

"Who's going to kill you?"

"What? Oh. Go slower. There's my turn. Right there, by the white mailbox."

Ty braked hard, glad the tires held on the wet pavement, and swerved onto a gravel driveway winding through some trees. The truck's lights framed a pretty, white, two-story farmhouse. When he rolled to a stop, an unattached garage stood unsteadily at the end of his high beams. The paint job it needed wouldn't be enough to hold it together. The house itself seemed okay. The lawn a tad untamed, scraggly weeds waving near the foundation of the porch. A light was on in what appeared to be a kitchen.

"This is it." Her voice was full of dread.

Ty put it in park. Swinging around, he caught her peering at the home. She was rubbing her wrist. He examined it closer. Was that shadow or bruise? He pulled her arm into a slice of light shining in the truck's cabin. Yep. A big, ugly bruise.

"Did that little punk do this to you?"

She hung her head and shook it. A teardrop hit him and when he peeked at it, he observed something else. He pushed the sleeve of her sweater above her elbow. Marching all up and down her arms were angry bruises. How did he not notice this in the diner? But he wasn't able to tear his focus from her face, other than the cursory appreciation of her figure.

"Who did this?"

She searched him then stared at the house. He scanned it, too. Someone had risen from the table and was coming to the window. The dark figure jerked aside the sheer, ripped curtain and leaned in, framing his vision with his hands. The wipers droned against the windshield, not enough rain at the moment to cushion them.

"I have to go." She hunted for the door's release, fumbling, never removing her attention from the figure. Still holding her, he felt her go cold and begin to tremble. "I have to go." Tears clung to her lashes again. "Thank you. Thank you for helping me with Jimmy and... For the ride..." She had found the handle and the door started to open.

Ty stretched over her and slammed it shut. Her gaze flew to him, eyes wide. "What...?"

"I'm not going to harm you." He swallowed, trying to regain his calm. "Let's stay in here and chat a second."

"I better not. I need to—" she broke off, taking note of his cut. "You're hurt."

He glanced and saw the skin of his knuckles was scraped away and blood was oozing from the area.

She grasped him tenderly. "Let me fix it. Do you have a first aid kit?"

"Huh? No. I..." he contorted his body, straining his muscles to reach across himself with his uninjured hand. "I have a bandana."

"Let me get it. Where? Back pocket?"

"Uh huh." He lifted his rear to give her access to retrieve the bandana. He held out his wounded fist, and she created a makeshift bandage. She was so pretty. Even like this, disheveled from her struggling with Jimmy. He cleared his throat. "You know, it's probably okay."

She looped it around, crossing it, and drawing the ends together again before tying it. "That okay? Does it hurt? I could probably get you a real bandage inside..."

"No," he said a hint too insistently. He knew he didn't have much more time with her, and the thought filled him with panic. "Melody..." he had to chance it. "Your dad did this, didn't he?"

She licked her lips and seemed about to deny it. She wouldn't look at him straight. "Things have been rough. He lost his job at the guitar string factory..."

Ty's gut clenched. "He worked at the factory?" He stared at the window, but the figure was gone.

She nodded. "He got fired when he got in a fight...and choked someone with the string from the line. He nearly killed the man."

That's all Ty needed to hear. "You're not going in there."

"What? No. I have to. He'll already be pissed."

"Listen, Melody." He touched her knee. Her skin was velvety smooth. Her warmth seduced him. He caressed her. "You can come with me." She started to protest, and he cut her off. "You don't have to stay here. You don't have to live like this." She parted her lovely lips to speak, and he couldn't help himself. He slipped his good hand behind her neck, and drew her to him. He took her lips—so soft—and his heart pounded, the blood raging in his veins. She smelled like heaven. He slid his bandaged fingers higher. She shoved him.

"Don't." Her gaze raked his face, tears swimming in her eyes. She pushed him again. "You're just like all the rest. Why can't people appreciate me for who I am? Not a body to fondle, or use as a punching bag. Me. Melody." She shook her head. "I thought maybe you were different."

His gut dropped and his heart became as heavy as his two-ton truck. *Why the hell did I have to go and kiss her? She didn't need that.*

She sobbed, scrambling to escape. Ty peered through the windshield. A man stood on a little, square side porch with three or four steps leading to the ground. A light above the entry illuminated him. He was big and wore a beard. His features were hard, fists stuffed in his pockets.

This wasn't happening. He threw the truck into reverse and then stretched to hold her door closed, gunning the engine. The truck didn't seem to move at first, as it was churning gravel. The man began to descend, the hands coming out of his pockets.

"What are you doing?" Mel screamed.

His jaw tightened. The tires caught and sped them erratically over the drive. "Put your seatbelt on."

"What are you doing? I'm not coming with you."

"Dammit, Mel. Put your seat belt on and be still before you kill us both."

She clamped her mouth shut and seemed to become frozen to her seat.

"Good enough." He clutched the steering wheel and got things more under control. He barreled onto the blacktop road. Lucky for them, no one was coming. They hightailed it away from there, leaving a white, dusty cloud of gravel in their wake. No one followed them. Mel was crying. *Dammit.* As soon as he saw a place to pull onto the shoulder, he did. She immediately clawed at the door and got it open, stumbling into the wet night.

"Shit." Ty undid his seatbelt and chased her. She was running across a field. The rain chose this time to let loose in torrents. Ty fought the water from his eyes so as not to lose track of her. She tripped and fell, hard. "Melody!"

When he caught up to her, she had flipped on her back. He bent to help her, but she punched him in the jaw, rocking him for a second. *Damn.* "Melody, stop." She beat at him furiously. He wrestled her to the ground, trapping her legs to avoid shots below the waist.

"Leave me alone. Leave me alone!" Thunder crashed. What the hell was he doing wrestling a wild cat in the rain and mud, his knuckles throbbing and his jaw now keeping tune? He got her wrists pinned.

"Mel, relax."

"You fucking relax!" she spat. Her hair was muddy, her lip bleeding where she must have bit it when she tripped. She still fought him, though crying.

"I'm not going to hurt you. I'm not here to hurt you. You have to believe me."

"Why should I?"

Why should she?

Rain pounded on the hard soil, making slapping noises in the mud. He realized they were in a farmer's field, evident by the lack of grass. Probably wheat in this part of the state. She still squirmed under him, and he fought to control the natural reaction his body took to her wriggling beneath him.

"I'm sorry, okay? Sorry I kissed you. That was wrong. But I don't want to hurt you. Or do anything you don't want. *Please*, just listen to me for a minute."

She was breathing hard. "You're hurting my arms."

He lightened up, but didn't release her. "Are you going to listen to me?"

"Well seeing as you're sitting on me I guess I don't have much of a choice, do I?"

He tilted his head, shaking the rain off. "Good point." He let her go, but remained cautious. He figured she was tired and regaining her strength before she took another whack at him. "I'm Ty Remkus. The singer? I own the string factory in town."

"*You* own Texas Twangs?"

"Yeah." The rain was still beating him, the cold stinging. "Do you think we could take this conversation back to the cab of my truck?"

"I don't know. Are you going to try anything again?"

He staggered to his feet. "No." He offered her his hand. "I promise."

She stared at him but finally let him help her to stand. Probably more because she was freezing than any real desire to talk to him, but he would take what he could get. They trudged side by side, she seemingly as weary as him. He peeked at her out of his peripheral vision. She was scanning the vicinity, no doubt choosing a getaway route.

"If you run, I'll be forced to tackle you again."

She frowned at him but continued walking. When they got to the truck, he opened the door for her. "Wow. How very gentlemanly."

He laughed. She was a pistol. He leaned against the vehicle. "Are you getting in?"

She peered into the cab and then down at her clothes. "I'm gonna get mud in your truck."

He shrugged. "Can't be helped. Climb in."

Once she was safely in, he walked slowly around the front of the pickup, keeping his gaze on her in case she should bolt. He slid behind the wheel. She was trying to wipe the mud from her face and smearing it everywhere.

"Don't. You're gonna get mud in your eyes." He snagged a flannel shirt from the bench seat in the rear. "Hold on. Let me get it." He moved to wash her forehead and she stopped him.

"Your bandana's gone."

He must have dropped it when they struggled. "Yep." He rubbed her gently and dabbed at her hair.

"But your cut."

"It's fine," he answered, irritated by her concern at this point.

"It'll get dirty."

He abandoned his efforts to dry her. Mud dripped from his wrists to his elbows and was smeared all over his palms and clothes. Despite his attempts at cleaning her, her ponytail was a sodden mess, her cheeks had dark swipes across them like Indian war paint, and she even had some mud in her ear. He drew a piece of wheat out of her hair, showing it to her, and she giggled. It became contagious. Whenever he got himself under control, he'd hear her laughter and lose it again. Then she'd rein it in and try to take a breath, but something would set her off.

"Whoo," he said finally, exhaling. "You're a mess, sugar."

"Well you're not exactly a movie star yourself." She chuckled again, picking some more wheat stubble from her skirt. "Wait. Ty Remkus? The country singer?"

He bowed his head. "One and the same." He considered her. "You recognize me?"

"Umm...no. I'm sorry. I'm more of a rock music fan."

He grunted. He noticed her shivering and started the engine, cranking up the heat.

"Not that I don't like country music, but... Okay. I hate country music. And I hate Texas Twangs."

He raised his brows as much as the stiffening mud would allow. "Why?"

"Because... I know it doesn't make any sense. My daddy deserved to be fired. But that's when he became real mean. Or maybe he was always mean, only he wasn't around much to show it."

"Well, that's gonna make it hard for me to offer you a job."

"What? You want me to work for you?"

He nodded. "I can tell you are smart and, believe it or not, I like your sass. You're a straight shooter and with so many people in my life telling me what they think I want to hear, I need that. I need you, Mel. Come to Phoenix and work for R&J Enterprises, Texas Twang's parent company." She was quiet, examining her grimy fingers. "I don't want you going back to him."

She folded her arms and looked away. "Oh. He ain't that bad..."

"Now you're not being straight with me." He gently took her chin, turning her to face him. "I've a suspicion he's worse."

She shrugged.

"Come work for me. I'll get you an apartment—"

She jerked her chin from his grasp at this and her jaw tightened. "No. Thank you, but no."

"Hold on. Let me explain what I mean. I'd get you a place, but there would be no strings attached." He almost touched her in a gesture to reassure, then realized it wouldn't be reassuring and put his hand on his knee. He peered through the windshield. The rain had lightened some, to a reasonable downpour. "I'm sorry I came on to you. It won't happen again. On my honor."

She stared out of the cab, too. "You're doing this because you feel sorry for me."

He studied her earnestly. "I'm doing it because I need you. I need someone I can trust."

"There's more to me. I'm not just a waitress or someone to bed. I want to be taken seriously."

He held up two fingers. "Scouts' honor. I will take you seriously, Melody. I will treat you fairly and with respect. I'll take care of you because you'll take care of me. I can sense that."

She swallowed. Her voice came out in a croak. "Okay, then."

"Okay." He smiled and put the truck in gear, steering it onto the road. It eased forward on its path to Phoenix, Arizona and a sunrise promising to be spectacular.

TO FIND OUT WHAT HAPPENS NEXT, PURCHASE MIDNIGHT MELODY TODAY!

ALSO FROM M.J. SCHILLER

ROMANTIC REALMS COLLECTION:
TAKEN BY STORM
AN UNCOMMON LOVE
LEAP INTO THE KNIGHT
LADY OF THE KNIGHT
A KNIGHT TO REMEMBER

ROCKING ROMANCE COLLECTION:
TRAPPED UNDER ICE
ABANDON ALL HOPE
BETWEEN ROCK AND A HARD PLACE
ROCK ME, GENTLY
MIDNIGHT MELODY

LOVE AND CHAOS SERIES:
ROCKED BY GRACE
ROCKED BY LOVE
ROCK IT TO THE MOON
ROCK OF SALVATION (Coming soon!)

REAL ROMANCE COLLECTION:
UPON A MIDNIGHT CLEAR
THE HEART TEACHES BEST
DAMAGE DONE
BLACKOUT
HOMETOWN HEARTACHE
TAKE A CHANCE ON ME

DEVILISH DESIRES SERIES:

TO HELL IN A COACH BAG
DAMNED IF I DO
THE DEVIL YOU KNOW
SATAN, LINE ONE
PITCHFORK IN THE ROAD
SIN WORTH THE PENANCE
HELL HATH NO FURY
TEN MINUTES IN THE SIN BIN
DEVIL'S IN THE DETAILS
DEVIL'S ADVOCATE
HADE'S NIGHT

INSATIABLE FIRE SERIES:

BEATING IN TIME
LEAD ME ON
ROCK WITH THE RHYTHM
BASSIST'S INSTINCTS

ABOUT THE AUTHOR

Bestselling author M.J. Schiller is a retired lunch lady/romance-romantic suspense writer. She enjoys writing novels whose characters include rock stars, desert princes, teachers, futuristic Knights, construction workers, cops, and a wide variety of others. In her mind everybody has a romance. She is the mother of a twenty-seven-year-old and three twenty-five-year-olds. That's right, triplets! So having recently taught four children to drive, she likes to escape from life on occasion by pretending to be a rock star at karaoke. However...you won't be seeing her name on any record labels soon.

www.ingramcontent.com/pod-product-compliance
Lightning Source LLC
Chambersburg PA
CBHW072236190626
46809CB00018B/2313

THE
CHILDERBRIDGE
MYSTERY

THE
CHILDERBRIDGE
MYSTERY

GUY BOOTHBY

WILDSIDE PRESS

THE CHILDERBRIDGE MYSTERY

Published by Wildside Press LLC.
www.wildsidebooks.com

CHAPTER I

One had only to look at William Standerton in order to realise that he was, what is usually termed, a success in life. His whole appearance gave one this impression; the bold un-flinching eyes, the square, resolute chin, the well-moulded lips, and the lofty forehead, showed a determination and ability to succeed that was beyond the ordinary.

The son of a hardworking country doctor, it had fallen to his lot to emigrate to Australia at the early age of sixteen. He had not a friend in that vast, but sparsely-populated, land, and was without influence of any sort to help him forward. When, therefore, in fifty years' time, he found himself worth upwards of half-a-million pounds sterling, he was able to tell himself that he owed his good fortune not only to his own industry, but also to his shrewd business capabilities. It is true that he had had the advantage of reaching the Colonies when they were in their infancy, but even with this fact taken into consideration, his was certainly a great performance. He had invested his money prudently, and the rich Stations, and the streets of House Property, were the result.

Above all things, William Standerton was a kindly-natured man. Success had not spoilt him in this respect. No genuine case of necessity ever appealed to him in vain. He gave liberally, but discriminatingly, and in so doing never advertised himself.

Strange to say, he was nearly thirty years of age before he even contemplated matrimony. The reason for this must be ascribed to the fact that his life had been essentially an active one, and up to that time he had not been brought very much into contact with the opposite sex. When, however, he fell in love with pretty Jane McCalmont—then employed as a governess on a neighbouring Property—he did so with an enthusiasm that amply made up for lost time.

She married him, and presented him with two children—a boy and a girl. Within three months of the latter's arrival into the world, the mother laid down her gentle life, leaving her husband a well nigh broken-hearted man. After her death the years passed slowly by with almost monotonous sameness. The boy James, and the girl Alice, in due course commenced their education, and in so doing left their childhood behind them. Their devotion to their father was only equalled by his love for them. He could scarcely bear them out of his sight, and entered into all their sports, their joys and troubles, as if he himself were a child once more.

It was not, however, until James was a tall, handsome young fellow of four-and-twenty, and Alice a winsome maid of twenty, that he arrived at the conclusion that his affairs no longer needed his personal supervision, and that he was at liberty to return to the Mother Country, and settle down in it, should he feel disposed to do so.

"It's all very well for you young folk to talk of my leaving Australia," he said, addressing his son and daughter; "but I shall be like a fish out of water in the Old Country. You forget that I have not seen her for half-a-century."

"All the more reason that you should lose no time in re-turning, father," observed Miss Alice, to whom a visit to England had been the one ambition of her life. "You shall take us about and show us everything; the little village in which you were born, the river in which you used to fish, and the wood in which the keeper so nearly caught you with the rabbit in your pocket. Then you shall buy an old-fashioned country house and we'll settle down. It will be lovely!"

Her father pinched her shapely little ear, and then looked away across the garden to where a railed enclosure was to be seen, on the crest of a slight eminence. He remembered that the woman lying there had more than once expressed a hope that, in the days then to come, they would be able to return to their native country together, and take their children with them.

"Well, well, my dear," he said, glancing down at the daughter who so much resembled her mother, "you shall have it your own way. We will go Home as soon as possible, and do just as you propose. I think we may be able to afford a house in the country, and perhaps, that is if you are a very dutiful daughter, another in London. It is just possible that there may be one or two people living who may remember William Standerton, and, for that reason, be kind to his son and daughter. But I fear it will be rather a wrench for me to leave these places that I have built up with my own hands, and to which I have devoted such a large portion of my life. However, one can be in harness too long, and when once Australia is left behind me, I have no doubt I shall enjoy my holiday as much as any one else."

In this manner the matter was settled. Competent and trustworthy managers were engaged, and the valuable properties, which had contributed so large a share to William Standerton's wealth, were handed over to their charge.

On the night before they were to leave Mudrapilla, their favourite and largest station, situated on the Darling River, in New South Wales, James Standerton, called Jim by his family and a multifarious collection of friends, was slowly making his way along the left bank of the River. He had ridden out to say good-bye to the manager of the Out Station, and as his horse picked his way along the bank, he was thinking of England, and of what his life was to be there. Suddenly he became aware of a man seated beneath a giant gum tree near the water's edge. From the fact that the individual in question had kindled a fire and was boiling his billy, he felt justified in assuming that he was preparing his camp for the night. He accordingly rode up and accosted him. The man was a Foot Traveller, or Swagman, and presented a somewhat singular appearance. Though he was seated, Jim could see that he was tall, though sparsely built. His age must have been about sixty years; his hair was streaked with grey, as also was his beard. Taken altogether his countenance was of the description usually described as "hatchet-faced." He was dressed after the swagman fashion, certainly no better, and perhaps a little worse. Yet with it all he had the appearance of having once been in better circumstances. He looked up as Jim approached, and nodded a "good evening." The latter returned the salutation in his customary pleasant fashion.

"How much further is it to the Head Station?" the man on the ground then enquired.

"Between four and five miles," Jim replied. "Are you making your way there?"

"That's my idea," the stranger answered. "I hear the owner is leaving for England, and I am desirous of having a few words with him before he goes."

"You know him then?"

"I've known him over thirty years," returned the other. "But he has gone up in the world while, as you will gather, I have done the opposite. Standerton was always one of Life's lucky ones; I am one of Her failures. Anything he puts his hand to prospers; while I, let it be ever so promising, have only to touch a bit of business, and it goes to pieces like a house of cards."

The stranger paused and took stock of the young man seated upon the horse.

"Now I come to think of it," he continued, after having regarded Jim intently for some seconds, "you're not unlike Standerton yourself. You've got the same eyes and chin, and the same cut of mouth."

"It's very probable, for I am his son," Jim replied. "What is it you want with my father?"

"That's best known to myself," the stranger returned, with a surliness in his tone that he had not exhibited before. "When you get home, just tell your governor that Richard Murbridge is on his way up the river to call upon him, and that he will try to put in an appearance at the Station early to-morrow morning. I don't fancy he'll be best pleased to see me, but I must have an interview with him before he leaves Australia, if I have to follow him round the country to get it."

"You had better be careful how you talk to my father," said Jim. "If you are as well acquainted with him as you pretend to be, you should know that he is not the sort of man to be trifled with."

"I know him as well as you do," the other answered, lifting his billy from the fire as he spoke. "William Standerton and I knew each other long before you were born. If it's only the distance you say to the Head Station, you can tell him I'll be there by breakfast time. I'm a bit foot-sore, it is true, but I can do the journey in an hour and a-half. On what day does the coach pass, going South?"

"To-morrow morning," Jim replied. "Do you want to catch it?"

"It's very probable I shall," said Murbridge. "Though I wasn't born in this cursed country, I'm Australian enough never to foot it when I can ride. Good Heavens! had any one told me, twenty-five years ago, that I should eventually become a Darling Whaler, I'd have knocked, what I should have thought then to be the lie, down their throats. But what I am you can see. Fate again, I suppose? However, I was always of a hopeful disposition, even when my affairs appeared to be at their worst, so I'll pin my faith on to-morrow. Must you be going? Well, in that case, I'll wish you good-night! Don't forget my message to your father."

Jim bade him good-night, and then continued his ride home. As he went he pondered upon his curious interview with the stranger he had just left, and while so doing, wondered as to his reasons for desiring to see his father.

"The fellow was associated with him in business at some time or another, I suppose?" he said to himself, "and, having failed, is now on his beam ends and wants assistance. Poor old Governor, there are times when he is called upon to pay pretty dearly for his success in life."

James Standerton was proud of his father, as he had good reason to be. He respected him above all living men, and woe betide the individual who might have anything to say against the sire in the son's hearing.

At last he reached the Home Paddock and cantered up the slope towards the cluster of houses, that resembled a small village, and surrendered his horse to a black boy in the stable yard. With a varied collection of dogs at his heels he made his way up the garden path, beneath the trellised vines to the house, in the broad verandah of which he could see his sister and father seated at tea.

"Well, my lad," said Standerton senior, when Jim joined them, "I suppose you've seen Riddington, and have bade him good-bye. It's my opinion he will miss you as much as any one in the neighbourhood. You two have always been such friends."

"That's just what Riddington said," James replied. "He wishes he were coming with us. Poor chap, he doesn't seem to think he'll ever see England again."

Alice looked up from the cup of tea she was pouring out for her brother.

"I fancy there is more in poor Mr. Riddington's case than meets the eye," she said sympathetically. "Nobody knows quite why he left England. He is always very reticent upon that point. I cannot help thinking, however, that there was a lady in the case."

"There always is," answered her brother. "There's a woman in every mystery, and when you've found her it's a mystery no longer. By the way, father, as I was coming home, I came across a fellow camped up the river. He asked me what the distance was to here, and said he was on his way to see you. He will be here the first thing to-morrow morning."

"He wants work, I suppose?"

"No, I shouldn't say that he did," James replied. "He said that he wanted to see you on important private business."

"Indeed? I wonder who it can be? A swagman who has important private business with me is a rara avis. He didn't happen to tell you his name, I suppose?"

"Yes, he did," Jim answered, placing his cup on the floor as he spoke. "His name is Richard Murbridge, or something like it."

The effect upon the elder man was electrical.

"Richard Murbridge?" he cried. "Camped on the river and coming here?"

His son and daughter watched him with the greatest astonishment depicted upon their faces. It was not often that their father gave way to so much emotion. At last with an effort he recovered himself, and, remarking that Murbridge was a man with whom he had had business in bygone days, and that he had not seen him for many years, went into the house.

"I wonder who this Murbridge can be?" said James to his sister, when they were alone together. "I didn't like the look of him, and if I were the Governor, I should send him about his business as quickly as possible."

When he had thus expressed himself, Jim left his sister and went off to enjoy that luxury so dear to the heart of a bushman after his day's work, a swim in the river. He was some time over it, and when he emerged, he was informed that his presence was required at the Store. Thither he repaired to arbitrate in the quarrel of two Boundary Riders. In consequence, more than an hour elapsed before he returned to the house. His sister greeted him at the gate with a frightened look upon her face.

"Have you seen father?" she enquired.

"No," he answered. "Isn't he in the house?"

"He went down the track just after you left, riding old Peter, and as he passed the gate he called to me not to keep dinner for him, as he did not know how long it might be before he would be back. Jim, I believe he is gone to see that man you told him of, and the thought frightens me."

"You needn't be alarmed," her brother answered. "Father is quite able to take care of himself."

But though he spoke with so much assurance, in his own mind he was not satisfied. He remembered that it had been his impression that the swagman bore his father a grudge, and the thought made him uneasy.

"Look here, Alice," he said, after he had considered the matter for some time, "I've a good mind to go back along the track, and to bring the Governor home with me. What do you think?"

"It would relieve me of a good deal of anxiety if you would," the girl replied. "I don't like the thought of his going off like this."

Jim accordingly went to the end of the verandah, and called to the stables for a horse. As soon as the animal was forthcoming he mounted it, and set off in the direction his father had taken. It was now quite dark, but so well did he know it, that he could have found his way along the track blindfolded, if necessary. It ran parallel with the river, the high trees on the banks of which could be seen, standing out like a black line against the starlit sky. He let himself out of the Home Paddock, passed the Woolshed, and eventually found himself approaching the spot where Murbridge had made his camp. Then the twinkle of the fire came into view, and a few seconds later he was able to distinguish his father standing beside his grey horse, talking to a man who was lying upon the ground near the fire. Not wishing to play the part of an eavesdropper, he was careful to remain out of earshot. It was only when he saw the man rise, heard him utter a threat, and then approach his father, that he rode up. Neither of the men became aware of his approach until he was close upon them, and then both turned in surprise.

"James, what is the meaning of this?" his father cried. "What are you doing here, my lad?"

For a moment the other scarcely knew what reply to make. At last he said:—

"I came to assure myself of your safety, father. Alice told me you had gone out, and I guessed your errand."

"A very dutiful son," sneered Murbridge. "You are to be congratulated upon him, William."

James stared at the individual before him with astonishment. What right had such a man to address his father by his Christian name?

"Be careful," said Standerton, speaking to the man before him. "You know what I said to you just now, and you are also aware that I never break my word. Fail to keep your part of the contract, and I shall no longer keep mine."

"You know that you have your heel upon my neck," the other retorted; "and also that I cannot help myself. But I pray that the time may come when I shall be able to be even with you. To think that I am tramping this infernal country, like a dead beat Sundowner, without a cent in my pocket, while you are enjoying all the luxuries and happiness that life and wealth can give. It's enough to make a man turn Anarchist right off."

"That will do," said William Standerton quietly. "Remember that to-morrow morning you will go back to the place whence you came; also bear in mind the fact that if you endeavour to molest me, or to communicate with me, or with any member of my family, I will carry out the threat I uttered just now. That is all I have to say to you."

Then Standerton mounted his horse, and turning to his son, said:—

"Let us return home, James. It is getting late, and your sister will be uneasy."

Without another word to the man beside the fire, they rode off, leaving him looking after them with an expression of deadly hatred upon his face. For some distance the two men rode in silence. Jim could see that his father was much agitated, and for that reason he forbore to put any question to him concerning the individual they had just left. Indeed it was not until they had passed the Woolshed once more, and had half completed their return journey that the elder man spoke.

"How much of my conversation with that man did you overhear?"

"Nothing but what I heard when Murbridge rose to his feet," James replied. "I should not have come near you had I not heard his threat and seen him approach you. Who is the man, father?"

"His name is Murbridge," said Standerton, with what was plainly an effort. "He is a person with whom I was on friendly terms many years ago, but he has now got into disgrace, and, I fear has sank very low indeed. I do not think he will trouble us any more, however, so we will not refer to him again."

All that evening William Standerton was visibly depressed. He excused himself from playing his usual game of cribbage with his daughter, on the plea that he had a headache. Next morning, however, he was quite himself. He went out to his last day's work in the bush as cheerfully as he had ever done. But had any one followed him, he, or she, would have discovered that the first thing he did was to ride to the spot where Richard Murbridge had slept on the previous night. The camp was deserted, and only a thin column of smoke, rising from the embers of the fire, remained to show that the place had been lately occupied.

"He has gone, then," said Standerton to himself. "Thank goodness! But I know him too well to be able to assure myself that I have seen the last of him. Next week, however, we shall put the High Seas between us, and then, please God, I shall see no more of him for the remainder of my existence."

At that moment the man of whom he was speaking, was tramping along the dusty track with a tempest of rage in his heart.

"He may travel wherever he pleases," he was muttering to himself, "but he won't get away from me. He may go to the end of the world, and I'll follow him and be at his elbow, just to remind him who I am, and of the claims I have upon him. Yes, William Standerton, you may make up your mind upon one point, and that is the fact that I'll be even with you yet!"

CHAPTER II

Childerbridge Manor is certainly one of the finest mansions in the County of Midlandshire. It stands in a finely-timbered park of about two hundred acres, which rises behind the house to a considerable elevation. The building itself dates back to the reign of Good Queen Bess, and is declared by competent authorities to be an excellent example of the architecture of that period. It is large, and presents a most imposing appearance as one approaches it by the carriage drive. The interior is picturesque in the extreme; the hall is large and square, panelled with oak, and having a massive staircase of the same wood leading from it to a music gallery above. There are other staircases in various parts of the building, curious corkscrew affairs, in ascending which one is in continual danger of knocking one's head against the ceiling and corners. There are long, and somewhat dark corridors, down which it would be almost possible to drive the proverbial coach and four, whilst there are also numerous secret passages, and a private chapel, with stained glass windows connected with the house by means of a short tunnel. That such a mansion should be provided with a family ghost, goes without saying. Indeed, Childerbridge Manor is reputed to possess a small army of them. Elderly gentlemen who carry their heads under their arms; beautiful women who glide down the corridors, weeping as they go; and last but not least, a deformity, invariably dressed in black, who is much given to sitting on the foot rails of beds, and pointing, with the first finger of his right hand, to the ceiling above. So well authenticated are the legends of these apparitions, that it would be almost an impossibility to induce any man, woman, or child, from the village, to enter the gates of Childerbridge Manor after dusk. Servants who arrived were told the stories afloat concerning their new abode; and the sound of the wind sighing round the house on a gusty night immediately set their imaginations to work, with the result of their giving notice of their intention to leave on the following morning. "They had seen the White Lady," they declared, had heard her pitiful death cry, and vowed that nothing could induce them to remain in such a house twenty-four hours longer. In fact, "As haunted as the Manor House" had become a popular expression in the neighbourhood.

When the Standerton's reached England, they set to work to discover for themselves a home. They explored the country from east to west, and from north to south, but without success. Eventually Childerbridge Manor was offered them by an Agent in London, and after they had spent a considerable portion of their time poring over photographs of the house and grounds, they arrived at the conclusion that they had discovered a place likely to suit them. On a lovely day in early summer they travelled down from London to inspect it, and were far from being disappointed in what they saw.

When they entered the gates the park lay before them, bathed in sunlight, the rooks cawed lazily in the trees, while the deer regarded them, from their couches in the bracken, with mild, contemplative eyes. After the scorched up plains of Australia, the picture was an exceedingly attractive one. The house itself, they could see would require a considerable outlay in repairs, but when that work was accomplished, it would be as perfect a residence as any that could be found. The stables were large enough to hold half a hundred horses, but for many years had been tenanted only by rats. The same might be said of the buildings of the Home Farm!

"However, taking one thing with another," said Mr. Standerton, after he had inspected everything, and arrived at a proper understanding of the possibilities of the place, "I think it will suit us. The Society of the neighbourhood, they tell me, is good, while the hunting is undeniable. It is within easy reach of London, and all matters taken into consideration, I don't think we shall better it."

In this manner it was settled. A contract for repairs and decorations was placed in the hands of a well-known Metropolitan firm, a vast amount was spent in furnishing, and in due course Childerbridge Manor House was once more occupied. The County immediately came to call, invitations rained in, and having been duly inspected and not found wanting, the newcomers were voted a decided acquisition to the neighbourhood. William Standerton's wealth soon became proverbial, and mothers, with marriageable sons and daughters, vied with each other in their attentions. James Standerton, as I have already said, was a presentable young man. His height was something over six feet, his shoulders were broad and muscular, as became a man who had lived his life doing hard work in the open air, his eyes were grey like his father's, and there was the same moulding of the mouth and chin. In fact, he was an individual with whom, one felt at first glance, it would be better to be on good terms than bad.

One evening a month or so after their arrival at the Manor House, Jim was driving home from the railway station He had been spending the day in London buying polo ponies, and was anxious to get home as quickly as possible. His horse was a magnificent animal, and spun the high dogcart along the road at a rattling pace. When he was scarcely more than half a mile from the lodge gates of his own home, he became aware of a lady walking along the footpath in front of him. She was accompanied by a mastiff puppy, who gambolled awkwardly beside her. As the dogcart approached them the puppy dashed out into the road, directly in front of the fast-trotting horse. As may be imagined the result was inevitable. The dog was knocked down, and it was only by a miracle that the horse did not go down also. The girl uttered a little scream, then the groom jumped from his seat and ran to the frightened animal's head. Jim also descended to ascertain the extent of injuries the horse and dog had sustained. Fortunately the former was unhurt; not so the author of the mischief, however. He had been kicked on the head, and one of his forepaws was crushed and bleeding.

"I cannot tell you how sorry I am," said Jim, apologetically to the young lady, when he had carried her pet to the footpath. "I am afraid I was very careless."

"You must not say that," she answered. "It was not your fault at all. If my silly dog had not run into the road it would not have happened. Do you think his leg is broken?"

Jim knelt on the edge of the path beside the dog and carefully examined his injuries. His bush life had given him a considerable insight into the science of surgery, and it stood him in good stead now.

"No," he said, when his examination was at an end, "his leg is not broken, though I'm afraid it is rather badly injured."

In spite of the young lady's protests, he took his handkerchief from his pocket and bound up the injured limb. The next thing to be decided was how to get the animal home. It could not walk, and it was manifestly impossible that the young lady should carry him.

"Won't you let me put him in the cart and drive you both home?" Jim asked. "I should be glad to do so, if I may."

As he said this he looked more closely at the girl before him, and realised that she was decidedly pretty.

"I am afraid there is nothing else to be done," she said, and then, as if she feared this might be considered an ungracious speech, she added: "But I fear I am putting you to a great deal of trouble, Mr. Standerton."

Jim looked at her in some surprise.

"You know my name, then?" he said.

"As you see," she answered, with a smile at his astonishment. "I called upon your sister yesterday. My name is Decie, and I live at the Dower House, with my guardian, Mr. Abraham Bursfield."

"In that case, as we are neighbours," said Jim, "and I must claim a neighbour's privilege in helping you. Allow me put the dog in the cart."

So saying he picked the animal up and carried it tenderly to the dogcart, under the seat of which he placed it. He then assisted Miss Decie to her seat and took his place beside her. When the groom had seated himself at the back, they set off in the direction of the Dower House, a curious rambling building, situated in a remote corner of Childerbridge Park. As they drove along they discussed the neighbourhood, the prospects of the shooting, and Jim learned, among other things, that Miss Decie was fond of riding, but that old Mr. Bursfield would not allow her a horse, that she preferred a country life to that of town, and incidentally that she had been eight years under her guardian's care. Almost before they knew where they were they had reached the cross roads that skirted the edge of the Park, and were approaching the Dower House. It was a curious old building, older perhaps than the Manor House, to which it had once belonged. In front it had a quaint description of courtyard, surrounded by high walls covered with ivy. A flagged path led from the gates, which, Jim discovered later, had not been opened for many years, to the front door, on either side of which was a roughly trimmed lawn. Pulling up at the gates, the young man descended, and helped Miss Decie to alight.

"You must allow me to carry your dog into the house for you," he said, as he lifted the poor beast from the cart.

A postern door admitted them to the courtyard and they made their way, side by side, along the flagged path to the house. When they had rung the bell the door was opened to them by an ancient man-servant, whose age could scarcely have been less than four-score. He looked from his mistress to the young man, as if he were unable to comprehend the situation.

"Isaac," said Miss Decie, "Tory has met with an accident, and Mr. Standerton has very kindly brought him home for me." Then to Jim she added:—"Please come in, Mr. Standerton, and let me relieve you of your burden."

But Jim would not hear of it. Accompanied by Miss Decie he carried the animal to the loose box in the deserted stables at the back of the house, where he had his quarters. This task accomplished, they returned to the house once more.

"I believe you have not yet met my guardian, Mr. Bursfield," said Miss Decie, as they passed along the oak-panelled hall. Then, as if to excuse the fact that the other had not paid the usual neighbourly call, she added: "He is a very old man, you know, and seldom leaves the house."

As she said this, she paused before a door, the handle of which she turned. The room in which Jim found himself a moment later was a fine one. The walls, like the rest of the house, were panelled, but owing to the number of books the room contained, very little of the oak was visible. There were books on the shelves, books on the tables, and books on the floor. In the centre of the room stood a large writing-table, at which an old man was seated. He was a strange-looking individual; his face was lined with innumerable wrinkles, his hair was snow-white and descended to his shoulders. He wore a rusty velvet coat and a skull cap of the same material.

He looked up as the pair entered, and his glance rested on Jim with some surprise.

"Grandfather," said Miss Decie, for, as Jim afterwards discovered, she invariably addressed the venerable gentleman by this title, though she was in no way related to him, "pray let me introduce you to Mr. Standerton, who has most kindly brought poor Tory home for me."

The old man extended a shrivelled hand.

"I am happy to make your acquaintance, Mr. Standerton," he said, "and I am grateful to you for the service you have rendered Miss Decie. I must apologise for not having paid you and your father the customary visit of courtesy, but, as you have perhaps heard, I am a recluse, and seldom venture from the house. I trust you like Childerbridge?"

"We are delighted with it," Jim replied. "It is a very beautiful and interesting old house. Unfortunately, however, we have been able to gather very little of its history. I have heard

it said that you know more about it than any one in the neighbourhood."

"I do indeed," Mr. Bursfield replied. "No one knows it better than I do. Until a hundred years ago it was the home of
my own family. My father sold it, reserving only the Dower
House for his own use. Since then the estate has fallen upon
evil times."

He paused for a moment and sat looking into the fireplace,
as if he had forgotten his visitor's presence. Then he added as
to himself:

"No one who has taken the place has prospered. There is a
curse upon it."

"I sincerely hope not," Jim answered. "It would be a bad
look out for us if that were so."

"I beg your pardon," the old man returned, almost hastily.
"For the moment I was not thinking of what I was saying. I
did not mean of course that the curse would affect your family. There is no sort of reason why it should. But the series of
coincidences, if by such a term we may designate them, have
certainly been remarkable. Sir Giles Shepfield purchased it
from my father, and was thrown from his horse, and killed at
his own front door. His son Peter was found dead in his bed,
some say murdered, others that he was frightened to death by
something, or someone, he had seen; while his second son,
William, was shot in a duel in Paris, the day after the news
reached him that he had come into the property. The Shep-
fields being only too anxious to dispose of it, it was sold to the
newly-made Lord Childerbridge, who was eager to acquire
it possibly on account of the name. He remained two years
there, but at the end of that period he also had had enough
of the place, and left it quite suddenly, vowing that he would
never enter its doors again. After that it was occupied off and
on by a variety of tenants, but for the last five years it has
been unoccupied. I hear that your father has worked wonders
with it, and that he has almost turned it into a new place."

"He has had the work done very carefully," Jim replied. "It is very difficult to repair an old mansion like Childerbridge without making such repairs too apparent."

"I quite agree with you," said the old man drily. "Your modern architect is no respecter of anything antiquated as a rule."

"And now I must bid you good-evening," said James. "My father and sister will be wondering what has become of me."

He shook hands with Mr. Bursfield, who begged him to excuse him for not accompanying him to the door, and then followed Miss Decie from the room. They bade each other adieu at the gate.

"I hope your dog will soon be himself again," said Jim, in the hope of being able to prolong the interview, if only for a few moments. "If you would like me to have him for a few days I would do what I could for him, and I would see that he is properly looked after."

"I could not think of giving you so much trouble," she returned. "I think he will be all right here. I feel certain I shall be able to do all that is necessary. Will you give my kind regards to your sister? I should like to tell you that I admire her very much, Mr. Standerton."

"It is very good of you to say so," he replied. Then clutching at the hope thus presented to him, he added, "I trust you and she will be great friends."

"I hope so," said Miss Decie, and thereupon bade him good-night.

As he went out to his cart he felt convinced in his own mind that he had just parted from the most charming girl he had ever met in his life. He reflected upon the matter as he completed the short distance that separated him from his home, and when he joined his sister in the drawing-room later, he questioned her concerning her new acquaintance.

"She must lead a very lonely life," said Jim. "I was introduced to the old gentleman she calls grandfather, and if his society is all she has to depend upon, then I do not envy her her lot."

His sister had a suspicion of what was in his mind though she did not say so. Like her brother she had taken a great liking to the girl, and there was every probability, as time went on, of their becoming firm friends.

"It may interest you to hear that she is coming to tea with me on Thursday," said Alice.

Jim was interested, and to prove it registered a mental vow that he would make a point of being at home that day. As a matter of fact he was, and was even more impressed than before.

From that day Miss Decie spent a large proportion of her time at the Manor House. In less than a month she had become Alice's own particular friend, and Jim felt that the whole current of his life had been changed. What Mr. Bursfield thought of the turn affairs had taken can be seen now, but at the time his views were only a matter of conjecture. That Jim and Miss Decie had managed to fall in love with each other was quite certain, and that William Standerton approved of his son's choice was another point that admitted of no doubt. Helen Decie with her pretty face, and charming manners, was a general favourite. At that stage their wooing was a matter-of-fact one in the extreme. Jim had no rival, and at the outset no difficulties worth dignifying with the name. He was permitted unlimited opportunities of seeing the object of his affections and, when the time was ripe, and he informed her of the state of his feelings towards herself, she gave him her hand, and promised, without any hysterical fuss, to be his wife, with the full intention of doing her utmost to make him happy.

"But, Jim," she said, "before you do anything else, you must see Mr. Bursfield and obtain his consent. He is my guardian, you know, and has been so good to me that I can do nothing without his approval."

"I will see him to-morrow morning," Jim replied, "and I fancy I can tell you what his answer will be. How could it be otherwise when he knows that your happiness is at stake?"

"I hope it will be as you say," she answered, but not with her usual cheerfulness. "Somehow or another grandfather always looks at things in a different light to other people."

"You may be sure I will do my best to get him to look at it as we want him to," her lover returned. "I will bring every argument I can think of to bear upon him."

Needless to say, Mr. Standerton, when he heard the news, was delighted, while Alice professed herself overjoyed at the thought of having Helen for her sister. In Jim's mind, however, there was the remembrance of Abraham Bursfield, and of the interview that had to be got through with that gentleman.

"It's no use beating about the bush or delaying matters," he said to himself. "I'll walk back with Helen and get it over to-night instead of to-morrow morning."

He informed his sweetheart of his intention. She signified her approval, and together they strolled across the Park towards the little gate that opened into the grounds of the Dower House. It was a lovely evening, and, as you may suppose, they were as happy a young couple as could have been found in the length and breadth of England. Their engagement had scarcely commenced, yet Jim was already full of plans for the future.

"I shall take you from that dreary old house," he said, nodding his head in the direction of the building they were approaching, "and we will find a place somewhere in the neighbourhood. How you have managed to exist here for eight years I cannot imagine."

"It has been dull certainly," she answered, "but I have the house and my grandfather to look after, so that my time is fairly well taken up."

"You must have felt that you were buried alive," he answered. "In the future, however, we'll change all that. You shall go where, and do, just as you please."

She shook her head.

"To make you happy," she said, "will be enough for me."

CHAPTER III

On reaching the house, Jim bade the butler inform his master that Mr. Standerton would like to see him. Isaac looked at him as if he were desirous of making sure of his business before he admitted him, then he hobbled off in the direction of his master's study, to presently return with the message that Mr. Bursfield would see Mr. Standerton if he would be pleased to step that way. Jim thereupon followed the old man into the room in which he had first made Abraham Bursfield's acquaintance some four months before. As on that memorable occasion, he found that gentleman seated at his desk, looking very much as if he had not moved from it in all that time.

"I wish you good evening, Mr. Standerton," he said, motioning his visitor to a chair. "To what may I attribute the honour of this visit?"

"I have come to you on a most important errand," Jim replied. "Its purport may surprise you, but I hope it will not disappoint you."

"May I ask that you will be good enough to tell me what that errand is," said the old gentleman drily. "I shall then be better able to give you my opinion."

"To sum it up in a few words," Jim answered, "I have this afternoon asked Miss Decie to become my wife, and she has promised to do so. I am here to ask your approval."

Bursfield was silent for a few moments. Then he looked sharply up at the young man.

"You are of course aware that Miss Decie is only my adopted granddaughter, and that she has not the least shadow of a claim, either upon me, or upon such remnants of property as I may possess."

"I am quite aware of it," Jim replied. "Miss Decie has told me of her position, and of your goodness to her."

"The latter of which she is endeavouring to repay by leaving me to spend the rest of my miserable existence alone. A pretty picture of gratitude, is it not? But it is the world all over!"

"I am sure she will always entertain a feeling of profound gratitude towards you," protested Jim. "She invariably speaks of you with the greatest affection."

"I am indeed indebted to her for her consideration," retorted the other with a sneer. "Unfortunately, shall I say, for you, I prefer something more than words. No, Mr. Standerton, I cannot give my consent to your engagement."

Jim could only stare in complete astonishment. He had never expected this.

"You do not mean that you are going to forbid it?" he ejaculated when he had recovered somewhat from his surprise.

"I am reluctantly compelled to admit that that is my intention. Believe me, I have the best of reasons for acting thus. Possibly my decision may cause you pain. It is irrevocable, however. At my death Helen will be able to do as she pleases, but until that event takes place, she must remain with me."

He took up his pen as if to continue his writing, and so end the interview.

"But, Mr. Bursfield, this is an unheard-of determination," cried the young man.

"That may be," was the reply. "I believe I have the reputation for being somewhat singular. My so-called granddaughter is a good girl, and if I know anything of her character, she will do as I wish in this matter."

Jim rose to his feet and crossed to the door as if to leave. When he reached it, however, he turned and faced Mr. Bursfield.

"You are quite sure that nothing I can say or do will induce you to alter your decision?" he enquired.

"Quite," the other replied.

"Then allow me to give you fair warning that I intend to marry Miss Decie," retorted Jim, who by this time had quite lost his temper.

"You are at liberty to do so when I am dead," Mr. Bursfield replied, and then continued his writing as if nothing out of the common had occurred.

Without another word Jim left the room. He had arranged that he should meet Helen in the garden afterwards. It was with a woe-begone face, however, that he greeted her.

"While he lives he absolutely refuses to sanction our engagement," he began. "For some reason of his own he declines to consider the matter for a moment. He says that at his death you are at liberty to do as you please, but until that event occurs, you are to remain with him. I consider it an act of the greatest selfishness."

Helen heaved a heavy sigh.

"I was afraid he would not look upon it as favourably as we hoped," she said. "I will see what I can do with him, however. I know him so well, and sometimes I can coax him to do things he would not dream of doing for any one else."

"Try, darling, then," said Jim, "and let us trust you will be successful."

They bade each other good-night, and then James set off on his walk across the Park. Dusk was falling by this time, and the landscape looked very beautiful in the evening light. As he strode along he thought of his position and of the injustice of Bursfield's decision. Then he fell to picturing what his future life would be like when the old man should have relented and Helen was his wife. He was still indulging in this day-dream when he noticed a shabbily-dressed man standing on the path a short distance ahead of him. Somehow the figure seemed familiar to him, and when he drew nearer he could not suppress an exclamation of astonishment. The individual was none other than the man he had seen lying beside the camp fire on the banks of the Darling River, and who, on a certain memorable evening, had caused his father so much emotion, Richard Murbridge. Whatever Jim's feelings might have been, Murbridge was at least equal to the occasion.

"Good evening, Mr. Standerton," he began, lifting his hat politely as he spoke. "You are doubtless surprised to see me in England."

"I am more than surprised," James replied, "and I am equally astonished at finding you on my father's premises after what he said to you in Australia. If you will be guided by me you will make yourself scarce without loss of time."

"You think so, do you? Then let me tell you that you have no notion of the situation, or of the character of Richard Murbridge. Far from making myself scarce, I am now on my way to see your father. I fear, however, he will not kill the fatted calf in my honour; but even that omission will not deter me. Tenacity of purpose has always been one of my chief characteristics."

"If you attempt to see him you will discover that my father has also some force of character," the other replied. "What is more, I refuse to allow you to do so. I am not going to permit him to be worried by you again."

"My young friend, you little know with whom you are dealing," Murbridge retorted. "I have travelled from the other side of the world to see your father, and if you think you can prevent me you are much mistaken. What is more, let me inform you that you would be doing him a very poor service by attempting to keep us apart. There is an excellent little inn in the village, whose landlord and I are already upon the best of terms. The Squire, William Standerton, late of Australia, but now of Childerbridge, is an important personage in the neighbourhood. Everything that is known about him is to his credit. It would be a pity if—"

"You scoundrel!" said Jim, approaching a step nearer the other, his fists clenched, as if ready for action, "If you dare to insinuate that you know anything to my father's discredit, I'll thrash you to within an inch of your life."

Then a fit of indescribable fear swept over him as he remembered the night in Australia, when his father had shown so much agitation on learning that the man was on his way to the station to see him. What could be the secret between them? But no! He knew his father too well to believe that the man before him could cast even the smallest slur upon his character. William Standerton's name was a synonym for sterling integrity throughout the Island Continent. It was, therefore, impossible that Murbridge could have any hold upon him.

"You had better leave the place at once by the way you came into it," Jim continued, "and take very good care that we don't see any more of you."

"You crow very loud, my young bantam," returned Murbridge, "but that does not alter my decision. Now let me tell you this. If you knew everything, you would just go down on your bended knees and pray to me to forgive you for your impudence. As I said a moment ago, it's not the least use your attempting to stop me from seeing your father, for see him I will, if I have to sit at his gate for a year and wait for him to come out."

"Then you'd better go and begin your watch at once, for you shall not see him at the house," retorted Jim.

"We'll see about that," said Murbridge, and then turned on his heel, and set off in the direction of the Park gates. James waited until he had seen him disappear, then he in his turn resumed his walk. He had to make up his mind before he reached the house as to whether he would tell his father of the discovery he had made or not. On mature consideration he came to the conclusion that it would be better for him to do so.

For this reason, when he reached the house he enquired for his father, and was informed that he had gone to his room to dress for dinner. He accordingly followed him thither, to discover him, brush in hand, at work upon his silver-grey hair. That night, for some reason, the simple appointments of that simple room struck Jim in a new and almost pathetic light. Each article was, like its owner, strong, simple and good.

"Well, my lad, what is it?" asked Standerton. "I hope your interview with Mr. Bursfield was satisfactory?"

"Far from it," Jim replied lugubriously; and then, to post-pone the fatal moment, he proceeded to describe to his father the interview he had had with the old gentleman.

"Never mind, my boy, don't be down-hearted about it," said Standerton, when he had heard his son out. "To-morrow I'll make it my business to go and see Mr. Bursfield. It will be strange if I can't talk him into a different way of thinking before I've done with him. But I can see from your face that there is something else you've got to tell me. What is it?"

Jim paused before he replied. He knew how upset his father would be at the news he had to impart.

"Father," he said, "I'm afraid I've got some bad news for you. I've been trying to make up my mind whether I should tell you or not."

"Tell me, James," answered the other. "I'll be bound it's not so very bad after all. You've probably been brooding over it, and have magnified its importance."

"I sincerely hope I have. I am afraid not, however. Do you remember the man we saw at Mudrapilla in the Five Mile Paddock, the night before we left? His name was Murbridge."

The shock to William Standerton was every bit as severe as James had feared it would be.

"What of him?" he cried. "You don't mean to say that he is in England?"

"I am sorry to say that he is," Jim returned. "I found him in the Park this evening on his way up to the house."

The elder man turned and walked to the fireplace, where he stood looking into it in silence. Then he faced his son once more.

"What did he say to you?" he enquired at last, his voice shaking with the anxiety he could not control or hide.

"He said that he wanted to see you, and that he would do so if he had to wait at the gates for a year."

"And he will," said Standerton bitterly; "that man will hunt me to my grave. I have been cursed with him for thirty years, and do what I will I cannot throw him off."

James approached his father, and placed his hand upon his shoulder.

"Father," he began, "why won't you let me share your trouble with you? Surely we should be able to find some way of ridding ourselves of this man?"

"No, there is no way," said Standerton. "He has got a hold upon me that nothing will ever shake off."

"I will not believe, father, that he knows anything to your discredit," cried Jim passionately.

"And you are right, my lad," his father replied. "He knows nothing to my discredit. I hope no one else does; but—but there—do not ask any more. Some day I will tell you the whole miserable story. But not now. You must not ask me. Believe me, dear lad, when I say that it would be better not."

"Then what will you do?"

"See him, and buy him off once more, I suppose. Then I shall have peace for a few months. Do you know where he is staying?"

"At the 'George and Dragon,'" Jim replied.

"Then I must send a note down to him and ask him to come up here," said Standerton. "Now go and dress. Don't trouble yourself about him."

All things considered, the dinner that night could not be described as a success. William Standerton was more silent than usual, and his son almost equalled him. Alice tried hard to cheer them both, but finding her efforts unsuccessful, she also lapsed into silence. A diversion, however, was caused before the meal was at an end. The butler had scarcely completed the circuit of the table with the port, before a piercing scream ran through the building, followed by another, and yet another.

"Good heavens! What's that?" cried Standerton, as he sprang to his feet, and hurried to the door, to be followed by his son and daughter.

"It came from upstairs, sir," said the butler, and immediately hurried up the broad oak staircase two steps at a time.

His statement proved to be correct, for, on reaching the gallery that runs round the hall, he found a maid-servant lying on the floor in a dead faint. Jim followed close behind him, and between them they picked the girl up, and carried her down to the hall, where she was laid upon a settee. The housekeeper was summoned, and the usual restoratives applied, but it was some time before her senses returned to her. When she was able to speak, she looked wildly about her, and asked if "it was gone?" When later she was able to tell her story more coherently, it was as follows.

In the fulfilment of her usual duties she had gone along the gallery to tidy Miss Standerton's bedroom. She had just finished her work, and was closing the door, when she saw, standing before her, not more than half-a-dozen paces distant, the little hump-backed ghost, of which she had so often heard mention made in the Servants' Hall. It looked at her, pointed its finger at her, and a second later vanished. "She knew now," she declared, "that it was all over with her, and that she was going to die. Nothing could save her." Having given utterance to this alarming prophecy, she indulged in a second fit of hysterics, on recovering from which she was removed by the butler and housekeeper to the latter's sitting-room, vowing as she went that she could not sleep in the house, and that she would never know happiness again. Having seen her depart, the others returned to the dining-room, and had just taken their places at the table once more, when there was a ring at the front door bell, and in due course the butler entered with the information that a person "of the name of Murbridge" had called and would be glad to see Mr. Standerton. James sprang to his feet.

"I told him he was not to come near the place," he said. "Let me go and see him, father."

"No, no, my boy," said Standerton. "I wrote to him before dinner, as I told you I should, telling him to come up to-night. Where is he, Wilkins?"

"In the library, sir," the butler replied.

"Very well. I will see him there."

He accordingly left the room.

A quarter of an hour later James and Alice heard Murbridge's voice in the hall.

"You dare to turn me out of your house?" he was saying, as if in a fit of uncontrollable rage. "You forbid me to speak to your son and daughter, do you?"

"Once and for all, I do," came Standerton's calm voice in reply. "Now leave the house, and never let me see your face again. Wilkins, open the door, and take care that this man is never again admitted to my house."

Murbridge must have gone down the steps, where, as Wilkins asserted later on, he stood shaking his fist at Mr. Standerton.

"Curse you, I'll make you pay for this," he cried. "You think yourself all-powerful because of your wealth, but whatever it costs me, I'll make you smart for the manner in which you've treated me to-night."

Then the door was closed abruptly, and no more was seen of him.

William Standerton's usually rubicund face was very pale when he joined his son and daughter later. It was plain that the interview he had had with Murbridge had upset him more than he cared to admit. Alice did her best to console him, and endeavoured to make him forget it, but her efforts were a failure.

"Poor old dad," she said, when she bade him good-night. "It hurts me to see you so troubled."

"You must not think about it then," was the answer. "I shall be myself again in the morning. Good-night, my girl, and may God bless you."

"God bless you, father," the girl replied earnestly.

"I do wish you'd let me help you," said Jim, when he and his father were alone together. "Why did you not let me interview that man?"

"It would have done no good," Standerton replied. "The fellow was desperate, and he even went so far as to threaten me. Thereupon I lost my temper and ordered him out of the house. I fear we shall have more trouble with him yet."

"Is it quite impossible for you to tell me the reason of it all?" James asked, after a moment's hesitation.

"Well, I have been thinking it over," said his father, "and I have come to the conclusion that perhaps it would be better, much as it will pain you, to let you know the truth. But not to-night, dear lad. Let it stand over, and I will tell you everything to-morrow. Now good-night."

They shook hands according to custom, and then departed to their respective rooms.

Next morning James was about early. He visited the Stables and the Home Farm, looked in at the kennels, and was back again at the home some three-quarters of an hour before breakfast. As he crossed the hall to ascend the stairs, in order to go to his own room, he met Wilkins coming down, his face white as death.

"My God, sir," he said hoarsely, "for mercy's sake come upstairs to your father's room."

"What is the matter with him?" cried James, realising from the butler's manner that something terrible had happened.

But Wilkins did not answer. He only led the way upstairs. Together they proceeded along the corridor and entered the Squire's bedroom. There they saw a sight that James will never forget as long as he lives. His father lay stretched out upon the bed, dead. His eyes were open, and stared horribly at the ceiling, while his hands were clenched, and on either side of his throat were discoloured patches.

These told their own tale.

William Standerton had been strangled.

CHAPTER IV

It would be almost impossible to describe in fitting words the effect produced upon James Standerton, by the terrible discovery he had made.

"What does it mean, Wilkins?" he asked in a voice surcharged with horror. "For God's sake, tell me what it means?"

"I don't know myself, sir," the man replied. "It's too terrible for all words. Who can have done it?"

Throwing himself on his knees beside his father's body, James took one of the cold hands in his.

"Father! father!" he cried, in an ecstasy of grief, and then broke down altogether. When calmness returned to him, he rose to his feet, clasped the hands of the dead man upon the breast, and tenderly closed the staring eyes.

"Send for Dr. Brenderton," he said, turning to Wilkins, "and let the messenger call at the police-station on the way and ask the officer in charge to come here without a moment's delay."

The man left him to carry out the order, and James silently withdrew from the room to perform what he knew would be the saddest task of his life. As he descended the stairs he could hear his sister singing in the breakfast-room below.

"You are very late," she said, as he entered the room. "And father too. I shall have to give him a talking-to when he does come down."

Then she must have realised that something was amiss, for she put down the letter which she had been reading, and took a step towards him. "Has anything happened, Jim?" she enquired, "your face is as white as death." Then Jim told her everything. The shock to her was even more terrible than it had been to her brother, but she did her best to bear up bravely.

The doctor and the police officer arrived almost simultaneously. Both were visibly upset at the intelligence they had received. Short though William Standerton's residence in the neighbourhood had been, it had, nevertheless, been long enough for them to arrive at a proper appreciation of his worth. He had been a good supporter of all the Local Institutions, a liberal landlord, and had won for himself the reputation of being an honest and just man.

"I sympathise with you more deeply than I can say," said the doctor, when he joined Jim in the library after he had made his examination. "If there is anything more I can do to help you, I hope you will command me."

"Thank you," said Jim simply, "there is not anything however you can do. Stay! There is one question you can answer. I want you to tell me how long you think my father has been dead?"

"Several hours," replied the medical man. "I should say at least six."

"Is there any sort of doubt in your mind as to the cause of his death?"

"None whatever," the other replied. "All outward appearances point to the fact that death is due to strangulation."

At that moment the police officer entered the room.

"I have taken the liberty, Mr. Standerton," he said, "of locking the door of the room and retaining the key in my possession. It will be necessary for me to report the matter to the Authorities at once, in order that an Inquest may be held. Before I do so, however, may I put one or two questions to you?"

"As many as you like," Jim replied. "I am, of course, more than anxious that the mystery surrounding my father's death shall be cleared up at once, and the murderer brought to Justice."

"In the first place," said the officer, "I see that the window of the bedroom is securely fastened on the inside, so that the assassin, whoever he was, could not have made his entrance by this means. Do you know whether your father was in the habit of locking his door at night?"

"I am sure he was not. A man who has led the sort of life he has done for fifty years does not lock his bedroom door on retiring to rest."

"In that case the murderer must have obtained access to the room through the house, and I must make it my business to ascertain whether any of the windows or doors were open this morning. One more question, Mr. Standerton, and I have finished for the present. Have you any reason to suppose that your father had an enemy?"

Jim remembered the suspicion that had been in his mind ever since he had made the ghastly discovery that morning.

"I have," he answered. "There was a man in Australia who hated my father with an undying hatred."

"Forgive my saying so, but a man in Australia could scarcely have committed murder in England last night."

"But the man is not in Australia now. He was here yesterday evening, and he and my father had a quarrel. The man was ordered out of the house, and went away declaring that, whatever it might cost, he would be revenged."

"In that case it looks as if the mystery were explained. I must make it my business to discover the whereabouts of the man you mention."

"He was staying at the 'George and Dragon' yesterday," said Jim. "By this time, however, he has probably left the neighbourhood. It should not be difficult to trace him, however; and if you consider a reward necessary, in order to bring about his apprehension more quickly, offer it, and I will pay it only too gladly. I shall know no peace until this dastardly crime has been avenged."

"I can quite understand that," the doctor remarked. "You will have the sympathy of the whole County."

"And now," said the police officer, "I must be going. I shall take a man with me and call at the 'George and Dragon.' The name of the person you mentioned to me is—"

"Richard Murbridge," said Jim, and thereupon furnished the officer with a description of the man in question.

"You will, of course, be able to identify him?"

"I should know him again if I did not see him for twenty years," Jim answered. "Wilkins, the butler, will also be glad to give you evidence as to his coming here last night."

"Thank you," the officer replied. "I will let you know as soon as I have anything to report."

The doctor and the police agent thereupon bade him good-day and took their departure, and Jim went in search of his grief-stricken sister. The terrible news had by this time permeated the whole household, and had caused the greatest consternation.

"I knew what it would be last night," said the cook. "Though Mr. Wilkins laughed at me, I felt certain that Mary Sampson did not see the Black Dwarf for nothing. Why, it's well known by everybody that whenever that horrible little man is seen in the house death follows within twenty-four hours."

The frightened maids to whom she spoke shuddered at her words.

"What's more," the cook continued, "they may talk about murderers as they please, but they forget that this is not the first time a man has been found strangled in this house. There is more in it than meets the eye, as the saying goes."

"Lor, Mrs. Ryan, you don't mean to say that you think it was the ghost that killed the poor master?" asked one of the maids, her eyes dilating with horror.

"I don't say as how it was, and I don't say as how it wasn't," that lady replied somewhat ambiguously, and then she added oracularly: "Time will show."

In the meantime Jim had written a short note to his sweetheart, telling her of the crime, and imploring her to come to his sister at once. A servant was despatched with it, and half-an-hour later Helen herself appeared in answer.

"Your poor father. I cannot believe it! It is too terrible," she said to her lover, when he greeted her in the drawing-room.

"Oh! Jim, my poor boy, how you must feel it. And Alice, too—pray let me go to her at once."

Jim conducted her to his sister's room, and then left the two women together, returning himself to the dead man's study on the floor below. There he sat himself down to wait, with what patience he could command, for news from the police station. In something less than an hour it came in the shape of a note from the inspector, to the effect that Murbridge had not returned to the "George and Dragon" until a late hour on the previous night, and that he had departed for London by the train leaving Childerbridge Junction shortly before five o'clock that morning. "However," said the writer, in conclusion, "I have wired to the Authorities in London, furnishing them with an exact description of him, and I have no doubt that before very long his arrest will be effected."

With this assurance Jim was perforce compelled to be content. Later came the intimation from the Coroner to the effect that the Inquest would be held at the George and Dragon Inn on the following morning.

Shortly after twelve o'clock Wilkins entered the study with the information that a person of "the name of Robins" desired to see his master on an important matter, if he would permit him an interview.

"Show him in," said Jim, forming as he did so a shrewd guess as to the man's business.

A few moments later a small, sombrely-dressed individual, resembling a Dissenting minister more than any one else, made his appearance in the room.

"Mr. Standerton, I believe," he began, speaking in a low, deep voice, that had almost a solemn ring about it.

"That is my name," the other replied. "What can I do for you?"

"I am a Scotland Yard detective," the stranger replied, "and I have been sent down to take charge of the case. I must apologise for intruding upon you at such a time, but if the murderer is to be brought to justice, no time mast be lost. I want you to tell me, if you will, all you can about the crime, keeping nothing back, however trivial you may consider it."

James thereupon proceeded to once more narrate what he knew regarding the murder. He discovered that the detective had already been informed as to the ominous suspicion that had attached itself to Murbridge.

"The first point to be settled," he said, when James had finished, "is the way in which the man got into the house. You have not cross-questioned the domestics upon the subject, I suppose?"

James shook his head.

"I have been too much upset to think of such a thing," he answered. "But if you deem such a proceeding necessary, you are, of course, quite at liberty to do so. Take what steps you think best; all I ask of you is to find my father's murderer."

"I presume you heard nothing suspicious during the night?"

"Nothing at all. But it is scarcely likely that I should do so, as my room is in another part of the house."

"Who is responsible for the locking up at night?"

"The butler, Wilkins."

"Has he been with you any length of time?"

"We ourselves have only been a few months in England," Jim replied, "but since he has been in our service we have found him a most careful and trustworthy man. There cannot be any shadow of suspicion against him."

"Very likely not," the detective answered. "But in my profession we often find criminals in the most unlikely quarters. Mind you, sir, I don't say that he had anything to do with the crime itself. It is not outside the bounds of possibility, however, that his honesty may have been tampered with, even to the extent of leaving a window unfastened, or a door unlocked. However, I have no doubt I shall soon learn all there is to be known about Mr. Wilkins."

When he had asked one or two other important questions, he withdrew to question the servants. From the account James received of the examination later, it would not appear to have been a very successful business.

Wilkins asserted most positively that he had made every door and window in the house secure before retiring to rest. He was as certain as a man could be that no lock, bolt, or bar had been moved from its place during the night, and the housekeeper corroborated his assertions. The detective's face wore a puzzled expression.

"I've been round every flower-bed outside the windows," he said to the police inspector, "and not a trace of a footprint can I find. And yet we know that Murbridge was away from the inn at a late hour, and there's evidence enough upstairs to show that somebody made his way into Mr. Standerton's room between midnight and daybreak. Later I'll go down to the village and make a few enquiries there. It's just possible somebody may have met the man upon the road."

He was as good as his word, and when he returned to the Manor House at a late hour he knew as much about Richard Murbridge's movements on the preceding evening as did any man in the neighbourhood.

Jim dined alone that night, though it would be almost a sarcasm to dignify his meal with such a name. He had spent the afternoon going through his father's papers, in the hope of being able to discover some clue that might ultimately enable him to solve the mystery concerning Murbridge. He was entirely unsuccessful, however. Among all the papers with which the drawers were filled, there was not one scrap of writing that could in anyway enlighten him. They were the plain records of a successful business man's career, and, so far as Murbridge was concerned, quite devoid of interest. I do not think James Standerton ever knew how much he loved his father until he went through that drawer. The neat little packets, so carefully tied up and labelled, spoke to him eloquently of the dead man, and, as he replaced them where he had found them, a wave of intense longing to be revenged on his father's cowardly assassin swept over him. He was in the act of closing the drawer, when there came a tap at the door, and Wilkins entered to inform him that the detective had returned and was at his service, should he desire to see him.

"Show him in, Wilkins," said James, locking the drawer of the table, and placing the key in his pocket as he spoke.

The butler disappeared, to return a few moments later accompanied by the individual in question.

"Well, Mr. Robins," said Jim, when they were alone together, "what have you discovered?"

"Nothing of very much importance, sir, I am afraid," the other replied. "I have found out that Murbridge left the park by the main gates almost on the stroke of half-past eight last night. I have also discovered that he was again seen within a few minutes of eleven o'clock, standing near the small stile at the further end of the park."

"I know the place," Jim replied. "Go on! What was he doing there!"

"Well, sir," continued the detective, "that's more than I can tell you. But if he were there at such an hour, you may be sure it was not with any good intention. I have made enquiries from the keepers, and they have informed me that it is quite possible to reach the house by the path that leads from the stile without being observed."

"It winds through the plantation," said Jim, "and it is very seldom used. Lying outside the village as it does, it is a very roundabout way of reaching the house. What have they to say about him at the inn?"

"Not very much, sir. But what little they do say is important. The landlord informs me that immediately after his arrival in the village he began to ask questions concerning the Squire. There is no doubt that your father was his enemy, and also that Murbridge cherished a bitter grudge against him. He did not tell the landlord who he was, or what his reasons were for being in the neighbourhood. It is certain, however, that had your father not been living here he would not have come near the place. On receipt of Mr. Standerton's letter, he set off for the house, and did not return to the inn until a late hour. In point of fact, it was between twelve and one o'clock when he did come in. The landlord is unable to give the exact time, for the reason that he was too sleepy to take much notice of it. He does remember, however, that Murbridge was in a very bad temper, and that he was excited about something. He called for some brandy, and moreover stated that his holiday was at an end, and that he was leaving for London by the early train next morning. This he did. That is as far as the landlord's tale goes. It seems to me that, unless we can prove something more definite against him than the evidence we have been able to obtain up to the present moment, it will be difficult to bring the crime home to him."

"But we must prove more," cried Jim, with considerable vehemence. "I am as certain in my own mind as I can be of anything that he was the man who killed my father, and if it costs me all I am worth in the world, and if I am compelled to spend the rest of my life in doing it, I'll bring the crime home to him somehow or another. It is impossible that he should be allowed to take that good, honest life, and get off scot free."

"I can quite understand your feelings, sir," said the detective, "and you may rest assured that, so far as we are concerned, no stone shall be left unturned to bring the guilty man to justice. Of course it is full early to speak like this, but if you will review the case in your own mind, you will see that, up to the present, there is really nothing tangible against the man. We know that he hated your father, and that he stated his intention of doing him a mischief, and also that on the night he uttered this threat the murder was committed. From this it would appear that he is responsible for it. But how are we to prove that he got into the house? No one saw him, and there are no suspicious footprints on the flower-beds outside. At the same time we know that he did not return to the inn until a late hour, and that, when he did, he was in an excited state. Yet why should he not have gone for a walk, and might not his excitement be attributed to resentment of the treatment he received at your father's hands? I am very much afraid it would be difficult to induce a Jury to convict on evidence such as we are, so far, able to bring against him. However, we shall hear what the Coroner has to say to-morrow. In the meantime, if you do not require my presence longer, I will return to the inn. It will be necessary for me to be early astir to-morrow."

James bade him good-night, and when he had departed, went upstairs to his sister's room. He found her more composed than she had been when he had last seen her, and able to talk of the dead man without breaking down as she had hitherto done. He informed her of the detective's visit, and of the information he had received from him. It was nearly midnight when he left her. The lamp in the hall was still burning, and he descended the great staircase with the intention of telling Wilkins that he could lock up the house and retire to rest. To his astonishment, when he reached the hall, he beheld the butler standing near the dining-room door, his face as white as the paper upon which I am now writing.

"What on earth is the matter, man?" asked James, who, for the moment, was compelled to entertain the notion that the other had been drinking.

"I've seen it, sir," said Wilkins in a voice that his master scarcely recognised. "I'd never believe it could be true, but now I've witnessed it with my own eyes."

"Witnessed what?" James enquired.

"The ghost, sir," Wilkins replied; "the ghost of the Little Black Dwarf."

Jim was in no humour for such talk then, and I very much regret to say he lost his temper.

"Nonsense," he answered. "You must have imagined that you saw it."

"No, sir, I will take my Bible Oath that I did not. I saw it as plain as I see you now. I'd been in to lock up the dining-room, and was standing just where I am now, never thinking of such a thing, when I happened to look up in the gallery, and there, sir, as sure as I'm alive, was the ghost, leaning on the rail, and looking down at me. His eyes were glaring like red-hot coals. Then he pointed upwards and disappeared. I will never laugh at another person again, when they say that they have seen him. May God defend us from further trouble!"

CHAPTER V

The inquest on the body of William Standerton was held next morning at the George and Dragon Inn in the village, and was attended by more than half the Neighbourhood. The affair had naturally caused an immense sensation in all ranks of Society, and, as the Coroner observed in his opening remarks, universal sympathy was felt for the bereaved family. Wilkins, who had not altogether recovered from the fright he had received on the night before, was the first witness. He stated that he had been the first to discover the murder, and then informed the coroner of the steps he had immediately taken. Questioned as to the visit paid to the Squire by Murbridge, he said that the latter was in a great rage when turned away from the house, and on being asked to do so, repeated the words he had made use of. In conclusion, he said that he was quite certain that no door or window in the house had been left unfastened on the night in question, and that he was equally certain that none were found either open, or showing signs of having been tampered with in the morning. Jim followed next, and corroborated what the butler had said. A sensation was caused when he informed the Coroner that Murbridge had threatened his father in his hearing in Australia. He described his meeting with the man in the park before dinner, and added that he had forbidden him to approach the house. Examined by the Coroner, he was unable to say anything concerning the nature of the quarrel between the two men. The doctor was next called, and gave evidence as to being summoned to the Manor House. He described the body, and gave it as his opinion that death was due to strangulation. Then followed the police officer. The landlord was the next witness, and he gave evidence to the effect that the man Murbridge had stayed at the inn, had been absent on the evening in question from eight o'clock until half-past twelve, and that he had departed for London by the first train on the following morning. The driver of the mail-cart, who had seen him standing beside the stile, was next called. He was quite sure that he had made no mistake as to the man's identity, for the reason that he had had a conversation with him at the George and Dragon Inn earlier in the evening. This completing the evidence, the jury, without leaving the room, brought in a verdict of "Wilful murder against some person or persons unknown," and for the time being the case was at an end.

"You must not be disappointed, my dear sir," said Robins, afterwards; "it is all you can possibly expect. The jury could do no more on such evidence. But we've got our warrant for the arrest of Murbridge, and, as soon as we are able to lay our hands upon him, we may be able to advance another and more important step. I am going up to London this afternoon, and I give you my assurance I shall not waste a moment in getting upon his track."

"And you will let me know how you succeed?"

"I will be sure to do so," Robins replied.

"In the meantime, there can be no harm in my putting an advertisement in the papers, offering a reward of five hundred pounds to anyone who will give such information as may lead to the discovery of the murderer."

"It is a large sum to offer, sir, and will be sure to bring you a lot of useless correspondence. Still, it may be of some use, and I would suggest that you send it to the daily papers without delay."

"It shall be done at once."

Jim thereupon bade the detective good-bye, and returned to the house to inform his sister of what had taken place at the inquest. She quite agreed with him on the matter of the reward, and an advertisement was accordingly despatched to the London newspapers, together with a cheque to cover the cost of the insertions.

Next day the mortal remains of William Standerton were conveyed to their last resting-place in the graveyard of the little village church. After the funeral Jim drove back to the Manor House, accompanied by his father's solicitor, who had travelled down from London for the ceremony. He was already aware that, by his father's death, he had become a rich man, but he had no idea how wealthy he would really be, until the will was read to him. When this had been done he was informed that he was worth upwards of half-a-million sterling. He shook his head sadly:

"I'd give it all up willingly, every penny of it," he answered, "to have my father alive. Even now I can scarcely believe that I shall never see him again. It seems an extraordinary thing to me that the police have, so far, not been able to obtain any clue as to the whereabouts of Murbridge. Look at this heap of letters," he continued, pointing to a pile of correspondence lying upon the writing table, "each one hails from somebody who has either seen Murbridge or professes to know where he is to be found. One knows just such a man working in a baker's shop in Shoreditch; another has lately returned with him on board a liner from America, and on receipt of the reward will give me his present address; a third says that he is a waiter in a popular restaurant in Oxford Street; a fourth avers that he is hiding near the Docks, and intends leaving England this week. So the tale goes on, and will increase, I suppose, every day."

"The effect of offering so large a reward," replied the lawyer. "My only hope is that it will not have the effect of driving him out of England. In which case the difficulty of laying hands upon him will be more than doubled."

"He need not think that flight will save him," Jim replied. "Let him go where he pleases, I will run him to earth."

* * * *

Helen had spent the day at the Manor House, trying to comfort Alice in her distress. At nine o'clock she decided to return to her own home, and Jim determined to accompany her. They accordingly set off together. So occupied were they by their own thoughts, that for some time neither of them spoke. Jim was the first to break the silence.

"Helen," he said, "I cannot thank you sufficiently for your goodness to Alice during this awful time. But for you I do not know how she would have come through it."

"Poor girl," Helen answered, "my heart aches for her."

"She was so fond of our father," James answered.

"Not more than you were, dear," Helen replied; "but you have borne your trouble so bravely—never once thinking of yourself."

The night was dark, and there was no one about, so why should he not have slipped his arm round her waist.

"Helen," he said, "the time has come for me to ask what our future is to be. Will you wait for Mr. Bursfield's death before you become my wife, or will you court his displeasure and trust yourself to me?"

"I would trust myself to you at any time," she answered. "But do you not see how I am situated? I owe everything to my Guardian. But for his care of me in all probability I should now be a governess, a music-mistress, or something of that sort. He has fed me, clothed me, and loved me, after his own fashion, for a number of years. Would it not, therefore, seem like an act of the basest ingratitude to leave him desolate, merely to promote my own happiness?"

"And does my happiness count for nothing?" Jim returned. "But let us talk the matter over dispassionately, and see what can be done. Don't think me heartless, Helen, when I say, that you must realise that Mr. Bursfield is a very old man. It is just possible, therefore, that the event we referred to a few moments ago may take place in the near future. Now, owing to my father's death, I ought not to be married for some time to come. I propose, therefore, that we wait until, say, the end of six months, and then make another appeal to your guardian? It is just possible he may be more inclined to listen to reason then. What do you say?

"I will do whatever you wish," she answered simply. "I fear, however, that, while Mr. Bursfield lives, he will take no other view of the case."

"We must hope that he will," Jim replied. "In the meantime, as long as I know that you are true to me, and love me as I love you, I shall be quite happy."

"You do believe that I love you, don't you, Jim?" she asked, looking up at her lover in the starlight.

"Of course I do," he answered. "God knows what a lucky man I deem myself for having been permitted to win your love. I am supremely thankful for one thing, and that is, the fact that my father learnt to know and love you before his death."

"As I had learnt to love him," she replied. "But there, who could help doing so?"

"One man at least," Jim replied. "Unhappily, we have the worst of reasons for knowing that there was one person in the world who bore him a mortal hatred."

"Have you heard anything yet from the police regarding Murbridge?"

"Not a word," Jim answered. "They have given me their most positive assurance that they are leaving no stone unturned to find the man, but, so far, they appear to have been entirely unsuccessful. If they do not soon run him down I shall take up the case myself, and see what I can do with it. And now here we are at the gate. You do not know how hard it is for me to let you go, even for so short a time. With the closing of that door the light seems to go out of my life."

"I hope and pray that you will always be able to say that," she answered solemnly.

Then they bade each other good-night, and she disappeared into the house, leaving Jim free to resume his walk. He had not gone many steps, however, before he heard his name called, and, turning round, beheld no less a person than Mr. Bursfield hurrying after him. He waited for the old gentleman to come up. It was the first time that Jim had known him to venture beyond the limits of his own grounds. The circumstance was as puzzling as it was unusual.

"Will you permit me a short conversation with you, Mr. Standerton?" Mr. Bursfield began. "I recognised your voice as you bade Miss Decie good-bye, and hurried after you in the hope of being able to see you."

For a moment Jim hoped that Mr. Bursfield had come after him in order to make amends, and to withdraw his decision regarding his marriage with Helen. This hope, however, was soon extinguished.

"Mr. Standerton," the old gentleman continued, "you may remember what I told you a few evenings since concerning the proposal you did me the honour of making on behalf of my ward, Miss Decie?"

"I remember it perfectly," Jim replied; "it is scarcely likely that I should forget."

"Since then I have given the matter careful consideration, and I may say that I have found no reason for deviating from my previous decision."

"I am sorry indeed to hear that. The more so as your ward and myself are quite convinced that our affections are such as will not change or grow weaker with time. Indeed, Mr. Bursfield, I have had another idea in my mind which I fancied might possibly commend itself to you, and induce you to reconsider your decision. You have already told me that Miss Decie's presence is necessary to your happiness. As a proof of what a good girl she is I might inform you that, only a few moments since, she told me that she could not consent to leave you, for the reason that she felt that she owed all she possessed to you."

"I am glad that Helen has at least a spark of gratitude," the other answered with a sneer. "It is a fact that she does owe everything to me. And now for this idea of yours."

"What I was going to propose is," said Jim, "that in six months' time, or so, you should permit me to marry your ward, and from that day forward should take up your residence with us."

The old man looked at him in astonishment. Then he burst into a torrent of speech.

"Such a thing is not to be thought of," he cried. "I could not consider it for a moment; it would be little short of madness. I am a recluse. I care less than nothing for society. My books are my only companions; I want, and will have, no others. Besides, I could not live in that house of yours, were you to offer me all the gold in the world."

Here he grasped Jim's arm so tightly that the young man almost winced.

"I have, of course, heard of your father's death," he continued. "It is said that he was murdered. But, surely, knowing what you do, you are not going to be foolish enough to believe that?"

"And why not?" Jim enquired in great surprise. "I can do nothing else, for every circumstance of the case points to murder. Good heavens! Mr. Bursfield, if my father were not murdered, how did he meet his death?"

The other was silent for a moment before he replied. Then he drew a step nearer, and, looking up at Jim, asked in a low voice:

"Have you forgotten what I said to you concerning the mystery of the house? Did I not tell you that one of the former owners was found dead in bed, having met his fate in identically the same manner as your father did? Does not this appear significant to you? If not, your understanding must indeed be dull."

The new explanation of the mystery was so extraordinary, that Jim did not know what to say or think about it. That his father's death had resulted from any supernatural agency had never crossed his mind.

"I fear I am not inclined to agree with you, Mr. Bursfield," he said somewhat coldly. "Even if one went so far as to believe in such things, the evidence given by the doctor at the inquest would be sufficient to refute the idea."

"In that case let us drop the subject," Bursfield answered. "My only desire was to warn you. It is rumoured in the village that on the night of your father's death one of your domestics was confronted by the spectre known as the Black Dwarf, and fainted in consequence. My old man-servant also told me this morning that your butler had seen it on another occasion. I believe the late Lord Childerbridge also saw it, and in consequence determined to be rid of the place at any cost. No one has been able to live there, and I ask you to be warned in time, Mr. Standerton. For my own part, as I have said before, though it is the home of my ancestors, I would not pass a night at Childerbridge for the wealth of all the Indies."

"In that case you must be more easily frightened than I am," said Jim. "On the two occasions you mention, the only evidence we have to rely upon is the word of a hysterical maid-servant, and the assurance of a butler, who, for all we know to the contrary, may have treated himself more liberally than usual, on that particular evening, to my father's port."

"Scoff as you will," Bursfield returned, "but so far as you are concerned I have done my duty. I have given you your warning, and if you do not care to profit by it, that has nothing to do with me. And now to return to the matter upon which I hastened after you this evening. I refer to your proposed marriage with my ward."

Jim said nothing, but waited for Mr. Bursfield to continue. He had a vague feeling that what he was about to hear would mean unhappiness for himself.

"I informed you the other day," the latter continued, "that it was impossible for me to sanction your proposal. I regret that I am still compelled to adhere to this decision. In point of fact, I feel that it is necessary for me to go even further, and to say that I must for the future ask you to refrain from addressing yourself to Miss Decie at all."

"Do you mean that you refuse me permission to see her or to speak with her?" Jim asked in amazement.

"If, by seeing her, you mean holding personal intercourse with her, I must confess that you have judged the situation correctly. I am desirous of preventing Miss Decie from falling into the error of believing that she will ever be your wife."

"But, my dear sir, this is an unheard-of proceeding. Why should you object to me in this way? You know nothing against me, and you are aware that I love your ward. You admitted, on the last occasion that I discussed the matter with you, that Miss Decie might expect little or nothing from you at your death. Why, therefore, in the name of Commonsense, are you so anxious to prevent her marrying the man she loves, and who is in a position to give her all the comfort and happiness wealth and love can bestow?"

"You have heard my decision," the other replied quietly. "I repeat that on no consideration will I consent to a marriage between my ward and yourself. And, as I said just now, I will go even further, and forbid you most positively for the future either to see or to communicate with her."

"And you will not give me your reasons for taking this extraordinary step?"

"I will not. That is all I have to say to you, and I have the honour to wish you a good evening."

"But I have not finished yet," said Jim, whose anger by this time had got the better of him. "Once and for all, let me tell you this, Mr. Bursfield: I have already informed you that I am determined, at any cost, to make Miss Decie my wife. I might add now, that your tyrannical behaviour will only make me the more anxious to do so. If the young lady deems it incumbent upon her to await your consent before marrying me, I will listen to her and not force the matter; but give her up I certainly will not so long as I live."

"Beware, sir, I warn you, beware!" the other almost shrieked.

"If that is all you have to say to me I will bid you good evening."

But Bursfield did not answer; he merely turned on his heel and strode back in the direction of the Dower House. Jim stood for a moment looking after his retreating figure, and when he could no longer distinguish it, turned and made his way homewards.

On reaching the Manor House he informed his sister of what had taken place between himself and Helen's guardian.

"He must be mad to treat you so," said Alice, when her brother had finished. "He knows that Helen loves you, and surely he cannot be so selfish as to prefer his own comfort to her happiness."

"I am afraid that is exactly what he does do," said Jim. "However, I suppose I must make allowances. Old age is apt to be selfish. Besides, we have to remember, as Helen says, that she owes much to him. No! we will do as we proposed, and wait six months, and see what happens then!"

But though he spoke so calmly he was by no means at ease in his own mind. He was made much happier, however, by a note which was brought to him as he was in the act of retiring to rest.

It was in Helen's handwriting, and he tore it open eagerly.

"My own dear love," it ran, "Mr. Bursfield has just informed me of what took place between you this evening. It is needless for me to say how sorry I am that such a thing should have occurred. I cannot understand his behaviour in this matter. That something more than any thought of his own personal comfort makes him withhold his consent, I feel certain. Whatever happens, however, you know that I will be true to you; and if I cannot be your wife, I will be wife to no other man.

"Your loving Helen."

CHAPTER VI

While the letter from Helen cheered James Standerton wonderfully, it did not in any way help him out of his difficulty with Mr. Bursfield. The latter had most decisively stated his intention not to give his consent to the marriage of his adopted granddaughter with the young Squire of Childerbridge. What his reasons were for taking such a step, neither Jim nor Helen could form any idea. It was a match that most guardians would have been only too thankful to have brought about. In spite of Helen's statements, he could only, after mature consideration, assign it to the old man's natural selfishness, and, however bitterly he might resent his treatment, in his own heart he knew there was nothing for it but to wait with such patience as he could command for a change in the other's feelings towards himself. He had the satisfaction of knowing, however, that Helen loved him, and that she would be true to him, happen what might. He was not a more than usually romantic young man, but I happen to know that he carried that letter about with him constantly, while he had read it so often that he must have assuredly known its contents by heart. All things considered, it is wonderful what comfort it is possible for a love-sick young man to derive from a few commonplace words written upon a sheet of notepaper.

After the momentous interview with Mr. Bursfield, the days went by with their usual sameness at Childerbridge. No news arrived from the detective, Robins. Apparently it was quite impossible for him to discover the smallest clue as to Murbridge's whereabouts. To all intents and purposes he had disappeared as completely as if he had been caught up into the skies. The reward, beyond bringing a vast amount of trouble and disappointment to Jim, had not proved of the least use to any one concerned.

Numerous half-witted folk, as is usual in such cases, had come forward and given themselves up, declaring that they had committed the murder, but the worthlessness of their stories was at once proved in every case. One man, it was discovered, had been on the high seas another had never been near Childerbridge in his life; while a third, and this was a still more remarkable case, was found to have been an inmate of one of Her Majesty's convict establishments at the time the murder was committed.

"Never mind," said Jim to himself; "he must be captured sooner or later. If the police authorities cannot catch him, I'll take up the case myself, and run him to ground, wherever he may be."

As he said this he looked up at the portrait of his father, which hung upon the wall of his study.

"Come what may, father," he continued, "if there is any justice in the world, your cruel murder shall be avenged."

Another month went by, and still the same want of success attended the search for Murbridge.

"Alice, I can stand it no longer," said Jim to his sister one evening, after he had read a communication from Robins. "I can gather from the tone of this letter that they are losing heart. I ought to have taken up the case myself at the commencement, and not have wasted all this precious time. The man may now be back in Australia, South America, or anywhere else."

Alice crossed the room and placed her hand on his shoulder.

"Dear old Jim," she said, "I am sure you know how I loved our father."

"Of course I do," said Jim, looking up at her. "No one knows better. But I can see there is something you want to say to me. What is it?"

"Don't be angry with me, Jim," she replied, seating herself on the arm of his chair "but deeply as that man has wronged us, I cannot help thinking that we should not always be praying for vengeance against him, as we are doing. Do you think it is what our father, with his noble nature, would have wished?"

Jim was silent for a moment. The desire for vengeance by this time had taken such a hold upon him, and had become such an integral part of his constitution, that he was staggered beyond measure by her words.

"Surely you don't mean to say, Alice," he stammered, "that you are willing to forgive the man who so cruelly killed our father?"

"I shall try to forgive him," the girl replied. "I say again, that I am sure it is what our father would have wished us to do."

"I am no such saint," Jim returned angrily. "I wish to see that man brought to justice, and, what's more, if no one else will, I mean to bring him. He took that noble life, and he must pay the penalty of his crime. An eye for an eye, and a tooth for a tooth, was the old law. Why should we change it?"

Alice rose and crossed the room to her own chair with a little sigh. She knew her brother well enough to be sure that, having once made up his mind, he would carry out his determination.

On the morning following this conversation, Jim was standing after breakfast at the window of his sister's boudoir, looking out upon the lawn, across which the leaves were being driven by the autumn wind. His brow was puckered with thought. As a matter of fact, he was wondering at the moment how he should commence his search for Murbridge. London was such a great city, and for an amateur to attempt to find a man in it, who desired to remain hidden, was very much like setting himself the task of hunting for a needle in a bundle of hay. He neither knew where or how to begin. While he was turning the question over in his mind, his quick eye detected the solitary figure of a man walking across the park in the direction of the house. He watched it pass the clump of rhododendrons, and then lost it again in the dip beyond the lake. Presently it reappeared, and within a few moments it was within easy distance of the house. At first Jim had watched the figure with but small interest; later, however, his sister noticed that he gradually became excited. When the stranger had passed the corner of the house he turned excitedly to his sister.

"Good gracious, Alice!" he cried, "it surely cannot be."

"What cannot be?" asked Alice, leaving her chair, and approaching the window.

"That man coming up the drive," Jim replied. "It doesn't seem possible that it can be he, yet I've often boasted that I should know his figure anywhere. If it were not the most improbable thing in the world, I should be prepared to swear that it's Terence O'Riley."

"But, my dear Jim, what could Terence be doing here, so many thousand miles from our old home?"

But Jim did not wait to answer the question. Almost before Alice had finished speaking he had reached the front door, had opened it, and was wildly shaking hands with a tall, spare man, with a humorous, yet hatchet-shaped face, so sunburnt as to be almost the colour of mahogany.

The newcomer, Terence O'Riley, was a character in his way. He boasted that he knew nothing of father or mother, or relations of any sort or kind. He had received his Hibernian patronymic from his first friend, a wild Irishman on the diggings where he was born. He had entered William Standerton's service at the age of twelve, as horse-boy, and for upwards of thirty years had remained his faithful henchman. In every respect he was a typical Bushman. He could track like a blackfellow, ride any horse that was ever foaled, find his way in the thickest country with unerring skill, was a first-class rifle shot, an unequalled judge of cattle, a trifle pugnacious at certain seasons, but, and this seems an anomaly, at other times he possessed a heart as tender as a little child. When William Standerton and his family had left Australia, his grief had been sincere. For weeks he had been inconsolable, and it meant a sure thrashing for any man who dared to mention James' name in his hearing.

"What on earth does this mean, Terence?" asked Jim, who could scarcely believe that it was their old servant who stood before him.

"It means a good many things, Master Jim," said Terence, with the drawl in his voice peculiar to Australian Bushmen. "It's a longish yarn, but, my word, I am just glad to see you again, and, bless me, there's Miss Alice too, looking as pretty as a grass parrot on a gum log."

With a smile of happiness on her face, that had certainly not been there since her father's death, Alice came forward and gave Terence her hand. He took it in his great palm, and I think, but am not quite sure, that there were tears in his eyes.

"Come in at once," said Jim. "You must tell us your tale from beginning to end. Even now I can scarcely realise that it is you. Every moment I expect to see you vanish into mid-air. If I had been asked where you were at this moment, I should have said 'out in one of the back paddocks, say the Bald Mountain, riding along the fence on old Smoker, with Dingo trotting at his heels.'"

"No, sir," Terence answered, looking round the great hall as he spoke, "I sold Smoker at Bourke before I came away, and one of the overseers has Dingo, poor old dog. The fact of the matter was, sir, after you left I got a bit lonesome, and the old place didn't seem like the same. I had put by a matter of between four and five hundred pounds, and, thinks I to myself, there's the Old Country, that they say is so beautiful, and to think that I've never set eyes on it. Why shouldn't I make the trip, and just drop in and see the Boss, and Master Jim, and Miss Alice in their new home. Who knows but that they might want a colt broken for them. As soon as I made up my mind, I packed my bag and set off for Melbourne, took a passage on board a ship that was sailing next day, and here I am, sir. I hope your father is well, sir?"

There was an awkward pause, during which Alice left the room.

"Is it possible you haven't heard, Terence?" Jim enquired, in a hushed voice.

"I've not heard anything, sir," Terence answered. "I was six weeks on the water, you see. I do hope, sir, there is nothing wrong."

Jim thereupon told Terence the whole story of his father's death. When he had finished the Bushman's consternation may be better imagined than described. For some moments it deprived him of speech. He could only stare at Jim in horrified amazement.

"Tell me, sir, that they've got the man who did it," he said at last, bringing his hand down with a bang on the table beside which he was seated. "Tell me that they're going to hang the blackguard who killed the kindest master in all the world, or I'll say that there's not a trooper in England that's fit to call himself a policeman."

The poor fellow was genuinely affected.

"They haven't caught him yet, Terence," said Jim. "The police have been searching for him everywhere for weeks past, but without success."

"But they must find him, run him down, and hang him, just as we used to string up the cowardly dingoes out back when they worried the sheep. If I have to track him like a Nyall blackfellow, I'll find him."

"Terence, I believe you've come at the right time," said Jim, holding out his hand. "Seeing the way the police Authorities are managing affairs, I've decided to take up the case myself. You were a faithful servant to my father, and you've known me all my life. You've got a head on your shoulders—do you remember who it was that found out who stole those sheep from Coobalah Out Station? Come with me, old friend, and we'll run the villain down together. I would not wish for a better companion."

"I'm thankful now that I came, sir," Terence replied. "You mark my words, we'll find him, wherever he's stowed himself away."

From that day Terence was made a member of the Childer-bridge household. In due course, accompanied by Jim, he inspected the stables and was more than a little impressed by the luxury with which the animals were surrounded.

"Very pretty," he muttered to himself, "and turned out like racehorses; all the same, I wouldn't like to ride 'em after cattle in the Ranges on a dark night."

The sedate head coachman could not understand the situation. He was puzzled as to what manner of man this might be, who, though so poorly dressed, while treating his master with the utmost respect, conversed with him on terms of perfect equality. His amazement, however, was turned into admiration later in the day when Mr. O'Riley favoured him with an exposition of the gentle art of horse-breaking.

"He's a bit too free and easy in his manners towards the governor for my likin'," he informed the head gardener afterwards, "but there's no denyin' the fact that he's amazin' clever with a youngster. They do say as 'ow he did all Mr. Standerton's horse-breaking in foreign parts."

It soon became apparent that Terence was destined to become one of the most popular personages at Childerbridge. His quaint mannerisms, extraordinary yarns, and readiness to take any sort of work, however hard, upon his shoulders, won for him a cordial welcome from the inhabitants of the Manor House. As for Jim and Alice, for some reason best known to themselves they derived a comfort from his presence that at any other time they would scarcely have believed possible.

On the day following Terence's arrival James stood on the steps at the front door, watching him school a young horse in the park. The high-spirited animal was inclined to be troublesome, but with infinite tact and patience Terence was gradually asserting his supremacy. Little by little, as he watched him, Jim's thoughts drifted away from Childerbridge, and another scene, equally familiar, rose before his eyes. He saw a long creeper-covered house, standing on the banks of a mighty river. A man was seated in the verandah, and that man was his father. Talking to him from the garden path was another—no less a person than Terence. Then he himself emerged from the house and stood by his father's side—a little boy of ten, dressed in brown holland, and wearing a broad-brimmed straw hat upon his head. Upon his coming his father rose, and, taking him by the hand, led him down to the stock-yard, accompanied by Terence. In the yard stood the prettiest pony that mortal boy had ever set eyes on.

"There, my boy," said his father, "that is my birthday present to you. Terence has broken him."

And now here was this self-same Terence in England, of all places in the world, making his hunters for him, while the father, who all his life had proved so generous to him, was lying in his grave, cruelly murdered. At that moment Alice came up behind him.

"What are you thinking of, Jim?" she enquired.

"I was thinking of Mudrapilla and the old days," he answered. "Seeing Terence out there on that horse brought it back to me so vividly that for a moment I had quite forgotten that I was in England. Do you know, Alice, that sometimes a wild longing to be back there takes possession of me. If only Helen were my wife, I'm not quite certain that I should not want to take you both back—if only for a trip. It seems to me that I would give anything to feel the hot sun upon my shoulders once again, to smell the smoke of a camp fire, to see the dust rise from the stock-yards, and to scent the perfume of the orange blossoms as we sit together in the verandah in the evening. Alice, that is the life of a man; this luxurious idleness makes me feel effeminate. But there, what am I talking about? I've got my duty to do in England before we go back to Mudrapilla."

At that moment Terence rode up, very satisfied with himself and with the animal upon whose back he was seated. He had scarcely departed in the direction of the stable before Jim descried a carriage entering the park. It proved to be a fly from the station, and in it Robins, the detective, was seated.

"Good afternoon, sir," he said, as he alighted; "in response to your letter, I have come down to see you personally."

"I am very glad you have done so," Jim replied, "for I have been most anxious to see you. Let us go into the house."

He thereupon led the way to his study, where he invited the detective to be seated.

"I hope you have some good news for me," Jim remarked, as he closed the door. "Have you made any discovery concerning Murbridge?"

The detective shook his head.

"I am sorry to say," he answered, "that our efforts have been entirely unsuccessful. We traced the man from Paddington to a small eating-house in the vicinity of the station, but after that we lost him altogether. We have kept a careful watch on the out-going ships, tried the hotels, lodging-houses, Salvation Army Shelters and such places, and have sent a description of him to every police station in the country, but so far without an atom of success. Once, when the body of a man was found in the river at Greenwich, I thought we had discovered him. The description given of the dead man tallied exactly with that of Murbridge. I was disappointed, however, for he turned out to be a chemist's assistant, who had been missing from Putney for upwards of a fortnight. Then a man gave himself up to the police at Bristol, but he was found to be a mad solicitor's clerk from Exeter. This is one of the deepest cases I have ever been concerned in, Mr. Standerton, and though I am not the sort of man who gives up very quickly, I am bound to confess that, up to the present, I have been beaten, and beaten badly."

"You are not going to abandon the case, I hope?" Jim asked anxiously. "Because you have been unsuccessful so far, you are surely not going to give it up altogether?"

"The law never abandons a case," the other observed sententiously. "Of course it's quite within the bounds of possibility that we may hit upon some clue that will ultimately lead to Murbridge's arrest; it is possible that he may give himself up in course of time; at the present, however, I must admit that both circumstances appear remarkably remote."

"Well," returned Jim, "I can assure you that, whatever else happens, I am not going to give up. If the authorities are going to do so, I shall take it up myself and see what I can do."

There was a suspicion of a smile upon the detective's face as he listened. Was it possible that an amateur could really believe himself to be capable of succeeding where the astute professionals of Scotland Yard had failed?

"I am afraid you will only be giving yourself needless trouble," he said.

"I should not consider it trouble to try and discover my father's murderer," Jim returned hotly. "Even if I am not more successful than the police have been, I shall have the satisfaction of knowing that I have done my best. May I trouble you for the name of the eating-house to which Murbridge proceeded on leaving Paddington?"

Taking a piece of paper from the writing-table, Robins wrote the name and address of the eating-house upon it, and handed it to Jim. The latter placed it carefully in his pocket-book, and felt that he must make the house in question his starting point.

When the detective took his departure half an hour later, Jim gave instructions that Terence should be sent to him.

"Terence," he began, when the other stood before him, "I am going up to London to-morrow morning to commence my search for Murbridge. I shall want you to accompany me."

"Very good, sir," Terence replied, "I've been hoping for this, and it'll go hard now if we can't track him somehow. But you must bear in mind, sir, that I've never been in London. If it was in the Bush, now, I won't say but what I should not be able to find him, but I don't know much about these big cities, so to speak. It will be like looking for a track of one particular sheep in a stock-yard after a mob of wild cattle have been turned into it."

Jim smiled. He saw that Terence had not the vaguest notion of what London was like.

That evening he informed Alice of the decision he had come to. She had been expecting it for some days past, and was not at all surprised by it. She only asked that he would permit her to accompany him.

"I could not remain here," she said, "and I'll promise that I'll not be in your way. It will be so desolate in this house without you, especially as Mr. Bursfield will not allow Helen to visit us, and I have no other companion."

"By all means come with me," said Jim, "I shall choose a quiet hotel in the West End, and you must amuse yourself as best you can while I am absent."

Later in the evening he wrote a note to his sweetheart informing her of his decision, and promising to let her know, day by day, what success attended his efforts.

Next morning they left Childerbridge Station at eleven o'clock for London. As the train steamed out of the village past the little churchyard, Jim looked down upon his father's grave, which he could just see on the eastern side of the church.

"Dear father," he muttered to himself, "If have to devote the rest of my life in bringing your murderer to justice, I'll do it."

CHAPTER VII

It was considerably past midday by the time Jim and his sister, accompanied by Terence, reached London. On arriving at Paddington, they engaged a cab and drove to the hotel they had selected, a private establishment leading out of Piccadilly. Terence's amazement at the size of London was curious to witness. Hitherto he had regarded Melbourne as stupendous, now it struck him that that town was a mere village compared with this giant Metropolis. When he noted the constant stream of traffic, the crowds that thronged the pavements, and the interminable streets, his heart misgave him concerning the enterprise upon which he had so confidently embarked.

"Bless my soul, how many people can there be in London?" he asked, as they drove up to the hotel.

"Something over five millions," Jim replied. "It's a fair-sized township."

"And we are going to look for one man," continued the other. "I guess it would be easier to find a scrubber in the mallee than to get on the track of a man who is hiding himself here."

"Nevertheless we've got to find him somehow," said Jim. "That's the end of the matter."

After lunch he sent word to Terence that he wished him to accompany him on his first excursion. Up to that time he had formed no definite plan of action, but it was borne in upon him that he could do nothing at all until he had visited the eating-house to which Murbridge had been traced after his arrival at Paddington Station. They accordingly made their way to the house in question. It proved to be an uninviting place, with a sawdust-covered floor, and half-a-dozen small tables arranged along one side. On the other was a counter upon which were displayed a variety of covered dishes and huge tea cups. At the moment of Jim's entering the proprietor was giving his attention to a steaming pan of frying onions.

"What can I do for you, sir?" he asked, as he removed the frying-pan from the gas and came forward.

"I want five minutes' conversation with you in private, if you will give it to me," Jim replied, and then in a lower voice he added: "I stand in need of some information which I have been told you are in a position to supply. I need not say that I shall be quite willing to recompense you for any loss of time or trouble you may be put to."

"In that case I shall be very happy to oblige you, sir," the man replied civilly enough. "That is to say, if it is in my power to do so. Will you be good enough to step this way?"

Pulling down his shirt-sleeves, which until that moment had been rolled up, and slipping on a greasy coat, he led the way from the shop to a tiny apartment leading out of it. It was very dirty and redolent of onions and bad tobacco. Its furniture was scanty, and comprised a table, covered with American cloth, a cupboard, and two wooden chairs, upon one of which James was invited to seat himself. Terence, who had followed them, took the other, while he surveyed its owner with evident disfavour.

"And now, sir," said that individual, "I should be glad if you can tell me what I can do for you. If it's about the Board School election, well, I'll tell you at once, straight out, as man to man, that I ain't a-goin' to vote for either party. There was a young wagabond that I engaged the other day. He had had a Board School edecation, and it had taught him enough to be able to humbug me with his takings. Thirteen and eleven-pence-'alfpenny was what he stole from me. And as I said to the missus only last night, 'No more Board School lads for me!' But there, sir, p'raps you ain't a-got nothing to do with them?"

"I certainly have not," James replied. "I am here on quite a different matter. Of course you remember the police visiting you a short time since, with regard to a man who was suspected of being the murderer of Mr. Standerton, at Childerbridge, in Midlandshire?"

"Remember it?" the man replied, "I should think I did. And haven't I got good cause to remember it? I was nigh being worritted to death by 'em. First it was one, and then it was another, hanging about here and asking questions. Had I seen the man? Did I know where he had gone? What was he like? Till with one thing and another I was most driven off my head. I won't say as how a detective oughtn't to ask questions, because we all know it's his duty, but when it comes to interferin' with a man's private business and drivin' his customers away from the shop—for I won't make no secrets with you that there is folks as eats at my table as is not in love with 'tecs—well, then I say, if it comes to that, it's about time a man put his foot down."

"My case is somewhat different," said James. "In the first place, I am not a detective, but the son of the gentleman who was murdered."

"Good gracious me! you don't say so," said the man, regarding him with astonishment and also with evident appreciation. "Now that makes all the difference. It's only fit and proper that a young gentleman should want to find out the man who, so to speak, had given him such a knock-down blow. Ask me what questions you like, sir, and I'll do my best to answer 'em."

"Well, first and foremost," said Jim, "I want to know how you became aware that the man in question hailed from Childerbridge? He wouldn't have been likely to say so."

"No, you're right there," the man replied. "He didn't say so, but I knew it, because after he had had his meal, my girl was giving him 'is change, I saw there was a Childerbridge label on the small bag he carried in his hand. I put it to you, sir, if he hadn't been there, would that label have been on the bag?"

"Of course it would not. And he answered to the description given you?"

"To a T, sir. Same sort of face, same sort of dress, snarly manner of speaking, spotted bird's-eye necktie and all."

"It must have been the man. And now another question. You informed the police, did you not, that you had no knowledge as to where he went after he left your shop?"

The man fidgetted uneasily in his chair for a moment, and drummed with his fingers upon the cover of the table. It was evident that he was keeping something back, and was trying to make up his mind as to whether he should divulge his information or not.

Here James played a good game, and with a knowledge of human character few people would have supposed him to possess, took from his pocket a sovereign, which he laid on the table before the other.

"There," he said, "is a sovereign. I can see that you are keeping something back from me. Now, that money is yours whether you tell me or not. If it is likely to affect your happiness don't let me know, but if you can, I shall be glad if you will tell me all you know."

"Spoken like a gentleman, sir," the other replied, "and I don't mind if I do tell you, though it may get me into trouble with some of my customers if you give me away. You see, sir, round about here in this neighbourhood, a man has to be careful of what he says and does. Suppose it was to come to the ears of some people that it was me as gave the information that got the bloke arrested, well then, they'd be sure to say to 'emselves, 'he's standin' in with the perlice, and we don't go near his shop again.' Do you take my meaning, sir?"

"I quite understand," James replied. "I appreciate your difficulty, but you may be quite sure that I will not mention your name in connection with any information you may give me."

"Spoken and acted like a gentleman again, sir," said the shopman. "Now I'll tell you what I know. I didn't tell the 'tecs, becos they didn't treat me any too well. But this is what I do know, sir. As he went out of the door he asked my little boy, Tommy, wot was playing on the pavement, how far it was to Great Medlum Street? The boy gave him the direction, and then he went off."

"Great Medlum Street?" said James, and made a note of the name in his pocket-book. "And how far may that be from here?"

"Not more than ten minutes' walk," the other replied. "Go along this street, then take the third turning to your left and the first on the right. You can't make no mistake about it."

"And what kind of a street is it?" Jim enquired. "I mean, what sort of character does it bear?"

"Well, sir, that's more than I can tell you," said the other. "For all I know to the contrary, it's a fairish sort of street, not so fust-class as some others I could name, but there's a few decent people living in it."

"And do you happen to have anything else to tell me about him?"

"That's all I know, sir," said the other. "I haven't set eyes on him from that blessed moment until this, and I don't know as I want to."

"I am very much obliged to you," said Jim, rising and putting his pocket-book away. "You have given me great assistance."

"I'm sure you're very welcome, sir," replied the man. "I am always ready to do anything I can for a gentleman. It's the Board School folk that—"

Before the man could finish his sentence, Jim was in the shop once more, and was making his way towards the door, closely followed by Terence.

"Now the first question to be decided," he said, when they were in the street, "is what is best for us to do? If I go to Great Medlum Street, it is more than likely that Murbridge will see me and make off again; while, if I wait to communicate with Robins, I may lose him altogether."

Eventually it was decided that he should not act on his own initiative, but should communicate with Detective Robins, and let him make enquiries in the neighbourhood in question. A note was accordingly despatched to the authorities at Scotland Yard. In it James informed them that it had come to his knowledge that the man Murbridge was supposed to be residing in Great Medlum Street, though in what house could not be stated. Later in the day Robins himself put in an appearance at the hotel.

"You received my letter?" James asked when they were alone together.

"I did, sir," the man answered, "and acted upon it at once."

"And with what result?"

"Only to discover that our man has slipped through our fingers once more," said the detective. "He left Great Medlum Street two days ago. Up to that time he had lodged at number eighteen. The landlady informs me that she knows nothing as to his present whereabouts. He passed under the name of Melbrook, and was supposed by the other lodgers to be an American."

"You are quite certain that it is our man?"

"There can be no doubt about it. He went to the house on the day that the murder was discovered. Now the next thing to find out is where he now is. From what his landlady told me, I should not think he was in the possession of much money. As a matter of fact, she suspected that he had been pawning his clothes, for the reason that his bag, which was comparatively heavy when he arrived, seemed to be almost empty when he left. To-morrow morning I shall make enquiries at the various pawnbrokers in the neighbourhood, and it is just possible we may get some further information from them."

Promising to communicate with Jim immediately he had anything of importance to impart, Robins took his departure, and Jim went in search of Alice to tell her the news. Next day word was brought to him to the effect that Murbridge had pawned several articles, but in no case were the proprietors able to furnish any information concerning his present whereabouts. Feeling that it was just possible, as in the case of the eating-house keeper near Paddington Station, that the detectives had not been able to acquire all the knowledge that was going, Jim, accompanied by the faithful Terence, set off in the afternoon for number eighteen, Great Medium Street. It proved to be a lodging-house of the common type.

In response to their ring the door was opened by the landlady, a voluble person of Irish descent. She looked her visitors up and down before admitting them, and having done so, enquired if they stood in need of apartments.

"I regret to say that we do not," said Jim blandly. "My friend and I have come to put a few questions to you concerning—"

"Not poor Mr. Melbrook, I hope," she answered. "Is all London gone mad? 'Twas but yesterday afternoon, just when I was settin' down to my bit o' tea that a gentleman comes to make enquiries about Mr. Melbrook. I told 'im he'd left the house, but that would not do. He wanted to know where he had gone, and when and why he had left, just for all the world as if he was his long-lost brother. Then this morning another comes. Wanted to know if I knew where Mr. Melbrook pawned his clothes? Did he appear to be in any trouble? Now here you are with your questions. D'ye think I've got nothing better to do than to be trapesing round talkin' about what don't concern me? What's the world coming to, I should like to know?"

"But, my good woman, I am most anxious to find Mr. Melbrook," said Jim, "and if you can put me into the possession of any information that will help me to do so, I shall be very pleased to reward you for your trouble."

"But I've got nothing to tell you," she replied, "more's the pity of it, since you speak so fair. From the time that Mr. Melbrook left my house until this very moment I've heard nothing of him. He may have gone back to America—if he was an American as they say—but there, he may be anywhere. He was one of them sort of men that says nothing about his business; he just kept himself to himself with his paper, and took his drop of gin and water at night the same as you and me might do. If I was to die next minute, that's all I can tell you about him."

Seeing that it was useless to question her further, Jim pressed some coins into the woman's willing hand, and bade her good-day. Then, more dispirited by his failure than he would admit, he drove back to his hotel. Alice met him in the hall with a telegram.

"This has just come for you," she said. "I was about to open it."

Taking it from her, he tore open the envelope, and withdrew the message. It was from Robins, and ran as follows:—

"Think am on right track—will report as soon as return."

It had been despatched from Waterloo Station.

"Why did he not say where he was going?" said Jim testily, "instead of keeping me in suspense."

"Because he does not like to commit himself before he has more to report, I suppose," said Alice. "Do not worry yourself about it, dear. You will hear everything in good time."

A long letter from Helen which arrived that evening helped to console Jim, while the writing of an answer to her enabled him to while away another half-hour. But it must be confessed that that evening Jim was far from being himself. He felt that he would have given anything to have accompanied the detective in his search. He went to bed at an early hour, to dream that he was chasing Murbridge round the world, and do what he would he could not come up with him. Next day there was no news, and it was not until the middle of the day following that he heard anything. Then another telegram arrived, stating that the detective would call at the hotel between eight and nine o'clock that evening. He did so, and the first glimpse of his face told Jim that his errand had as usual been fruitless.

"I can see," he said, "that you have not met with any success. Is that not so?"

"I'm sorry, sir," the man answered. "Information was brought me the day before yesterday that a man answering in every way the description of the person we wanted had pawned a small portmanteau at a shop in the Mile End Road, and on making enquiries there, I heard that he had come to lodge at a house in one of the streets in the vicinity. Accompanied by one of my mates, I went to the house in question, only to discover that we were too late again, and that the man had left for Southampton that morning, intending to catch the out-going boat for South Africa. Procuring a cab, I set off for Waterloo, and on my arrival there sent that telegram to you, sir, and then went down to Southampton by the next train. Unfortunately the two hours' delay had given him his chance, for when I reached Southampton it was only to find that the vessel had sailed half-an-hour before. I went at once to the Agent's office, where I discovered that a man whose appearance tallied exactly with the description given had booked a steerage passage at the last moment, and had sailed aboard her. But if he's got out of England safely, we'll catch him at Madeira. The police there will arrest him, and hold him for us until we can get him handed over. He does not know that I am upon his track, and for that reason he'll be sure to think he's got safely away."

"We must hope to catch him at Madeira then. The vessel does not touch at any port between, I suppose?"

Robins shook his head.

"No, Madeira is the first port of call. And now, sir, I'll bid you good-night, if you don't mind. I've had a long day of it, and I'm tired. To-morrow morning I've got to be abroad early on another little case which is causing me a considerable amount of anxiety."

Jim bade him good-night and then went in search of his sister, only to find that she had a bad headache, and had gone to bed. After the excitement of the day bed was out of the question, so donning a hat and coat he left the hotel for a stroll. He walked quietly along Piccadilly, smoking his cigar, and thinking of the girl who had promised to be his wife, and who, at the moment, was probably thinking of him in the quiet little Midlandshire village. How delightful life would be when she would be his wife. He tried to picture himself in the capacity of Helen's husband. From Helen his thoughts turned to Murbridge, and he tried to imagine the guilty wretch, flying across the seas, flattering himself continually that he had escaped the punishment he so richly deserved, finding more security in every mile of water the vessel left behind her, little dreaming that justice was aware of his flight, and that Nemesis was waiting for him so short a time ahead.

Reaching Piccadilly Circus, he walked on until he arrived at Leicester Square. As the sky had become overcast, and a thin drizzle was beginning to fall, he called a hansom, and bade the driver take him back to his hotel. The horse started off, and they were soon proceeding at a fast pace in the direction of Piccadilly. Just as they reached the Criterion Theatre, a man stepped from the pavement, and began to cross the road. Had not the cabman sharply pulled his horse to one side, nothing could have saved him from being knocked down. So near a thing was it that Jim sprang to his feet, and threw open the apron, feeling sure that the man was down. But near though it was, the pedestrian had escaped, and, turning round, was shaking his fist in a paroxysm of rage at the cabman. At that moment he saw Jim, and stood for a second or two as if turned to stone; then, gathering his faculties together, he ducked between two cabs and disappeared.

That man was Richard Murbridge!

CHAPTER VIII

Before Jim could recover from his astonishment at seeing the man whom he had been led to believe was upon the high seas, standing before him, the cabman had whipped up his horse once more, and was half across the Circus. Springing to his feet, he pushed up the shutter, and bade the driver pull up as quickly as possible. Then, jumping from the cab, he gave the man the first coin he took from his pocket.

"Did you see which way that fellow went we so nearly knocked down?" he cried.

"Went away towards Regent Street, I believe," answered the cabman. "He had a narrow shave and it isn't his fault he isn't in hospital now."

Jim waited to hear no more, but made his way back to the policeman he had noticed standing beside the fountain in the centre of the Circus.

"Did you see that man who was so nearly knocked down by a cab a few minutes ago?" he enquired, scarcely able to speak for excitement.

"I did," the officer answered laconically. "What about him?"

"Only that you must endeavour to find him, and arrest him at once," said Jim. "There is not a moment to be lost. He may have got away by this time."

"And he's precious lucky if he has," said the policeman. "Never saw a closer thing in my life."

"But don't you hear me? You must find him at once. Every second we waste is giving him the chance of getting away."

"Come, come, there's no such hurry: what's he done that you should be so anxious to get hold of him?"

By this time Jim was nearly beside himself with rage at the other's stupidity.

"That man was the Childerbridge murderer," he replied. "I am as certain of it as I am that I see you standing before me now."

"Come, come, Sir, that's all very well you know," said the policeman, with what was plainly a kindly intent, "but you go along home and get to bed quietly; you'll be better in the morning and will have forgotten all about this 'ere murderer."

After which, without another word, he walked away.

"Well, of all the insane idiots in the world," muttered Jim, "that fellow should come first. But I am not going to be baulked; I'll search for Murbridge myself."

He thereupon set off along Regent Street, but before he had gone half the length of the street the folly of such a proceeding became apparent to him. He knew that Murbridge had seen him, and, for this reason, would most likely betake himself to the quiet of the back streets. To attempt to find him, therefore, under cover of darkness, and at such an hour, would be well-nigh an impossibility. Then another idea occurred to him. Hailing a cab, he set off for Scotland Yard. On arrival there, he handed in his card, and in due course was received most courteously by the chief officer on duty. He explained his errand, and in doing so showed the mistake under which Detective-sergeant Robins had been and was still labouring.

"He shall be communicated with at once," said the official. "I suppose you are quite certain of the identity of the man you saw in Piccadilly Circus, Mr. Standerton?"

"As certain as I am of anything," Jim replied. "I should recognise him anywhere. I was permitted a full view of his face, and I am quite sure that I am not making a mistake. If only the cabman had pulled up a few moments earlier, I might have been able to have stopped him."

"In that case, you should be able to give us some details of his present personal appearance, which would afford us considerable assistance in our search for him."

"He was wearing a black felt hat, and a brown overcoat, the collar of which was turned up."

The officer made a note of these particulars, and promised that the information should be dispersed in all directions without loss of time. Then, feeling that nothing more could be done Jim bade him good-night, and drove back to his hotel. In spite of the work he had done that day he was not destined to obtain a wink of sleep all night, but tumbled and tossed in his bed, brooding continually over the chance he had missed of securing his father's murderer. If only he had alighted when the cabman first stopped, he might have been able to have secured Murbridge. Now his capture seemed as remote as ever; further, indeed, than if he had been, as Robins supposed, on board the vessel bound for South Africa.

Jim had just finished his breakfast next morning when Robins called to see him.

"This is a nice sort of surprise you have given us, sir," said the detective, when he had made a few commonplace remarks, "I mean your seeing Murbridge last night; I don't know what to think of it. It seems to me to be more of a mystery than ever now."

"The only thing you can think of it is that Murbridge is in London, and not on board the mail boat as you supposed," Jim replied. "You must have got upon a wrong track again. I suppose there is no further news of him this morning?"

"There was none when I left the Yard," the other replied. "At present we are over-hauling all the doss-houses and shelters, and it is possible we may make a discovery before long. When you think of the description we have of him—a man wearing a brown coat and a felt hat—it is not very much to go upon. There must be hundreds of men dressed like that in London. If only we had a photograph of him it would make the labour a good deal easier."

This set Jim thinking. In the lumber-room at Childerbridge there was, as he remembered, a number of cases containing books, photograph albums, etc., which his father had brought with him from Australia, but which had never been unpacked. He recalled the fact that his father had told him that he had been on intimate terms with Murbridge many years before. Was it not possible, therefore, that among his collections there might be some portrait of that individual. He felt inclined to run down and turn the boxes over. What was more, if he did so, he might chance to obtain an interview with Helen. He explained his hopes with regard to the photograph to the detective, who instantly agreed that it might be worth his while to make the search.

"In that case I will go down by the eleven o'clock train, and if I discover anything, I will wire you and post the photograph on to you by the evening mail."

"It is unnecessary for me to assure you it would be an inestimable help to us in our search," the other answered; "we should have something more definite to go upon then."

True to this arrangement, therefore Jim, Alice, and Terence returned to Childerbridge by the morning train. A carriage met them at the station, and in it they drove through the village. As they were drawing near the park gates, an exclamation from Alice roused Jim from the reverie into which he had fallen, and caused him to glance up the lane that led from the main road. To his unspeakable joy, he discovered that Helen was coming towards them. In a moment the carriage was stopped, and Jim alighted and hastened to meet her.

"My darling," he cried, "I never counted upon having the happiness of seeing you so soon. This is most fortunate."

"But what brings you back to-day, Jim?" Helen replied. "From your letter I gathered that I should not see you for at least a week. There is nothing wrong, I hope?"

She scanned his face with anxious eyes, and as she did so it occurred to Jim that she herself was looking far from well.

"Nothing is the matter," he answered. "We have merely come down to try and find some photographs that would help us in our search. But, Helen, you are not looking at all well. Your face frightens me."

"I am alright," was the reply. "I have been a little worried lately about my grandfather, and that probably accounts for my appearance, but we will not talk of that now. I must say 'How do you do' to Alice."

She accordingly approached the carriage, and held out her hand to her friend. They conversed together for a few moments, and then Alice proposed that Helen should return with them to the Hall, but this being, for more reasons than one, impossible, it was arranged that Jim should see her home across the park, a suggestion which, you may be sure, he was not slow to take advantage of. They accordingly watched the carriage pass through the lodge gates, and then themselves set out for the Dower House. As they walked Jim told his sweetheart of the ill success that had attended his mission to London.

"But, Helen," he said at last, as they approached the house, "you have not told me what it is that is worrying you about your grandfather. I hope he has not been making you unhappy?"

She hung her head but did not answer.

"Ah, I can see that he has," he exclaimed, "and I suppose it was something to do with me. I wonder whether I should be right if I hazarded a guess that Mr. Bursfield had been trying again to force you into giving me up? Is that the case, Helen?"

"I am afraid in a measure it is," she replied, but with some diffidence. "You may be quite sure, however, that whatever he may do it will not influence me. You know how truly I love you?"

"Yes, I know that," he answered, "and I am quite content to trust you. I know that nothing Mr. Bursfield can say will induce you to do as he proposes."

"Remember that always," she said. "But, oh, Jim, I wish he were not so determined in his opposition to our marriage. Sometimes I feel that I am acting not only like a traitor to him, but to you as well."

"That you could never be," Jim returned. "However, keep up a good heart, dear, and you may be sure all will come right in the end. In the future we shall look back upon these little troubles, and wonder why we so worried about them."

A few minutes later they reached the gates leading into the grounds of the Dower House. Here Jim bade his sweetheart good-bye, and, having arranged another meeting for the morrow, set off on his walk to his own home. Immediately upon his arrival there, he made his way, accompanied by Alice, to the lumber-room on the top story of the house, in which the boxes he had come down to over-haul had been placed. How well he could recall the day in Australia on which his father had packed them. Little had he imagined then that those boxes would next be opened in order to discover a portrait of the same kind father's murderer. When the first box had been overhauled it was found to contain unimportant papers connected with the dead man's various properties in Australia. In the second was a miscellaneous collection; which consisted of a variety of account books, with specimens of ore, wool, and other products of the Island Continent. It was not until they had opened the third box that they began to think they were on the right track. In this were a few engravings, perhaps half-a-dozen sketch books, filled with pen-and-ink drawings by Jim's mother, upwards of a hundred novels between thirty and forty years old, and at the bottom a large album filled with photographs, each of which looked out upon a forgetful world from a floral setting. Jim took it to a window, where he sat down on a box to examine it.

To my thinking there is nothing more pathetic than an old album. What memories it recalls of long-forgotten friends; as one looks upon the faded pictures, how clearly old scenes rise before one.

On the first page was a photograph of William Standerton himself, taken when he was a young man. His coat was of a strange cut, his trousers were of the peg-top description, while a magnificent pair of "Dundreary" whiskers decorated his manly face. With a sigh Jim turned the page, to discover a portrait of his mother, which had been taken on her wedding day. Then followed a long succession of relatives and personal friends, each clad in the same fashion, and nearly all taken in the same constrained attitude. But examine each picture as he would, no representation of the man he wanted could he discover.

"Well, I'm afraid that's all," said Jim to Alice, as he replaced the album in his box. "I am disappointed, though I cannot say that I hoped to be very successful. I shall have to write to Robins and tell him that I have found nothing."

Having relocked the boxes, they descended to the hall once more. It was growing dark, and the dressing bell for dinner had already sounded. They accordingly separated, and went to their respective rooms. If the truth must be confessed, Jim was more disappointed by the failure of his search than he cared to admit.

"It would have been of inestimable value," he said to himself, "to have a portrait of Murbridge just now."

He had tied one end of his tie and was in the act of performing the same operation with the other, when he stopped and stared at the wall before him with half-closed eyes.

"By Jove!" he said, "I believe I've hit it. I think I know where there is a portrait of him."

He recalled a scene that had taken place at Mudrapilla one winter's evening, many years before, when Alice and he were children. The lamp had been lighted, and to amuse them before they went to bed, their father had promised a prize to whichever one of the pair should recognise and describe by name the greater number of the portraits in the very album he had been looking through that afternoon. Jim remembered how on that occasion he had chanced upon a certain carte de visite, showing a tall young man leaning, hat in hand, against a marble pillar.

"Who is this, father?" He had enquired for he was not able to recognise the individual portrayed in the picture.

"Do not ask me," returned his father in a tone that the children never forgot, so stern and harsh was it. Then, drawing the portrait from the page, he placed it in the pocket at the end of the book. After that the game had recommenced, but was played with less vigour than before.

"I wonder if it could have been the same man?" said Jim. "I cannot remember father ever having expressed such a dislike for any one else save Murbridge. After dinner I'll go up and endeavour to find it. It was there for many years, for I can recall how I used to creep into the drawing-room and peep at it on the sly, wondering what sort of villainy he had committed that was sufficient to prevent his name being mentioned to us. Poor father, it is certain that he was not deceived in him after all."

Throughout dinner that evening his mind dwelt on the remembrance of that scene at Mudrapilla, and as soon as they rose from the table he begged Alice to excuse him, and went upstairs candle in hand, to recommence his search. He left his sister in the drawing-room, and the household were at supper in the servants' hall, so that, so far as the disposition of the house went, he had all the upper floors to himself. Entering the lumber-room, he knelt down and unlocked the box which contained the album. To take the book from the box, and to turn to the pocket in question was the work of a moment. It had been placed there for the purpose of holding loose photographs, and it extended the whole width of the cover. With a half fear that it might not be contained therein, Jim thrust his hand into the receptacle. He was not to be disappointed this time, however, for a card was certainly there, and he withdrew it and held it up to the light with a feeling of triumph. Yes, it was the picture he remembered, and, better still, it was the portrait of Richard Murbridge. Though it had been taken when the latter was a young man, Jim recognised his enemy at once. There was the same crafty look in his eyes, the same carping expression about the mouth. The man who had been so nearly knocked down by the cab on the previous evening was the same person who, in the picture, posed himself so gracefully beside the marble pillar "This must go to Robins to-night," said Jim, to himself, "copies of it can then be distributed broadcast. It will be strange after that if we do not manage to lay hands upon him."

So saying, he replaced the album in the box, locked the latter, and then placed the photograph in his pocket, and prepared to return to Alice once more. As he descended the stairs, he extinguished the candle, for the hanging lamp in the hall below gave sufficient light for him to see his way. He was only a few steps from the bottom when a curious noise, which seemed to come from the gallery above, attracted his attention. It resembled the creaking of a rusty hinge, more than anything else. He had just time to wonder what had occasioned it, when, to his amazement, he became aware of a little black figure passing swiftly along the corridor in the direction of the further wing. A moment later it had vanished, and he was left to place such construction as he pleased upon what he had seen. For a space, during which a man might have counted twenty, he stood as if rooted to the spot, scarcely able to believe the evidence of his senses.

"Good heavens! The Black Dwarf," he muttered to himself. "I must find out what it means."

Then he set off in pursuit.

CHAPTER IX

Hastening round the gallery of the hall, Jim endeavoured to discover some traces of the mysterious visitor, spectre or human, whom he had seen. The corridor, however, leading to the oldest and western portion of the house, was quite empty. Like the remainder of the building, it was panelled with dark oak, some portion of it being curiously, though richly carved. He searched it up and down, stopping every now and then to listen, but save for the wind sighing round the house, and an occasional burst of laughter ascending from the servants' hall, he could hear nothing. At the end of the long corridor a flight of stone steps led to the domestic offices below. These he descended, and having reached the servants' hall, called Wilkins, the butler, to him. When the latter emerged, Jim led him a short distance down the passage before he spoke.

"Wilkins," he said, "do you remember the night when you thought you saw the Black Dwarf on the landing?"

"I shall never forget it, sir," the other replied. "I can never go along that corridor now without a shudder. What about it, sir?"

"Only that I have just seen the figure myself," James replied. "I had been up to the lumber-room, and was descending the stairs when it passed along the further side of the gallery, in the direction of the west corridor. Now, Wilkins, I have come down to find out whether you would be afraid to come upstairs with me in order that we may discover whether we can come to any understanding of the mystery?"

"Yes, sir, of course I will come with you," said Wilkins. "At the same time I am not going to say that I am not a bit frightened, for it would not be the truth. However, sir, I am not going to let you go alone."

"Come along then," said Jim, "and bring a light of some kind with you."

Wilkins procured a candle, and then they ascended to the floor above. As they reached the corridor Jim turned and caught a glimpse of his companion's face. It looked very white and frightened in the dim light.

"Cheer up, my man," said he; "if it's a ghost it won't hurt you, and if it's a human being you and I should be more than a match for him."

As he said this he opened the door of the first room on the corridor. It was empty, and quite devoid of either the natural or the supernatural.

"Nothing here," said Jim as they passed out into the passage, and into the next room. This was used as a sewing-room for the female servants, and was furnished with a long table and half-a-dozen chairs. They explored it thoroughly, and having done so, voted it above suspicion. The next room was a bedroom, and had only been once used since the Standertons had come into possession of the house. The walls were panelled, and there was a curious recess on the side opposite the door. Jim overhauled each panel, and carefully examined the recess, but without discovering anything suspicious. Thus they proceeded from room to room searching every nook and cranny, and endeavouring in every possible way to account for the creaking noise which had first attracted Jim's attention. The carving of the corridor itself was carefully examined, every panel of the wainscoting was tested, until at last, having reached the gallery of the hall, they were compelled to own themselves beaten. The fact that they had not been able to discover anything only added to Wilkins' belief in the supernatural agency of the Dwarf. Jim, however, had the recollection of that creaking hinge, before mentioned, continually before him. There might be ghostly bodies he argued, but he had never heard of ghostly hinges.

"Well, it doesn't appear as if we are destined to capture him to-night," said Jim, when they had finished their labours. "Now one word of advice; just keep the fact of his appearance to yourself, Wilkins. If the maid-servants come to hear of it we shall have no end of trouble."

Wilkins promised that he would say nothing about the occurrence, and then returned to the Servants' Hall, leaving Jim standing on the gallery ruminating on the behaviour of the figure he had seen.

"One thing is quite certain, and that is the fact that he disappeared in the corridor," he said to himself reflectingly. "Now I wonder where he came from?"

The only room on that side of the gallery then in use was Alice's bedroom, and to this Jim forthwith made his way. It was a strange scene that met his eyes when he opened the door. As he had good reason to know, Alice was always a most methodical and neat young lady; now everything was in confusion. The drawers of the dressing-table stood open and their contents were strewed upon the table and the floor. The writing-table in the further corner of the room was in much the same condition, while the wardrobe doors were open, and the dresses, which usually hung upon the pegs, were piled in a heap upon the floor.

"Good gracious! what on earth does this mean?" said Jim to himself as he gazed upon the scene of confusion. "Has Alice gone mad, or has the Black Dwarf been trying to see how untidy he can make the place? She must not see the room in this condition, or it may frighten her."

Thereupon he placed the candle upon the table and did his best to restore something like order. This task accomplished, he went downstairs to the drawing-room, where he found his sister seated beside the fire reading.

"You have been a long time upstairs," she remarked. "What have you been doing?"

For a moment Jim had forgotten the important discovery he had made. In reply he withdrew the photograph from his pocket and handed it to her. She took it with what was almost a shudder. Somewhat to Jim's surprise, she returned it without commenting upon it. He replaced it in his pocket, also without a word, and then stood before the fire, wondering how he should tell her of what he had seen. He knew it would cause her some uneasiness, but at the same time he felt that he ought to place her upon her guard.

"Alice," he said at last, "do you make a point of locking your bedroom door at night?"

"Lock my bedroom door at night?" she repeated. "No! Why should I?"

"I can't exactly say why you should," he answered, "but I want you to do so for the future. This is a big, lonely house, and we have to remember that you and I are the only people on this side. I wish my room were nearer yours, but as it is not, I think it would be safer if you were to do as I suggest."

"But what makes you say this to-night?" she asked. "What is it, or who is it, you suspect?"

"I suspect nobody," he replied. "You must not think that. But there are such people as burglars, and it would only be an ordinary act of common sense to make yourself safe, while you are permitted the opportunity. Ever since that terrible night I have been nervous about you, and for that reason I have decided upon something, which at first you may think strange."

"What is it?" she enquired.

"For the future," he answered, "I intend that Terence shall sleep in the room next to yours. Then, if any one makes trouble, and help were needed, we should have a sure ally at our beck and call."

"But I hope no one will ever attempt to make trouble, as you describe it," she replied, looking at him with startled eyes as she spoke.

"I also sincerely hope not," he continued. "Now I am going to see Terence about the matter."

He thereupon left her, and went to his study and rang the bell. On the butler making his appearance he instructed him to bring O'Riley at once. A few minutes later Terence put in appearance.

"You had better remain also, Wilkins," said Jim. "Just close the door behind you, in case any one should chance to overhear us. Now, Terence, I have something to say to you. Doubtless, since you have been in the neighbourhood, you have heard certain stories connected with this house. I suppose you have been told that it has the reputation of being haunted."

"Lor' bless you, sir," Terence replied, "I've heard all sorts of yarns about it. There's folk down in the Township yonder, as would no more think of coming up here after dark than they would of lying down in front of the train and having their heads cut off."

"You're not a believer in ghosts, I suppose?"

"Not as I knows on," said Terence candidly. "Though I don't mind sayin' as how there are things as have never been explained to my satisfaction. 'Twas said, as you may remember, sir, as how there was a ghost of an old man to be seen, some nights in the year, waiting to get over at the Thirty-Mile Crossing up the river. Then there was the ghost outside Sydney, that used to get on the fence beside the road, and ask everybody who would listen to him to have him properly buried."

James knew that the man before him was as brave as a lion. He was the possessor of nerves of iron, and did not know the meaning of the word fear.

"Well," he went on after a moment's pause, "the long and the short of the matter is, Terence, some little time ago a maid-servant saw what she thought to be the ghost of the Little Black Dwarf up in the gallery outside. Wilkins here was the next to see it. I thought at the time he must have been mistaken, but this evening I know that he was not, for I have seen it myself."

"You don't mean that, sir?" said Terence, while Wilkins plainly showed the triumph he felt. "And what may he have been like, sir?"

"I had no time to see that," Jim answered. "He disappeared into the western corridor almost as soon as I caught sight of him. At the same time I heard the sound of a creaking hinge. What would you think of that?"

"I should say that it was no ghost, sir," said Terence. "I've been told that this old house is full of secret passages, and, if you ask me, I should say it was somebody playing a game with you."

Wilkins stared disdainfully at him. He was quite convinced in his own mind of the ghostly nature of the mysterious visitor.

"I am inclined to agree with you, Terence," Jim replied. "The more so as, since I parted with you, Wilkins, I have made a curious discovery. At what time was Miss Alice's room made tidy?"

"While you were at dinner, sir, according to custom," replied the butler. "I saw the maid coming out just as I left the dining-room, and she would not be likely to leave it—"

"To leave it in an untidy state?" Jim put in.

"Of course she would not, sir," the other replied. "She would hear of it from the housekeeper if she did. No, she's a nice, steady girl, sir, and I'm told she does her work to the best of her ability."

"Well, it seems curious that when I entered the room after you had left me, I found it in a state of the wildest confusion. The contents of the drawers of the dressing-table were lying scattered upon the floor, as were the dresses in the wardrobe. Now I feel quite certain in my own mind that it was from Miss Alice's bedroom that the figure I saw emerged. I am equally sure of one thing, and that is that it is no ghost—at least," and he added this with a smile, "no respectable ghost, of course, would dream of playing such tricks with a lady's wearing apparel."

"Then, sir, whom do you suspect?" Wilkins enquired. "I can assure you that none of the staff would dare to take such a liberty."

"I am quite sure of that," Jim replied. "Yet the fact remains that somebody must be, and is, responsible for it. Now what

I intend to do is to lay myself out to capture that somebody, and to make an example of him when I have got him. For that reason, Terence, I am going to ask you to sleep in the house, in the room next to that occupied by Miss Alice. It will go hard, then, if between us we cannot lay our hands upon the gentleman, whoever he may be, who is playing these tricks upon us."

Terence willingly agreed to the proposal, and that night occupied the room in question. His watchfulness availed him nothing, however, for no further sign of the Black Dwarf.

Next morning Robins received the photograph of Murbridge, and from that moment Jim awaited tidings from him in a fever of expectation. Day after day, however, went by, and still no good news came to reward his patience. The only consolation he derived was from sundry mysterious interviews which he had with Helen in a wooded corner of the park. With the cunning of lovers they had arranged a plan of meeting, and those little tête-à-têtes were to Jim as the breath of life. No sooner was one at an end than he hungered for the next. But he was destined ere long to receive a fright, such as he had never received in his life before. Winter was fast approaching, and the afternoons drew in quickly. When he reached the rendezvous on this occasion it was nearly five o'clock, and almost dark. Helen had arrived there before him, and he discovered her pacing up and down the little glade, in what was plainly an agitated frame of mind.

"Oh, I am so thankful that you have come, Jim dear," she said, as she came forward to greet him. "I have been counting the minutes until I should see you."

"Why, what on earth is the matter?" he asked, placing his arm round her waist and drawing her to him. "You are excited about something. Tell me, dear, what it is."

"Something so dreadful that it has upset me terribly," she answered. "I scarcely know how to tell you."

He led her towards a fallen tree upon which they had often seated themselves on previous occasions.

"Now let me know everything," he said.

She looked about over her shoulder in a frightened way. Then she began almost in a whisper:

"Jim, what I have to say to you concerns my grandfather. I am very much alarmed about him."

"I hope he has not been making himself disagreeable to you again on my account," Jim replied. Then he continued angrily: "If so, I think I shall have to call upon him."

"Hush, hush," she said, "do not speak so loud, you do not know who may be listening."

"I will be all discretion, dear, now go on!"

"Well, this afternoon I was playing the piano in the drawing-room when a message was brought to me by Isaac to the effect that my grandfather desired to see me in his study at once. I went to him there, to find him seated at his desk as usual, at work upon his book, the 'History of the County,' you know. He signed to me to be seated by the fire, and when I had done so resumed his writing, not putting down his pen until I had been some minutes in the room. Then he looked at me with a very thoughtful face, in which I imagined I could detect an expression that I had never seen there before. Taken altogether, his manner frightened me. It was so strange, and so utterly unlike himself, that I did not know what to think. Then he took off his spectacles, and laid them on the desk before him, remarking as he did so, 'I am given to understand that you are still in correspondence with Mr. Standerton, Miss?' Then, before I could answer him, he continued—'and I hear that you have secret meetings with him in the park. Is this so?' I admitted that it was, and went on to say that as we were betrothed I could see no harm in it."

"And what did he say to that?"

"He rose from his chair and paced the room for a few minutes without speaking. Then he reseated himself. As he did so he said, 'You are not engaged, and you know it as well as I do. Never let me hear you say such a thing again.' After that he began to pace the room once more, and finally hurled at me such a torrent of abuse that I was almost stupefied by it. He accused me of the most outrageous things, until I could bear it no longer, and rose to leave him. By this time, as you may suppose, I had come to the conclusion that the life of retirement he had lived for so long had turned his brain. No man could have said the things he did without his mind being a little affected."

"My darling, this is more serious than you suppose," said Jim anxiously.

"But you have not heard the worst yet. It appears that before I had entered the room he had drawn up a document which he now desired me to sign. It was to the effect that I would bind myself never to speak to you or see you again, and contained my promise that I would abandon all thought of ever becoming your wife. 'Sign that,' he said, 'or the consequences will be more terrible than you suppose. I am an old man, but remember even old men can be dangerous at times.' With that he handed me a pen, but I refused to take it."

"And then?"

"I cannot tell you how he looked at me as I said it. I could never have believed that his face could have undergone such a change. But I still refused to sign the document, and at last he discovered that it was impossible to force me to do so. 'Very well,' he said, 'since you refuse, the consequences of your action be upon your own head.' With that, opening the door, he bade me leave him. You can imagine for yourself how thankful I was to do so."

"And then you came on here," said Jim. "You were most imprudent, dear. He may try to revenge himself upon you when you return to the house."

"I don't think he will hurt me," she replied. "I am only afraid for you."

"There is no need for fear on my account," Jim answered, with a short laugh. "I do not think it is possible for the poor old gentleman to do me any harm. But the idea that you are shut up in the house with a madman, for a madman he must surely be, frightens me beyond all measure. You must see for yourself that you have no longer any reason to remain with him. He has threatened you, and that will be sufficient excuse for you to leave him."

"No, no," she answered, shaking her head. "If he is losing his reason, he should not be blamed, and it is all the more necessary for his comfort that I shall remain with him. I feel sure I shall be quite safe. He is angry with me at present, but he will calm down. It is above all necessary, however, that you should not come near him. It will only irritate him and make him more excited than before. Think how good he has been to me, dear, for the past eight years, and try not to be angry with him."

"But I am not angry with him," said Jim. "I am only trying to be just. One thing is quite certain, I shall know no peace as long as you are in that house with him."

"Will it satisfy you if I give you my promise that, should he become very bad, I will at once send for you?"

"If you persist on going back there, I suppose I must be content with that promise," Jim replied, but with no good grace. "And now you had better be running in. If he finds that you are out, he might suppose that you are with me, and have another paroxysm of rage. In that case there is no knowing what might happen."

Helen accordingly bade him good-bye and left him, returning by the path to the Dower House. Jim watched her until she had disappeared and then turned homeward with a heavy heart. He felt that he had already enough anxiety upon his shoulders without this additional burden. He had never trusted Mr. Bursfield, but he was at a loss to understand his present malignity, unless it were to be accounted for by the fact that his brain had given way.

When he reached his home he let himself in by a side door, and made his way to the drawing-room, where he found Alice.

"How late you are," she said. "The gong sounded some time ago. You will scarcely have time to dress."

"Then dinner must wait," replied Jim. "Alice, I have bad news for you."

"Why, what is the matter now?" she asked.

Jim thereupon proceeded to furnish her with an abstract of his interview with Helen. She heard him without a word, but it was to be easily seen how distressed she was for her friend.

"My dear Jim," she remarked when he had finished, "this is indeed serious. What do you propose doing?"

"I scarcely know," Jim answered. "The case is an extremely delicate one. The old man has taken a decided dislike to me, and if I interfere between Helen and himself it will have the effect of adding to his wrath and do more harm than good. And yet I cannot allow her to remain there, and perhaps run a daily risk of her life."

"What does she think about it herself?"

"She has an absurd notion that her duty lies in standing by Bursfield in his trouble. That, of course, is all very well in its way, but no one could possibly expect her to turn herself into a keeper for a madman."

Alice, seeing the tired look on his face, crossed the room and placed her arm round his neck.

"Dear old Jim," she said, "you must not worry yourself too much about it. All will come right in the end. Helen is a girl of very marked character, and it is quite probable that, under her influence, Mr. Bursfield's condition may improve. Were I in your place, I should trust matters to her for a little while. You know that she loves you, and you may be quite sure that she will keep her promise, and let you know directly anything is very wrong. But there! what am I thinking about? I should have told you when you first came in that there is a telegram waiting for you. Here it is."

As she spoke she took an envelope from the mantelpiece, and handed it to him.

"I wonder who it is from?" he remarked as he tore it open.

Having withdrawn the contents, he read as follows:—

"Standerton, Childerbridge.

"Murbridge found. Come at once.

"13, Upper Bellington Street. Robins."

CHAPTER X

"Murbridge found," said Jim to himself as he stood holding the telegram in his hand. "At last, thank goodness, at last!"

Alice, however, said nothing. She had more of her dead father's forgiving spirit in her, and she was aware that he would have been the last to have desired vengeance on his assailant.

"What do you mean to do?" she asked.

"Catch the 8.40 train up to Town," said Jim, "and see Murbridge as soon as possible. The telegram says 'Come at once.' That is sufficient evidence that there is no time to be lost. Perhaps he has been wounded in a desperate struggle with the police. In fact, there are a thousand possibilities."

He gave the necessary instructions for dinner to be hurried forward, his bag to be packed, and the carriage to be ready immediately afterwards to take him to the station.

"You will not mind being left alone for one evening, will you, Alice?" he said to his sister, half apologetically. "Terence will be in the house and will keep a careful eye upon you. If you think you will be lonely I will take you up to Town with me, drop you at the hotel, and then I will go on to Upper Bellington Street."

Alice, however, would not hear of this arrangement. She declared that she would be quite content to remain where she was.

"Besides," she said, "if any news were to come from Helen, I should be here to receive it. It would not be wise for both of us to be away at this juncture."

Jim thereupon went out and sent word to Terence to come to him in his study.

"I am called up to Town to-night, Terence," he said, "and I am going to leave Miss Alice in your charge. I know she could not be in a better."

"You may be very sure of that, sir," Terence replied; "I wouldn't stand by and see anything happen to Miss Alice, and I think she knows it."

"I am sure she does," Jim returned, and then went on to explain the reason for the journey he was about to undertake.

An hour and a-half later he was seated in a railway carriage and being whirled along towards London at something like fifty miles an hour. If ever a young man in this world was furnished with material for thought, James Standerton that evening was that one. There was his errand to London in the first place to be considered, the singular behaviour of the Black Dwarf a few nights before for another, and the declaration that Helen had made to him that afternoon for a third. In the light of this last catastrophe the finding of the man whom he felt sure was his father's murderer sank into comparative insignificance.

What if the madman should wreak his vengeance upon her? What if in a sudden fit of fury he should drive her from his house? If the latter were to come to pass, however, he felt certain that the place she would fly to would be the Manor House, and in that case Alice would take her in and Terence would see that she was safe from the old man's fury.

It was nearly eleven o'clock when he reached Paddington. Hailing a cab, he bade the man drive him first to his hotel, where he engaged his usual room. When he had consulted a directory, he made his way into the street again. His cabman, whom he had told to wait, professed to be familiar with Upper Bellington Street, but later confessed his entire ignorance of its locality. Jim set him right, and then, taking his place in the cab, bade him drive him thither with all speed. Once more they set off, down Piccadilly, through Leicester Square, and so by way of Long Acre into Holborn. Then the route became somewhat more complicated. Through street after street they passed until Jim lost all idea of the direction in which they were proceeding. Some of the streets were broad and stately, others squalid and dejected, some wood paved, others cobble-stones, in which the rain that had fallen an hour previous stood in filthy puddles.

How long they were driving, Jim had no sort of idea, nor could he have told you in what portion of the town he was then in. At last however they entered a street which appeared to have no ending. It was illumined by flaring lamps from coster barrows, drawn up beside the pavement, while the night was made hideous by the raucous cries of the vendors of winkles baked potatoes and roasted chestnuts.

"This is Upper Bellington Street, sir," said the cabman, through the shutter. "At what number shall I pull up?"

"Thirteen," Jim replied; "but you will never be able to find it in this crowd. Put me down anywhere here, and I'll look for it myself."

The cabman did as he was directed, and presently Jim found himself making his way along the greasy pavement—which even at that late hour was crowded with pedestrians—in search of the number in question. It was as miserable an evening as ever he could remember. A thin drizzle was falling; the sights and sounds around him were sordid and depressing in the extreme; while the very errand that had brought him to that neighbourhood was of a kind calculated to lower the spirits of the average man to below the mental zero.

After an examination of the numbers of the various houses and shops in the vicinity, he came to the conclusion that Thirteen must be situated at the further end of the street. This proved to be the case. When he reached it, he knocked upon the grimy door, which was immediately opened to him by a police officer.

"What is your name?" asked that official.

"James Standerton," Jim replied. "I received a telegram from Detective-sergeant Robins this evening asking me to come up."

"That's all right, sir," the man answered. "Come in; we have been expecting you this hour or more."

"But how is it your prisoner is here, and not at the police station?"

"I doubt if he'll ever trouble any police station again," returned the officer. "He's just about done for. In fact, I shouldn't be surprised if he wasn't dead by now."

"What is the matter with him?"

"Pneumonia, sir, the doctor says. He says he can't last out the night."

At that moment Robins himself appeared at the head of the dirty stairs that descended to the hall, and invited him to ascend. Jim accordingly did so.

"Good evening, Mr. Standerton," he said, "I regret having to inform you that we have caught our bird too late. We discovered him at midday, and he was then at the point of death. He was too ill to be moved, and as he had no one to look after him, we got a doctor and a nurse in at once. But I fear it is a hopeless case."

"Will it be possible for me to see him, do you think?"

"Oh yes, sir; he's been calling for you ever since we found him, so I took the liberty of telegraphing to you to come up."

"I am glad you did," said Jim. "There are some questions I must put to him."

"In that case, please step this way, sir, and I'll speak to the doctor. You shall not be kept waiting any longer than I can help."

He led Jim along the landing, then opened a door and disappeared into a room at the further end. While he was absent Jim looked about him and took stock of his position. The small gas-jet that lit up the well of the staircase, served to show the dirty walls in all their dreariness. The sound of voices reached him from above and below, while the cries of the hawkers in the street came faintly in and added to the general squalor. Then as he stood there he recalled that first meeting with Murbridge beside the Darling River. In his mind's eye he saw the evening sun illumining the gums on the opposite bank, the soft breeze ruffling the surface of the river, an old pelican fishing for his evening meal in the backwater, and lastly, Richard Murbridge stretched out beside his newly-lighted fire. This would be their third meeting; and in what a place, and under what terribly changed circumstances! He was indulging in this reverie when the door opened once more, and a small, grey-haired man emerged.

"Good evening, my dear sir," he said, "I understand that you're Mr. Standerton, the son of the man the poor wretch inside is suspected of having murdered. However, they have captured him too late."

"You mean, I suppose, that he will not live?" said Jim, interrogatively.

"If he sees the light of morning I shall be very much surprised," said the doctor; "in point of fact he is sinking fast. You wish to see him, do you not?"

"I do," said Jim. "There is some mystery connected with him that I am very desirous of clearing up."

"I see," said the medico, "and in that case I presume that you would wish to see him alone?"

"If you can permit it," Jim replied.

"I think it might be managed," answered the other. "But if you will stay here for a moment I will let you know."

He returned to the room, and when he stood before Jim once more, invited him to follow him. He did so, to find himself in a small apartment, some ten feet long by eight feet wide. It was uncarpeted, and its furniture consisted of a broken chair, a box on which stood an enamelled basin, and a bed which was covered with frowsy blankets. On this bed lay a man whom, in spite the change that had come over him, Jim recognised at once as being Richard Murbridge. A nurse was standing beside him, and Robins was at the foot of the bed.

"Do not make the interview any longer than you can help," whispered the doctor, and then beckoned to the detective and the nurse to leave the room with him. They did so, and the door closed behind them. Then Jim went forward and seated himself upon the chair by the bedside of the dying man. The latter looked up at him with a scowl.

"So they sent for you after all?" he said in a voice that was little above a whisper. "They even took that trouble?"

"I received the message just before dinner, and came away immediately afterwards."

"Left your luxurious mansion to visit Upper Bellington Street? How self-denying of you! Good Lord, to think that it should be my luck to die in such a hole as this! I suppose you know that I am dying?"

"I have been informed that your recovery is unlikely," Jim replied. "That fact made me doubly anxious to speak to you."

There was a little pause, during which Murbridge watched him intently.

"You mean about the murder, I suppose?" he whispered.

"Yes!" Jim answered. "God forgive me for feeling revengeful at such a moment, but you took from me and my sister the kindest and best father that man ever had."

"You still think that it was I who committed the murder, then?"

"I am certain of it," Jim answered. "You were at the house that night; you cherished a deadly hatred against my father; you vowed that you would be even with him, happen what might, and you ran away from Childerbridge immediately afterwards. Surely those facts are black enough to convict any man?"

"They would have gone some way with a Jury, I have no doubt," the other replied. "But, as a matter of fact, I did not commit the murder. Bitterly as I hated your father, I am not responsible for his death."

Jim looked at him incredulously.

"Ah, I can see you do not believe me. Now, listen, James Standerton, and pay attention to what I say, for I shan't be able to say it again. I've been a pretty tough sort of customer all my life. There have not been many villainies I haven't committed, and still fewer that I wouldn't have committed if they tended to my advantage. The record I shall carry aloft with me will not bear much looking into. But on the word of a dying man, may"—(here he swore an awful oath which I feel would be better not set down)—"if I am not absolutely guiltless of your father's death. Will you believe me now?"

But still Jim looked incredulous.

"Ah, I can see that you still doubt me. How can I convince you? Think for a moment, what have I to gain or lose by saying such a thing? I shall be gone hence in a few hours, perhaps minutes. Even if I were the murderer, the police could not take me now. With old Bony behind me I can laugh at them and at you."

"But why did you run away if you were innocent?"

"Because I saw what a hole I had got myself into. You remember that I went up to the house and had an interview with your father? He turned me out, and in the hearing of yourself and the servant I vowed to be even with him. That vow I certainly should have kept, had not somebody else that night stepped in and took the case out of my hands. When I left the house, I went for a long walk. I knew my own temper, and also that I dared not trust myself with human beings just then. Good heavens, man! You don't know how desperate I was. I had followed your father to England, and the voyage had taken nearly all my money. What little was left I spent in liquor, and then went down to Childerbridge to screw more from your father. He refused point blank to help me except on certain conditions, which I would not comply with. Knowing his stubbornness of old, I cleared out of Childerbridge by the first train, vowing that I would be even with him by some means. Then in an evening paper I saw that he had been murdered. In a flash I realised my position, and saw that if I was not very careful I should find myself in Queer Street. Then came your reward, and from that moment I hid myself like a 'possum in a gum log. I didn't care very much about my miserable neck, but—but—well, you see, strange though it may seem, I was a gentleman once."

Jim did not know what to say. If this man's tale were true, and it bore the impression of truth, then they had been on a false scent from the first.

"I wonder what your mother would have said had she been alive to see it all," said Murbridge, after a pause. "Good Lord, to think that Jane Standerton's brother should end his days in a hole like this."

"What?" cried Jim, scarcely believing that he had heard aright. "Whose brother did you say?"

"Why, your own mother's to be sure," returned Murbridge. "Do you mean to say that your father never told you after all?"

"Can such a thing be possible?" Jim continued, in an awed voice.

"Yes; I am Jane Standerton's brother sure enough. If you look in that old bag under the bed, you will find evidence enough to convince you of that fact. My real name is Richard McCalmont, though you wouldn't think it to look at me, would you? That was how I got my hold upon your father, don't you see? I was convicted of forgery at the age of twenty-one"— (the man spoke as if he were proud of it)—"and did my three years. For a while after that I went straight, but at twenty-six there was another little mistake, with the details of which I will not trouble you, but which was sufficient, nevertheless, to again cause me to spend some years in durance vile. At the age of thirty-two they tried to convict me of an Insurance Fraud, combined with a suspicion of murder. They would have done so but for certain technicalities that were brought forward by my Counsel, who, by the way, was employed by your father. You see I am perfectly candid with you."

"And you are my mother's brother?" said Jim slowly, as if he were still trying to believe it.

"And your father's brother-in-law, too. And your uncle. Don't forget that, James," said the other. "Lord! How your father hated me! On certain occasions I made it my custom to call upon him in a friendly way. At the end of my last term of exile, I found that my sister was dead, and that you and Alice were growing up. It was my desire to play the part of the kindly uncle. But your father made himself objectionable, and vowed that if ever I dared to betray my relationship to you he would cut off supplies. As there was never a time in my life in which I did not stand in need of money, I was perforce compelled to deprive you of a life's history that would certainly have proved interesting, if not instructive, to you. However, I now have the satisfaction of knowing that I shall not die without having accomplished that task."

Here he was interrupted by a violent fit of coughing, which left him speechless for upwards of a minute. As for Jim, he was thinking of the mental agony his father must have suffered, year after year, with this despicable creature, the brother of the woman he loved so fondly, continually holding this threat over his children's heads.

"God help you for a miserable man," he muttered at last. "Why didn't my poor father tell me this before? He might have known that this would not have made the least difference."

"He was too proud," replied the other, when he recovered his speech. "Well, it doesn't matter much now, and in a little while it will matter still less. The police and I have been on the most friendly terms all our lives, and it gives one a homely sort of feeling to know that even my last moments will be watched over by their tender care."

He tried to laugh at his own hideous joke, but the attempt was a failure.

"For my mother's sake, is there anything I can do for you?" Jim enquired, drawing a little closer to the bed.

The other only shook his head. The effort he had made to talk had proved too much for him, and had materially hastened the end.

Seeing that his condition was growing desperate, Jim rose and went in search of the doctor. He found him in an apartment close at hand.

"I believe he is sinking fast," said Jim. "I think you had better go to him."

The doctor accordingly returned to the sick-room, leaving Jim alone with Robins.

"Well, sir," asked the latter, "did he confess?"

"We have been deceived," said Jim. "The man is as innocent of the crime as I am. I am convinced of that!"

"God bless my soul, you don't mean to say so," said the astonished detective, and asked the same questions Jim had put to the dying man. Jim answered them as the other had done.

"Well, this is the most extraordinary case I have ever had to do with," said Robins. "If Murbridge had wanted to place a halter round his neck he could not have gone to work in a better fashion. If he is not the man, then where are we to look for the real murderer?"

"Goodness only knows," replied Jim. "The case is now shrouded in even greater mystery than before."

Half an hour went by, then an hour, and still they waited. At two o'clock the doctor rejoined them.

"It is all over," he said solemnly. "He is dead."

CHAPTER XI

Between the time of Murbridge's funeral and his own arrival at Childerbridge, Jim had plenty of leisure to consider his position, and to make up his mind as to how much he should let Alice know of the other's story.

After mature consideration, he decided that he had better tell her everything. Yet it had been such a painful shock to himself that he could well understand how it would affect her.

It was mid-morning when he arrived at Childerbridge, and Alice had walked down to the gates to meet him. He alighted from the carriage on seeing her, and they strolled across the park together.

"I have been so anxious to hear from you," she said, linking her arm through her brother's. "What have you to tell me? Did you find that wretched man?"

"Yes, I found him," he answered, "and he was dying."

She paused for a moment before she put the next question. "And did he confess?"

"No," said Jim. "I firmly believe I wronged him in suspecting him of—of what happened. But I made another discovery, and one, I fear, that will cause you some astonishment and not a little pain. I learnt from him that his name was not Murbridge, but McCalmont."

"McCalmont?" she echoed, as if she did not understand. "But that was our mother's maiden name."

"Exactly," said Jim, "and he was her brother!"

Alice looked at him in horrified surprise.

"Oh, Jim," she answered, "surely such a thing cannot be possible?"

"I am afraid it is only too true," Jim replied. "His story was most circumstantial. He was our mother's youngest brother, and was, I am very much afraid, a disgrace to the family."

"But if he had been our mother's brother, why did he entertain such a deadly hatred for our father?" she asked.

"For the simple reason that father had been successful, while he had been the reverse," Jim replied. "I rather fancy the poor old governor had helped him out of one or two of his worst scrapes, and such being the perverse nature of mankind, he hated him for the very benefits he had received from him."

They walked some distance in silence.

"Poor, wretched man," said Alice at last. "Oh, Jim, you don't know how thankful I am that he was not the author of that terrible crime. And now, before we say anything further, there's one thing I must talk to you about."

"What is that?" he enquired.

"It is about Helen," she answered. "I met her in the village this morning. I don't want to frighten you, but she is looking very ill. She seems to have come to look years older within the last few days. There is a frightened expression on her face that haunts me even now."

Jim was troubled. This was bad news indeed.

"Did she give you any reason for it?" he enquired.

"She tried to account for it by saying that her grandfather had not been at all well lately, and that she had had rather a trying time with him."

"Alice," said Jim, after the short pause that ensued, "I have come to the conclusion that old Bursfield is insane. Helen did not tell you, I suppose, that he uttered all sorts of threats against me the other day. For some reason or another he has taken an intense dislike to me."

"She said nothing about it," Alice answered. "I am sorry for her. What is best to be done, do you think?"

"It is difficult to say," Jim answered. "One thing is quite certain. She cannot go on living with him if he is to continue in this strain. Under such circumstances there is a limit even to a woman's fidelity. I must endeavour to see her as soon as possible."

"Would it do for me to go and see her, do you think?" asked Alice. "I should then be able to tell you something definite about Mr. Bursfield's condition."

Jim shook his head.

"No," he said, "such a thing would not be wise. I must think the matter over and see what is best to be done."

By the time he reached the house he had arrived at a conclusion.

"Do you remember, Alice," he said, "that clever young doctor that we met at the Caltrops on the evening that we dined with them, soon after our arrival in England? His name was Weston. Mrs. Caltrop declared that, before many years were past, he would be a recognised authority on mental diseases."

"I remember him quite well," Alice answered. "He took me in to dinner, and was so interested in Australia. He had a brother in Sydney, I think. What about him."

"Well, I have made up my mind to telegraph to Mrs. Caltrop for his address, and having got it, to wire and ask him to come down and see Mr. Bursfield. He would be able to tell me then whether or not it is safe for Helen to go on living with him. If he says not, then she must leave him at once."

"I should think it would be a very good plan, provided always that you can get Mr. Bursfield to see him. You will find that the difficulty."

"Not at all," Jim answered. "I have a scheme that I think will answer. At any rate we will try it."

A telegram was accordingly despatched to Mrs. Caltrop, asking her to forward the address of the doctor in question. This done, Jim sent for Terence.

"Well, Terence," he said, when the latter made his appearance, "any sign of the Black Dwarf during my absence?"

"Never a one, sir," Terence replied. "I kept my eyes and ears open all night, and waited about after dark, but there's not been so much as a mouse stirring."

"I am glad to hear it," Jim remarked, and then gave Terence a brief description of his visit to London, and of what he had discovered there.

"Then if it wasn't he as did it," said Terence, "who could it have been?"

Before he answered, Jim looked at the door, as if to make sure that it was closed.

"Terence," he said, "I am gradually coming to the conclusion that the Black Dwarf, whoever he may be, was responsible for it."

"I've thought of that myself, sir," Terence replied.

"In the first place, he was seen by one of the maid-servants in the gallery on the night that my father was murdered."

"Don't they say, sir, as how another gentleman was murdered in the same way in this house?"

"I believe there is some legend to that effect," said Jim, "but how true it is, I cannot say. I don't think, however, we need take that circumstance into consideration."

"Then what are we to do, sir?"

"Watch and wait until we catch him," Jim replied. "When we've done that we shall be satisfied whether he is flesh or blood or not, and if he is, by what right he dares to enter my house."

There was a lengthy pause, then with a diffidence that was somewhat unusual with him, Terence said:

"You'll excuse me, sir, I hope, for saying such a thing, but between you and me, sir, I cannot help thinking that we was happier at Mudrapilla."

Jim heaved a heavy sigh. A longing to be back in the old home, and to be engaged in the pursuits he had been brought up to from a boy, had been with him a great deal of late.

"Yes," he said. "I think we were happier at Gundawurra. I must go back there soon, Terence, if only for a whiff of Bush air. I am very much afraid that playing the fine gentleman in England does not suit me."

When the other had left the room, Jim lay back in his chair and fell into a reverie. He closed his eyes, and was transported back to the old home where he had been born, and where he had spent his happiest days. How sweet it would be to settle down there some day, with Helen as his wife. He tried hard to realise the day's work upon the run; the home-coming at night, to find Helen at the gate waiting for him; the evenings spent in the cool verandah, with the moon rising above the river timber. Then he came back to the very real anxieties of the present. An hour later a message came from Mrs. Caltrop. It was as follows:

"Doctor Weston, Harley Street."

Whereupon he took another telegraph form and wired to the doctor to the effect that he would be grateful if he could make it convenient to travel down to Childerbridge that afternoon. In order that the latter might understand from whom the message emanated, he added the words, "Met you at dinner at Mrs. Caltrop's." Luncheon was scarcely finished before a message arrived from the doctor saying that he would endeavour to be at Childerbridge at four o'clock. Accordingly at half-past three Jim drove to the railway station to await his coming. Punctual to the moment the train steamed into the station, and he looked about among the passengers for the man he wanted.

Presently he descried him coming along the platform—a tall, good-looking man, resembling a soldier more than a Harley Street physician.

"Mr. Standerton, I believe," he said as he approached Jim.

"And you are Doctor Weston, of course," the latter answered with a smile.

"Now," said the doctor, "I will commence, Mr. Standerton, by saying that it is absolutely necessary that I should catch the six o'clock train back to London."

"I will arrange that you do so," Jim replied, and then the doctor surrendered his ticket and they strolled out of the station. "Now, perhaps, I had better tell you my reasons for asking you to come down to-day. Shall we walk a little way along the road. I have no desire to be overheard. I will now make you acquainted with the facts of the case, in order that you may go direct to the house of the gentleman I want you to see."

"He is not a member of your own family, then?" the doctor enquired.

"No, he is no sort of relation. In fact, I had not seen him until a few months ago."

They paused beside a gate and faced each other.

"I gather that it is rather an unusual case?" the doctor remarked.

"A very unusual one," Jim replied. "The matter stands in this way. I am engaged to a young lady who is the adopted granddaughter of the gentleman in question."

The doctor nodded, but said nothing. He listened attentively, while Jim told his tale, explained his fears for Helen's safety, and described the threats the old gentleman had made use of concerning himself.

When he had finished Dr. Weston drew some lines on the ground with the point of his umbrella, as if he were working out a difficult calculation.

"This is certainly a singular case, Mr. Standerton," he said at last. "You are no connected with this gentleman in any way, and he, not approving of your marriage with his granddaughter, has forbidden you his house. The young lady's only reason for believing him to be a little weak in his intellect is his treatment of you. I really do not know whether, under the circumstances, I should be justified in seeing him."

Jim's heart sank. He had not looked at the matter from this point of view. Observing his disappointment, the doctor smiled.

"Nevertheless," he continued, "I will see him, provided you will give me your promise that my report shall be considered a purely confidential one."

"Am I to understand that I am not to acquaint Miss Decie or my sister with your decision?"

"Of course, I will allow you to tell them, and equally, of course, provided it goes no further."

"In that case I will give you my promise most willingly," said Jim.

"And now the question comes as to how I can obtain my interview with him."

"I have thought out a plan that should enable you to do that," Jim replied. "I happen to know that for a long time past he has been engaged in writing a history of the neighbourhood, and my house in particular which at one time was the property of his family."

"Quite so; and the ruins a mile or two back, what are they called?"

"Clevedon Castle," Jim answered. "I believe it was destroyed by Cromwell."

"That should answer my purpose. And now with your permission I will drive to his house—not in your carriage, but in a cab. I shall see you afterwards, I presume?"

"I will wait for you here, or at my own house, whichever you please," said Jim.

"Your house, I think, would be better," the doctor answered. "I will drive there directly I leave Mr.—. By-the-way, you have not told me his name or given me his address."

Jim furnished him with both, and then the doctor hailed a fly and drove away.

It was nearly half-past five before Jim was informed by Wilkins that Dr. Weston had called, and that he had been shown to the study.

He immediately proceeded thither, to find the doctor sitting before the fire.

"Well, Mr. Standerton," he began, "I have seen Mr. Bursfield, and have had rather a curious interview with him."

"And what decision have you come to?"

"Well, I think your supposition is correct. Not to be technical, I might say that he is not really responsible for his actions. While we discussed archæology, and the history of the neighbourhood, he was rational enough, but when I chanced to touch upon this house, and your connection with it, his whole demeanour changed. If I were in your place I should avoid him as much as possible, for there can be no doubt that he would do you a mischief if he could. As for Miss Decie, I would not advise you to persuade her to leave him, at least not at present. It would in all probability immediately produce unfavourable results, and in so doing might snap the frail link that still connects him with Sanity. The influence she exerts over him, where you are not concerned, is undoubtedly a beneficial one."

"Am I to consider that she is safe with him?"

"I should say so," the doctor replied. "Of course, if he has many more of these paroxysms of rage it might be necessary for her to leave him. But she must be the best judge of that. Doubtless you can arrange that with her. And now I must be getting back to the railway station; if I wish to catch my train I have not much time to lose."

"I am exceedingly obliged to you, Doctor Weston," said Jim gratefully. "I cannot say that you have made my mind easier, but you have at least let me know exactly how matters stand with Mr. Bursfield."

"I am glad to have been of service," said the doctor.

James handed him an envelope containing his fee, and escorted him to the door. When he had seen him depart he returned to the drawing-room and communicated his intelligence to his sister.

"Poor Helen," said Alice, "it is no wonder that she looks anxious. What will you do now, Jim?"

"I must take the night to think the matter over," he answered. "Since the old man is undoubtedly mad, and not only mad, but dangerously so, I cannot bear to contemplate her remaining with him, and yet I have no desire to hasten the crisis."

All the evening Jim brooded over the matter, imagining all sorts of dangers for the woman he loved. At last the time came for them to retire to rest. He was in the act of lighting

Alice's candle in the hall, when the sound of steps on the gravel path outside attracted his attention.

"Good gracious!" cried Jim, "who on earth can it be at this time of the night?"

So saying, he hastened to the door. The lights from the hall shone on the steps, and showed him Helen Decie, standing, bareheaded, before him. For a moment the shock at seeing her there at such an hour, and in such a plight, deprived him of speech. Alice was the first to break the silence.

"Helen, my dear girl," she cried, "what does this mean?"

Then Helen stepped into the hall, and James closed the door behind her. He had scarcely done so, before she gave a little cry and fell to the floor in a dead faint. Picking her up, Jim carried her to the big settee in the centre.

"My poor girl," he cried, "what has he done to you?" Then, turning to Alice, he added, "What can have happened?"

She did not answer him, but sped upstairs to her bedroom, to presently return with a bottle of smelling salts. Under their restorative influence, consciousness very soon returned, and Helen looked about her in a dazed fashion, as if she could not realise where she was.

"Do you feel well enough to tell what has taken place, dear?" Jim asked, when she had so far recovered as to be able to sit up. "What has brought you here bareheaded at this time of night?"

"My grandfather has turned me out of his house," she answered falteringly.

"Turned you out of the house?" repeated both Jim and Alice together. Then Alice added: "Surely not? He ought to be turned out himself."

"You must not be angry with him," said Helen. "I really don't think he knows what he is doing."

"But this is an unheard-of thing," Jim said angrily. "He must have taken leave of his senses."

"He accused me of being in league with you to poison him, and bade me come to an instant decision as to whether I would give you up or leave the house."

"And my noble girl refused to give me up?" said James, kissing her hand.

"Helen acted nobly," said Alice. "Never mind, dear, you know where your real friends are, don't you?"

"But whatever shall I do?" the girl put in. "He bade me leave the house and never come back again."

"We will arrange all that to-morrow," Jim replied. "For to-night, Alice will take care of you. Do not worry, dear heart, all will come right in the end."

Then he proceeded to inform her of Dr. Weston's visit that afternoon, and of the report that gentleman had given of the old gentleman's mental condition.

"I cannot tell why," she said, "but I had some sort of sus-picion that he came for that purpose. Poor grandfather, how sad it is to think of his being like this. Since he does not know what he is doing, we should not be angry with him for acting as he did."

At this juncture Alice departed to make arrangements for her friend's comfort for the night.

"Oh, Jim dear, what do you think will become of me?" Helen asked. "Think for me, for I cannot think for myself."

"I think I can hazard a very good guess what your fate will be," said Jim. "To-morrow morning I shall go up to London to obtain a special license, and the day after you shall become my wife."

CHAPTER XII

Unexpected as the events of the evening had been, Jim Standerton, as he stood in his bedroom before retiring to rest, could not declare that he altogether regretted the turn they had taken. On the morrow he would go to London, and afterwards, armed with the Law's authority, he would make Helen Decie his wife without delay. From that moment Mr. Bursfield might do his worst. Before retiring to his room he had visited Terence, and had received from him a positive assurance that so far all was right for the night. Knowing that he might trust the latter implicitly, he had given him an account of what had happened that evening.

"The sooner, sir, they put that old man under lock and key the better it will be for everybody," said Terence. "Let him just come playing his little game round here, and he'll have me on his track like a Nyall blackfellow."

Half-an-hour later, Jim was in bed and asleep, dreaming that he was back in the Bush once more, and that he and Terence were chasing wild horses through a mountain range, and that, on the foremost horse, Helen was seated, clinging to his mane, as if for dear life. He was galloping after her as fast as his horse could carry him, when suddenly a hand clutched him by the throat, and tried to lift him out of the saddle.

At that moment, however, he woke to find that this was no dream, but the most horrible reality he had ever known in his life. Bony fingers were clutching tightly at his windpipe, rendering it impossible for him to breathe. He endeavoured to rise and to seize his assailant, whoever he might be, and throw him off. But his efforts were unavailing. Still those talon-like fingers retained their hold; try as he would he could not weaken their terrible grip. Little by little he felt himself sinking. The room was in such total darkness that it was impossible to discover whom his antagonist might be. In the last extremity of his agony he rolled from the bed and lay helpless upon the floor, entangled in the clothes. With the fall, his assailant lost his grip of his throat. Then something must have startled him, for a moment later the door opened, and he was gone. Disengaging himself as quickly as possible from the bed-clothes, Jim staggered to his feet, half stunned by the fall and the terrific conflict in which he had so lately been engaged. As soon as he recovered he lit a candle, hastened to the door, opened it and passed out into the gallery. No one was to be seen there, but he had not gone many paces before he heard the same clicking noise that had arrested his attention on the first occasion of his seeing the Black Dwarf. Making his way round the gallery, he reached the room occupied by Terence. The door stood ajar, and from the noises that proceeded from within, he gathered that his trusty servant was not only in bed, but fast asleep. He crossed and shook him by the shoulders.

"Get up, Terence," he whispered softly. "Get up at once."

"What's the matter?" asked the half-awakened man. "Why, it's you, sir. Is there anything wrong?"

"I should rather think so," Jim replied. "Look at my throat and see if you can detect any marks upon it."

The other held up the candle as he was directed. On either side of his throat were a number of bruises and scratches, and some of the latter were bleeding profusely.

"My gracious, sir!" said Terence; "it looks as if somebody had been trying to strangle you."

"You've hit it exactly," Jim replied. "Good heavens! Terence, I've been nearly murdered. You've no idea what a fight of it I've had in the dark. The man, whoever he was, finding that he couldn't finish me, bolted, and has gone down some secret passage in the gallery. Terence, we must catch him somehow."

Terence sprang out of bed, and while he was dressing, Jim hastened back to his room and also donned some clothes. This done, he returned to Terence's bedroom, to discover that worthy in the act of lacing his boots.

"It's a funny business this, sir!" Terence remarked. "I wish I had been behind that gentleman when he was trying to settle you. I'd have given him one for his precious nob, ghost or no ghost."

"I expect you would. Now be as quick as you can, for there is not a moment to lose if we want to catch him."

Terence immediately announced himself as ready, and then, taking their candles, they set off round the gallery towards the corridor where Jim felt sure his mysterious assailant had disappeared. Inspection showed them that the door of the stairs at the further end, leading down to the domestic offices, was securely fastened on the other side. Having made sure of this, they tried, as on a previous occasion, the various rooms along the corridor, searching each one most carefully. But no success attended their efforts.

"It is quite certain that he is not in any of these rooms," said Jim. "Now what we have to do is to discover the entrance to that secret passage. I shall not rest content until we have found that."

They accordingly returned to the corridor, where they set to work once more to over-haul the wainscotting. Beginning at one end, they worked to the other; their efforts, however, met with no more success than they had done in the searching of the rooms. Every panel of the wainscotting seemed as hollow as its fellow—each projection as firmly secured.

"And yet I am as certain that it is somewhere about here that he disappeared," said Jim.

At the entrance to the corridor from the gallery were two square pillars elaborately carved with fruit. Jim had explored his side, having pressed and pulled every pear and apple, with the usual result. Suddenly Terence touched him on the arm.

"Look here, sir," he whispered, "what's this? It seems to me that this grape is not very firm."

Jim turned to him and knelt down beside the bunch of fruit indicated. It certainly did seem as if the lowest grape of the bunch were loose. It shook under his finger, and yet showed no sign of coming off.

"I believe we've got it at last," he said, pressing upon the grape, as he spoke, with all his strength. Yet it did not move. He endeavoured to push it in the direction of the gallery, but still it remained immovable. He tried forcing it from him towards the corridor, when to his amazement it left its place and moved half an inch or so away. As it did so there was a heavy creaking noise, and a portion of the panelling of the corridor, some three feet in width and six feet high, swung inwards, disclosing a black cavity, which might either have been a well or a staircase. Both men drew back in astonishment, half expecting that Jim's assailant, if he were concealed within, would dash out upon them.

"We've found the place at last," said Jim. "Now, if I'm not mistaken, we shall be able to solve the mystery of the famous Childerbridge ghosts. Hold your candle aloft, Terence, so that we can see what we are doing, and we'll descend and discover where it leads to."

"Let me go first, sir," Terence returned. "After the fight you had upstairs, you may not be up to the mark, and I'm dying to have a turn with him, if he's as big as a church."

But Jim would not hear of this, and bade the other follow him. Holding their lights aloft, they descended the narrow stone steps. They were longer than they expected to find them, and when they reached the bottom Jim knew that they must be some distance beneath the level of the foundations of the house. They were then standing in a passage, some four feet wide by seven in height. The walls and ceiling were of brick, the floor composed of huge blocks of stone. Everything reeked with damp while the air was as close and musty as a vault. Being resolved to leave no part of it unexplored, Jim pushed on closely followed by Terence. For economy's sake they blew out one of the candles, not knowing how far they might have to travel, or what might happen to them by the way. They had not been more than three minutes in the passage before Jim stopped, and turning to his companion, held up his hand.

"What's up?" he asked.

A sound as of heavy blows upon stone reached them from above.

"I can tell you what it is, sir," said Terence, after a moment's reflection. "It's the horses, and it means that we're under the stables."

"In that case it must run the entire width of the house and burrow under the courtyard. It means also that the direction is due east. This is growing interesting. Come along."

After this discovery they pushed on with increased speed, but the passage showed no signs of coming to an end. The air was close, but now and again draughts poured in upon them to prove that though they could not see them, there must be vent holes somewhere.

"I wouldn't have believed such a place could have existed," said Jim. "It seems as if we have come miles. By Jove, what's that?"

As he spoke the light of his candle shone upon a dark mass huddled upon the floor. A second later it became apparent that it was the figure of a man.

"Take care, sir," said Terence, as Jim hastened towards the prostrate form, "it may be the man we want, and he's as like as not shamming."

"We'll soon find that out," answered Jim, and knelt down beside the prostrate figure.

While Terence held the candle, Jim rolled the figure over until they were able to see the face. Then he uttered a cry of horror. The man lying before them was none other than Abraham Bursfield!

"Good heavens, this is too terrible," said Jim, after the long pause which followed, during which he had assured himself that he had made no mistake as to the other's identity. "Is he dead, do you think, Terence?"

"Quite dead, sir," Terence replied, after he too had knelt down and examined him. "If he's the man who tried to kill you, he'll never do any more mischief to anybody again."

But Jim did not answer. A sickening feeling of giddiness was taking possession of him. If it were Abraham Bursfield who had done his best to murder him that night, it was only logical to conclude that he was also the man who had murdered his father. Doctor Weston had declared him to be a madman that afternoon. Now he had certainly proved himself to be one of the most dangerous type. If that were the case what a narrow escape Helen had had.

"What's to be done, Terence?—what's to be done?" Jim asked almost piteously. "We could not have made a more terrible discovery."

"There'll have to be an Inquest, sir," said Terence.

"When it will be found that he entered my house and endeavoured to murder me. Then it will be remembered how my father died. Two and two will be put together, and the terrible truth will come out. That would break Miss Decie's heart."

"Good heavens! sir, I see what you mean," said Terence. "I never thought of that."

"He was mad, Terence, hopelessly mad, and therefore not responsible for his actions. Poor Miss Decie!"

"Aye, poor young lady. If she was so fond of the old gentleman, it would break her heart to know what he has been trying to do."

"She must never know," said Jim, who by this time had made up his mind. "I can trust you, Terence."

"To the death, sir, and I think you know it. I've served you, sir, and I served your father before you, and I don't think you ever found me wanting. Tell me what you think of doing."

"We must get him back to his own house, if possible," said Jim, "and let him be found dead there. No one but our two selves will know the truth, and if we keep silence, no one need ever know that we found him here. I cannot let Miss Decie be made more unhappy than she is."

"I don't know but that you are right, sir," Terence answered. "But how are we going to get him to the Dower House?"

"We must go along the passage and see where it leads to. If I am not mistaken it will take us there. This place must have been made years ago, when the two properties were one. We will leave the body here, and, if I am right in my conjecture, we can come back for it."

They accordingly allowed the remains of Mr. Bursfield to lie where they had found them, and proceeded on their tour of exploration. As it transpired, they had still a considerable distance to go before they reached the end of the tunnel. At last, however, they found themselves at the foot of a flight of stone steps, similar to those by which they had descended at the Manor House.

"Tread very quietly," Jim whispered to his companion. "We must on no account rouse the servants."

They noiselessly ascended the stairs until they found themselves at the top, and confronted by a door.

"I'll get you to stay here, Terence," Jim whispered, "while I open this door and see where we are."

He soon discovered what appeared to be a spring in the middle of the door, and when he had pressed it, had the satisfaction of seeing the door swing inwards. Shading the candle with his hand, Jim stepped into the room he found before him. His surprise at finding himself in Mr. Bursfield's study, the same room in which he had his last unpleasant interview with the old gentleman, can be better imagined than described. The secret door, he observed, formed part of the panelling on one side of the fireplace, a fragment of carving in the setting of the chimney-piece being the means of opening it. The old man's papers and books were littered about the table just as he had left them; a grandfather clock ticked solemnly in the further right-hand corner, while a little mouse watched Jim from beneath the sofa, as if it were endeavouring to ascertain his errand there at such an hour.

Having made sure of his whereabouts, Jim returned to the passage, closing the door carefully behind him.

"We must lose no time," he whispered to Terence; "it is already a quarter to three. Heaven grant that Isaac, his man-servant, does not take it into his head to look in upon his master during the night. He would then find him absent, and that would make it rather difficult to explain the fact of his being found dead in his chair in the morning."

By this time their first candle had expired, and it became necessary to light that Terence was carrying.

"If we are not very careful we shall be compelled to make our way back in the dark, after we have carried him up here," said Jim. "This candle will scarcely see us through."

"Never mind that, sir, so long as we can get him in here safely," said Terence. "I have got a box of matches in my pocket, and we can fumble our way back somehow."

They accordingly set off, and in due course reached the place where they had left the old man's body.

"How are we to carry him?" asked Jim.

"Oh, you leave that to me, sir. I can manage it," answered Terence. "If you'll go ahead with the light, I'll follow you."

So saying, he picked up the frail body, as if its weight were a matter of no concern to him, and they set off on their return journey to the Dower House. If the distance had appeared a long one before, it was doubly so now. At last, however, they reached the steps, climbed them, and a few moments later were standing in the dead man's study once more. In spite of his assertions to the contrary, it was plain that his exertions had taxed Terence's strength to its utmost. Between them they placed the body in the chair before the table.

This done, they left the room as quietly as they had entered it, and made their way down the steps once more. Jim's prophecy that the return journey would have to be made in darkness was fulfilled, for they had scarcely reached the place where they had discovered the body ere the candle fluttered out and they found themselves in inky darkness.

Terence struck a match, but its feeble flicker was of little or no use to them. Fumbling their way along by the wall they continued to progress, until a muttered exclamation from Terence, who was leading, proclaimed the fact that they had reached the steps at the further end.

"Bad cess to 'em," said he, "I've barked my shins so that I shall have good cause to remember them to my dying day."

He thereupon lit another match, and by means of this modest illumination they climbed to the door in the corridor above.

"Heaven be thanked! we're safe home once more," said Jim, as they stepped into the passage. "I trust I may never experience another night like this."

Whispering to Terence to follow him quietly, he led the way round the gallery and downstairs to the dining-room, where he unlocked the Tantalus and poured out a glass of spirits for Terence and another for himself. Both stood in need of some sort of stimulant after all they had been through.

"Not a word must be breathed to any living being of this, Terence," he said, as he put his glass down. "Remember, I trust my secret to you implicitly."

"I give you my word, sir, that nobody shall ever hear it from me," answered Terence, and then the two men solemnly shook hands.

"Now, before we go to bed, I'll get you to come to my room and have a look at my throat," said Jim; "it's uncommonly sore."

This proved to be the case. And small wonder was it, for the finger marks were fast turning to bruises, while the scratches showed up as fiery-red as ever. Jim shuddered again and again as he recalled that awful struggle and compared his escape with his father's cruel fate.

"Another moment and in all probability he would have done for me too," he said to himself, and then added somewhat inconsequently, "Poor Helen!"

When his wounds had been dressed, he despatched Terence to bed; for his own part, however, he knew that sleep was impossible. In fact, he did not attempt to seek it, but seating himself in a comfortable chair, proceeded to read, with what attention he could bestow upon the operation, until daylight.

When the sun rose he dressed himself and went out, wearing a scarf instead of a collar, in order that the wounds he had received might not be apparent to the world. The memory of that hateful passage under the park haunted him like an evil dream. He determined to have it closed at once for good and all. While he remained the owner of Childerbridge no one should ever set foot in it again. He was still wondering how he could best carry out the work without exciting suspicion or comment, when he observed an old man crossing the park towards him. As he drew nearer, Jim became aware that it was old Isaac, Mr. Bursfield's man-servant and general factotum. It was also to be seen that he was in a very agitated state.

"God have mercy upon us, sir!" he said, as he came up to Jim; "I've had such a fright. Is Miss Helen with you?"

"She is," Jim replied, and then endeavouring to speak unconcernedly, he added—"Has Mr. Bursfield sent you to find her?"

"The poor gentleman will never send me on another errand," Isaac replied solemnly; "he has been sent for himself. He is dead!"

CHAPTER XIII

"What's that you say?" cried Jim, trying to appear as if he were scarcely able to believe that he heard aright. "Do you mean to tell me that Mr. Bursfield is dead?"

"Yes, sir," said the old man; "when I went into his study this morning to open the shutters, I found him seated at his table in the arm-chair stone dead. I ran up at once to Miss Helen's room to tell her, only to find that her bed had not been slept in. Me and my wife searched the house for her, but she is not to be found anywhere. Oh, sir, what does it all mean?"

"It means that Miss Decie came to my house last night at about eleven o'clock. Mr. Bursfield's condition was such that she was afraid to remain in the house with him any longer. You must have noticed that he has been very strange of late?"

"The poor old gentleman has been ailing for some days past," Isaac replied. "He always was quick tempered, but for the last month or so he doesn't seem to have been able to control himself. Perhaps it isn't right for a servant to say it, sir, but there 'ave been times lately when I 'ave been afraid that his reason 'ave been a-failing him. There was a time when he couldn't make enough of Miss Helen, but lately he's been scarce able to speak civil to her. It's a sad thing, sir, a very sad thing, especially for a servant that's worked for him true and faithful for nigh upon forty years."

"His fit of rage last night must have hastened the end," said Jim. "The news you bring will affect Miss Decie very painfully. You had better go back and send at once for the doctor; I will return to the Manor House and tell Miss Decie."

"I humbly thank you for your kindness, sir," the man replied. "I will do what you say, and perhaps you will be kind enough to come over later."

When he had extracted the other's promise he hobbled off, and Jim returned to his own house. He found Helen and Alice in the hall, standing before the great fireplace in earnest conversation. He bade them as cheery a good morning as was possible under the circumstances, and when he had done so his sister enquired why his throat was wrapped up so closely.

"It's a trifle sore this morning," Jim replied, with some truth. "That's all. It will be all right very soon."

He then suggested that they should go in to breakfast. He had determined to break the news of Mr. Bursfield's death to Helen after the meal. This he did with great gentleness. The shock, however, was a severe one, nevertheless, but she did her best to meet it bravely.

"Poor old grandfather," she said after a while, "I always feared that his death would come like this. Oh how sorry I am that he should have died believing that I had ceased to love him."

"He could not have done that," Jim replied. "In his inmost heart he must have known that your affection was one that could never change."

She shook her head, however.

"Will you take me to him?" she enquired, and Jim, feeling that it would not be wise not to do so, consented to go with her to the Dower House. Side by side they crossed the park by the path they had come to know so well, entered the house by the little postern door, and were met in the hall by the village doctor whom Isaac had summoned.

"My dear Miss Decie," he said as they shook hands, "will you accept my heartfelt sympathy for you in your trouble. I fear it must have been a terrible shock."

"It has affected me more than I can say," she answered. "I had no idea, though I was aware that his heart was in a very weak state, that the end was so near."

"One thing I can tell you if it will make you any happier," said the doctor, "and that is, that I am certain his end was a peaceful and painless one."

Thanking the doctor for his sympathy, Helen left the room and went upstairs to the dead man's bedroom. Jim and the doctor went into the study.

"I suppose it will be necessary to hold an Inquest," said Jim, when they were alone together.

"I am very much afraid so," the doctor replied. "But it will be quite a formal affair. There are two circumstances, however, Mr. Standerton, about the affair, that I must confess puzzle me more than a little."

Jim felt himself turning cold. Had he left anything undone, or had he made any mistake?

"What are those two circumstances?" he enquired.

"Well, in the first place," said the doctor, "the old gentleman seldom went outside the house, not once a month at most, and only then on fine days. Yesterday, his man-servant tells me, he did not stir beyond the study door. Isaac is certain that he was wearing his carpet slippers at dinner time, and also when he looked in upon him before retiring, yet when he was found this morning he was wearing boots."

"That is most curious, certainly," said Jim, "but I must confess I fail to see anything remarkable in it."

"Not perhaps in the fact of his wearing the boots," said the medical gentleman, "but there is another point which, taken in conjunction with it, makes one pause to think. On the first finger of the right hand I found that the nail had been recently broken, and in a painful fashion. What is more, the second and third fingers had smears of blood upon them. Now with the exception of the nail to which I have alluded and which did not bleed, he had not a trace of a wound on either finger. That I am quite certain of, for I searched diligently. Moreover, there is not a trace of blood upon the table at which he was seated. And there is one thing stranger still."

"What is that?"

"As you are aware, it commenced to rain at a late hour last night. Unfortunately I know it, for the reason that I was compelled to be out in it. The roads were plastered with mud. Now though Mr. Bursfield, for some reason of his own, had put on his boots, he could not have ventured outside, for there is not a speck of mud upon them. In that case, why the boots, and where did the blood come from?"

"You are perfectly sure that he died of heart disease?"

"As sure as I can be of anything," said the doctor. "Nevertheless, it's altogether a mysterious affair."

This also proved to be the opinion of the Coroner's Jury, and as there was no one forthcoming to clear it up, a mystery it was likely to remain for all time. Had the Coroner and his Jury, however, known the history of the bruises under the thick bandage which the young Squire of Childerbridge wore round his throat, they would have been enlightened.

As nobody was able to account for anything save the doctor, however, a verdict of "Death from Natural Causes" was returned, and three days later, Abraham Bursfield was laid to rest with his forefathers in the little churchyard, scarcely fifty paces away from the grave of the man who had fallen by his hands.

"Jim," said Alice on the evening of the funeral, when they had brought Helen back to the Manor House, "I have a proposal to make to you. I am going to suggest that I should take Helen away for a few weeks to the seaside. The anxieties and sorrow of the past two months have been too much for her. I can see that she stands in need of a thorough change. If you have no objection to raise, I thought we could start to-morrow morning. We shall be away a month, and by that time she should be quite restored to health."

"And pray what am I going to do with myself while you are away?" he asked. "I gather you mean when you say that you are both going away that I am not to accompany you?"

"No; all things considered, I think it would be better not," said Alice. "But if you are very good you shall come down to us for two or three days during the month. Then if Helen agrees, and I have no doubt you will be able to induce her to do so, you could obtain a Special License, and be quietly married at the end of that time."

Jim, who regarded it quite possible that the marriage might be postponed for some time, clutched eagerly at the straw of hope held out to him, and willingly agreed to her suggestion.

"And now one other matter, Alice," he said. "I, on my side, have a proposal to make. Whether you will prove as complaisant as I have done is another matter."

"What is your proposal?"

"It can be resolved into one word," he answered, "That word is Mudrapilla."

He heard her catch her breath, and then she looked pleadingly at him.

"Jim," she whispered, "Oh Jim, dear, you don't mean it, do you?"

"If you and Helen will accompany me, I do," he answered. "Terence I am quite sure will not object. Will you agree, my sister?"

The answer she vouchsafed might have meant anything or nothing. It was:—

"Only to think of seeing dear old Mudrapilla again!"

So it was settled. Helen and Alice departed next day to a tiny seaside place in Devonshire, where Jim was under orders to join them for three days at the week end once during their stay. As soon as they were gone, he in his turn set off for London. His first act on reaching the City, and when he had deposited his bag at the hotel, was to drive to the office of the Estate Agent with whom his father had negotiated the purchase of Childerbridge. That portly, suave gentleman received him with the respect due to a man worth half a million of money, and the owner of such a palatial mansion and estate.

"But, my dear sir," he began, when he had heard what James had to say, "you surely don't mean to say that you are desirous of selling Childerbridge. You have only been there a few months."

"I am most anxious to be rid of the place as soon as possible," Jim replied. "As you may suppose it has the most painful recollections for me. Besides I am thinking of returning to Australia almost immediately, and scarcely know when I shall visit England again."

"In that case I must do the best I can for you," said the other. "At the same time I feel that I should warn you that the Estate Market is not in a very flourishing condition at present, and that a large number of properties that have been placed upon the market have not sold nearly as well as they should have done."

"I must take my chance of not getting its value," said Jim. "Find me a purchaser and I don't think he will be able to complain that I have not met him fairly."

The agent promised to do his best, and for the next fortnight Jim amused himself in a lazy fashion travelling about England, purchasing a variety of stock for his Australian stations, and longing for the time to come when he should be at liberty to present himself in Devonshire. At last, however, the day arrived. It was morning when he left London, it was evening when he reached his destination. It was winter when he left Waterloo, dull, dismal and foggy; when he reached Devonshire it was, in his eyes at least, perpetual summer. Both Helen and Alice were at the railway station to greet him, and immediately he saw them he realised the fact that a change for the better had taken place in his sweetheart. The old colour had come back to her cheeks, the old sparkle was in her eyes. She greeted him very lovingly, but if possible a little shyly. There were such lots of news to hear, and still more to be told, that it seemed as if they would never have done talking.

The village had proved itself a delightful little place. It was far from the track of the tripper, and had not then been spoilt by the wealthy tourist. High cliffs hemmed it in on either side, and the sea broke upon the beach of shingles. They returned to their lodgings for tea, a charming thatched cottage, within a stone's throw of the primitive little jetty, beside which the fisher boats were moored. Afterwards the lovers went for a walk upon the cliffs.

"Helen, my darling," said Jim, "I can scarcely realise that it is only a fortnight since I saw you. It seems as if years had passed. You can have no idea how happy it makes me to see you looking like your own dear self once more."

"I could not help being well here," she answered. "Besides, Alice has been so good and kind to me. I should be ungrateful indeed were I to show no improvement."

But Jim had not brought his sweetheart out on the cliff to discuss his sister's good qualities.

"Helen," he said at last, "is it possible for you to be my wife in a fortnight's time?"

He took her little hand in his and looked into her eyes. The veriest tyro might have seen that the young man was terribly in earnest.

"It might be possible," she said softly, but without looking at him. "Are you quite sure you do wish it?"

"If you talk like that I shall go back to London to-night," he answered. "You know very well that to make you my wife has been my ambition ever since I first saw you."

And then he went on to tell her of his dreams, winding up with this question—"I wonder whether you will like Australia?"

"I shall like any place where you may be," she replied.

Could any young woman say more to her lover than that? At any rate Jim appeared to be satisfied.

On the Monday following he returned to London to learn from the agent that a probable, though unexpected, purchaser had been found for Childerbridge. He proved to be a wealthy American, who was not only prepared to take over the estate at a valuation, but also to purchase the furniture and effects as they stood.

On the day following the receipt of this news, Jim travelled down with the would-be buyer, conducted him over the property, and was in a position to assure himself, when the other had departed, that Childerbridge would be very soon off his hands. To the agent's horror the matter was conducted on both sides with unusual promptness, and in consequence, when, a fortnight later, Jim stepped into the Devonshire train with a special marriage license in his pocket, the sale was as good as effected.

The wedding was solemnised next day in the quaint little village church, and excited no comment from the humble fisher folk. The only persons present were the bride and bridegroom, Alice, and the family lawyer, who had travelled down from London expressly to give the bride away. Then, no impediment being offered, James Standerton, bachelor, took to himself for wife Helen Decie, spinster. The worthy old gentleman pocketed his fee with a smiling face, congratulated both parties, and then hurried off to another parish to bury a fisherman who had been drowned in the bay a few days before. An hour later Jim and Helen started for Exeter, en route for Scotland, while Alice accompanied the lawyer, whose wife's guest she was to be, to London, to wait there until her brother and sister-in-law should return from the north.

Four years have elapsed since that terrible night when Abraham Bursfield was found dead in the secret passage leading from Childerbridge Manor House to the Dower House in the corner of the Park. Those four years have certainly worked wondrous changes in at least four lives. One short sketch must serve to illustrate this fact, and to bring my story to a conclusion. The scene is no longer laid in England but on a rough Bush track on a very hot Australian afternoon. A tall good-looking man is jogging contentedly along, apparently oblivious to all that goes on around him. It is easily seen that he and his horse are on the very best terms with each other. He passes the Pelican Lake, descends into the hollow of what was perhaps a continuation of the same lake, and on gaining the summit of the next rise finds himself looking upon what, at first glance, would appear to be a small village. This village is the station of Mudrapilla, and the giant gums which can just be discerned some five miles or so to the right, indicate the spot where on a certain eventful evening, James Standerton first came face to face with Richard Murbridge. This same James Standerton, for it is he who is the rider of the horse, increases his pace as soon as the station itself comes into view. He passes the men's quarters, the store, the blacksmith's shop, and finally approaches a long and extremely comfortable looking one-storied residence, whose broad verandahs are confronted by orange groves on the one side, and the brave old river on the other. As he rides up one of the overseers emerges from the barracks, and hastens forward to greet his employer, and to take his horse from him. That overseer is no less a person than our old friend, Terence O'Riley, looking just the same as ever. Jim gives him a few directions concerning the sheep in the Mountain Paddock, which he has visited that afternoon, and then dismounts and strolls on through the gates, and up the garden path towards the house. In the broad verandah a lady is seated in a long comfortable chair, and playing beside her on the floor is a chubby urchin upwards of two years of age. Helen, for as may be supposed, it is none other than she, rises on hearing her husband's step on the path, and catching up the infant brings him forward to greet his father with a kiss.

"I didn't expect you for half-an-hour at least, dear," she says, when she in her turn has kissed him. "The boy and I have been patiently awaiting your arrival. Did you meet the mail?"

"I did," he answered, "and I opened the bag upon the road. There are two letters for you, one I see is from Alice."

"And you?" she asks, as she takes the letters from him.

"Well, I had one of some importance," he replied. "It is from Fairlight—my old solicitor in England, you remember him—and what do you think he tells me?"

Helen, very naturally, could not guess.

"Well, he says that Childerbridge Manor was burnt down by fire three months ago and totally destroyed. The American, the owner, is going to rebuild it at once on a scale of unparalleled magnificence."

There was a pause for a few moments, then Helen said:—

"What do you think about it, Jim?"

"All things considered I am not sorry," he answered. "Yet, perhaps, I should not say that, for it brought me the greatest blessing a man can have."

"And that blessing?" she asked innocently.

"Is a good wife," he answered, stooping to kiss her. After which he disappeared into the house.

"And pray what does Alice say?" he asked, when he returned a few minutes later.

"She gives us such good news," Helen replied. "She and Jack will spend Christmas with us. She declares she is the happiest woman in the world. Jack is a paragon."

In case the reader should fail to understand who Jack is, I might remark that he is no less a person than Jack Riddington, the overseer, mentioned at the commencement of my story, and who was supposed to be Jim's best friend. Alice, after they were engaged, admitted that she had always entertained a liking for him, while it was well known that he had always been head over ears in love with her. During Jim's absence in England he had come into a large sum of money, had purchased a station one hundred and fifty miles south of Gundawurra, had married Alice within six months of her return, and was now living a life of undoubted felicity.

"They may be happy," said Helen, "but they can never be as happy as we are. That is quite certain, husband mine."

THE END

www.ingramcontent.com/pod-product-compliance
Lightning Source LLC
Chambersburg PA
CBHW030232180626
46810CB00008B/3093